LASS' VALOR

The Pith Trilogy - Book Three

KARA GRIFFIN

LASS' VALOR

The Pith Trilogy - Book Three

All Rights Reserved.
Copyright © 2012 Kara Griffin – 1st edition
Copyright @ 2020 Kara Griffin – 2nd edition

Cover Photo © 2020 All rights reserved – to be used with permission.
Cover design by Sheri L. McGathy -
http://coverdesign.sherimcgathy.com/

This book may not be reproduced, transmitted, or stored in whole or in part by any means, including graphic, electronic, or mechanical without the express written consent of the publisher except in the case of brief quotations embodied in critical articles and reviews.

This is a work of fiction. Names, characters, businesses, places, events, and incidents are either the products of the author's imagination or used in a fictitious manner. Any resemblance to actual persons, living or dead, or actual events is purely coincidental or used in historical view or context.

This book contains adult material, reader discretion is advised.

AISN: B007M0OLGK
ISBN-13: 9798609356987

DEDICATION

This story is dedicated to those who make it their goal to
protect children no matter what the cost.
And to Trixie for 19 years of love and friendship.

*In men of the highest character and noblest genius,
there is to be found an insatiable desire for honor, command,
power, and glory.* ~Ciecero

LASS' VALOR

The Pith Trilogy - Book Three

Kaitlin Stanhope learns of her father's death delivered with a strange medallion and a cryptic message. He warns, *beware the friend with the black heart*. Wrenched from her beloved home, she's sent to live with her vile guardian. Escaping his clutches, she embarks on a dangerous mission, one that could mean the death of both her and the child she rescues. A believer in the ancient ways, Kaitlin has a vision of a warrior which brings comfort and many questions.

Brendan MacKinnon, the protector of his clan and doting uncle, is devastated when his niece goes missing. His mission is to find her however long it takes. When he comes across Kaitlin, the violet-eyed fairy enchants him. The woman risked everything to save his niece's life, and courageously she stands up to his obstinate nature.

How can the LASS' VALOR not touch his heart? Yet is it enough to win him over to the idea of a happily ever after?

PROLOGUE

Whitehall Castle, England
June 1221

"Hell, I'm caught." The edge of Henry's golden threaded gray cape caught the bottom of a lance held by a vacant suit of armor that stood sentry beside the wall. He sighed woefully and yanked his cape free, rattling the armor, and hurried on. His official crowning as king was delayed until he reached his majority. At six and ten, he wasn't old enough to sit on the throne, and the regency ruled the kingdom. Steven Langton and Pope Innocent influenced Hugh de Burg—the highest regent. Hugh complied with their demands lest he sent the country into an uproar again with the church. England couldn't risk excommunication again. Clergymen had recently accepted the edict was lifted and returned. England came into the church's good graces just before his father, King John, had died.

Henry put aside his thoughts of England's turmoil as he turned the corner of the hallway. He was beside himself because his beloved cousin, Julianna MacKinnon, had come for a visit. Henry met her in his father's court when he'd turned nine. She lived in Scotland, but they kept in contact through letters.

He'd just received word of her arrival and was restless for her visit. Julianna came with her husband, Colin MacKinnon, a powerful Highland laird, and their daughter, Bonnie. Bonnie just turned seven-winters old. Henry loved the little girl more than anything. Even when she poured milk on his chair on purpose, all she had to do was pout with her innocent eyes and say it was an accident. Who was he to dispute it? He chuckled—he being the unofficial King of England.

Sweet, sweet Bonnie. The adorable girl looked like her mother with her light-colored hair and bright blue eyes. Who would ever think she'd do something so wicked? Alas, the truth was—the little lady was a hellion. She made him smile with her endearing antics. It had been a year and a half since he'd visited them, so he'd sent a summons for them to come during his summer retreat. He laughed aloud at that because his cousin wasn't one to abide his summons, nor his father's when he'd been alive.

Now that Julianna was here, he would discuss the lands held in her name, which became the heated debate among his council. Henry spent most of the morning cloistered with several lords, all spoke on their behalf for the grant of those lands. The most arrogant lord, Richard de Morris, insisted he be given the property bordering his, but Henry wanted to speak to Julianna before he allowed the Regent's proceedings.

He scurried down the hall and rapped at the door. Colin MacKinnon opened the door and scowled. Highlanders were an ornery bunch.

"Colin, you're here at last." Henry strode past him. "Where's my sweet, lovely lady?"

Julianna held out her arms, but he bypassed her. He didn't stop until he reached his dear-heart. Henry lifted Bonnie in his arms and threw her high in the air. She squealed when she landed against his chest, and he placed a loving kiss on her baby-soft cheek.

"Sweeten, give me a hug."

Bonnie wrapped her hands around his neck and giggled in delight. "I missed you, Honey."

Her nickname broadened his grin. Henry nodded to Julianna. "Greetings."

"You finally welcome us, Henry. We shouldn't have bothered to come, Colin, we should've just sent Bonnie for a visit." Julianna laughed heartily.

Henry smiled in his roguish way, much like his father had. Even though he dressed in regal flamboyant fabrics, the trend of the courtiers, he tried to be cordial. He continued to hold Bonnie and gave her another hug.

"I'm glad you're here, Julianna, and you too, Colin, but I've missed this little minx. Have you behaved, sweeten?"

"Oh, aye, Honey, I've been a good lass. Papa hasn't punished me since yesterday." Bonnie's innocent tone told him she must've caused trouble on the journey.

"What did you do to warrant punishment?" He smiled then frowned at her father. "Colin, you're being too harsh on the poor little mite."

"Poor little mite! She knotted my horse's reins so badly, I had to remove them and get a new harness, but I can't stay angry with her. Look at her innocent face, she's my bonny button." Colin's affection softened his usual gruff manner.

"Perhaps 'tis a good idea to be strict. How are you, Julianna? Are you well since delivering Colin his son?" Henry took a whiff of Bonnie's sweet scent.

"Aye, I'm well. Kevin is well, and safely at home. He's too young to travel yet. I had to beg Colin to let Bonnie come. He doesn't want our children away from our home, and it was bad enough traveling with…" Julianna ceased her ramble when Bonnie's attention perked.

Henry squeezed Bonnie and laughed. "It's good to see you, all of you. My heart is pleased at your happiness, Julianna. Father would have been fond of your children."

"You're well? All goes well in your kingdom, Henry?" Julianna asked.

"Hugh rarely advises me on the happenings, but there

3

are ways to enforce my rule. I don't worry too much about it yet. Now, I have a surprise for you, we've invited many to a tourney, even those Scots you favor, Colin. I must settle a betrothal contract for a woman whose father died in the holy lands and I'm considering Angus Barclay. What do you know of him?"

"Only that he's a rough sort and causes a bit of mischief among the nearby clans."

Henry sighed because he didn't want to place the woman in a bad situation. Her father was a great noble. "Is Angus honorable, there's rumor of his clan's raids on the borders?"

Colin nodded. "As honorable as any other. I'm not aware of his activities."

"Well, we shall attend the parties and games and I'll assess this Angus Barclay for myself and decide whether to gift him with the lady later. I want you to enjoy yourself whilst you are here. How long do you plan to stay?"

"I thought we would stay a fortnight." Colin stood beside Julianna and took her hand.

"Then we shall have a long visit. I'll sit with you at supper. We must speak of your mother's lands, Julianna. Hugh wants to gift them to a knight in his service, but we can discuss it later. Get rest from your travel." Henry left, elated his family arrived.

The next day, the castle filled with fanfare as Henry's summer festival began. Bonnie stood by her nurse and gawked at the boisterous activity. A group of men played beautiful melodies, their chairs cascaded the steps that swept the palace's lawn. Everyone hurried outside because the weather was sunny and warm. Trumpeters sounded in the distance and declared Henry's arrival at an event. Games were played on the expanse of the lawn, and an archery contest held in the lower courtyard drew crowds of spectators. Knights placed their names on the lists for the event of the day, the joust. Their shiny armor reflected the sun and sent blinding streaks toward the onlookers.

Bonnie couldn't contain her glee as arrows flew through the air. She ran off, and in her excitement, she forgot her nurse. Her attendant, Emma, couldn't keep up with her. Emma held her skirts and chased after her all morning.

She pulled Bonnie along and held fast to her arm. "Now you're in for it. If I can't get you to listen to me, I'm sure your laird father will."

"Pray, Emma, don't tell Papa on me."

"You haven't listened once this morn, wee lass. I've chased after you eight times, no more. You'll answer to your papa now," Emma chided and gave her a 'you're-in-trouble-now' scowl.

Her plea hadn't worked. Papa would be disappointed. Emma tugged her along, and she tried to pry her arm free. They reached the tent where she was pulled inside. When they entered, Bonnie snickered because Papa kissed Mama. She hoped Papa was in a good mood, he usually was after kissing Mama. He turned to give her a warning glance.

Mama strode to her and knelt. "Bonnie, listen to your papa, now give me a kiss."

Bonnie kissed Mama's soft cheek, and she waved goodbye as Mama exited the tent. Emma, in the meantime, regaled the tale to Papa. Bonnie fiddled with her tartan and waited for his attention.

"Papa," she called.

"Don't Papa me, lass. Emma says you keep running off. You're supposed to stay with her for your safety. What do you have to say for yourself?"

She was glad they weren't home, because she would surely be put in Papa's chair. The chair was uncomfortable, and she didn't like sitting on it because there was nothing to do but wait until Papa said she was punished enough.

"Aye, Papa, I know och..." Bonnie didn't finish giving her excuse, because Papa frowned and she didn't like it when he frowned.

Bonnie lowered her eyes, gave her sweet little pout, and

tried her hardest to mellow him. She hoped it would make him forget her punishment. Papa looked as though he wanted to laugh, but he didn't. His melodic voice was soft, but he wasn't pleased.

"I will have to punish you, lass. Where is that bloody chair when you need it? You'll stay inside the tent for an hour. Give poor Emma a wee break, take a rest, Button."

"Aye, Papa, I'll rest, but I want to see the people on the sticks."

"Sticks? Oh, you mean the stilt walkers." Bonnie nodded. "All right, I'll take you myself if you pledge that you'll behave and rest for an hour."

"Really, Papa, you'll take me?"

Papa lifted her. She always liked when Papa picked her up and held her in his strong arms. His familiar scent and love in his eyes comforted her. Even though she was about to be punished, she hugged him.

"Aye, now give me your pledge."

Bonnie smiled with her face against his neck and took a whiff of his scent. He always smelled good. "I give my pledge, Papa."

"Pledge what, Button?"

Papa always made her repeat her punishment and promises, something he'd learned the hard way—he'd told her. He hid his smile because she reminded him of her mother, or so he'd said many times. She smiled widely and had no choice but to obey.

"I'm supposed to rest and give poor Emma a wee break."

"That's right, lass. Give me a kiss and I'll come back for you later."

Bonnie lifted her head and gave him a wet kiss on his rough cheek. Papa set her down, and she scrambled to the pallet. She placed her head on the tartan atop a pile of coverings, and as was her habit, she pulled nubs of lint from her cover and rubbed them on her face. Papa smiled at her action and soon after, he left the tent.

LASS' VALOR

The tent grew hot and Bonnie grew restless awaiting Emma. Her nurse nodded off and snored loudly. She snickered in laughter at the sound. Bonnie looked across the tent but wasn't at all tired. An idea came and she slunk to the tent's flap and peeked outside. People walked around, and she heard laughter from across the grounds. Excitement called and not one to wait, she slipped through the opening.

Bonnie gawked as she skipped along. She looked everywhere at once and didn't notice the man who followed closely. A row of high green yew shrubs blocked her view of the tournament. She rounded the corner of a hedge when a man yanked her from the grass. At first, she thought it was Papa and she turned to him. Only it wasn't Papa. The man's hand clamped over her mouth when she tried to scream. She kicked and squirmed to no avail. The man ran and jostled her. He almost dropped her as he ran to his tethered horse and settled her across his lap.

"Be quiet and I won't hurt ye."

Bonnie was scared, butterflies fluttered in her tummy. She couldn't get free from the man's grip and twisted as the view of the castle drew away. Tears streamed from her fear-stricken eyes and she whimpered against the hand that covered her mouth. How she wished she listened to Papa and stayed in the tent with Emma. Papa would be angry when he returned and found her gone.

CHAPTER ONE

Cheshire, England
July 1221

Bright wildflowers speckled the green fields that lay beyond Kaitlin Stanhope's home. Fifty men-at-arms protected the small fief, but the modest home didn't attract attention by passing knights. Twelve flags flew, bearing the family's coat of arms and that of its overlord, Aldwyn de Guylet's insignia. Cheshire's brilliant sunshine made for a glorious day. Various makeshift tents nestled between trees, where a caravan of travelers occupied the land with Kate's permission. With her father gone, she allowed the nomads to camp on her land, because none would gainsay her.

She stepped around a group of acrobats who practiced for the night's performance. Variegated meals cooked on open pots and caldrons and filled the air with enticing aromas which caused her stomach to grumble. An animal performer, with his head wrapped in a white cloth, pulled the rope tied to an enormous bird. She'd never seen such a creature with its overlong neck and broad beak. The performer offered to let the children ride on the bird's feathered back. She'd been told the animal was an ostrich and came from a faraway land in the east. Kate witnessed many unusual sights in the village, but nothing compared to the animals the visitors brought. The bright hues of the tent she sought came into view and she hurried inside.

"Madam Serena? Madam, are you here?" Kate pulled aside a fashioned curtain inside the tent and entered the personal area of her longtime friend. The scents of rosemary and incense drifted throughout the confines.

"Darling, I'm glad you're here. Come, sit, Kate." Madam Serena waved her hand over a table laden with the tools of her trade: cauldrons, spheres, daggers, sand, candles, and herbs. She even used cards with pictures depicting kings, queens, knights, jesters, and such, in determining the lives who sought her wise guidance.

Kate smiled at the aged woman. "I've seen the vision again."

Madam smiled in return and placed a clear sphere on the table. "It does my heart good the spirits use ye. My old Gaelic Grandma used to say that about me." Madam Serena cackled. "Speak of your vision, darling, while I look at my ball. Mayhap I can answer you this time."

"The dark-haired warrior floated like a ghost in the night, Madam, but I wasn't afraid. He frowned at me, yet I sensed he tried to tell me something. Do you think this has to do with my father?"

Madam shook her head. "Ah, it's a sign from the spirits, but alas, it's not about your father. Go on, continue."

Kate nodded. "I couldn't make him out, but he appeared to be a mighty warrior. His stance suggested he was fierce and strong. Yet, he comforted me. Will he reveal himself to me?"

Madam Serena's dark eyebrows furrowed. "Oh, dear, this is worrisome."

"What?" Kate sat forward. "What is it?"

"It involves a child. You will come across the warrior when ye meet the child."

"How will that happen?" Kate was confused. "There are no children here."

"You must tell me more." Madam pushed back the grayed locks of her hair, took a handful of wrinkled linen to reposition her garment, and leaned back.

"I sat in my circle and just placed my candles when the vision came. He has dark hair, dark as night, and light eyes, blue, or perhaps gray. He seemed unearthly. I sensed he wasn't pleased with me."

Serena's eyes twinkled. "This man will cause much grief, but don't despair for it's well-meant. Perhaps 'tis kismet. I sense nothing else about your vision, Kate."

"I don't understand why this vision comes, but I thank you for trying. It has plagued me for so long, since my father left. That is why I assumed the vision has to do with my father."

"All shall be revealed when ye meet the child. Have you heard any news about your father?"

Kate sighed with despair. "Nay, it's been four years now, and still, no word since his letter last year. I worry so. Can you see anything?"

Madam placed her hands above her eyes then glanced down into the glass sphere. After a few minutes of reflection, she spoke, "I sense doom. Evil lurks around your father's spirit. I am sorry, Kate, but I don't believe your father lives. He's been gone for a time."

"How did he die?"

Madam looked sadly at the globe. "Beware the friend with the black heart."

"What does that mean?"

"It, too, shall come to ye."

"Madam, you're being evasive. It's unlike you not to reveal the truth. Please, don't hold back. I can handle the truth."

"Greed is the motive. Your father won't return from the strange land."

Kate's lower lip trembled. "I have sensed that as well and shall miss him. We had a lovely last day together. I shall always remember it."

"Tell me about it."

"I had just put away my herbs when he came with news of the missive from Aldwyn. Our overlord requested he leave at once for the excursion to Egypt. He was to relieve the knights... He called me his fairy, and we talked about my marriage. I tried to tell him I didn't want to leave our home or him, but he wouldn't listen and made me promise to write to him with my choice. We both knew that I wouldn't."

Madam Serena looked at her with her dark eyes and smoothed Kate's flaxen hair with a touch of her hand. She sighed. "Kate, I shall not see ye again. You will embark on a somber mission, and I shan't be here when you return."

"Where are you going? What kind of mission will I go on?"

"Your questions shall be answered when ye meet the child, and you will know where to go. Your life will forever be changed. I shall miss ye, darling."

"I will miss you, too, Madam." Kate placed her hand upon Madam's wrinkled hand and squeezed it. "Thank you for your guidance these past years. I learned much from you. You've been a wonderful teacher."

"I packed a trunk full of objects. Take and use them."

"Oh, Madam, your lovely things. I cannot, please, take them back." She sensed sadness in Madam's dark-brown eyes.

"You need the objects more than I." Serena scratched her silver-streaked raven hair. "I am leaving the area to visit my brother."

"But you never travel."

"I fear my age won't allow me to continue as I am. I will retire from advising these good people and shan't return."

"How will we ever get along without you?"

"They will survive, just as you will." Madam stood. "Go now and remember all I have foretold. Here." Madam handed her the small trunk.

Kate placed the trunk aside and hugged Madam. After, she picked up the trunk and rushed through the curtain. She glanced back at the tent in sadness she'd miss her dear friend, but Madam aged and needed rest. Her grandmother was Madam's childhood friend, and she promised to show her the ways of their ancestors. She was glad Madam retired, but she seemed immortal to her and had enlightened people for years, even before Kate was born.

Kate reached the manor and ambled to her chamber. She placed the chest beside the door and lit a candle. Once she erected a circle in the center of the room, she readied for her morning ritual. She sat inside the circle and held a shiny golden goblet high—an offer to the Goddess. Candles sat around her, with four others outside the rope pointed to the cardinal directions: north, south, east, and west. She meditated with her eyes closed and concentrated on the silence with her cat curled into a ball beside her.

She hoped the vision would come again. It haunted her repeatedly since she'd turned four and ten. If Madam Serena's prophecy came true, she would meet the warrior in the flesh. Yet, he didn't come while she prayed.

Each morning, the same prayers and queries crossed her lips. She prayed her father would return and she would meet the warrior. She appealed to the gentle spirits to guide her in her choice of husband, yet she worried her guardian would select someone unsuitable. Her father said he would take her to court when he returned, but now that wouldn't happen.

Kate receded deeper within herself and chanted the Celtic prayers taught to her by her mother, grandmother, and Madam Serena. After a time, she opened her eyes to find her beloved nurse by the door. Lolly's frail figure was barely noticeable as thin as she was. She wore her silver hair knotted at the nape and those startling green eyes often reflected motherly adoration. Something was wrong, Kate sensed it, and upon closer inspection, Lolly's face downcast.

"Lolly, what brings you here?"

"Good morn, my girl, I must speak with you, but if you're busy, I shall return later."

"Nay, you're always welcome. Come inside and sit with me. You work too hard. I told you to have others see to the chores. We should take care of you."

"Bah, I wouldn't know what to do with myself. 'Tis not fair tidings I bring. Manik returned with news of your father."

A sudden chill made Kate shiver. "Oh, dear, come and sit next to me, Lolly. I suppose he hasn't brought good tidings." She sat on her pallet and waited for Lolly to join her.

Lolly took her hand. "Dear sweet girl, I fear you'll become distraught when I tell you—"

"My father is dead. Go on, tell me the news, I am prepared to hear it."

Lolly took a deep breath. "Perhaps you should read the missives he gave to Manik, ere he died." She opened a scroll written in Lord Hawk's hand and read:

Dearest fairy, I've been on this excursion for years, yet I tire of fighting the heathens and destroying their homes. My heart is heavy. Death surrounds me, likewise, I fear for my own. We've made progress and moved our forces along the river. This morning, my regiment was chased by a score of soldiers into the jungle. I only tell you this because we retreated to a cave hidden behind strange-looking trees. We crawled on our knees into the cavern and once inside, we were able to stand. I lit a torch, but couldn't see much. The walls were wet with slime and emitted a sulfuric smell.

Lolly stopped reading and looked at her.

"Oh, goodness, Lolly, that sounds horrible. Pray, continue."

Creatures hung on the ceiling above us; red eyes glowed in the darkest part of the cave. All I could see was blackness. I'm sorry to say this, fairy, but I thought I entered hell for all the sins I have committed. We followed rugged corridors and didn't know which direction to take. We went into the bowels of obscurity and stopped at a dead end. Worry not, but I received a wound on my leg. I leaned against the wall for support and knocked something loose. When I lifted the strange object, it gleamed in the torchlight. I didn't have time to view it and shoved the object in my pouch.

Kate interrupted, "What do you think it was, Lolly?"

"Let me continue." She lifted the parchment closer to her eyes.

A guard found a way for us to leave the cave. We crawled through a hole in the rock. When we reached the outside, we were in a jungle of sorts, not lush with green, but enough to give us cover. We ran back to camp and I had my leg tended to by the camp healer, and remembered the object. I pulled it from my pouch and studied it. It was a medallion with a strange spider-like symbol on the front. I flipped it over and found a smooth surface on the back. There was a hole on the back and I pried it open. Inside, I found a map with unusual writings and symbols, but I couldn't read the heathen's language. How fortunate am I to have found it? Your loving father, HS.

Kate stood and turned to Lolly. "What do you think the object is? Do you deem it caused my father's death? What did Manik say?"

"Manik shall come to you after you read the letters. There is only one more. Shall I read it?"

"Aye, please." Kate took her place again next to Lolly.

My sweet fairy, I write with such discontent. Richard de Morris, my comrade, became interested in my find. He has threatened to take the medallion. I should never have confided in him, and now I regret showing it to him. He has attached himself to finding it and claims we shall be rich men. I just want to return home to you, and don't know what will happen. I refuse to give Richard the medallion. If anything should happen to me, Katie, I warn you. Beware the friend with the black heart. I hope to be home with you soon, HS.

Kate's eyes widened. "Madam spoke those very words this morn. She said to beware the friend with the black heart. Richard must've killed my father for the medallion."

"Mayhap. I'll have Manik come. I loved Hawk like a son. He was a sweet lad. How I shall miss him. Will you be all right?"

"Aye, Lolly, I expected this news, and Madam's visions confirmed my fears."

"Did she tell ye he was dead?"

"Aye, she said there was evil afoot and many other things, but you know Madam. Lolly, she's leaving, retiring to her brother's."

"Serena's leaving? Oh, dear, I must go see her before she

goes and bid farewell."

As Lolly left, Manik entered the chamber. His manner was sullen.

He shook his dark-haired head when she stood. "Nay, My Lady, please sit. I must talk to you privately."

Kate couldn't sit. "Manik, I'm glad you made it home safely. Are you well?"

"Aye, I'm well. I'm sorry, My Lady, but your father is dead."

Kate's head lightened as she sat on the bed. "Papa is dead. I didn't want to believe…"

"My Lady, he asked me to give you this." Manik handed her a wrapped cloth.

She held it but kept her gaze to the floor. "How did he die?" Shock lodged its unemotional bearing inside her, and coldness sat in the pit of her stomach.

"Your father gave me the item and told me to hide it. I put it with my belongings, and when I returned, he was injured. He told me to go, but I didn't want to leave him, My Lady, but he commanded me to," his voice grew thick with emotion.

"Who killed him?" Kate looked at the cloth she held. She didn't want to believe her dear papa was gone. It seemed unreal, as though she'd dreamt it.

"I know not, My Lady, the heathens came and a battle ensued outside the tent. Lord Hawk told me to tell you he loved you and then he yelled at me to leave. He was a good man, the Hawk."

Kate saddened because he'd been fond of her father. "Manik, you were brave. I'm sure Father thought so, too. What does Lord Richard have to do with this?"

"When Lord Hawk returned from battle, I took his gear to clean it. The healer tended his leg, and I saw Lord Richard and my lord talking, they were heated. After Lord Richard left, Hawk ordered me to hide the object. When I returned, he lay dying." His dark eyes glossed.

"Did you see Richard?"

"Nay. Hawk fought to stay alert, but the sound of soldiers' shouts bore down on us. He bade me to leave, so I lifted the edge of the tent to escape. There was little I could do for him. Before I slipped out, I saw a large man enter the tent. I waited for the blow that would surely end my lord's life, but I admit my fear, and I quickly left the tent. Look at the object. My lord said he wrote a message."

Kate unwrapped the cloth and found the medallion, it looked old but lustrous. She turned it over and back again.

"My lord put the note inside, open it."

Kate turned it over, took the dagger Manik held out to her, and pressed the tiny clasp, it clicked open. She removed the folded parchment and read it.

Beware the friend with the black heart. "Where was Lord Richard when this happened?" She didn't trust Richard, not after her father's words implied he'd wanted the medallion.

"I know not, when I returned, Hawk was alone." Manik's face turned bleak.

"We'll have to keep this a secret until I can figure it out. Pray, don't let on that I have it. I sense evil afoot. I don't trust Richard."

"I shan't tell a soul, My Lady. I was unable to protect my lord. I'll never be able to…"

"It's not your fault, Manik, don't hold guilt. You're back with us and that's all that matters. My father wouldn't want you to hold yourself accountable."

"Thank you, My Lady, for your kindness." Manik opened the door and left.

Kate sat on the bed and stared at the medallion. She glanced at the note again and recognized her father's hand. Why wouldn't he tell her whom he referred to outright? Until she uncovered its importance, she would be wary.

Kate stood in stunned silence. Immediately upon his unexpected arrival, Richard de Morris handed her a missive which she read with furrowed brows.

LASS' VALOR

Lady Stanhope, Regrettably your father is presumed dead. His tent was found burned to the ground and we could not locate his whereabouts. I will remain in Egypt for some time and give guardianship to my vassal, Lord Richard de Morris. On my return, I shall turn your father's lands over to your husband which the king has selected. His Grace betrothed you to a Scot, and your marriage will take place upon my return. Condolences, de Guylet.

Apparently, her betrothed wasn't knighted or titled and likely landless. The most astounding news was that he lived in Scotland. Her worst fear came true. She was betrothed to a man not worthy of her rank, but the king chose him so she hoped he was prosperous. With shaky hands, she rolled the missive and handed it back. She was forlorn but resisted the tears gathered in her eyes. If only she might flee the hall and retreat to her chamber. There, she'd soothe her restlessness and pray to the spirits.

"Lady Kaitlin, I'm sorry for your grief." Richard stood next to her and spoke with a gentle voice, "I cared for your father as much as you did. 'Tis sorrow for us all."

"Thank you, Lord Richard. I shall go to my chamber and pray for his soul." Kate turned to leave.

"Wait, ah, I regret not coming sooner. I've been home for several months but had business to attend and when the regent sent for me, I hadn't known Hawk was killed. This is dreadful. I should have stayed to protect him. Is there aught I can do to make you feel better?" Richard folded his hands behind him and walked beside her. "If I hadn't gone to Henry's court months ago, I would've been here to comfort you."

Kate sensed he wanted to say more, and he'd feigned concern for her father's death. His eyes gave him away; they didn't hold compassion, only coldness.

"I thank you for your concern, Lord Richard, but I must retire. Please, there's no need to account for yourself. I'm sure you would've protected my father were you there." She almost blanched at the untruth of those words. Kate needed to be alone, needed to think over what Richard told her, but most of all; she needed the comfort of the Goddess.

"Be ready to leave on the morrow."

"Why would I leave here?" She stopped at the steps.

"Aldwyn gave me guardianship and we shall travel to my home at once. You won't stay here alone…unprotected."

"I don't wish to leave my home. Surely, you'll allow me to stay until I wed, and then my husband will take over as lord here. Lord de Guylet stated the king selected my husband. I don't wish to be bothersome or cause you unnecessary hardship."

"I won't allow it, child. You will live with me until your overlord returns. I have written to Aldwyn and expressed the king's choice for your husband is unacceptable. He shall agree and select another. Your father wouldn't accept the arrangement, to a Scot of all men. The king is biased in his opinion of this man and your overlord will right this as soon as he returns."

Was that supposed to assuage Kate? She wasn't sure why he told her that, but she nodded.

"You shall pack your belongings and be ready to leave in the morn. I'll call Lolly to help." He told her nurse to ready for Kate's departure.

Kate's eyes filled with unshed tears. She didn't want to go with him and didn't trust the wretched man. Yet, she wouldn't disobey his command. Until her overlord returned, she would be at his mercy. She lowered her gaze and hid her repugnance.

"I wondered, Lady Kaitlin, did your father send you any keepsakes?"

"Keepsakes? Nay, My Lord."

"We found many treasures in Egypt. There were riches, and I thought… Nay?"

Kate eyed him warily and tried to sense if he was privy to the details of her father's death. Richard turned and was about to walk away when curiosity got the better of her.

"Treasures?"

Richard turned back, his face emotionless. "I thought

mayhap he sent you something before he...died. I sent my wife gold necklaces and trinkets. Would you like one?"

"Oh? Nay, Lord Richard." Kate shook her head. "I want no reminders of that horrid place. My father sent me nothing."

"I recall him showing me a golden medallion. He said that he would send it to you. It was beautiful with a spider etched on it. Did you not receive it?"

"Nay, I didn't," she lied. She tried to remain calm and lowered her eyes. Did he believe her? She couldn't tell. He remained unemotional, not even a blink to show his interest.

"Well, I shall give you a trinket. It's the least I can do since Hawk didn't send you anything. I'll return in the morning." He smiled and turned to leave.

"Farewell, My Lord."

After Richard strode from the hall, Kate ran up the stairs to her chamber. She swung the door open, ran to the bed, and sobbed for several minutes. Her gentle, loving father was dead, killed in a war that had no bearing on their lives. The news made Kate despise her country for its subterfuge.

She erected her rope circle and sat inside it. Contentment came with prayers spoken to the Goddess. Once again, the vision of the warrior came. If only he was her betrothed, she would be protected. His powerful aura relieved her, though she didn't understand why. The vision didn't matter now. She'd be sent to her unknown betrothed, especially if Aldwyn didn't change the king's decree. During the restless night, thoughts of her betrothed, her father's death, Richard's treachery, and Madam's forsooth, replayed in her head. She had to garner courage and face what was to come. After a restless night, she readied for her journey.

The next morning, Kate rode to Richard's keep. Deep sorrow embedded inside her and caused her detachment. The zealous late-summer day did little to warm her insides or her spirit. Richard had thirty soldiers escort her, who kept to themselves throughout the journey. She wasn't thrilled at the prospect of going to his home. Her father's last words prevented her from feeling safe. She had to beware the friend with the black heart—Richard. She tensed unknowing of what to expect.

Richard's land lay south of Londontown in the wooded forests of Surrey. They arrived after the noon hour. Smoke billowed from the manor's chimney and blackened the air. No landscape adorned the front of the manor. Large plain bricks in four steps led to the manor's entrance. Richard stood on the steps and received his steward. He looked at her with a spurious smile. Richard didn't possess a good character, of that she was certain.

"Welcome to my home, Lady Kaitlin. Come inside and take rest from your journey."

His sweet words sickened her. Richard was a thin man with dark hair, grayed on the sides, with wafts of hair stuck out beside his ears. He appeared to have wings but walked as if in pain, and she wouldn't venture a guess how old he was. He was slight, though tall. She stepped past and held her satchel in a death grip and entered the hall.

Her father's fief was much smaller but cozier and cleaner. Kate was unimpressed by the look of his home. Tables covered with layers of grime, almost blackened by soot. The tapestries on the walls tattered and faded. Designs were unrecognizable. She chanced a glance at the floors, and the rushes cracked when she walked on them. Stale ale smelled rancid, and she suppressed a gag. Must she live here?

She would write to King Henry as soon as possible and beg him to intercede on her behalf. Hopefully, he'd persuade the Regent to settle her elsewhere. If only they overturned Lord de Guylet's command and choose another guardian. Even staying with her betrothed had to be an improvement. She was appalled by the hall's lack of cleanliness.

"Lady Kaitlin, welcome," a lady called from her seat at the table. "I'm Lady Hilda, Lord Richard's wife. My husband was a good friend of your father's and we're regretful for your loss."

"Lady de Morris, it's a pleasure to meet you." Kate

swallowed hard while she assessed her.

"I'll have you shown to a chamber. I'm pleased to have another lady here. It's been a long time since we entertained. I find I'm excited to have another lady at our manor."

The lady's thin hair, worn in curls atop her head, matted and flattened. Though Lady de Morris was supposedly young, her rumpled appearance made her appear aged. The chartreuse color of her gown was unbecoming. Kate shook her head. It wasn't polite to judge the lady so, Goddess forgive her, she pleaded, for being uncompassionate. She tried to find something pleasant about the woman, but even her high-pitched voice unnerved Kate. What did the lady say? She remembered now.

"Aye, My Lady, I'm tired from my journey and need rest."

At that moment, her cat made her presence known when she popped her head from the carryall Kate held. Lady de Morris' shriek was likely heard all the way to Londontown by the sound of it.

"What is that?" Lady de Morris jumped onto the bench that flanked the table and lifted her skirts high enough to show her knees. "Someone get a sword, kill it. Kill it!"

"It's my cat, Trixie. I'm sorry she frightened you. She's harmless, I assure you." Kate petted her cat and tried to soothe her. Trixie clawed at the carryall and attempted to free herself.

"Be gone with that rodent." Lady de Morris' demand came in another shriek.

Kate's first thought was that an animal living within the keep wouldn't make much difference, her second, to calm the horrid lady. The lady continued to hold her gown above her ankles.

"Lady de Morris, if you'll allow me, I shall keep my pet in my bedchamber. She'll not be bothersome. She's not a rodent, but a feline. I promise she'll behave."

"See that, that creature stays in there. I don't want it walking around my keep, the filthy, vile beastie."

"Aye, My Lady." Kate raised her eyes heavenward. Cats were revered and respected for their mystical aura. But the lady probably didn't hold with such beliefs. After all, cleanliness was next to Godliness.

Lady de Morris showed her to a large bedchamber on the second level. Several young boys brought her trunks and other baggage into the room. She set Trixie on the floor and closed the door behind the servants. Finally alone, she was thankful the chamber wasn't as filthy as the hall. The chamber contained a large canopied bed with clean linens tucked neatly at the corners. A table flanked the bedside, on which, sat a bowl and a pitcher. A tall screen stood in the corner of the room. It was a rather nice room considering what the hall looked like.

She wandered to the wardrobe and placed her garments inside. Trixie jumped on the bed, curled into a ball, and purred. Kate finished her chores and joined her friend on the bed. Trixie soothed her and made her feel not so very alone. She petted her and closed her eyes.

Kate opened her eyes and noticed the window-casement darkened. She fell asleep, but something woke her. Someone yelled in the adjacent chamber and made thumping sounds. Lady de Morris' high-pitched voice reverberated through the wall.

"You will eat," Lady de Morris' voice hardened.

A child's bawl followed and she wondered who the child was since the de Morris' had no children. Lady de Morris' yell rattled the wall again.

"Ye best get used to being here, little savage. This is your home now. If this food is not eaten, you will be punished again. I don't know why I care for the likes of ye. Starve yourself for all I care."

The door banged and the lady's footsteps retreated. Her first opinion was accurate—the lady didn't possess a good character. The child sobbed loudly and her heart ached. The child's cries diminished a few minutes later, and the night grew quiet once again.

Early the next morning, Kate awoke in her new home. She dressed and readied for the day. Trixie continued to slumber on the bed and wouldn't wake until noon. Kate gave her a pat betwixt her ears, for which she received a loathsome look. She always rose early, near to sunrise, and rushed to the hall for her morning meal. The hall was surprisingly empty, so she sat at the table and a servant girl entered with a tray of food balanced on her hip. She wore a brown frock tied at the waist. The girl seemed pleasant.

"Good morn, My Lady, I'm Susie." She set the food down and curtseyed.

"Did you prepare my room?"

"I tried to make it welcoming, not that Lady de Morris asked. Please, don't let on. My Lady doesn't like it when we tarry over our chores."

Kate frowned but nodded. "The room was a welcome relief from travel. I appreciate the food. Is there anyone about yet? Have Lady and Lord de Morris risen?"

"Oh, nay, My Lady, the de Morris' don't rise for another few hours yet. They are late sleepers. Lady de Morris is lazy…" Susie's eyes widened. "Forgive me, My Lady, I shouldn't have said that. Pray, don't tell Lady de Morris I said such. She would grumble at me for the rest of the day."

Kate's eyes crinkled. "I shan't tell her."

Susie lifted the hem of her frock, curtseyed, and strode away.

Kate ate a light breakfast then she snatched an apple from the trencher, and returned to her chamber. She crept down the hall and stopped outside the room next to hers. With her ear pressed against the wood, she listened for sounds from within. She turned the handle and opened the door.

Though it was dark inside, she made out the outline of a window on the far wall. She walked to it and pulled the worn tapestry aside. Light filtered in and brightened the room. Beams of sunlight filled with dust and streamed across the chamber. Kate waved at the dust and held her breath. She glanced around the room. A pile of covers sat in the corner. The small hearth on the opposite side was empty, save for a few cobwebs. There was a chill in the room.

Had she dreamt of the child's presence last evening?

Kate stooped beside the covers and stifled a gasp when a beautiful child unveiled herself from beneath the pile. Her tiny hands rubbed the sleep from her eyes. She couldn't tell if the child had light or dark hair, but peered at her beautiful blue eyes. The child looked frightened. Her fear made Kate empathize, and she knelt beside her.

"I'm Kate. Who are you?" She gentled her voice, but the little girl didn't answer and scooted back. "I'd like to be your friend. Would you like that, too?" She hoped to soothe the child. Still, the child didn't speak. Mayhap she wouldn't speak? Perhaps she didn't understand English?

"Be not afraid. Are you well, unharmed?" The child nodded. "All right, sweeten, you must eat something. I brought an apple. If you eat it, I'll bring you a surprise." Kate handed the apple to her and the girl reached with her shaky hand and took it. She held it but didn't raise it to her mouth. "You eat your apple and I'll return in a few minutes with your surprise."

Kate rose slowly so she wouldn't frighten the girl and left the chamber. *A child.* Was she the child Madam Serena spoke of in her prophecy? Kate scoffed, it couldn't be. She returned to her chamber to get her cat. When she reached the child's room, she placed Trixie next to the girl. The child slunk away and held the half-eaten apple.

"Don't be afraid. This is my friend Trixie. She's my best friend. Do you want to know why?" Kate smiled and continued to pet her cat.

The little girl nodded. It was progress.

"She likes to purr and listen to me talk. I talk to her all the time and do you know what? Never once has she told my secrets." The little girl giggled a delightful sound that made Kate smile. She continued to pet Trixie and sensed the girl's ease. "I need a favor because the lady here doesn't want

Trixie in her hall. Might I leave her here with you? You shall keep her company when I'm unable to be with her. She likes people." Kate fibbed because Trixie didn't like anyone, save her, but she hoped the cat would make the girl smile.

The child nodded again. It was a start.

"All right, I'll leave her here. She likes to be petted like this." Kate stroked Trixie's back to the tip of her tail and showed her how to pet her. She left the room again and hoped the cat would pull the girl out of her glumness. The poor thing looked pale and thin. Kate was determined to find out about her, how she came to be with the de Morris', and why she'd been kept in the room. Questions racked her mind. She would search out Lady de Morris later and get those answers.

A child, here at the de Morris' keep. Who would have thought such a thing was possible? Kate considered what Madam bespoke; she'd meet the warrior when she met the child. Having dismissed the comments Madam made, what with the news of her father's death, the betrothal announcement, and her sudden departure from home, she hadn't given it much thought. What were the chances she would meet a child and a warrior? Yet she met a child. Would she meet the warrior?

CHAPTER TWO

The warrior haunted her visions.

Kate returned to her chamber, cleaned up a bit, unpacked her candles and rope, and sat in her circle. Once again, the vision of the warrior came. He never moved, only appeared to look sternly at her with his arms crossed. She shook him from her mind, not wanting to venture there. Instead, she prayed to the Goddess for guidance on how to aid her. It was a futile effort because the dark-haired warrior kept intruding. His rigid stance and gray eyes troubled Kate. She wouldn't get answers this morning, not with the warrior haunting her. After she'd completed her morning ritual, she returned to the hall.

Lady de Morris called to her when she entered. Kate approached and looked to make sure the bench was clean before she sat on it.

"What have you been doing this morning, Lady Kaitlin?"

"I've unpacked and settled in, My Lady."

"How do you find the keep? It's magnificent, is it not?" Lady de Morris sounded proud of the derelict residence.

Kate almost choked on the piece of cheese she'd stuck in her mouth. She picked up a goblet and drank and swallowed the cheese caught in her throat. "It's...lovely. I would be glad to help in the keeping of it. I took care of my—"

Lady de Morris interrupted, "Nay, my girl, that's the servants' tasks. I won't have ye lifting a finger. Now, tell me, how old are you?"

Kate wasn't at all impressed with her manners. "I just turned nine and ten, My Lady."

"How is it you're not married?" Lady de Morris poured more ale in her cup.

"My father was called to Damietta five years ago and didn't make arrangements before he left. I was only four and ten and there was no time to see to it."

"My husband has influential contacts in Londontown. In fact, he just returned from a tourney at his majesty's summer palace." She boasted her husband's position as if it would impress Kate.

Kate wasn't affected in the least. "Will we be going to such events?"

"Perhaps, you shall. You'll attend with Richard. I fear I don't have the stamina for such a journey and nor do I wish to go to court. Richard won't return to court for a while, but he will help you find a worthy husband."

"Thank you, Lady de Morris, but King Henry betrothed me, and when Lord Aldwyn returns, I shall go to him." Why did it sound distressful? Her future husband awaited, whether Lord Richard insisted Aldwyn influence the king's decision. Perhaps the man was a gentleman and would be a kind husband. The king wouldn't betroth her to someone of ill bearing. Although she'd only met the king once, she hoped he remembered her.

Lady de Morris nodded. "I had forgotten that. Richard told me of the betrothal and his dislike of the circumstances. Have no fear, Richard will right it. Have you eaten, child?"

"Aye, I rise early and have eaten. I heard you speaking to a child last night, in the room next to mine. Who is she?"

Lady de Morris' eyes narrowed and her face scrunched. "Child?"

"Aye, a child...in the room next to mine."

"Oh, that child. Forgive me, I had forgotten about her.

She's an orphaned servant's child. I've taken the poor girl in and gave her a home. Yet, she won't speak. Perhaps she's mute. I'll begin training her, but she's young and troublesome."

"That is kind of you, Lady, to take her in. Perhaps I can help."

"Mayhap you can get her to eat. She'll not come out of the room, and I want to begin her training soon. There's plenty of work to do."

Kate knew she'd lied because the woman yelled at the girl the night before. "I'd be happy to see to her adjustment. I haven't anything else to do and adore children." She tried to sound unenthusiastic.

"You can begin by taking her food. She hasn't eaten yet this day. I don't want the servants near her, because she's frightened. She's a timid thing."

"How long has she been here?" Kate feared to question her, but the lady seemed forthcoming.

"Almost three months."

If the child had eaten little since she'd come, no wonder she looked thin. She would make sure the child ate and would fatten her up.

"I'll see you later, dear child, I'm off to the village." Lady de Morris strode from the hall and left Kate sitting at the table alone.

She left soon after and ambled to the kitchens. After placing foodstuff in a sack, she grabbed a small basin from a table. She took the stairs and walked the filthy corridor that led to the sleeping chambers. When the girl didn't answer her knock, Kate opened the door and peeked inside. The girl sat in the corner, petting her cat, and slunk back when Kate entered.

"Don't be afraid, lovey, I won't hurt you." Kate set down the basin and removed the sack from over her shoulder. She sat next to her and smiled in hopes to relieve the child's fear.

"I know you speak English because you understood me

earlier. I want to be your friend, and like Trixie, I can keep secrets, too." The child didn't move or speak. "Why don't we start with our names? You remember, I told you my name is Kate. What's your name?" Seconds passed before the girl uttered a sound.

"B-Bonnie," the little girl uttered.

"Bonnie, that's a beautiful name. We're going to be fast friends. Where are you from?"

"T-the H-highlands. Scotland."

"Scotland? I've never been there before. Is it nice there?"

She nodded and stuttered, "'Tis h-home."

"Where are your parents?"

"At Honey's."

"Who is Honey?" Kate placed her hand under Trixie's chin and scratched her.

"Mama's cousin."

"Where does she live, in Scotland, too?"

"Nay, England. Cousin Honey is a he."

"How did you come here? The lady said…" Kate was stunned. Hadn't Lady de Morris said the girl was an orphaned servant's child? How could a servant's child be from Scotland?

"T-the mean m-man…took me."

"Took you? Do you mean her husband?"

Bonnie nodded.

Kate sobered. "Do you mean he was asked to bring you here and—"

Bonnie shook her head. "Nay, I was supposed to rest, Papa said so."

"Aye, and…" She waited for her to continue.

"I snuck out, and the mean m-man…took me."

"He picked you up and took you?" Kate realized she'd raised her voice and blew a dejected sigh.

Bonnie moved away. "Aye, he put me on his horse and rided away. I tried to scream, but no one could hear me."

"Will your parents be upset that you're gone?"

"Aye, Mama will cry and Papa will look for me."

Bonnie's eyes watered, and her little body shuddered.

"Do they know where you are?"

"Nay," she sobbed and shook her head.

"You've been here for a long time? Three months?"

"Aye, I'm scared and miss Papa."

"Bonnie, do you want to go home?"

"I want Mama and Papa." Tears rolled down her face, and she wailed.

Kate realized she was crying, too. She lifted Bonnie and settled her on her lap and held the girl in her arms, and tried to comfort her.

"Don't worry, we'll get you home. I'll take you there myself if I have to. You can trust me, Bonnie. Can you stay with me until I figure out a way to get you home?"

Bonnie nodded and sniffled with another shudder.

"I promise we'll go on a great quest." She swiped the tears from Bonnie's face and hugged her close.

"I like adventure, Papa always says so."

Kate laughed. "Well, we're alike in that. Now, we must get you cleaned, and you must eat. You need to get nice and fat before we go on our journey." She tickled her tummy and Bonnie giggled.

She thought to wash the girl and reached for the basin, but the child needed a bath. Instead, Kate returned to the kitchen and instructed a bath to be sent to her room. She returned to Bonnie's room and took her to her chamber. When the bath arrived, she undressed Bonnie and put her in the tub. Bruises spotted the poor girl's back and legs. Someone beat her. Kate suppressed her rage, or at least she tried to.

"Who beat you, Bonnie?"

"The l-lady."

That harridan hurt the poor child. She hid her fury, but her cheeks burned with anger. "I shall get even with her."

She washed the girl, dried her, and put her into a fresh gown, one that was slightly tight on her and no longer fit properly. Even so, the gown was too large for the little girl.

She cut the bottom hem where it ended at her feet and shortened the sleeves. A mending would make for a better fit, but she'd have to see to it later. Bonnie looked silly in the overlarge garment.

Kate combed her long hair, likely never cut once in her short life. Once dried, the ends curled, giving her an innocent look. She and Bonnie spent the day tidying Kate's chamber. After the midday meal, they sat on the bed. Trixie lay next to them, her purr filled the room.

"You're nice and clean. You'll sleep better now."

"C-can I stay with you?"

"There's more than enough room." Kate changed into her nightdress behind the screen and when they settled in bed, she asked Bonnie to tell her about Scotland and her family. Was that ever a mistake? The child who hadn't spoken suddenly found her voice.

"Mama is pretty, Papa says so. He loves her. Papa is laird. I'm a MacKinnon."

"Tell me about your family."

"I have a brother, his name is Kevin. He's just a bairn, och I help Mama take care of him." Bonnie couldn't sit still and fiddled with the covers. "Sometimes I get into trouble and Papa punishes me. He doesn't want to and says he has to. Mama always laughs 'cause Papa tries to think of new punishments, but he always does the same thing—makes me sit in his chair. I don't like to sit in Papa's chair, but it's the best one. 'Cause you know why?"

Kate shook her head.

"'Cause Papa's laird." Bonnie's voice became arrogant as if Kate should've known that.

Kate laughed and hugged her.

"Uncle Brendan, that's Papa's brother. He's going to be angry with me for gettin' lost. He looks scary, but I'm not 'ascared of him. You know why?"

"Nay, why, lovey?" Kate closed her eyes. As she listened to the girl, she couldn't help wonder why Lord Richard would abduct her. There had to be a reason, and it certainly wasn't because they needed servants. She wondered if something happened at the king's castle which caused Lord Richard's ire, and he took Bonnie for revenge. Lord Richard was an evil knave. Somehow, she had to help Bonnie. She opened her eyes and found Bonnie gazing at her.

"'Cause he has a good heart. He told me not to tell anyone. Oops, I shouldn't have told you that, now Uncle will be angry." Bonnie placed her hand over her mouth, her eyes twinkled with mischief.

"I won't tell your uncle, your secret is safe."

"Papa has a big family. They live with us and they're our clan. Uncle Robin married Mama's friend, Tess. She's bonny, just like Mama, and she gaved Uncle a bairn, too. You know what his name is?"

"Nay, what?" Kate yawned.

"Robert. Mama calls him Robbie, 'cause his Papa's name is Robin." Bonnie yawned, too. "I have a pet named George."

"Is George a dog?"

"Nay." Bonnie giggled. "He's a goat. Mama loves 'em, but he's 'badder than me sometimes. You know what?"

"What?"

"He likes to eat Mama's tablecloths. She smacks him and he runs away." Bonnie giggled again. "Mama says he plays games with her."

When she finally quieted, Kate thought about what the little girl told her. Bonnie was abducted by her guardian and she had a loving family who was, at this very minute, desperate to find her. Kate knew why the Goddess sent her there now: she had to save Bonnie and return her to her family. How would she be able to do that? Madam said she would go on a somber mission. How was the warrior connected to the child? She'd met the child, but where was the warrior? She needed to get inside her circle but would wait until Bonnie fell asleep. She hoped Bonnie's family searched nearby so she could return her.

Somehow, Kate would get even with Lady de Morris for hurting Bonnie, and she would begin the very next morning.

And get even, she would. No woman or man would hurt a child if she had anything to do with it. A sennight passed since Kate's arrival to the de Morris manor. She and Bonnie spent every waking moment together. Kate took her out on walks in the fresh air for exercise, being cooped up in that chamber for such a long time made Bonnie pale. This day, they picnicked in the outlying area beyond the manor where the grass grew thicker, and they sat upon an old cloth taken from the bedchamber. At least outside, they didn't have to contend with Lady de Morris, her loathsome looks at Bonnie, or the stench of the hall.

Kate got an idea. "Bonnie, are you afraid of insects?"

"What kind of insects?"

"Big, ugly beetle insects." Kate laughed.

"Nay, why?"

"I want to collect them and put them in the lady's bed."

Bonnie giggled. "Aye, that would be fun. Where do we find 'em?"

"Just go along this high brush." Kate knelt and plucked an insect from the blade of grass. She placed it in the basket she'd brought. The creature felt strange and vile, but it was worth touching them, knowing what she would do with them.

They put any kind of insects they found in the basket. When they found an ugly insect, they shouted with glee. Bonnie found the biggest beetle Kate had ever seen. They hated touching the insects, but it would be worth it. Lady de Morris would be in for a surprise this night. Kate and Bonnie skipped back to the manor, their trick secure inside the basket. When they entered, Lady de Morris sat in her usual place.

Mayhap Kate should pity her. Alas, Lady de Morris had an evil spirit and wouldn't get compassion from her, not after seeing what she did to Bonnie. Nay, the woman didn't deserve a kind word, let alone sympathy. She was fortunate Kate didn't use her skills to cause harm, for if she had, the lady would be dead by now. But Kate never used her powers to cast spells in ill against others. It was something Madam enforced, and Kate had too gentle a heart to want to hurt anyone, even someone as vile as Lady de Morris. Although harming the woman crossed her mind several times since she'd seen Bonnie's back.

She and Bonnie returned to the chamber they now shared. It neared the evening meal, so they changed and washed. Kate disliked eating in the hall, but the lady forbade them from eating in their chamber. Once they were ready, they retreated down the stairs for the meal. Kate sat next to Bonnie and put meat on her tray. Pigeon, veal, and a variety of vegetables were served. Kate thought it odd, because she didn't think the de Morris' were well to do, yet the food served was of quality. She piled her tray with vegetables and avoided the high piled meats. The smell of it made her nauseous. As they ate, the hall's silence became palpable.

Lord Richard joined them for the meal. It was the first time he'd eaten with them since Kate's arrival. He gave her looks of loathing, which made her uncomfortable. She avoided his gaze and concentrated on finishing her food. Kate and Bonnie left the hall as soon as the meal ended. They hurried to take care of their little chore of releasing the creatures.

Kate entered her room and grabbed the basket. "I have them, Bonnie, let's go."

"Aye, Kate."

They tiptoed down the hall to the lady's room. The empty chamber darkened because the sun faded, which produced a hazy atmosphere. Dimness added to the shabbiness of the abode. When they approached the bed, Bonnie pulled back the covers and Kate dumped the contents onto the bed, shaking the basket until all the creatures were out. Insects crawled in various directions.

"Hurry, pull back the covers."

After they finished the chore, they crept toward the door. Someone's footsteps sounded in the hallway. Kate grasped Bonnie's hand and pulled her behind the door. She cracked the door open to peek and they held their breath. A servant hummed as she passed by, laden with a pile of wash. They slipped from the room, and once they were inside their chamber, they fell on the bed in a riot of laughter.

"Kate, if Papa knowed what we did, he would make us both sit in his chair for a whole day." Bonnie giggled.

"I can't wait until she comes. Let us ready for bed." Kate opened the wardrobe and took a nightrail.

They finished washing and changed into their nightclothes. She read to Bonnie from a large tome she'd bought from home. Bonnie seemed to enjoy being read to. After reading a few pages, they heard the lady in the corridor. They scrambled from the bed and ran to the door. Kate cracked the door open, their ears pressed against the wood and listened. The lady entered her room, the door creaked.

They waited.

"A few more minutes," Kate whispered.

All quieted, but then Bonnie let out a low giggle.

"Shhh." Kate held the door ajar.

In a sudden rush, the lady's door opened, and she ran down the hall shrieking. Kate closed the door and she and Bonnie fell into a fit of laughter. Bonnie's giggle lightened the chamber as they both tried to fall asleep.

Early the next morning, they entered the hall to break their fast and found Lady D there in her usual place. They now referred to her as 'Lady D.' She slept in the hall the night before and looked groggy.

"Kaitlin, have you seen any insects in your room? I was beset by the vile beasts last eve. They overtook my chamber, and I'm having Suzie give it a thorough scrubbing."

Kate stifled her laughter. "I haven't noticed any." She regretted Suzie would have to clean Lady D's room, but that couldn't be helped.

Bonnie stood next to her and hid her smile. They ate breakfast and spent the day thinking of nasty things to do to her.

The next day, they collected toads all afternoon by the pond beyond the village. It was fun, and they were soaking wet from their jaunt. They placed fifteen toads in the ale barrel just before the evening meal. Lady D happened to open the barrel to refill her goblet. Her scream caused many men-at-arms to run inside the manor. Lady D glared at Kate, but she held herself circumspect because the lady couldn't prove that she'd done it.

"Kaitlin, Lord Richard was called away to a tenant's home." Lady D placed food on her tray, and Kate didn't think she wanted a response, so she kept quiet.

Kate was glad he'd left because he repulsed her with his glares and ogles. She tried not to look at him, but his stare made her uneasy. At least, the meal that night would be more enjoyable without his company.

Later that day, Kate threw her basin water out the window. Luckily, Lady D stood below it. She stuck her head out the window and yelled down, "Oh, My Lady, I didn't know you were walking by. I apologize." She and Bonnie had a fit of laughter over that. Kate enjoyed torturing her and anticipated the next day.

When Kate arrived in the hall the next morning, it was vacant. After she poured herself and Bonnie a bowl of pottage, she mixed dried mandrake and yarrow roots in the porridge pot that sat on the fire. It would cause the lady to have stomach cramps for the rest of the day. Lady D came down to break her fast. Kate hoped she would pour herself a heaping bowlful, as she normally did.

"Kaitlin, will you get me a cup of ale?"

"Of course, My Lady." Kate couldn't resist, she put grounded raspberry leaves in the cup.

Lady D would run from the room. Likely, she'd spend the rest of the day in the garderobes. It had been a long time since she'd pulled such pranks. She sobered because it reminded her of when she was young and carefree, living at home with her beloved father, Lolly, and Madam Serena. How she missed her father's keep and him. He often remarked jovially about her pranks, though she didn't do such vile things to him or the servants. She knew that she needed to form a plan to return Bonnie to her home, and she had a few ideas.

Lady D's shout interrupted her thoughts. "This porridge is horrible, take it away." She sipped the ale Kate gave her.

Kate watched, not smiling outwardly, but inside she burst with giddiness.

"What are you girls about this day?"

Kate kept her expression serene. "We're going to the village for a while. We'll return later, and I will begin instruction on sewing."

"'Tis time the girl learned to sew," Lady D agreed.

The two girls walked the mile to the village. Kate wanted to talk to the smithy. Master Hemmings seemed a kind old soul. Kate hoped he would offer to help her. She entered the smithy's hut and found him at his work. He hit a flaming mass with a large maillot, tapping pieces of steel. When he noticed her, he stopped his banging. Her ears rang from the deafening sound.

"My Lady, what can I do for ye?"

"Master Hemmings, I'm Lady Stanhope, a ward of Lord Richard's. I need your help."

"I'll help if I can. What do ye need?"

"I need a good, sturdy horse. I have a few jewels as payment. Do you know where or how I can go about getting one? Is there a hostler in the village?"

"Aye, there be, My Lady. I can take care of that." He seemed proud that she asked him.

"Thank you, Master Hemmings. I need the horse as soon as you can arrange it. When might you be free to take care of this matter?"

"I'd be free this noon. Would that be soon enough?"

"Oh, aye. Can you keep the horse tethered out back?"

"Aye, My Lady. Why do ye need a horse, there's plenty at the manor?" He flushed at his insolence.

Kate was alarmed by his question, her mind raced,

searching for an answer. "Um...I will teach the young one to ride. She's always wanted to learn and—"

"Why he need be sturdy then? They have horses at my lord's manor." He stepped toward her with his brows raised.

"Master Hemmings, I beg your pardon, but I'm a good judge of horseflesh. Please be sure it can handle a tough hand and a rough ride." Kate's tone became stringent.

He swallowed hard at her words. "Of course, My Lady, I didn't mean to offend ye."

"Very well." She smiled and handed him the jewels, but kept the coins. She realized that she should placate him before she left. "Please, don't say a word about this...you see, it's meant to be a surprise. They adore the child, her being the relative of my lady's and I want to teach her in private."

"I understand," he said.

She hated lying to the old man, but she couldn't tell him the truth. She and Bonnie walked around the village, and they waved to those who passed by. Kate removed the cloak she placed around Bonnie because the day grew warm.

She was responsible for the girl and had to find a way to return her to the caring arms of her family. The need to leave pressed on her. Lord Richard looked at her oddly when he ate the evening meal with them the other night. He had been gone for two days and expected to return today. She knew she'd have to leave soon. Tomorrow, they would begin their journey. She had an idea of where they would go and would take the child to Honey's, wherever that was. It was after all, still in England. Kate had never traveled all the way to Scotland.

They stopped at the miller's hut where Kate bought a large saddlebag to hold their belongings. She carried the thick leather bag and left it behind Master Hemmings' hut. They headed toward Madam Flichard's hut down the path. She enjoyed Madam's bread and hoped the lady would give them a loaf or two for their journey. When she asked if she had any extra bread, she was given three fresh loaves. The woman beamed with pride over Kate's compliments on her baking.

She stopped back at Master Hemmings' hut and noticed the horse tethered out back. The gelding was beautiful, dark-brown, with black spots. He was sound and docile, with a strong sturdy girth around his middle. The horse nibbled at the grass along the path.

"Will he do?" Master Hemmings came outside, shielding his eyes from the bright early-afternoon sun.

"Aye, thank you. What's his name?"

"His name be Ralph, but you can call him anything ye want. He's yours, right and tight."

Kate laughed. Ralph was as fine a name as any. "You'll leave him tethered here? We shall return on the morrow for the lessons."

"Of course, My Lady, as ye asked."

They left the smithy's hut and walked back to the manor. For the rest of the day, they sat in the hall practicing sewing. Kate tried to keep calm because Lady D would suspect something if she was agitated. Lady D's chair sat empty, and that gave Kate another idea. She and Bonnie strolled outside and walked along the keep's walls.

"Where are we going, Kate?"

"I'm looking for a plant."

"What's it for?"

"Lady D. It has three leaves and whatever you do, don't touch it. You'll break out in a rash that'll have you itching for a week."

"What are we going to do with it?"

"I'm going to rub it on Lady D's chair, it's what she deserves." Kate knelt down and spotted the weed she sought. She used her gown to pull out a big stem.

They skipped back to the hall. Kate hurried and rubbed the leaves over the lady's chair. Bonnie pointed to the spots she missed. She was thorough, making sure that if the lady's skin touched anywhere on the chair, she'd be itching by the end of the night.

The day wore on, and Kate was grateful it passed quickly. Her stomach fluttered madly. She wanted to retire and have the morning come. Supper became a tumultuous affair because Lord Richard returned. He sat at the end of the table, sending peculiar glances at her. She ignored him as best she could. At last, supper ended with Lord Richard's departure. She took Bonnie's hand and stood to leave, but Lady D stopped them. Blotches of redness streaked her hands and arms, making her scratch. Not only that, but her face was blotchy, too.

"Are you unwell, Lady de Morris?" Kate feigned concern.

"Oh, aye, I seem to be itchy, must be this new material. My dear husband brought this fabric from Londontown, and I had it made into this gown. I believe I'll go and have a bath."

Kate smiled. As soon as her body touched the water, the rash would spread and she would itch all over, but Kate kept that thought to herself. "Aye, a nice warm bath."

"I need the young one to go to the kitchens and peel onions for tomorrow's stew."

"I'll help her." Kate took Bonnie's hand, but Lady D pulled her away.

"Nay, you rest. You've been with the child all day. It won't take her long, there are not many to peel, and cook cut himself this morn. He needs help."

Kate nodded. "All right, don't be too long, Bonnie."

Bonnie nodded because she'd never spoke in the lady's presence. Bonnie hesitated to leave her side, but she had no choice. She had to obey Lady D, and send her to the kitchens.

The light faded and night approached, Bonnie would have to walk back in the dark. She wanted to retrieve her when she finished her tasks. Kate hurried to her chamber and gathered the items they needed for the journey. She pulled the satchel aside and placed inside: a dagger she'd taken from the hall, a small bow her father gave her when she was younger, arrows, and a few garments for them both. Once the large satchel crammed with their belongings, she set the satchel by the door.

LASS' VALOR

Kate positioned her rope on the floor, set the candles in place, and then sat. She folded her legs beneath her, closed her eyes and waited. Trixie took her place beside her. Kate hummed a light tune and tried to ease the tension from her body.

And then it came, the vision of the gray-eyed, dark-haired warrior. Kate shook her head. "Please, Goddess, send me a vision about the journey. Will we be safe? Will I get the child home?" She hummed again, but the warrior's silhouette framed in sunlight came to her. Answers wouldn't come this night, not with his vision intruding. Was he trying to tell her something with his austere frown?

Kate jumped when her door banged open. Lord Richard stepped inside and closed the door behind him. He gave her an indignant glance.

She froze.

"What do you want?" She frowned at him from her position on the floor.

"What every man wants. My wife suggested you might enjoy it. Lord knows she's no good at it. You'll make me a fine wife once I rid myself of—"

"S-surely you don't m-mean what you just s-said," she stammered. She hastily picked up the rope, doused the candles, and set them aside.

"Aye, I do, Kaitlin. You will remove your garments and do my bidding. You are indebted to me for letting you come here. As your guardian, I command you to do it."

Kate's face reddened. "Nay, I'll do no such thing. I don't understand what…you mean by this. I shall never submit to you. I will never marry you, and besides, the king has betrothed me."

He laughed coarsely. "A betrothal that shall be set aside. You'll obey me or the child will suffer. I've seen how fond you are of her." Richard crossed the room, his eyes glared like a wolf's in the night.

Kate backed away. "Nay, you'll not hurt that child."

"Then you'll do as I say, now remove your garments. I'll

not hurt you if you do my will."

She walked away from him, stalling, hoping to think of a means of escape, but he blocked the path to the door. An intense pain settled in her chest as panic seized control over her.

"B-but I-I am betrothed. You wouldn't go against the king." It was all that came to her.

"The king is a sniveling fool. Your betrothal won't come to pass. Aldwyn will listen to me. Ah, my dear Kaitlin, there are things we need to discuss, but after we enjoy our pleasure. One of which is the medallion, I know you have it. You believe me a fool, don't you?"

His voice lowered to such a pitch that it frightened Kate. Fear mingled with panic in her stomach, and she thought she'd be ill. Just what had he intended when he brought her to his home? Surely he wouldn't go against the king and refute her betrothal?

"I don't know what you speak of, Lord Richard. What medallion?"

Richard reached out and slapped her across her cheek. The force of it sent Kate to the floor. She cried out but didn't move. She tried to abate the sting in her cheek by rubbing it. Richard grabbed her arm and jerked her to him.

"Don't lie to me, I know you have it. Where is it?"

"I'll never give it to you, never. You're a blackheart. My father told me not to trust you. I'll die before I give it to you." She pulled away from him.

Richard laughed snidely. "If that's your wish, Kaitlin. I shall find the medallion amongst your belongings, but first, I'll enjoy myself. You've become rather appealing. Now remove your garments or I'll have the child fetched so she can witness your downfall."

Kate searched the room with a quick glance, her mind raced. Terror spread throughout her insides, shaking every nerve in her body. He stalked about the room and removed his robe. When he stood before her, she withheld the urge to gag. The man was downright dreadful.

He reached out and grasped her arm. Kate struggled and tried to get free from his clutch, but he threw her on the bed and laid his body atop hers. He pulled at her garments, his hands moved over her body touching her lewdly. She screamed, but his chilling laughter banished her panic.

Kate focused on the canopy above and fumbled to reach behind her. If only she found something, anything to use as a weapon on the bedside stand. Why couldn't she have left the dagger on the table? She felt a quill used for writing—that wouldn't do. Then she fingered the book she'd read to Bonnie. The tomb was heavy and she barely lifted it with one hand. She held it with both hands now.

Richard pawed her breast and kissed her face. How she withstood it, she had no notion. He pressed his body against her, mindless to what she was doing. She gripped the book and brought it down upon his head as hard as she could. A loud whacking noise followed and he stilled.

Had she killed him? Her breath rasped from the exertion and she pushed him off her. She grabbed the tie from his robe and bound his wrists and gagged him with a belt. She hadn't killed him she realized when his breath rose his chest. At least she'd made it so he'd spend the night there. He wouldn't give an alert that she fled. That was until someone found him in the morning. Her chest rose and fell with excitement.

Kate stumbled to the basin and splashed water on her face. The vile man touched her. She was appalled and tried to calm her indignation. Her torn garment drew her notice, so she donned a cloak. She picked up her satchel, threw in her rope and candles, clutched Trixie under her belly then ran for her life.

She reached the kitchens and called to Bonnie. "Bonnie, lovey, we have to go now." Kate was amazed at how calm she sounded.

"Where are we going, Kate?"

"Home, but we must hasten. We have to run. Can you do that, Bonnie?"

"To Ralph?"

"That's right…to Ralph." The village was a mile or so from the manor house. Nightfall gave cover from anyone trailing them, so they stopped a few times to catch their breath. Kate held Bonnie's hand and pulled her along.

"Kate, I can't run anymore."

"I will slow down, but we must keep moving." They continued, and after making more progress, the young girl slowed again. Kate finally picked her up. They ran the rest of the way. Bonnie didn't weigh much, so it wasn't too difficult, but holding her belongings and making sure she didn't jostle Trixie, was a difficult task. When they reached the smithy's hut, there, as promised, waited Ralph.

CHAPTER THREE

Kate lifted Bonnie onto the horse's back and secured the satchel to the harness by the horse's forelegs. Trixie jumped into the satchel so Kate wouldn't worry her. She touched the medallion covered by cloth on a string, tied around her pet's neck. The only clue to her father's death was secure. She had all she needed. Thank goodness she'd made plans this day, for if she waited, Richard would've hurt her, perhaps have even killed her. She wouldn't have been able to get Bonnie to safety. Kate kicked her heels into Ralph's flanks.

All Kate wanted was to get far away from the evil place. They were in southern England west of Londontown. Kate headed north, not knowing where to go. She held the sleepy child and rode through the night.

They made a good distance as the sun rose. The hues of yellow and pink indicated it would be a hot day. She had a hard time keeping her eyes open and needed to stop. Kate thought it safe to rest for a spell. After she lifted Bonnie down, she tethered Ralph.

"Bonnie, sit beside me and don't move for any reason."

"Aye, Kate."

"If there's trouble or you hear someone, wake me."

"Aye, Kate."

"And Bonnie, don't let me sleep long."

"Aye, Kate." Bonnie nodded at her instructions.

As Kate lay sleeping, Bonnie made a fire. Papa taught her how, and she couldn't wait to tell him she did it all by herself. She found flint in Kate's satchel and struck it against the rock as her uncle showed her. When the kindling caught, she shouted but quieted and realized her loudness. She took the bow and arrows from the satchel. Uncle Brendan taught her how to use them, but this bow was larger than the one Uncle made for her. She had trouble notching the arrow and keeping her aim fastened on the clearing.

Kate would be surprised when she awoke. Bonnie sat in a secluded dell and waited. Uncle told her she had to have… What did he say? Oh, aye, patience. He'd told her you had to wait a long time before a target came.

Then she spotted it, a very large hare hopped into the small glen not too far from where she sat. She pulled the arrow back, scrunched her eyes closed, then let go. Amazingly it hit the target. In awe, she smiled. "Wait until Papa hears this."

Kate lay on a grassy spot covered by a small counterpane, and Bonnie smiled at the pretty lady who saved her. Kate was tired, but it got late, and she shook her.

"Not now, Lolly," Kate grumbled.

"Kate, wake up," Bonnie whispered. "Please."

Kate shot up and remembered that she slept in the forest. She listened to the approach of dusk. Only the sound of birds on their return flight to their nests sounded nearby. Sighing relief, she released her bated breath. "Lovey, are you all right?"

"Aye, but the day is gone."

"You're right about that. Why didn't you wake me sooner? What do you have there?" A furry creature clutched in her hand.

"'Tis a hare. I used your bow," Bonnie explained.

"I cannot believe you notched the arrow, the bow is almost larger than you." Kate laughed in disbelief of the girl's ability. "Did anyone ever tell you you're a remarkable girl? Where'd you learn to shoot an arrow?"

"Uncle Brendan taught me," Bonnie said proudly.

"You mean the one with a heart?"

"Aye, don't tell him I told you. He will be angry at me."

Kate laughed. At least, the poor man's niece thought kindly of him and she sensed no one else did. So he didn't want anyone to know he had a kind heart, did he? "I won't tell, I promise."

She then noticed the fire. It was small with perhaps four logs caught with flame. "Now I am amazed. How old did you say you were? Are you certain it wasn't ten?"

Bonnie giggled. "Nay, I'm this many." She held up both hands and showed seven.

Kate pulled the dagger from the satchel and thought to keep it close. She used it to skin the hare and once that was done, she placed the hare on the fire with a makeshift spit. Hunger overrode her guilt for eating the animal.

"Bonnie, where does Honey live?"

"In the castle—"

Kate grabbed her shoulders and turned the girl toward her. "Who is Honey, Bonnie?"

"Mama's cousin, King Henry."

"Oh, Goddess above, you're the king's cousin? Why didn't I realize that before?" Kate placed her hands on her head. "What to do, what to do?"

"Aye, Mama, Papa, and me visited. Cousin Honey was happy we came. He was happy, I know he was. He had a festival for us. What if they went home without me? What if Mama and Papa aren't looking for me?" Bonnie's eyes lowered, her lips turned, and she wept.

"They wouldn't do that, Bonnie. We're a long way from London. I don't know if we—"

"We were at Honey's summer castle, that's what Mama said."

"Do you know where the summer castle is?"

"Nay." She shook her head. "Somewhere in Londontown."

"All right, then. Think…think… I can't chance to take you to Londontown, we would have to pass right by…we'd risk getting caught. Nay, I must take you to Scotland."

"Yay," Bonnie shouted.

"Shhh, be quiet."

"You can come home with me, Kate. You can meet Mama and Papa."

"It won't be easy. We'll keep going north until you recognize the land. The distance is greater and will be a long journey and it might very well be dangerous."

Bonnie set her head on Kate's lap. "Don't worry so, Kate. When we get to Scotland, we can get someone to take us home."

"No wonder you're such a clever girl, you're related to the king."

After eating the hare, they put out the fire and mounted Ralph. Kate tugged on the reins and headed in the direction she thought was north.

"Kate, are we on our way to the Highlands?"

"Aye, lovey, we are. I hope we're not being followed, and we make it to the border before he catches up with us."

"The mean man?"

Kate nodded. The night grew darker, but she needed to keep riding through the night. Not enough distance was put behind them and she needed to be more vigilant during the darkest part of the night. She wouldn't let her guard down, at least until they were farther away.

Their second day was uneventful and the quiet forest and gentle breeze calmed Kate. She only had about six hours of sleep in two days and was exhausted, but she pushed onward. Ralph continued on, as she drifted off to sleep on his back. Bonnie nudged her.

"Kate, wake up, you fell asleep again."

"We better stop. I'm too tired to continue."

"Do you want me to build a fire again?"

"Nay, not tonight, something is not right. I'll hide Ralph." She took him to a closed-off spot, tied his reins to a bush, and returned to Bonnie.

"I don't feel safe, let's move under that thicket. Be careful of the thorns."

She placed a cover on the ground. The spot was tight, and they squeezed together. Bonnie curled up against her and they fell asleep minutes later.

Kate awoke to the sound of horses pounding the ground, and by the sound of it, there were many. Was it men from Lord Richard's keep? She put her hand over Bonnie's mouth and prayed they didn't find Ralph. As the horses flew by, Kate held her breath until she no longer heard them. She and Bonnie continued to rest until morning and set out as soon as it lightened enough to see.

For the next five days, they rode over the dusty roads and through the forests. They were tired and dirty. Kate had several coins tucked in the seam of her gown, and she hoped to find a village or an inn. Instead, they settled for a stream and slept on the soft high grass. They stopped early that day because they both grew weary. After a bath in the stream, they finished the remains of their foodstuff. Kate refilled the flask with water. She gave Ralph a well-deserved rest and rubbed him down. Trixie stalked away, in search of her meal. Kate rested beside Bonnie on the ground, her back was sore, and her muscles ached because she'd never ridden so long. She groaned and rubbed the ache in her lower back.

"You know what, Kate?"

"Nay, what, Bonnie?"

"I can't wait to see Papa and Mama," she said sadly.

"We'll get there soon, lovey. I hope we can find someone who will direct us because I haven't figured out if we're headed the right way."

"Papa will make me sit in his chair."

"If he does, Bonnie, I'll sit with you." Kate hugged her.

"Uncle Brendan won't let Papa punish me."

"Why not?"

"He always gets me out of it. He says that I'm just a wee fairy who likes venturing."

"My father used to call me a fairy," Kate said sadly. "Your uncle sounds like a nice man." She wished her betrothed was just as kindhearted as Bonnie's uncle sounded.

Bonnie rolled on the ground, held her tummy, and giggled.

"What's so funny?" Kate smiled at the delightful sound of her gaiety.

"He's not nice—he's mean. Mama says ladies don't like 'em cause he frowns too much, but he only frowns at me when I do something to 'em."

Kate didn't like that he frowned. "What have you done to him?"

"Once, a longed time ago, when I was wee, I stoled into his bed."

"Stole," Kate corrected her.

Bonnie continued. "It was late when he came to bed, and I scairt 'em, and he swore loudly."

"Scared," Kate corrected her again.

Bonnie nodded and resumed her story, "Mama came running, och when she got there, she standed there staring at Uncle. That's when Papa came and yelled at Uncle Brendan. He swore, too. Then he said I had to contemplate and sit in his chair the whole next day. I don't know what contemplate meant so I just played with George."

"Why was your Papa mad?"

"Oh, 'cause Uncle didn't have clothes on and Mama sawed him. Papa pulled her out of the room. Every time Mama saw Uncle after that she got a red face."

Kate laughed. "I can't wait to meet your family, sweeten. They sound fun."

"Aye, Uncle Brendan will like you."

"Why do you say that?"

"'Cause you're bonny, but you'll be scairt of him. Most ladies are."

"Scared," Kate corrected her again. "Nay, I won't be afraid of him, I promise. Let's get sleep now, we have a lot more riding to do, I think."

They fell asleep, and it grew chilly during the night, but at least it was dry. It had rained little since they began their trek. When they awoke in the morning, Kate's stomach growled.

"I'm hungry," Bonnie complained, as she scooped up the cover from the ground.

"Me, too. I'll think of a way to get food. We could catch another hare."

"I can fish. Mama's uncle taught me how when he was alive."

"Taught," Kate corrected her. "What do you need?"

"A big stick. Can you make a point on the end? That's what Uncle Walden used."

Kate found a narrow branch that fell from a birch tree on the ground. She whittled the end until it was sharpened into a point. "Now what?"

Bonnie laughed. "You have to stand in the water until a fish swims near. Then drop the spear fast and try to catch 'em. 'Tis hard, Uncle Walden used to swear and shout."

Kate removed her slippers, lifted her hem, and wadded in the stream. Her gown billowed atop the water's surface. She waded knee-deep in the water, the soggy stream's bottom slimy beneath her feet, but thankfully, the water wasn't too cold.

"Bonnie, did your uncle say how long this takes?"

"Shhh, Kate, you will scare away the fish. It takes a longed time. I used to sit for hours and wait for 'em."

Kate watched a fish swim by and she tried to spear it, but it got away. Its scales brushed against the skin of her leg. "Damn."

Bonnie chuckled at her curse.

Another large speckled-trout came toward her and she

tried not to move. She positioned the spear just right—she would get this one. Slamming the spear downward, it pierced its middle. The caught fish wiggled on the spike when she lifted it from the water.

Kate jumped up and shouted. "I got it, I got it!"

"Yay, I knowed you could do it, Kate."

"I'll catch another one. Here, put this on the bank." She handed the fish to her. Bonnie used both hands to carry it. The fish wiggled and jerked from her hold. Bonnie flipped the fish onto the grass, where it lay still. The child was resourceful.

After a few tries, Kate caught another fish, and a good-sized one, at that. They would be full for the rest of the day. The fish tasted bland, but it would suffice as a meal.

"Who is your Uncle Walden? Does he live within your clan?" Kate used a leaf to wipe her hands.

"Mama's uncle. Mama was sad when he died and Aunt Mathilda cried."

"That's sad, I'm sorry he died."

"Aye, me too. Mama said he had a good life."

"He's with the Gods now, probably showing them how to use the spear. Thanks for the idea." After she cleaned up the campfire, she collected Trixie, and they moved on, going farther north.

"Kate, how long do you think it will take now?"

"I hope not too long, but we must keep moving."

"I can't wait to get home. Papa will be angry and Mama will cry."

"Lovey, your Papa will be so happy to see you, it won't matter. You'll see." Kate hugged her.

Kate couldn't sleep that night. The image of the warrior floated in the recess of her mind. She didn't understand how he was connected to Bonnie or if she would ever meet him. Try as she might, the image wouldn't go away. She didn't fall asleep until the middle of the night, but Bonnie slept soundly.

In the morning, she realized they were past the border. The terrain changed, and Bonnie insisted they were closer to home. How would a seven-year-old know that? Kate felt safer with the distance they'd put behind them. They had left England behind and the land hillier. Richard wouldn't find them in the deep woods and expanse of Scotland. She grew tired from sitting on the horse and decided it would do them good to stretch their legs.

Kate dismounted and helped Bonnie down then she released Trixie from the satchel.

"Do you deem we're in the Highlands?" Bonnie skipped beside her.

"Mayhap, it's eerily quiet and the birds aren't making any noise. Why do you suppose that is?" Kate searched ahead for danger but saw nothing amiss.

"I'm scairt, Kate." Bonnie moved closer and took her hand.

"I'm certain it's only my imagination running wild. Trixie seems to have run off."

She searched along the trees for her. They continued to walk and after a few minutes, Trixie returned with a small creature in her mouth. Kate found a trail a half-hour later. The forest remained eerily quiet, but they walked along silently.

A man jumped out from a bush and stood with his sword aimed at her. Not just any man—but a daemon. To protect Bonnie, Kate shoved her behind her. She stood mesmerized and bit her lower lip so she wouldn't yell out. She was afraid—terrified, was more like it.

"Good Goddess above." The man was a barbarian, painted like a heathen. He would kill her and make off with Bonnie. How would she ever get Bonnie home now?

The warrior stood in a hostile manner and held the largest sword she'd ever seen. Several men strode from the thick forest and surrounded them, seeming to magically appear. All of them, including the warrior, wore blue painted symbols on every part of their bodies, except for the parts covered by their tartans. Kate swallowed the lump that formed in her throat. Bonnie pressed against her back, holding her up. She was thankful for that. If not, she'd probably be on the ground at the heathen's mercy. Swooning seemed a reasonable reaction to the horrifying situation, but she wouldn't dare.

His eyes, made even colder by the dark paint that covered his face, pierced hers. Kate turned to see if there was a way to bypass him when she noticed the man motioned to the others to stay back. They obeyed.

"Lass, don't be afraid, I mean no harm."

"I'm n-not a-afraid."

The warrior laughed.

"Aye, you are, don't be. Why do you travel alone in the darkened forest? Are you by chance a damsel in distress or a fairy bent on trouble?"

The warrior's laughter drew an odd look from his men.

"I'm Lady Kaitlin Stanhope, and I'm on my way to the MacKinnon clan's holding." She couldn't believe she spoke to the man. Was she still standing? Nay, she hadn't swooned, as she thought she might have. Bonnie continued to press against her legs and tried to get around her, but Kate held her back.

"You are?" He sounded surprised. The warrior turned and gave a look to the others, but they remained quiet.

"Aye, and if you would be good enough to point me in the right direction, I'd be grateful."

"Why, lass? Are you a friend of Julianna's?"

"Julianna, um...nay. Can you direct us?" She hoped the warrior would accommodate her, and at the very least, give direction, but he wasn't compliant. He stood there with a scowl drawing his brows close, and shook his head.

Bonnie peeked around Kate's skirts and screeched loudly. She ran full force at the warrior. Kate was dizzy, an overwhelming sense of faintness struck her, and she wavered on her feet.

"Bonnie, don't." Kate tried to pull her back, but she was already out of her reach.

"Bonnie?" The warrior stepped forward.

"Aye, Uncle, 'tis me."

"Oh, Bonnie, lass!" He lifted her high in the air and hugged her close then kissed her face. "Oh, fairy, I missed you. Don't ever scare me like that again."

"I'm s-sorry, Uncle. I j-just..." Bonnie's lip trembled and she cried.

"Where have you been? Your Mama and Papa are worried sick." The warrior continued to hold her close and petted her hair. His face gave the impression he disbelieved he held his sweet niece in his arms.

"I been with Kate."

"It's a long story." Kate stood by and watched their reunion, still reeled with dizziness.

He turned back to the men and spoke in a stern voice. "Make camp."

The men turned hastily and set to make a fire and placed their bedrolls. Kate stood shocked to the ground, not wanting to move for anything. The warrior was Bonnie's uncle? Good Goddess, he intimidated her more than she'd admit. She hoped she didn't show signs of fear and tried to calm her rapid heartbeat. *Please, please, Goddess, get me out of here.*

"Lass, who's the lady?" He spoke in Gaelic to Bonnie.

Bonnie turned to look at her. "That's Kate, she saved me."

"She did?"

"Aye, and you know what?"

"Nay, what, fairy?"

"She brung me home."

"Aye, she certainly did."

The warrior gazed at her and stared intently as if he judged her. Kate felt awkward under his scrutiny, but she also felt the sudden urge to run.

He scowled and motioned to her. "Lady, join us."

She walked slowly to where he stood with Bonnie.

"How did you come to have Bonnie in your care?"

A lump formed in her throat and Kate's voice refused to cooperate, robbed of all her senses. The man was a huge warrior covered in paint for Goddess's sake. She couldn't even tell what he looked like. His hair matted down with paint, and no skin showed on his face, arms or legs. He wore a tartan around his waist and had a huge sword in a scabbard by his side. The man made Kate feel uncomfortable with him towered above her. Her blood crept to her neck and heated her skin.

"Lady, I asked you, how did you come to have Bonnie?" his voice hardened.

"I-I uh..." Kate couldn't get a word out, her throat closed, and her heart beat madly.

"Uncle, I'll tell you." Bonnie turned his face toward her.

"All right, lass, I wish someone would explain."

"Papa's going to make me sit in his chair 'cause I was supposed to rest, giving poor Emma a wee break, but I didn't. I left the tent and a mean man picked me up. He took me to his home and I was there a longed time before Kate came. She promised to bring me home and you know what?"

The warrior silently listened to his niece's babble.

"Nay, what?"

"She did. She's bonny, too." Bonnie spoke in Gaelic, and Kate didn't understand a word she said. She barely paid attention, because her body stiffened and heat rose within her. A situation made worse when the warrior stood ridged with his gaze fastened on her.

The warrior hesitated as if he tried to make sense of what his niece told him. He didn't introduce himself, which she thought was rude, but he certainly daunted her. She wanted to ask what Bonnie had told him, but she kept quiet. Besides, Bonnie mustn't have finished, because she took a breath and regaled him with more unknown words.

"Kate and I ran to the horse. We got away, and now you found us, Uncle." Bonnie yawned and her eyes drooped.

"You will explain now, lady." He nearly shouted and his eyes blazed with fury.

Kate watched the warrior turn into two images then both waved before her eyes. The thump of her heart pounded in her ears and her eyes teared. She searched for something to grab hold of, but the closest thing was the obstinate warrior. Darkness took hold and she fainted dead away.

CHAPTER FOUR

Brendan MacKinnon muttered a curse and set Bonnie on the ground. He knelt beside the lady, knowing his camouflage frightened her. He should have told her he and his men did so to respect their ancestors and for their amusement, not to frighten damsels. She'd fainted, and he wasn't sure what to do about it. His comrade, Gil, handed him a flask of ale, which he poured on the woman's face. She sputtered and lay back groaning.

He used his instincts to discern the woman's character, and if what his niece told him was the truth, he owed her much. Brendan kept his gaze on the woman, whom he thought had to be the most beautiful lass he'd ever seen. His talent for keeping his emotions hidden came into play. He eyed her skeptically and disheartened at her fear. He supposed he shouldn't frighten her more than she already was.

"Are you all right? You swooned."

"I did?" She closed her eyes.

The woman didn't speak further, and yet, Bonnie wept over her as if she'd died. He didn't know how to deal with either female and watched them with reverence. Brendan scooped his niece into his arms again and held her tightly. When he held Bonnie's wee body securely in his arms, all the pain of the last months subsided. He searched for her, as had her father and most of the clan, never dreaming she would find him. Now that he held her, he couldn't put her down. His mind whirled with questions: who took her, where she had been all this time, and what the lady had to do with her abduction.

But Brendan couldn't ask and stood there in mass confusion. The woman took his breath away, at least he didn't draw breath while he beheld her. She had the most appealing hair, as light as the color of the sun. The men behind him gawked and their restlessness brought him back to reality.

He stretched his hand at her and offered assistance from the ground. She placed her dainty hand in his and he helped her to stand. Their touch startled him because he'd never been as affected by a woman before.

"Lady, I can't thank you enough—"

"My Lord, I'm happy to return Bonnie to her family."

Brendan listened to her voice, the soft sound caressed him, and an unfamiliar sentiment overcame him. He looked at her eyes which appeared violet and with her pale hair…a sudden urge to smile tug at his lips. She was a fairy, aye, a bean-sith who saved his niece. Her beauty caused one of his men to whistle low and he turned to scowl at his rudeness.

"I'll be going now that Bonnie is safe." The woman turned and walked away. He heard her mumble, "Just get your cat, jump on your horse, and get the hell out of here."

Brendan stood in front of her before she took two steps.

"Lass, I can't let you go." For some reason, his words sounded romantic. Perhaps it was the way he'd said them, mayhap it was the truth, veritably he was being outlandish.

"Why not?" She couldn't keep the garish tone from her voice, which made him grin.

"Because you must explain to my brother what happened to his daughter. He'll want to speak to you. You will come with us."

"You can explain it to him. I'm going home." She turned

and walked away.

Brendan handed Bonnie to one of his men and stalked after her. "Nay, wait. I cannot let you walk off alone in the forest without protection. Come, you look tired and need rest. We'll protect you, have no fear. My brother will expect an explanation and you must give him your account. What of Bonnie? Surely you want to make certain she reaches home."

She sighed and gazed at the forest's distance. Brendan continued to frown. She didn't seem to know where to go, and she didn't appear to appreciate being at his mercy. When he didn't back down, she shrugged her shoulders and ambled forward to Bonnie. Seeing how she looked at Bonnie, Brendan suspected she wouldn't leave until his niece arrived home. At least, that's why he demanded that she return with them. Mayhap that wasn't exactly why he'd asked her to stay—he didn't want her to leave. He determined her character and sensed she was a gentle, sweet lass.

Brendan watched her settle down next to Bonnie. Gil, his longtime friend, approached, but Brendan shook his head before he spoke. He didn't want to disturb them. Exhausted, both his niece and the lady lay on a bedroll. He wondered what they had gone through. The lady was English and he wondered if they'd come that far. Bonnie was abducted in London from the king's castle. His brother, Colin, stayed in England and searched for her. Brendan needed to send someone to fetch Colin and called two of his men forward. His brother and sister-in-law would be elated at the news that he'd found Bonnie.

His brother would be overjoyed and most eager to leave England. Neither he, nor his brother, enjoyed visits to England, and he regretted his decision not to protect them when they'd gone for a visit to Henry's summer castle. If he hadn't been occupied helping his cousin, Douglas, with his difficulties, he probably would have gone, and his sweet niece wouldn't have been abducted. Too late now to feel guilt, at least he'd found her and she was safe.

He took a tartan from Gil and covered them. Something

rubbed against his leg and he glanced down at his feet and glimpsed a cat, a very fluffy cat that meowed at him. He opened his pouch, took out dried meat and fed the animal. A string around the animal's neck drew his regard. He held the covered object and studied it. The cat hissed, lay with its mistress, and cleaned itself.

Never in a hundred years had Brendan thought he'd camp in the woods with a bean-sith, a feline, and his niece slumbered beside him. He gave a hand signal to Gil to do the rounds. Until Bonnie was safely tucked away on their land, he wouldn't rest. Brendan leaned back against a tree and listened for sounds of danger. A smile came to him—a very unusual occurrence.

CHAPTER FIVE

Kate awoke in her typically cheerful manner until the coldness from the ground chilled her. She opened her eyes and saw the warriors stood beside their mounts. With a pierced scream, she gripped the covers to her chest. She'd forgotten where she was, that warriors were present and that she fled for her life. Everything, all she'd endured, trickled back to her mind. The soldiers ran near with their swords drawn and her eyes widened in horror. The dark warrior motioned them back and scowled as she stood.

He scoffed as he approached. "Why did you scream? Is there danger?"

Danger, was he serious? "I-I uh…forgot where I was, and the men frightened me and… I didn't mean to scream."

The man kept a staid gawk on her and studied her from her head to her toes. She pursed her lips and wanted to scold his boorish behavior.

"We might look a wee bit frightening with our paint, but we only do it for our amusement. Our ancestors painted each other and we… I only tell you because we don't mean to scare you."

"I see. Thank you for explaining, I shan't fear you any longer." Kate was sure the Goddess shook her head at her fabrication. Even if they washed away their camouflage, they'd still intimidate her.

"Fix your gown, you show a wee too much skin. I don't want the men to ogle you, and they certainly will because you're—"

"Oh, Goddess above." Kate straightened her garments, and her face reddened. No wonder he scrutinized her. The warrior sounded possessive, which irritated her too. Before she countered him, he shoved food at her.

"Eat."

She shook her head. "Nay, thank you, sir."

He shoved the food at her again. "You will eat, now."

"I don't usually eat this early, perhaps later. Do we have far to travel?"

"Aye, very far."

Kate realized he was a man of few words. He continued to stare. Did the warrior always wear such a fierce look? Even though the paint on his face hid his regard, she discerned his scowl. Too cowardly to ask, she refrained from asking his name. She prayed he was Robin, the man who married Bonnie's mother's friend. He had to be because she wouldn't travel with an arrogant, sexy as hell man who wasn't at least married. She was tempted to curse him or make a potion that would render him silly and lighten his foreboded manner. The thought of that made her smile.

"How many more days?" She grumbled under her breath.

"A few. Bonnie will ride with Gil, you'll ride with me."

Kate didn't appreciate his commanding tone. Her usual pleasant personality took on a cranky nature. "I will do no such thing. I have a horse, My Lord."

"Lass, that's not a horse. He's old and will never make it up the incline."

She glanced at Ralph and had to agree. Poor Ralph rode a great distance, and he wasn't bred for the hilly terrain they traveled. "What should I do with him?"

He narrowed his eyes. "Set 'em free."

"Aye, he deserves it. He brought us this far and for that

I'm thankful." She went to Ralph and removed her belongings. "You've been a big, brave boy. Thank you, my friend." She smacked his rump, and Ralph walked away. Kate watched him until he disappeared beyond the thicket. When she turned around, the warrior stood right behind her. She bumped into him and craned her neck to see his face. He was tall, and his smoky eyes peered back.

Gray eyes. Still, she couldn't tell what color his hair was. She hoped he wasn't the warrior from her visions. The Goddess wouldn't be as cruel to send her the fearsome man. She wondered which uncle he was. Was he the one who had a heart, but didn't want anyone to know about it? Brendan MacKinnon? He had gray eyes. Was it a sign? Kate shook her head, stepped backward and almost fell. He reached out to catch her, his big hand settled on her lower back.

"Aye, it's going to be a rough ride home."

He grumbled that statement, and Kate pretended not to hear it. Something about the warrior struck her heart. She didn't know why, but she felt oddly safe with him. He seemed to shake himself as if he'd been deep in thought. Goddess help her, she wouldn't survive another few days with him, let alone riding with him.

"Lady Kate, these are my men, Gil and Benjamin. I'll introduce the rest later."

Kate wondered why he hadn't told her his name. She wanted to ask but kept quiet. He walked away without another word. The men waited for them, most sat upon their steeds, including Bonnie, who happily talked to Gil in their language. Gil, hmm, she thought.

She placed Trixie inside her satchel and folded the cover they slept on. One man came forward and took it from her. All was ready, and she stood by not knowing what to do. The warrior rode to her on a huge white warhorse. Its coat was pristine and unblemished and appeared cared for. The warrior took pity on her and before she might make a fool of herself. He lifted her around her waist and placed her in front of him.

Kate sat straight with her spine as unbending as a lance.

She hadn't ever been held as inappropriately by a man before, even her father let her have her own mount to ride. With her eyes focused forward, she pretended he wasn't there. Try as she might, his presence couldn't be overlooked by anyone. He shifted his position, while she held on for dear life. He whistled for the men to proceed.

After hours of riding, she thought her back would break from holding herself rigidly. If only she had time to meditate and calm her inner spirit. She was uneasy at not having completed her morning ritual, and her inner turmoil increased with each mile.

Kate wasn't sure if she should trust the warrior. She wondered what she would tell Bonnie's father about where she was kept and by whom. If she wanted to seek justice for her father's death she had to keep Richard's name a secret. With the medallion secure, she needed to find a way to speak to King Henry and gain his assurance to question Richard. Now the only problem was how to avoid telling them her guardian's name?

CHAPTER SIX

Brendan's body flinched with her every movement. He wanted to pull her against him, but it would only cause trouble. He had enough of a hard time with her sitting on his lap. Aye, the last time a lass rode with him, he recalled being irked about it because Isabel was meant to be his cousin, Douglas' wife. Now, here he was with a lass of his own. Where had that irrational thought come from? She wasn't his, nor had she shown the slightest interest. Would that matter? Nay, he granted, it wouldn't.

She distracted him from his thoughts when she shifted her position. He held her tightly, looked into her bonny eyes, and set his mouth close to hers, a mere scant from her soft-looking lips. He waited for her to speak and tried to measure the passion in her eyes.

"My Lord, may we stop to rest?"

"Aye," Brendan called a halt. He'd misread her look and smiled at the way she ambled away.

Bonnie ran to Kate as soon as her feet touched the ground. She took her hand and led her into the woods. His niece danced around and he smiled, knowing why.

"She's bonny." Gil stood next to him and watched them disappear through the shrubs.

Brendan disliked Gil's grin, but he ignored his obvious

chaff.

"You're a lucky man."

"What do you mean by that?" Brendan shoved him and knocked him back a step. Gil's arms flailed.

"I see the way she looks at you."

"How does she look at me?" Brendan's jaw twitched, and he wondered why he was aggravated. He should be pleased the woman looked at him at all.

"You know like she's interested."

"With all this paint on? Nay, it's your imagination. Don't pull that cosh with me, Gil. I'm not as easy to dupe as my brothers or Douglas. They might fall for that cosh about women looking at them a certain way, but I won't. Don't start trouble."

"If you don't want her, say so." Gil laughed. "What do you plan to do with her?"

Brendan scowled. "I'm taking her home. What the hell do you think I'm doing with her?"

"That's telling, Brendan. Aye, telling indeed."

"Go to hell, Gil." He stomped away. If there was one thing Brendan couldn't tolerate, it was teasing from his comrades. He put up with it from his brothers for years, but wouldn't take banter from his friends. Finally, the lass and his niece returned from the shrubs, and they could be on their way.

During the long day, Kate seemed to get their names all mixed up. Gil mentioned her blunders a few times when they stopped, and that she'd called him by other names. The last time they stopped, Gil said he corrected her, but she still called him Gregory or Graham. Brendan grinned at her delightful absentmindedness.

The sunset brought the cooler night, and they camped beside a wide stream. Brendan laughed when Kate whisked Bonnie away for a bath and made her eat a good amount of food before she settled his niece for the night. Some men joined them by the fire. He watched his men converse with Kate, and he couldn't withhold his grin when she mumbled something about them not being heathens. She probably thought they'd been out raiding the countryside. England was rife with rumors of pillaging, some true, some not. Many Scottish clans raided the border region, especially the Barclays.

"Lady Stanhope, where are you from?"

Gil sat next to her, a little too close in his opinion. Brendan listened as he sharpened his sword with a stone. He tried to appear uninterested in their conversation.

"Cheshire. Gerald, where exactly is the MacKinnons' land located?"

"Milady, I'm Gil or Gilbert, not Gerald. Their land is located in the Highlands, past the black bracken of the hills of the northeast region. 'Tis a good distance from the border."

Brendan almost laughed at Gil's insulted tone.

"Oh, I cannot wait until we get there. We've traveled for days and I know Bonnie wants to get home. She misses her family. Will it take us much longer?"

"Another day or so."

That night at camp, Brendan listened to her tell Bonnie a story. He wanted to question her further about the details of their flight from England and suspected there was more to tell. The lass was English, so he presumed that's where they fled from. He wasn't usually patient, but soon enough he'd have answers to his many questions once they reached home. Brendan didn't press her for the details. She was troubled enough, without him plying her with questions. Besides, Colin would ply her with enough to make her bonny head spin.

Bonnie curled next to her savior. Aye, that's what the lass called Kate—her savior. Brendan longed to lie next to her too, but there he was on the other side of camp, watching like a randy lad from afar. His men watched her too, which made him angry. He had no claim on the lady, and he detested their attention bothered him. The only reason he insisted she travel with them was because of Bonnie and the explanation Colin would expect.

Who was he jesting? He didn't want her to leave him. His niece was attached to her, the way Kate held his niece during sleep made his heart tense. They must've had a difficult time. He owed her his protection, and wouldn't admit it was more than her safety which concerned him. Once he reached their holding, he would free himself of her, he promised. She'd be safe, and besides, he didn't want to get involved with a troublesome lass, even though she captivated him.

The ride the next day was the most grueling. Brendan wanted to wrap his arms around her, feel her next to him, and pretend for a moment she was his, and so he did. She didn't push his arms away, and he held her close. As she relaxed against him, her sweet fragrance engulfed him. She smelled of summer roses, and she entranced him with her alluring eyes. He might well be besotted for the first time in his life.

The day ended with shadows darkening the forest, and they stopped to make camp again close to their home by the loch. Brendan lightened at the way she held Bonnie in her arms until she fell asleep. The warmth from the campfire chased the cold away. She set Bonnie next to her and covered her small body with a tartan and lifted her cat onto her lap.

"Oh, the heat feels good. The Goddess' elements always make me feel peaceful." Kate rubbed her hands together.

He smiled at the softness of her voice, but he couldn't help but wonder what she meant about the Goddess. Something about her was mysterious, and she hid many sides of herself from him. She continued to pet the cat.

"Lady Kate, is that your animal?"

She startled, not knowing that he'd sat next to her. "Aye, it is."

"I saw it the first night and thought it might be yours. What's that around its neck?"

"Ah, just a...ah, trinket." She continued to pet the cat's fur. "Will we reach the MacKinnon's holding soon?"

He regarded her for a moment before he answered. She tried not to fluster over his question, but she didn't do a good job of it. Whatever was around that cat's neck was of obvious import.

"We should reach home on the morrow. Why are you eager to reach my clan? Are you being followed?" He leaned casually on his bared knees. Her eyes widened, but she shifted her gaze to a safer place. He held her eyes with his and wanted to laugh at her delightful bashfulness.

"Nay, I only want to get Bonnie home. I promised her I would see her arrive safely. Then I must go."

"Where must you go?"

"To King Henry. I must see him about my father's…about my wardship and other matters."

"Are you married, Lady Kate?"

"Nay, that's another matter which I must speak to Henry about. Another painful issue piled atop the rest." Her face saddened.

Brendan acted casually and fiddled with the ties on his boots. Now that he was on Highland soil, he removed the dirt he'd placed in them before he'd left home. It was his long-standing habit to put Highland soil in his boots whenever he left the Highlands, that way his feet never left his beloved country's soil. As he dumped his boots, he continued the conversation.

"Why do you want to talk to Henry about marriage?"

She looked at him oddly, while he finished his chore.

"He settled a betrothal for me and I'll soon marry. My father's lands lay unprotected because my overlord is away. I cannot await his return, and I intended to ask the king to place me with my betrothed."

"There's much more to this story?"

"I shouldn't discuss it and must see the king at the soonest. I'll speak to Bonnie's father and then be on my way." Kate lay next to Bonnie and closed her eyes.

Brendan fumed silently. He didn't like what she told him. What the hell was going on? The lass was supposed to wed and was betrothed? Well, hell. Why did the thought of her marrying make him incensed? She had lands in England? The lass must be an heiress akin to Julianna. Did all women in England come with such dowries? He didn't know the goings-on of that land. He despised England and didn't venture there if he could help it, but he wouldn't dislike the lass because she came from the hated country. Nay, he liked her just fine. A smile tugged at his lips.

Gil approached Brendan from across the camp. "Ah, hell, Brendan, are you smiling? You're in for it now, the lass will turn you upside down. I'm glad because you need a woman. Aye, she'll make you smile and laugh, not to mention being a fine—"

Brendan cut him off and gestured in a lewd manner, which Gil laughed at. Brendan kept his eyes on Kate, while Gil baited him. It was true; he rarely laughed or smiled, but the woman's presence lightened him.

"Shhh, quiet, Gil. Don't wake them, and cease carping about this cosh. Have you set someone to the watch? I'm going to do sentry and perhaps bathe in the loch after."

Gil nodded but continued to bait him. "The lady seems to like you. At least, she didn't run away when she first saw you. I know she probably wanted to because you're not the type to attract a lass. Nay, you scare them witless. Come to think about it, she swooned when she first met you."

Brendan's jaw clenched, but he didn't comment on Gil's view. He was coarse and crass, yet underneath, he was a good man with a slightly sensitive side, rarely shown to anyone. His true nature wasn't something he wanted known. He'd spent most of his life training to be a warrior. Nay, he wasn't suitable for many women, but he was prideful in that he could at least protect his clan. He and his brothers were raised under their father's formidable rules. Since his father died, their clan prospered and his brother, Colin, became a well-respected laird.

Though Brendan mainly kept to himself because of his father's uncaring mien, his brothers were important to him, as were their wives and children. Over time, he lost some of his abrasiveness, but he couldn't help keeping his true self hidden. He supposed it became more of a habit to be contentious.

Gil spent much time with him, and Brendan considered him his closest friend. Since Brendan's brothers married and started families, he spent more time carousing with Gil's laird, Douglas Kerr. When Bonnie went missing, Douglas gave Gil leave to aid in the search. Though they were similar in size, his friend had lighter hair, and always smiled. That damned smile irritated him because it usually flocked the ladies to him. Brendan neither attracted the ladies nor was he cheerful. But they were similar in their tastes, which made gallivanting with Gil enjoyable. Gil relished at his blunders in dealing with the lady. Gil would assist any way he could, and torment him to no end.

Brendan felt the burden of his niece's plight ease from his insides now that she was safely home. Once he reached his land, he purposely camped at the loch so the men might wash before they reached the keep. He stripped his tartan away and scrubbed the paint from his body. After the chore was finished, he pulled soap from his pouch and washed until he was finally clean. He lay on the bank and closed his eyes, drying himself in the late-night air. The coolness felt pleasant on his skin and calmed him. He was happy to be home again.

"Brendan?"

He glanced up and saw Gil. "Aye?"

"What are you going to do about the lass?"

"What should I do about her? She's here to explain to Colin what happened to Bonnie. There's nothing more to it than that." He sat up and frowned at him, questioning his manner.

"Well, if you're not interested, then—"

"I don't know if I am or not," Brendan admitted to himself, more so to Gil.

"Aye, you are."

"Then why are you asking?"

"Just checking." Gil threw his tartan at him and chuckled.

"Don't you have a lady waiting for you at Douglas' keep?"

"Mayhap I do, at least I hope Romy is there when I return." Gil leaned forward on his knees and kept his eyes on the loch. Brendan punched his arm. Gil spoke of the woman he'd met at the asylum where Douglas' wife, Isabel, had been sent by her father. They'd gone to aid Douglas in rescuing her when he promised to retrieve his sister Candace's friend, namely Isabel. They married and his cousin seemed content with his wife.

Brendan grinned and remembered the weeks that followed with Gil talking excessively about Romy. He claimed he'd fallen in love and Brendan thought him as mad as his brothers. Still, Gil hadn't returned to his clan, and he didn't seem to be in a rush to do so. Brendan sobered and recalled a similar conversation about women with his cousin, Douglas, that he'd just had with Gil about Katie.

He disregarded Gil and relaxed back and let the loch ease him. It felt good being home and he'd missed the solitude. He had searched for Bonnie for months and never considered he'd find her. He hoped to hear news of her abduction then send word to Colin in Londontown, but he was glad the ordeal was over. His sweet niece was safe and sound and Colin would be happy when he returned.

Brendan came to the realization that he'd never be a family man as his brothers had become. Mayhap he'd spent too much time training as a warrior, or maybe he wasn't the sort to marry and have a family. He had to admit though Lady Kate was beautiful enough, sweet enough, and courageous enough to make him change his mind.

CHAPTER SEVEN

They reached the MacKinnon holding the next day just before late afternoon. Kate held Bonnie and covered her with the tartan her uncle gave her to keep the sun from burning her tender skin. A guardsman at the portcullis frowned while the warrior spoke to him rapidly in another language, probably stated whom he had with him. The man's face lit with a smile, he then shouted unknown words to the men who stood behind them and walked away. The warrior turned to help Kate from his horse, careful not to rouse his niece.

"I see you've returned, lad."

Kate turned at the sound of another man's approach. A dark-haired man with gray eyes who resembled the man in her vision stood near. Perhaps he was the man with the heart that didn't want anyone to know about it. He appeared older than he had in her vision and differed in his physique.

"Walt, it's good to be home. How goes it?"

The man, Walt, clapped the man on the back. "I'm doing well. Who is this?"

"This is Lady Kaitlin Stanhope." The warrior turned to her. "This is Walt, our good friend, and commander-in-arms."

"My lady." Walt bowed and placed a hand on the man's shoulder. "Come by later, lad. I want to talk to you and haven't seen you in months. Have you heard a word of Bonnie?"

The warrior nodded. "Aye, I found her, she's beneath the cover. Her mother will raise the keep with her crying when she sees her."

Walt smiled broadly. "God Almighty, 'tis good news, lad. Best go then and see Julianna." He walked away and whistled.

"Keep Bonnie covered until we tell Julianna about her. I don't want her to die from shock." He motioned to her to enter the keep.

Kate did as she was told and kept Bonnie concealed beneath the tartan. She entered a large hall that was clean and adorned with banners. The castle had a homey feel to it. A fire in the hearth lent warmth to the coziness. The warrior gestured for her to sit and he left. She sat alone in the hall and idly surveyed the surroundings. She noticed the floor reflected a shine, and the furnishings gleamed. Kate readjusted Bonnie on her lap, but the child slept like a baby and drooled on her bodice. If Bonnie knew where she was, she'd yell down the keep.

He returned with a beautiful lady whose long hair was pulled back with a tie. Kate noticed it's length swung behind her. She thought to rise to greet her, but the warrior motioned for her to remain seated. Kate did as he requested, and the lady sat next to her. Her face reflected an odd look, as though she tried to reason why Kate was there.

"Welcome to our home, I'm Julianna MacKinnon. Brendan tells me you brought a gift."

Kate's eyes widened when she spoke his name. She'd been with Bonnie's Uncle Brendan all the while, the man with a heart who hid his demeanor. He stood next to her, and she turned a frown at him. "You're the man with a...oh, good Goddess, save me."

"Pardon me, what did you say?" Julianna's brows furrowed at Kate's rude remark.

If the warrior had a heart beneath his hard-looking body, she'd be stewed for supper. She smacked her forehead and realized she judged him most inaccurately. So the man painted his body like a heathen, but wasn't it similar to her praying to her ancestor's spirits, the Goddess and Gods? Nay, he definitely wasn't of the same gentle manner as she. Besides, he raided her country, and he was too arduous. Why was she attracted to him? Was she attracted to him?

"Good Goddess, I am."

"Lady Kaitlin?" Julianna called.

Kate blushed at her affront. She hadn't realized she prayed and spoken aloud, or that she became immersed in her thoughts.

"Oh, uh...I apologize, Lady MacKinnon. Please forgive me for my lack of manners. I am happy to meet you. I'm Kaitlin Stanhope of Cheshire, England and I have brought something you've been in search of."

"Kaitlin, what a bonny name. What have you there?" Julianna leaned close with a look of dismay on her pretty face.

The lady seemed in shock to have an Englishwoman at her table, probably because her brother-in-law, Brendan brought her home. She likely considered her to be a lady of vulgar manners or ill repute. Lady Julianna glanced from her to Brendan.

Brendan took the seat next to her. She grimaced at the way he sat too close on the bench, and it made for an awkward moment. His body pressed against hers and forced her to move aside.

"Julianna, God sent this lass to Bonnie and—"

"Bonnie? Oh, my...is she...she dead?" Julianna wept into her hands.

"Nay, nay, My Lady. She's well, truly. In fact—"

"You've seen her? Where is she?"

"Julianna, let the lass finish and she'll tell you all." Brendan's voice rose with impatience.

Kate gave him a hard glance for speaking to Lady Julianna that way.

"Oh, I apologize, Lady Kaitlin, please continue."

Kate smiled. "I have brought your daughter home."

"You have? Where is she then?" Julianna stood and glanced at the door. "Is she outside?"

"Nay, she's right here beneath the cover." She pulled back the woolen tartan to reveal the sleeping child. Lady Julianna's eyes widened when she viewed her daughter. Kate placed Bonnie in her mother's arms and she gazed lovingly at her daughter but continued to weep.

"She looks thin and frail. Oh, her wee face is so sweet. It's hard to believe I am truly holding her, seeing her." Julianna whispered and tried not to wake her daughter. "It has been months since she went missing and I never thought to see her again." She cried harder, and her shaking woke Bonnie.

Bonnie opened her eyes and fat tears streamed her cheeks. She wept and said, "Mama."

They hugged and bawled, oblivious to Brendan and Kate.

"Darling, I've missed you. You don't know how happy I am to see you," Julianna whispered against her daughter's head.

"Mama, I missed you, too. I'm sorry I didn't listen and stay in the tent. Is Papa angry?"

Julianna smiled and hugged her tightly. "Nay, love, he's not angry with you. In fact, you're going to make him most joyful." Her eyes rose to Kate's and beheld a look of love.

"Where is he?" Bonnie shouted as loud as she could. "Papa, Papa, I'm home."

"He's still in England searching for you, Button. Brendan will you send someone—"

"I already have, several days ago, when I found these two in the woods. I met Burk at the gate and told him to expect Colin's arrival." Brendan remained stone-faced.

Kate couldn't believe he wasn't affected by the mother and daughter's reunion. She was about to cry buckets over the joy of it. Nay, she definitely shouldn't be attracted to him. Why would she even consider such foolishness?

"How did you find her, Lady Kaitlin?"

"I'm sorry, Lady MacKinnon, but we should await your husband's return before I divulge all that happened. It's a long story. Do you mind if we await him?"

Julianna's gaze pivoted to Brendan's before she answered. "Nay, I have my daughter back, that's all that matters. Just look at you, you both need tender care. I'll have a bath and food sent up. Bonnie, let's show Kaitlin your chamber." Bonnie shuffled from her mama's lap and took Kate's hand. They left without a word to Brendan.

Kate stood in the hall and waited for Lady MacKinnon's return. She admired the beautifully sewn banners that hung on the walls and thought about her plan. Calling them by different names would aid in not having to reveal Lord Richard's name. She wanted to reach King Henry first and gain his promise to investigate her father's death. If she told the MacKinnons, Lord Richard's name, she would never know if he had truly killed her father. Desperation to find the truth outweighed her sensibility. If the Highlanders found out his name, they would search for him and kill him before she proved Richard's guilt. The truth would die with him. Kate's keen sense impelled Richard's culpability, and somehow she would verify his treachery. She owed that to her father, didn't she?

She was deep in thought and hadn't noticed Brendan stood by the door. When she turned, she startled at his appearance. Kate stared attentively and realized she looked at her living-breathing vision. Her vision stood before her very eyes, the gray-eyed, dark-haired warrior. Why hadn't she realized it before? This morn when she'd awakened, she was preoccupied with arriving at the MacKinnon keep. She hadn't noticed he'd washed the war-paint from his body. She hadn't dared to pay attention to his form. Even his body resembled that of her vision. With the door opened wide, and what with the way he stood with his arms folded over his chest and the sun shone behind him… He appeared exactly as her vision.

Goddess help her, a dizzy sense overtook her. Kate swayed on her feet and was about to fall to the floor. He startled her when he reached her side before she took two steps.

"Are you unwell, Lady Kaitlin?"

His strong hands supported her, and she assessed him. Lord, he was a tall, well-built man. His muscles bulged against his tunic. His hair dark was nearly black. With his hair and body cleaned of its paint, she took him in. She realized her mouth was agape and closed it. He made her knees weak, her heart thump madly, and her pulse race. Was it fear or something else which caused her intense reaction? Unfamiliar emotions stirred a mixture of havoc within her.

"Good Goddess, my vision in the flesh." Had she said that aloud?

Brendan threw back his head and laughed. She blushed in her embarrassment. When he ceased his laughter, he released her and stepped back. She would recover once she got over the shock of seeing him in the flesh. As she surveyed him, she tried to see kindness in his eyes, but only saw coldness. Several people entered the hall, but none disturbed the two of them surmising each other. The cool color of his eyes bespoke sadness, and she almost empathized with him.

Voices sounded behind her, but she couldn't take her eyes from him.

"Uncle, please don't let Papa make me sit in his chair." Bonnie pleaded as she came down the stairs. She tugged on his tartan, and he snapped from his trance to answer her.

"Nay, bean-sith, I won't."

Kate moved to sit at the table. Brendan sat across from her and resumed his stare. She stared back. The feeling of serenity overcame her as she gawked at her living, breathing vision. Even though his cold gray eyes scrutinized her, all those years of seeing him through her mind overrode his boorish manner. She swore he wouldn't intimidate her, but he was more menacing now without his war-paint. She wanted to be courageous and appear so to him. Well, she was brave.

Hadn't she saved his niece? That had to count for something.

"You're taller than most ladies I know, Lady Kate," he said suddenly.

She was taller than most ladies, but his comment irritated her. Nay, she wasn't a dainty lady, well as dainty as some. As if he was acquainted with many ladies, she almost snorted at that. He didn't appear to be the sort many ladies would get close enough to since his frowns probably sent them in flee of their lives. Bonnie mentioned something about his frowns on their journey.

Kate shivered and tried to hide her chill. It wasn't too cold and she considered the coldness inside her was caused by the icy glare Brendan gave her. She rubbed the chill on her bared arms. Her light-brown gown barely covered her and did little to warm her. Lady Juliana insisted she wear it, and she even arranged her hair atop her head. But Brendan didn't appear to notice her appearance, because he continued to scowl. She was bold in her observation of him and wanted to smile. She wasn't one to cower. Be courageous, she reminded herself, and cleared her throat, because it had gone dry. Had she lost her voice and her courage?

Julianna entered and noted their stare-match. She smiled and broke the silence, "Brendan, she brought my bairn home, you be nice."

"Aye, I am being nice," was all he said.

Gil approached the table and sat on the other side of her. He grinned at Brendan and bellowed.

"Well, hell." Brendan cursed and gave Gil a formidable frown.

Lady Julianna laughed.

"What did you say, Brendan? Did you blaspheme in front of the ladies?" Gil asked.

"Aye, so I did." He tapped his finger against his cup. As if he were lordly, the servant hurried to refill his cup. His manner struck a chord of admiration in her, mayhap he could be considered highborn if he didn't look so mean.

"He said, well, hell," Bonnie repeated happily. "Well,

hell, he swore, Mama."

Everyone ignored Bonnie, and Julianna didn't seem to have the heart to reprimand her when she'd only returned from her mysterious disappearance. Instead, she asked, "Did the men leave yet to get Colin?"

"Aye, they left right off days ago. I told Burk that Colin would arrive home soon for good. I expect he should be here within a day or so. He'll hasten here when he gets my message."

"Good, I hope he—"

"Julianna," a man shouted, as he walked into the hall. Walt stood beside him, and they stopped upon seeing everyone at the table.

Julianna stood with her daughter in her arms. "Colin, I'm glad you're home. Brendan found Bonnie."

The man drew a deep rasped breath. He glanced at Julianna, and in a sprint, he ran across the hall and took Bonnie into his arms. He squeezed her tightly against his chest, and his throat grew thick as he uttered her name. One arm held her, and the other moved to caress her hair, arms, and legs.

"I'm home, Papa."

The man appeared shaken to behold Bonnie alive and well. He smelled her hair. His daughter held onto him and cried, and soaked his tunic. Everyone spoke at once. Colin held his hand up for silence. He looked as though he wanted to hold his daughter for now. Kate thought he might weep because his eyes misted, and he swung Bonnie in his arms.

Kate's heart wrenched as she viewed Colin MacKinnon's reunion with his daughter. Colin was a handsome man, his hair was lighter than his brother's, and his eyes were green, unlike the gray ones that seared her, even now. She chanced a glance at Brendan and caught him observing his brother. He remained expressionless with his standoffish manner.

"Papa, I'm sorry I didn't—"

"Nay, shhh, lass. I love you, Button, and missed you. Are you well, unharmed?" Colin whispered against her ear, but the hall quieted and everyone listened.

"Aye, Papa, I'm well 'cause Kate saved me. She brung me home." Bonnie placed her hand on his face and turned it to her. Colin searched his wife's face for an explanation. "Papa, don't make me and Kate sit in your chair."

"Nay, lass, I wouldn't make you or Kate sit in my chair. Why would I do that?" Colin's shock must've addled him because he seemed to want to laugh at her request. "Did I hear you correctly? My Button is home safe and sound, alive and well, and yet, you're concerned about having to sit in my chair?"

"'Cause me and Kate, we were bad lassies, Papa. We did bad things to um, the lady—"

"Nay, you're never bad, Button. Now, who is Kate?"

They spoke in Gaelic, and though Kate didn't understand them, she heard her name. Her heart lightened, seeing father and daughter hug and whisper closely. Their closeness made her miss her own father and her eyes dampened with tears. She wanted to bawl, but she fought to keep her lips from trembling.

"That's Kate." Bonnie pointed to her.

"Kate, I'm Laird MacKinnon. You've my thanks for returning my daughter." Colin's voice deepened and rolled with a heavy accent, yet it cracked with emotion that snuck into his gratitude.

Kate blushed and shook her head. "Your thanks is unnecessary, Laird MacKinnon. We should all protect the children."

"You're right about that." He placed Bonnie back on her mother's lap and kissed his wife. "I've missed you. Are you well? Kevin?"

"Aye, we're all well, now." Julianna smiled.

"It's good to be home. We need to send word to Henry. He was despondent when I left him and blames himself."

"Aye, I'll take care of it and will send him a missive. Brendan sent men to alert you Bonnie returned days ago. You must have missed them," Julianna said.

"I was on my way home for a visit when I ran into them, and they told me about Bonnie." Colin gawked at his brother and Gil. Brendan scowled and Gil had a fat smile placed on his face. He glanced back at Kate, and he whispered to his wife. "The woman's beauty must be causing problems. I'll give up my tartan for a month in a wager that these two are taken with her."

Lady Julianna nodded. Kate blushed but didn't understand what he said in the unknown language. No one in the room spoke, and everyone stared at her, even Colin MacKinnon. Kate grew abashed at their attention. Bonnie took pity on her, the sweet child, and drew their notice when she began talking.

"Papa." She tugged his tunic. "I was too a bad lass and I left the tent 'cause I wanted to see the stickmen. I searched for you and Mama, och a man picked me up. I tried to scream, even though I wasn't supposed to. I remembered you told me no more screaming."

Colin looked appalled as she recited the event. He retook her in his arms and waited for her to continue, and petted her head.

"But I tried to scream anyway. The mean man put me on a horse and rided away. He took me to his home and his wife was mean too. She didn't like me 'cause I was Scots, and she spanked me 'cause I wouldn't eat. I didn't eat it 'cause I was a scairt. I'm sorry, Papa."

No one spoke or moved during the girl's reminiscence. She continued with the retelling after sighing. "I was there for a longed time afore Kate came. She heard me cry and came in my room. She became the ward of the man that took me, and she brung her cat to me. She told me I could hold it and pet it. Kate said Trixie was good at keeping secrets. And, you know what?"

"Nay, what, Button?" Colin's voice shook.

"She was aright, 'cause she didn't tell anyone my secrets. Kate took care of me. She's good, Papa, och the lady, she was mean. But Kate and me, we got back at her. Papa, I'm sorry I was a bad lass and did those things to the lady."

"What did you do, Button?"

"Oh, no one wants to hear about that, Bonnie." Kate tried to get her to stop talking and shook her head. She hoped she wouldn't continue. Of course, the girl's admissions were spoken in English for all to hear.

"I want to hear it. Bonnie?" His face immediately expressed his, 'you-better-do-as-I-say' mien. Unfortunately, Bonnie complied.

"We put all kinds of insects in the lady's bed. Kate said I was the best insect catcher. You know why? 'Cause I catched the biggest insects. Then Kate poured her basin water on the lady's head. Her hair looked pitiful, at least that's what Kate said. Then we put powder in the lady's porridge and it gave her pains, but we weren't finished, were we, Kate?"

Kate was mortified, and couldn't believe Bonnie told them all the things they had done. "Nay, Bonnie, we weren't done." Remarkably, she sounded proud.

"We catched fifteen toads and put 'em in the lady's ale barrel. That was fun 'cause the toads were hard to catch and were slimy, right Kate?"

Kate nodded.

Colin, Julianna, Brendan, Gil, and Walter, roared with laughter.

"Lass, you weren't bad at all, the lady deserved it."

"Papa, that's not all. Then Kate put the leaves on the lady's chair, and she got a rash all over. We laughed 'cause she itched and looked pitiful, just pitiful." Bonnie scrunched her face.

Colin turned to Kate. "Our clan owes you a great debt for bringing our daughter home." He returned Bonnie to her mama.

"Nay, truly, Laird MacKinnon, I just wanted to get her home safely. Now that she's here, I can be on my way. It was a pleasure meeting you all." Kate rose to take her leave. She needed to abscond because the hall closed in on her and she thought she'd suffocate. Strangers often provoked her apprehension, but being around them wasn't what caused her to worry. They would want answers—answers she was unwilling to give.

"Not yet, I need to know who took her," Colin said low.

She stiffened at his hard words. "I'm uh...sorry I can't... I can't recall his name. You see, I'm terrible with names and uh... I shall send word if I recall. I really must leave." Kate stepped around her chair and walked to the door. When she reached it, Brendan MacKinnon stood in the center of it. How had he gotten there so quickly? And she hadn't even noticed he moved from his seat.

"Katie, sit back down," Brendan spoke low so only she caught his words.

She colored at the way he'd said her name. "I must leave, sir, please...move out of my way." Panic ensued because they weren't going to let her leave. Her chest tightened, and she flustered in distress of what to do.

"How far do you think you're going to get, lass? You have no horse and no escort. Are you planning to walk back to England? You'll likely get lost." Brendan's snide voice stiffened her spine.

She hadn't anywhere to go and the likelihood of reaching Henry was slim, especially if she had no way of traveling or no knowledge of where she was headed. A sob tore from her mouth and she wanted to cry. A rush of failure washed over her.

"You're not leaving. Come back to the table before you fall to the floor in exhaustion." He took her arm and seemed surprised when he didn't have to drag her back.

"Lady Kaitlin, please, you must stay here. You have traveled a great length. At least rest yourself for a time before you return to England." Julianna kept her eyes on Kate until she nodded her agreement.

Kate retook her seat and tried to maintain dignity. "Laird MacKinnon, I would appreciate the rest and you are right, the travel will be great. I should take time before returning, but I must return to King Henry and relay... I need to get myself settled because I can't go back to Lord…" She stumbled over her words and muddled her explanation badly.

"I would be happy to send a missive to King Henry for you, Lady Kaitlin. I'm sure he would be honored to help you." Julianna peered at her husband. "Colin will have someone take it to him when we send him the news of Bonnie's return."

"Where was Bonnie taken?" Colin asked hotly.

"I'm terrible with directions. Why I'm certain it took us many more days to get here because of my bad sense of direction. I can't tell you where or who, I'm sorry."

"Our clan must repay the miscreant for what he caused our family. You must tell me who he is and why he took my daughter." Colin shouted and slammed the table with his fist.

"Colin, please don't yell at Lady Stanhope. If she says that she doesn't know the name or the direction, you shouldn't press her." Julianna touched her husband's arm to soothe him.

Something strange happened then because Colin's demeanor completely changed. He looked at her oddly and laughed as though he'd gone addled. He hastily wiped his eyes from laughing so hard. Whatever had overtaken him subsided and he quieted.

"Laird MacKinnon, I'm unaware of why he took Bonnie and I'm sorry, I can't tell you who he is because I have to… If you don't want me to stay, I shall be on my way." She tried to leave again and rose, but felt Brendan's hand on her shoulder. She turned and gave him a 'get-your-hands-off-me' look, but he returned his attention to Colin. He squeezed her shoulder firmly and forced her to sit back down.

"Lady Kaitlin, I apologize for yelling. Please stay, you are welcome here. Julianna will set you up in a cottage. Stay as long as you wish, and I want you to call us by our given names. My name is Colin and my wife is Julianna."

"Oh, thank you, Conner. I'm so happy you're letting me stay."

Colin ground his teeth. "It's Colin, lass, not Conner."

"Forget it, Colin, it won't do any good," Gil told him.

"What do you mean?"

Gil grinned. "I'll tell you later."

Kate regarded him skeptically and wondered if he suspected her ploy.

"Julianna, we're in for a celebration. We'll make it for two days hence. Will that give you enough time to prepare?" Colin motioned to her for Bonnie, but Julianna wouldn't let her go.

"Aye, but will you send word to Steven and Sara? They'll want to come." Julianna leaned toward her. "Kate, Sara is my closest friend and is married to Laird KirkConnell. Their land borders ours."

"Aye, get Kate settled. Let me have Bonnie for a while. I want to hold her." Colin took his daughter from his wife.

Julianna motioned for her to follow, but Kate held Brendan's eyes for a moment before she trailed behind her. His stare tensed her back as she made her way through the doorway. She definitely didn't want to be attracted to him.

CHAPTER EIGHT

Bonnie settled on Colin's lap and appeared to slumber. Colin rejoiced at his daughter's return, and now that she was safely home, he would make certain she stayed there. His family was once again together, which he hadn't believed would ever happen. He'd thought he lost his wee Button forever. When his men told him Brendan found her and she was home, he was astounded by the news. When he walked into the keep and saw her, he didn't react well. Fortune assuredly befell on their clan.

He smiled smugly and glanced at Brendan and contemplated how he'd break the news to him. When he heard Julianna speak Kate's full name, he realized who she was. Before he'd left London, Henry told him he'd settled the issue over Julianna's land and gifted it to Angus Barclay, now betrothed to Kaitlin Stanhope. Henry wanted the Barclays to cease their raids on the borderlands, and decided maybe if they had land of their own, they would heed his warnings.

Colin was sure the news would cause his brother's ire, but perhaps not.

"She's something, is she not?" Gil waited for the ladies to leave before he made that comment.

"Aye, she's bonny." Colin whistled. "But you didn't notice that, did you?"

The men laughed.

"If I was a younger man," Walt said and flashed a grin.

"She drove me daft on the way here. Brendan found her at the crossing, near the Gordons' holding. They were ragged. She's bad with names and called me Gerald, George, and God knows what else along the way. 'Tis likely she doesn't recall the name of her guardian."

"I see that you couldn't handle one wee woman." Colin laughed and settled back with his arms around Bonnie's wee body.

"Damned if we didn't try. The lass wasn't impressed with me, because she gave Brendan a look-see and hasn't noticed me since. You should've seen him—"

Brendan cut him short. "She held my stare longer than any other lass. She's got guts, you know how the ladies' run—"

"Aye, Brendan, we know," Walt said.

"I deem Brendan's doing a little running himself, but that's about to end. Is it not?" Colin baited him. Hell, before Brendan walked as a wee lad he'd teased him. Now, however, the teasing would aid him in gaining Brendan's agreement regardless of his discord.

"What are you talking about, Colin? Just what am I running from?" Brendan sat back and folded his arms over his chest. Though he appeared relaxed, his shoulders tensed and he had a rigid demeanor about him Colin knew well.

"I have news from Londontown and from Henry."

"Oh? What does the king have to say?"

Colin grinned at Brendan's surliness. If there was one person whom Brendan didn't get along with, it was King Henry, not that his brother got along with many. Brendan often fought with men at whatever keep they visited. Yet he and Henry had somewhat of a rivalry, the two of them harassed each other when Henry came for visits. Although, now that Colin thought about it, Brendan and Henry seemed to respect each other's talents. Henry was considered diplomatic and entertaining, and Brendan was branded a guerrilla for his combative skills and perseverance.

"Before I give you the news, there's something I want to know?"

"Which is?"

Colin slid his hand over his daughter's back and continued to hold her against his chest. "I take it you approve of Lady Kaitlin?"

Brendan's frown intensified. "What does that have to do with anything? Will you get on with the news? I don't have time for this cosh. Does the news have something to do with me? If not, I should get back to training."

"I'd say the news might be of interest if you have a fondness for Lady Kaitlin?" Colin almost laughed at his brother's expression. His frown disappeared, and he mellowed.

"What do you mean by fondness? Do I think she's beautiful? Hell, aye. Is she courageous? She saved Bonnie, so aye. What man wouldn't be fond of her? What else can I say? Aye, I'm fond of her." Brendan placed his hands on the table and leaned forward in his most threatened manner, but Colin didn't take it as seriously as others might have. "Now, give me the damned news from Henry so I can go to the barracks."

"Walt, will you retrieve the missive he wrote to Julianna? It's in my saddlebag. It's a rolled parchment with the king's seal on it."

Walt left to run the errand. In the meantime, Colin continued to bait Brendan.

"So you think she's beautiful, aye?"

"Did I not say so? I don't want to talk about Katie. What is Henry's news? You read the missive, so why don't you just tell me? Why make me wait?"

"I trust it's best you wait to read his missive for yourself. I'll say this though, Henry doesn't know what slipped through his hands, and neither do the Barclays." Colin grinned at his brother's impatience.

"Hurry the hell up, Walt." Brendan's bellow caused

Bonnie to wince.

Walt returned and threw the parchment on the table and retook his seat. "Here, lad."

Colin suspected Walt read the missive because he wore a telling smile. "Well, open it." He couldn't refrain from grinning widely as well. The news would cause his brother's reaction, and he wanted to see what that reaction would be.

Brendan hastily unrolled the parchment and scanned the words. His eyes didn't change at all during the reading and remained focused. If anyone watched for a sign of his surprise, they wouldn't surmise the missive affected him. Colin knew Brendan better than anyone and recognized the shift in his arms. Brendan gripped the parchment with his fist.

He glanced up from the missive. "Why would he do this to the poor lass?"

"He said he owed Barclay the favor and because his father caused their clan hardship. Henry wants to repay the debt and also wants the Barclay to cease their raids on the borderlands."

"So he's betrothed the poor woman to that swine? Why would he force any woman to marry that knave? I should never have saved Henry's arse down by the loch."

Colin laughed and snatched the parchment from him. "Well, her fate is settled, and she will wed the Barclay as her king bids. Now, what's this about you saving Henry?"

"When he last visited some soldiers took his garments whilst he bathed and left him to dry in the breeze. I happened by and saw the poor lad shivering. When he asked me to give him my tartan, I did. Henry owes me. This is how he repays me by betrothing Katie to another man?"

"Aye, but he wasn't aware of your interest, now was he? I'd say you might want to send Henry a missive of your own."

"To hell with that. She has nothing to do with me, Colin. What do I care if she's betrothed to the Barclay? I found Bonnie, now I can go about my business." Brendan's look was as cross as he'd ever seen.

"Aye, you're right. None of these doings have anything to do with you. I cannot believe my men took the king's garments. I wonder why Henry said nothing about it." Colin wanted to laugh at his brother's dour mood. Brendan never told him what happened at the loch, neither had Henry.

"Why would he do such an atrocious thing to Katie? I cannot see her with a man such as Barclay, even if she is a wee brave." Brendan's incredulous tone attested to his ire.

"He's her king, and she has a duty to follow his dictate."

"I don't give a damn if he's her king. Well, he's not my king. I can't let her marry him."

Colin kept his voice from rising. "Why the hell not? Henry decreed it and she must obey. She's fortunate in his choice. At least he didn't choose you. She's beautiful, courageous, and deserves… We should escort her to Londontown for her wedding. It's the least we can do."

"Aye, return her to England. That's what she wants. I don't know her well, but I think she's a wee bit absentminded." Brendan took his cup with a quick swipe and chugged it.

Colin laughed at Brendan's discontent. One minute he wouldn't let the woman marry Henry's chosen groom and the next he wanted her gone. He hadn't misjudged his brother and didn't believe for a second Brendan would let the woman from his sight. He'd thought Brendan would do the right thing, but there was no getting Brendan to do something he didn't want to. In time, he'd come around and until then, Colin would do everything within his power to keep her there.

"But before I send her back, I want the name of the man who took my daughter. Who will befriend the lass and find out for me?" Colin sensed Brendan's attraction to the lass and considered he wouldn't let anyone near her. Besides, Brendan had a thirst for blood and vengeance. He wouldn't let anyone else take on the chore of gaining their enemy's name. Before Brendan reasoned it in his mind, Gil gave him a look.

"I'll do it, Laird MacKinnon. She's too bonny by far, mayhap she'll succumb to my charms since Brendan doesn't want her." Gil laughed and slapped Brendan on the shoulder. "I wouldn't mind saving her from the dastardly Barclays."

Colin glanced at his brother and waited. He gave Brendan a chance to interject before he gave permission to Gil to woo her. Only, Brendan sat there with a scowl and didn't show interest in the conversation. Yet Colin caught the little signs that showed Brendan was knocked on his arse by Henry's news. If his brother was standing, surely he would pace the room—a habit which drove Colin daft.

"Well, Colin, what say you?" Gil asked.

"You must woo the lass and get her to trust you, Gil. You'll have to spend a lot of time with her. Do you deem you can handle her?"

"Aye, I can handle her. It'll be my pleasure to woo the lass. I vow to be a gentleman, Colin, and only steal a few kisses from her." Gil snickered jokingly.

"Wait." Brendan stood.

Colin, Walt, and Gil's eyes shot to Brendan. Brendan's temper was as cross as they'd ever seen it. "What?" they asked in unison.

"You'll not do it, Gil, it's my niece the swine took and I'm her uncle. I should make the sacrifice." Brendan's eyes glared at them when he spoke.

"Sacrifice?" Colin and Gil asked at the same time.

Colin laughed and wouldn't cease his absurd tirade. His brother had a strange expression on his face, one he'd never seen before. Brendan's betrothal was on as far as Colin was concerned, even if Brendan wouldn't admit it.

"Are you certain, Brendan? It would mean you'll have to put away your scowl."

Brendan glowered. He snatched his cup and drank the remaining ale, and set it down with a bang. "Cosh, I won't have to do anything. I'll get the swine's name from her by nightfall. You'll see, it won't take long at all." With that, Brendan marched from the hall.

CHAPTER NINE

Her plan to be elusive wouldn't be easy.
Kate walked beside Julianna along the trail to the cottages that dotted the slope below the main keep. She felt awkward and unsure of how to act around the strangers. It seemed they lived a peaceful life until Lord Richard ruined it. Julianna showed her to a cottage with a thatched roof and dirt floors. The two-roomed cottage had an extensive area for eating and such, and one small sleeping area. It was clean and certainly large enough for her.

"I'll come to help you clean it on the morrow."

"Thank you, Jennifer, I appreciate your kindness. The cottage is lovely."

"Nay, it's Julianna," she reminded her and smiled. "There's clean bedding on the table. I'll get you some items to fix it up a wee bit nicer."

"That's kind of you. I hope I have put no one out of their home."

"Nay, the cottage has been empty for a while. Do you want to come to the keep with me? You can take your meals with us. We'll have the evening meal soon. Then you can get rest. You must be exhausted from the journey."

When they left the cottage, Julianna showed her how to find her way back to the keep. Kate noticed the trees surrounding the stone castle because the saplings didn't appear to be deep-rooted.

"Did you plant the trees?"

"Aye, there were no trees when I came, the landscape was barren. I had Colin dig these trees up and replanted them here." She laughed. "I don't deem he enjoyed the task though. I like to work outside often. Mayhap you would like to help?"

"I'd be glad to help any way I can. I tended to my father's grounds for many years before he died." The mention of her father saddened Kate.

"I'm sorry. Has it been long since he passed?"

"He died warring in the holy land. He was a wonderful father and I shall miss him."

"I'm sorry for your loss. You will consider our clan your family. I never thought to see Bonnie again and if it wasn't for you… Losing someone you love is never easy. Let's talk about something else. Do you want to help with the celebration? It will give you something to do."

"Of course, I'd be glad to help."

"I shouldn't ask because you're our guest of honor."

"I'd be pleased to help if I can, but there's no need to honor me." Kate walked beside her and memorized the way back.

They returned to the great hall and the evening meal was served. Colin sat at the head of the table awaiting his wife. When she reached his side, she whispered in his ear.

Kate couldn't hear what she said, nor understand her because she spoke hastily and in the unknown language. She noticed the room filled with MacKinnon men-at-arms. She met Bonnie's Uncle Robin and his wife, Tess. Their bairn was tended to by a young girl at the other end of the hall.

Everyone joyously greeted Bonnie, and Emma, her nurse, blubbered and carried on for several minutes about Bonnie's return. Emma attended to Bonnie when she disappeared, and she held guilt for not being more attentive. Kate thought her a kindly woman.

LASS' VALOR

The clan's people kissed and hugged Bonnie, and she loved all the attention. Their show of affection lightened her heart, and she gave the Goddess a silent blessing of thankfulness. She did the right thing. Bonnie was back where she belonged. After she finished eating, Kate sat back and listened to the gaiety of the people around her, though she didn't understand much of anything. Brendan viewed her from afar, and she blushed at the way his eyes followed her. Luckily, Tess sat beside her and distracted her from the cursed warrior.

"We're thankful you brought Bonnie back. Would you like to meet my Robbie?"

"Aye, that would be nice, Tara." Kate tried not to laugh at her guise.

Tess continued to smile and handed the baby to her. Kate looked at the sweet babe. "He's adorable." Robbie cooed, and her heart skipped a beat. She handed the babe back to his mother.

"You're from England?"

"I am." Kate reached for the baby's hand and held it gently.

"Julianna was from there."

"She sounds as though she was born here." Kate was astounded because Julianna looked every bit a Highland chieftain's wife.

"She's always been a Scot in her heart."

"I'm going to retire. It was nice meeting you." She stood and went to bid Colin and Julianna a goodnight. Bonnie heard her give a farewell and jumped from her mother's lap. She ran to her. Kate wrapped her arms around Bonnie's shoulders and she held onto her legs.

"Kate, you're leaving me? Are you going home?"

"Nay, lovey, I've been given my very own cottage. I'll rest there. Don't weep." She knelt to whisper her explanation and touched her head to Bonnie's.

"I'll miss you. I love you, Kate."

A tear tried to sneak out the corner of her eye, but Kate

resisted the sentiment. "I love you, too, but I'm only going to bed. I'll return in the morn and we'll eat our meal together. Will you show me what you do for fun?"

"Aye, I know what we'll do," Bonnie told her in a whisper.

"I'll see you on the morrow then."

Bonnie hugged her tight around her neck and wouldn't let go. She placed a kiss on her head, set Bonnie away from her, and turned to leave the hall.

Kate stepped outside and stood under the expanse of the star-flecked sky. She sobbed at the heartbreak of leaving the child. How would she bear to leave Bonnie when the time came? She would miss her terribly and became attached to her. Someone called her name, and she turned to find Brendan behind her. She quickly turned away and swiped tears from her eyes.

"Katie, I'll walk you to your cottage."

"I'm sure I can find my way, Bryan."

He grabbed her hand and gave her a hard look. She tried to pull away, but he tightened his grip and tugged her along. They reached her cottage a few minutes later, and she opened the door. He told her to wait. Brendan strolled inside and lit a candle, while she stood with her back against the doorjamb and waited for him to leave. He strode to her, placed his hand against the doorframe next to her head and peered down at her.

"Thanks for walking me—" Before she finished, he lowered his head and kissed her. Her back pressed against the door with nowhere to go. His other hand pulled at her chin until she opened her mouth. He slipped in his tongue and lightly caressed hers. She kissed him back and liked the sudden warmth that overcame her.

Brendan pulled back and stared into her eyes. His eyes gave the impression he read her thoughts and she blushed. Her stomach fluttered madly, and she took a deep breath. The earthly essence and his manly scent engulfed her senses. She was stunned by his kiss and hadn't known people kissed in such a way. She longed to wrap her arms around him and kiss him again. He grinned boyishly and set her back on the ground. Everything about him muddled her.

"Good night, fair Katie."

"Good night, Boyd."

Brendan blanched when she misused his name. Trixie appeared out of nowhere and meowed. He looked down and her cat wrapped around his boot. Kate picked Trixie up and as he walked away, she couldn't help but notice his bare muscled calves. She waited until he disappeared before she closed the door.

"Trixie, how did you get here? Did you see him?"

"Meow."

Kate laughed. She took a small bowl from her satchel and filled it with the meat she'd taken from the table in the hall. Trixie purred loudly, content to eat her food. She glimpsed a pitcher of water on the table and wondered where it came from. Then she noticed the cottage. She walked to the table which now covered with a beautiful linen cloth that matched the fabric that covered the window. Logs stacked neatly beside the hearth and two chairs flanked the table. Someone placed linens on the bed and two pillows at the top.

Humbled by their kindness, she tried to keep her emotions from brimming to her eyes. Everything looked lovely, and there was even an arrangement of flowers on the small table beside the bed. There were several garments of clothing lying on the bed: long and short-sleeved gowns, nightrails, and even slippers. She picked up a nightdress and set it on the table, then undressed and readied for bed. With the kindle set, the logs caught fire in no time and warmth permeated the cottage.

After such a grueling journey, all she wanted was a good night's sleep. She pulled back the covers on the bed and slipped inside and snuggled into the warmth. Trixie jumped upon the bed and made herself comfortable and kneaded her paws on the covers. The medallion dangled at her cat's chest and she touched it and sighed at the thought of what it meant. She didn't want to think such sorrowful thoughts this night, not when she'd returned Bonnie to her loving family.

Kate thought about Brendan's kiss. She found the warrior of her vision at last—her own gentle warrior. But he wasn't gentle—far from it. It was her last thought as her mind drifted to sleep.

He was a rogue and that was that. Kate came to that realization by the end of the next day.

She awoke to the sunshine and dressed quickly. With her promise in mind, she ran to the hall to meet Bonnie. The cool air chilled her, but it would warm once the sun rose higher. She entered the castle and was almost knocked over by Bonnie, who stood in wait of her inside the doorway.

"You didn't leave me."

"Nay, lovey, I told you I wouldn't."

"Come and sit with me. Papa said I can't leave the table until I finish my food."

"That's good, you need to fatten up." Kate tickled her tummy, and Bonnie's smile made her feel carefree. She missed being near her, and she supposed she would miss her because she hadn't let the child from her sight in many weeks.

"Good morn, Laird MacKinnon." Kate greeted Colin when she entered the hall.

"Nay, it's Colin. Please, call me Colin."

"I'm sorry, I forgot." Kate smiled at his chafed tone. "Is Lady Josephine about yet?"

"You mean Julianna? She's tending to Kevin and will be down soon." He smiled and motioned his daughter back to the table. "Button, you need to finish eating."

A ruckus outside drew their attention. Colin stood and readied to go see to it when Brendan strode in holding her cat by its nape.

"Katie, I demand you not let your animal loose. The horses are afraid of small critters and Benjamin was unseated by his horse." Brendan grunted. "He's darned incensed, too, because it happened in front of most of your soldiers, Colin."

Kate frowned because of the way he held her pet, and she was about to tell him not to be so brutish with her cat when Bonnie tapped her arm.

"Oh, nay, Kate, Papa's going to make you sit in his chair," Bonnie said low.

"Bonnie, I can't punish Kate or make her sit in my chair. She's not my daughter," Colin explained. "Finish your food."

"Oh, Kate, you're lucky Papa cannot punish you." Then she turned and asked her father, "Can anyone punish her, Papa?"

"Nay, Button, not yet, anyway."

"Who gets to punish her?"

"Her husband, when she marries."

"Kate, never get married." Bonnie expressed her notion in a serious tone, which made her want to laugh at the sweet remark.

"All right, I won't."

Brendan scowled and dropped Trixie on her lap. He sat next to her and poured ale into a goblet, but he kept glancing at Colin. As usual, he crowded her with his large body. Kate couldn't help but look at him. He was attractive in his own reticent sort of way. He moved closer, so much so, she smelled his wonderful outdoorsy scent. She closed her eyes and savored the aroma of his earthiness. She reminded herself not to be attracted to him, but a fat lot of good that did.

"Button, have you recalled the man's name?"

Kate gasped when she heard Colin, but she studied Bonnie's face and prayed she hadn't remembered.

"It's D, we called the lady, Lady D, right, Kate?"

"Now, let me see? What was it? Dennison, Dunston, darned, I can't recall. I'm sorry, Conway."

Colin glanced at his brother. "We'll wait until you remember. Button, let's go see your mama." He got up from his seat and stretched his hand to Bonnie.

"But I didn't finish my food yet, Papa."

"It'll be here when we return." He lifted her from the

bench and set her on the floor.

Kate sat alone at the table with Brendan. He leaned back with his arm extended on the tabletop. Lord, he was a handsome devil. A blush crept up her neck. Brendan watched her again, too. At least, she felt pretty this morning with her hair braided into rolls and pinned upon her head. She continued to eye him and recalled how his eyes filled with passion when he'd kissed her the night before. When his eyes moved to her mouth, she instinctively licked her lips. Heat coiled inside her and wound its way to her heart.

"What are you about today, Katie?"

Kate was absorbed in her own thoughts and hadn't paid attention.

He asked again, "What do you want to do this day?"

"I thought to look around the keep. Why?" Kate listened to his gruff voice, which somehow softened and almost sounded lyrical. Trixie stood and set her paws on her shoulder, but Kate settled her back on her lap.

"Would you like me to show you around?"

"You don't have to do that, Bryce. Don't you have training to do?" She made her voice sound curt and hoped he'd leave. When he was near, her mind and thoughts scattered. If only she could keep the fact that she was attracted to him to herself, she might avoid him altogether.

"Brendan, my name is Brendan." He sounded somewhat annoyed she didn't recall his name. Then she heard him say under his breath, "The lass is out of her mind."

She held in her laughter. "Oh, I'm sorry. I'm terrible with names."

"I'll walk you, anyway." He grabbed her hand and pulled her from her seat. Trixie jumped from her lap just in time. She placed her hand against his chest to stop herself from falling against him. He was solid, she'd give him that.

They walked outside and he continued to hold her hand, not that she had the strength to get him to release it. He introduced her to the clans' people they passed, and even though she wouldn't remember their names, he told her anyway. The people greeted her with friendliness and smiles. Most she didn't understand, because they spoke to her in Gaelic, but she nodded and returned their smiles. He showed her where she could walk and where she couldn't. Obviously, she wouldn't walk on the training field. Did he think her totally without sense?

Brendan led her away from the courtyard. The farther away from people they walked, the more nervous she became. "Where are we going?"

"Down to the loch. We can rest beside the water." He led her through broad-leafed trees that extended to the bank of the loch. They continued to walk for several minutes, and he remained silent as they stepped beneath the shaded terrace of trees.

She didn't know what to say to him either, so she kept quiet. Once they reached the loch, she was startled by its pristine beauty. Various trees: pines, birch, and oaks towered to the sky. Water moved seemingly at its own pace, flowing rapidly in places, while still in others.

"It's beautiful here."

"It's not as bonny as you."

She swallowed and shyness overtook her, being alone with him. Had he given her a compliment—the scowling warrior? "What?"

"I said you're beautiful. I haven't thanked you for bringing my niece home. You're a brave lass, you know that?" Brendan pulled her to the embankment, pushed her down gently, and sat next to her.

"Thank you, Bryce, but truly, I was glad to help Bonnie. It's serene here. I am relieved and—"

"Brendan, lass, it's Brendan. Say it." His eyes narrowed at her gall, and his lips pressed together and looked hard.

She'd angered him. "Say what?"

"My name, say my name."

"Brendan." She conceded only because she was uncertain what he'd do if she willfully disobeyed him, and not knowing him well enough, she didn't want to test her lot.

"Aye, say it again."

"Brendan."

"You won't forget it again."

"Nay, I shan't." She smiled at his cranky spirit. Why he got angry over her not using his name was beyond her. She considered it for a moment and concentrated on his nearness. Why did he have to sit so close?

Brendan leaned toward her, and she shimmied back a few inches. He supported his body on his hands and set his arms on each side of her body. She fell against the grass and couldn't get away. He didn't seem to want to talk. Would he kiss her senseless again? He moved his mouth above hers, hovering as though he would. When he touched his lips to hers, she tried to move her head away, but his hands stilled her.

She allowed him one kiss and returned it with as much passion as she possessed. She whimpered into his mouth at the way he overwhelmed her. It must have edged him on, and he pressed his body against hers, willing her response. Her breasts crushed against his chest, and her body betrayed her. She'd never experienced such passion before.

Realization struck Kate. She panicked at the erratic emotions that overcame her. Something told her to be afraid, and she listened. She jammed her knee between his legs and pushed him off her. She stood and faced him with her back to the loch.

"How dare you? Don't ever…do that again." She hoped the fury in her voice made him understand he'd frightened her and she didn't know how to react.

Brendan groaned at the pain she'd inflicted upon him. He sat up slowly. "Lass, you—"

"Don't you lass me, Brendan MacKinnon. I'm not a… You can't maul me and think to—"

"Lass, you're going to—"

"Nay, don't speak. For the love of the Goddess, I'm betrothed and won't do that with the likes of you." Kate couldn't resist raising her voice and pointing her finger at him accusingly. She needed space, lots of space. He overwhelmed her with his overbearing kiss and his domineered nature. She stepped back to do just that.

Brendan rose, and she backed up another step. She didn't realize she was close to the bank. Before he reached for her, she lost her footing and fell backward into the loch. Kate gasped and sucked in water. She flailed her arms and tried to reach the edge. The weight of her garments pulled at her and made it difficult to keep her head above the water. As she rose above the water line again, she coughed and her breath hastened.

He fell back onto the grass and laughed his arse off, but he stopped abruptly as if he didn't want anyone to hear him. His pain forgotten—her reaction to falling must've been beyond hilarious.

"Katie?" Brendan called her. He called her name a few more times. "Well, hell."

He ripped his tartan from his chest and dove into the loch and swam toward the bottom. The loch had to be at least twenty feet or so deep. He flapped around the murky depths for her gown and grabbed it, and encircled his arm around her waist. He pulled her to the water's surface and pushed her onto the embankment.

She lay unmoving in shock at what happened. A strange numbness came over her, yet she heard his rasped breath.

"Damn, she's drowned," he muttered. Brendan pulled her arms away from her body and used his hands to compress her stomach and chest. "What the hell should I do?" He pushed on her chest again and she coughed from the force he used.

Kate gasped and filled herself with deep breaths. She rolled over and spit out the taste of the water. "Ugh." She wiped her mouth with the back of her hand. "Get off me, you lout."

He stayed right where he was. "I saved you. You drowned. You don't know how to swim?"

"Nay, I never learned. I never had to…" She coughed

again.

"Are you alright, lass?"

"Aye, oh you're all wet." Kate groaned when she realized how attractive he looked with his wet hair hung in his face and his muscles covered with droplets of water. "Thank you for saving me. I probably would've drowned if you hadn't jumped in. I apologize." Her tone suggested she really was sorry. She hoped he understood.

"I tried to tell you that you were in danger of falling."

"Nay, not about that…for striking you…there. I apologize if I hurt you." Her cheeks burned acknowledging such a thing.

"Are you blushing because you almost drowned or because you struck me there?" He continued to lean over her and his face was but an inch from hers. Droplets of water from his hair dripped on her breast and he looked down but returned his gaze to her eyes. She wasn't sure what the look meant.

Kate moaned and tried to push him off her.

"It's already forgotten. Just do me a favor, hmm? Next time you want to strike me, hit me anywhere but there." He smiled when her cheeks brightened even more.

Kate giggled. "I am truly sorry, but you made me feel funny. I didn't like it."

"You didn't?" He sounded incredulous.

"Nay." She peered at him, her eyes shone with laughter.

"You sure as hell will." Brendan stared into her eyes with a serious mien.

"I doubt that." Kate shifted her legs and groaned from his weight. She shoved his chest and tried to make him move. "Will you get off me?"

Brendan grunted at the way her hands pushed him away. "I never laugh, and here I am laughing for the second time this day. Aye, I'm not sure I like this turn-about."

She narrowed her eyes at his comment. Was his grunt a laugh? Why didn't he laugh? She supposed it wasn't something a warrior would do. He helped her up, and she shivered from her now soaked garments. He grabbed his tartan from the ground and wrapped it around her shoulders.

"T-thanks," she muttered between her now chattering teeth. He placed his arm around her shoulder to provide warmth and they walked back to the keep.

When they entered the hall, Colin and Julianna gasped at the sight of them.

"What the hell happened to you?" Colin approached when they strode in.

They stood in the hall and dripped water on the floor. Brendan stood bare-chested, and Kate had his tartan wrapped around her. What did his brother think happened? Kate tried not to let her teeth chatter from being cold, and she decided to let Brendan give their excuses.

"Katie fell into the loch." Brendan gave her a gentle look.

Kate lowered her face so they couldn't see how embarrassed she was. She noticed Colin glance at his wife, who smiled at them.

"Are you alright, Kate? Were you harmed?" Julianna asked.

"I'm well. Brendan saved me."

"How is it you remember his name?" Colin placed his arm around Julianna and grinned at Brendan oddly.

She spoke up, "He made me say it several times so I wouldn't forget."

Colin nodded and moved his eyes to Brendan for a second. "Why didn't I think of that? How did you fall into the loch, Kate?"

"I, uh…lost my footing—"

"She was upset because I kissed—"

Kate covered his mouth with her hand. "I lost my footing, Brendan, that's all."

Colin and Julianna laughed.

Brendan took her hand away from his mouth and kissed the delicate skin on her palm before he released her. She was strangely aware of the looks his brother and sister-in-law gave.

"I would gladly stay and torment you further, Kate, but I need to change." Brendan gave his brother a fleeted look before he left.

"I better change, too." Kate picked up Trixie and followed him out.

Kate returned to her cottage and changed her clothing. She'd forgotten she promised to help Julianna with the planning of the celebration and hurried back to the keep. Trixie trailed behind her with her fluffy fur waving in the breeze. Julianna directed a few women in the hall when she entered. For the rest of the afternoon, she helped clean and prepare food. They worked hard and scrubbed the floors and tables, not that they appeared to need cleaning. Julianna insisted the hall be spotless for the celebration. It was a habit she'd learned from her aunty, she'd said.

Later that day, they stood by the hearth. "It's much cleaner and smells good. Thank you for your help, Kate."

"It does smell good in here." She set a broom next to the woodpile and waited while Julianna finished her chore of cleaning the cinders from the threshold.

"It won't for long, not with those warriors spilling ale on my floor this night."

Kate laughed at her remark.

"What do you think of Brendan?"

"Brendan, oh, he's nice, I suppose," Kate said absently. She hadn't paid attention to what Julianna asked and realized what she'd said a moment later.

Julianna burst with laughter. "He's been called many things, Kate, nice wasn't ever mentioned. I'll let you in on a wee secret. Brendan has a big heart but rarely shows it. But it's there all the same. You won't break it, will you?"

"Break it? I have no intention of trying to capture that warrior's heart. Why ever would I do that?" Kate stepped away from the hearth and avoided her new friend's gaze.

"He's never acted strangely before. I think he's enamored of you."

"He is not attracted to me and I'll not let him close again."

"Kate, you won't have a choice. If a MacKinnon wants you, he'll have you." Though she thought Julianna jested with her, she looked quite serious.

"I don't want to be taken or anything of the sort. I just want to return to England and see the king so I can show him the…"

"Colin sent off my missive to King Henry and I made sure to mention your wish for his counsel. Why do you want to see Henry? Show him what? You mentioned that you wanted to tell him about your guardian. I get the feeling there's more you're not telling."

Colin and Brendan walked in and stood behind them, neither made a sound and listened attentively.

Kate had her back to them and hadn't seen them enter. She didn't think it would hurt to tell Julianna a few details, but sooner or later she'd have to return home. Regardless of whether she was attracted to Brendan MacKinnon, she had to think of her father and her people. There was no sense in letting her attraction for the scowling warrior interfere with her plan. Even if the king put aside her betrothal, Brendan wouldn't leave his homeland. She couldn't imagine him living in England, running her father's lands, and befriending their crofters. When she returned to Henry, she would continue with her plan and secure her father's holdings.

"My father's lands lay unprotected. The king arranged an acceptable marriage for me and I must return."

"Do you know whom you're to marry?"

"Nay, but I'm certain the king would marry me well. I shall ask him to arrange my marriage at the soonest so I won't have to return to my guardian. I will speak to him about my father's death."

"So you want to marry?"

"Aye, I need protection from…my guardian. I have lands, and my husband will gain wealth, at least, I think he will. Lord Aldwyn de Guylet, my father's overlord, all but said my husband would take over my father's lands upon our marriage."

"What about your guardian?"

"Aldwyn made him my guardian until he returns from the holy lands."

Julianna touched her shoulder affectionately. "Why did you not ask your guardian to contact Henry and arrange for an immediate counsel?"

"I was going to, but I seriously doubt he would have done so."

"Why do you say that? Did he tell you so?"

Kate shook her head. "Because the night Bonnie and I escaped, my guardian came to my room and told me to submit to him, that he was going to marry me himself. He said he would have my overlord tell King Henry that my betrothal was unacceptable. He uncovered himself and attacked me, but I hit him over the head with a book to get him off me. I had to tie him up to make my escape."

"That's awful. My poor bairn was held by a monster. You don't know why he took her?" Julianna's expression turned to dismay.

"Nay, I don't. He didn't speak about Bonnie that night, only that he would have her brought to witness my downfall if I didn't submit to him."

Brendan and Colin shared a heated look before they returned their eyes to her.

Kate shook from reliving that night. "That's when I knew I had to get Bonnie to safety. If anything happened to me, her chances of returning were naught. We ran a mile or so before we made it to the horse. I arranged ownership of the horse that day because I planned to leave the next day. I carried Bonnie and ran until I reached the horse. I was glad to get away from there." She lowered her gaze and her cheeks heated with embarrassment.

"What happened then?"

"We rode for days. I had no idea where I was going, and traveled north hoping to find my way to Scotland. I couldn't go to Londontown to see the king, because I would have had to pass by my guardian's keep and I didn't want to risk Bonnie's safety and possibly being caught."

Julianna's hand moved down Kate's arm to her hand. She clasped it and gave her a reassuring squeeze. "So you rode into the night not knowing where you were going?"

"I had to. Bonnie is an amazing child. You should be proud of her. She built a fire and hunted a hare. She even showed me how to fish." Kate's tears streamed her face. Why now, had her tears chosen to fall? She didn't want to cry, but she couldn't help it.

Colin stepped around Kate and hugged her, not too gently either. "Aye, we are proud of her. Thank you, Kate, for saving our daughter. Our debt is great. We will repay you somehow." He stepped away from her, took his wife's hand, and led her from the room.

Brendan looked taken aback by her confession and stood with a stare at her as if he was in shock. Kate considered kicking him to bring him out of his state, but she wouldn't do anything so unladylike. He snapped out of it a moment later. He took her hand and pulled her to the bench, where he set her on his lap. She continued to weep with quiet sobs.

"Don't cry, Katie. I don't like it."

Of all the harebrained things to say, his words caused her to weep even more. He hugged her to him and she let him comfort her. It felt good to be held and she wouldn't release him. She soaked his tunic with her tears. When she calmed, she settled her head on his shoulder. He readjusted her on his lap and tilted her face to look at him.

"Katie, he's a knave. You've done so much for us, let me help you. You saved my niece, och there's no way to repay you. Give me the name of your guardian, and I'll make him pay for causing you pain."

"I cannot. I must get myself settled first. I have to see the king, it's the only way I can… If you kill Lord…the king won't—"

"Tell me, Katie, be honest." Brendan looked into her

eyes and willed her to say the name.

"Are you done wooing Kate, yet, Uncle Brendan?" Bonnie skipped down the stairs and stopped at the bottom.

They looked up to see her watching them. She held her tartan bunched in her arms, the edge touched the floor.

"What, lass?"

"Are you done wooing Kate? That's what you told Papa. You said you would woo her to get the man's name. Remember?"

Kate hastily retreated from Brendan's lap. She slapped his face with force and ran from the hall and kept running until she reached her cottage. The door slammed behind her and she ran to her bed. She looked around for Trixie and realized she'd left her at the keep. Trixie always soothed her, and she needed her friend's comfort right now. Her anger made her want to scream to the rafters. How dare he use her? She thought he was being kind, but all he wanted was Richard's name. What she needed was the Goddess's solace. She erected a circle and sat in the center, then chanted the words needed to evoke the Goddess' presence.

At that moment, she was definitely not attracted to Brendan MacKinnon.

CHAPTER TEN

She appealed even more to him now.

Kate had courage, and if her beauty wasn't enough to bring him around, her valor would. Brendan's cheek burned from her slap and he rubbed his skin in disbelief. He'd stood there with his mouth agape in shock that Kate struck him again. She didn't seem the sort to become so angry. His niece's sobs drew his attention, and he realized he might have upset her with his fierce frown. He softened his expression and walked to Bonnie. She cast her gaze to the floor because he was disgruntled. Now he had to comfort her, or there would be no living with the lass. Lord knew what she'd do to him. After he discovered what she and Kate did to the knave's wife, he'd be beset with pranks aplenty.

He picked Bonnie up and hugged her. "You weren't supposed to tell about that." Brendan sat in Colin's chair and placed Bonnie on his lap.

"Is Kate angry with you now?"

"Aye, she's very…furious."

"I'm sorry, Uncle, I didn't know I wasn't supposed to tell. Are you angry with me?"

She placed her wee face against his neck and cried. Brendan sighed, mindful she was contrite. "Nay, fairy, I'm never angry with you. I'll see you later." He gave her a kiss on the cheek and set her on the punishment chair and hoped she would stay there. Colin came down the steps, and Brendan waved as he strode out the door.

Colin stopped at the bottom of the steps and observed his daughter. She sat in the punishment chair and her sweet wee face downcast. She was troubled about something.

"Button, why are you sitting in my chair?"

"Oh, Papa, I did something bad." She wept softly.

"You did? When? You've only been down a few minutes. Who told you to sit in my chair?"

"No one, Papa, I knowed you would make me 'cause…"

"What did you do?"

"I asked Uncle if he was done wooing Kate to get the man's name."

"That is very…bad. What happened?"

"Kate smacked him. She never gets mad, Papa, even when she saw my hurt back, she didn't yell or scream. But she was mad 'cause she turned red. She said she would get even with the lady for hitting me. That's why we put insects in the lady's bed and did those things."

"I see." Colin couldn't believe what his daughter told him. He swallowed his ire and closed his eyes at the vision of it. He owed Kate more than he realized.

"Come here, Button."

She jumped from the chair and ambled to him. Colin lifted her and kissed her lightly on her lips. He couldn't help it but hugged her tightly. He was thankful she wasn't harmed, and each time he thought about it, he'd tense again.

"I'm glad you're unharmed. We have Kate to thank for that. She's a woman of valor. Do you know what that means, Button?"

Bonnie shook her head. "Nay, Papa, what?"

"It means she's courageous and brave."

"Is that good, Papa?"

Colin chuckled. "Aye, it's very good. There is a way you can make it up to her." He caressed her hair and gave her a reassuring smile.

"How, Papa?"

"There, you see." He pointed to the cat that lay by the hearth, licking its long fur. "I say you take it to her later. While you're there, you'll tell her you were mistaken. Brendan told me he was going to woo Kate. I asked him to try, try to get the man's name. Now, tell me what you will do?"

Bonnie repeated word for word his instructions as she usually did when she did something wrong. Colin nodded; satisfied she accepted what she must do.

Later that night, Brendan walked with Colin and Bonnie to Kate's cottage. He stood outside and waited for Bonnie to enter. If this harebrained scheme worked, he would owe Colin a cask of brew and would have to beg Scottie Gordon, their ally, for it. The Gordon's produced a drink finer than any other in the Highlands.

Kate's anger would delay him in gaining the man's name, and he couldn't have that. He wanted revenge and wanted it now. Brendan paced impatiently along the pathway and waited for his niece to come out. A few minutes later, she skipped through the doorway.

"Well?" Brendan waited for her report.

Colin laughed and picked up his daughter.

Bonnie smiled at her father. "She said she wasn't angry with me, Papa."

"There, Brendan, I told you it would work. She's not angry anymore, right Button?"

"Kate might still be angry with Uncle, 'cause she said he was the last person she wanted to see." She placed her head on Colin's shoulder and closed her eyes.

Brendan chuckled. "Aye, it worked all right, to the minx's benefit. Better get her to bed, Colin. I'll see you on the morrow." He waited until they reached the hill before he looked inside the cottage. Once the inside darkened, he assumed Kate retired for the night. He would wait a few more minutes before he entered.

What the hell would he do? She wanted to marry her betrothed, the damned Barclay and would ask Henry to arrange it as soon as possible. He wasn't good at wooing. Mayhap he should talk to Robin. Robin had been a ladies' man before he married Tess. Brendan decided against talking to Colin or Gil because they would tease him. Colin convinced Julianna to marry him after she'd run out of the chapel on their wedding day. At least, Colin knew how to handle her. Nay, it was unthinkable, because Colin would tease him unmercifully.

Lassies always followed his cousin Douglas around, but he didn't have time to ride to his cousin's land. For the first time in his life, Brendan had no idea how to proceed. Well hell, he didn't want her to marry another. She belonged to him. After all, just because Henry decreed her betrothal to another, didn't mean it was set in stone. At first, he wouldn't accept the king's word about Kate's betrothal to the Barclay, and now he was certain it wouldn't happen. He'd be a fool not to marry her himself.

Now all he had to do was secure Katie's agreement. But would she accept her fate?

The king has arranged an acceptable marriage for me. He'd cringed when she had spoken those words. She was right? He was unacceptable, and he'd never be able to convince her to wed him. He needed to talk to Robin and soon.

Brendan opened the door and quietly entered the cottage. A chill set the air. She snuggled beneath her covers. The hearth lit the room in a light glow. He was careful not to touch her when he slipped beside her, but she slept soundlessly and wasn't awakened by his movements. His blood simmered being so near her. He noticed her creamy skin, her little ears, and beautiful chin. Then his eyes moved to her breasts. Her breasts were perfect in his opinion, not too large, not too small. He cleared his throat and tried to get a hold of himself.

Katie shifted on the bed and rolled close to him and ended up on her back. He leaned to kiss her softly on the lips, but she grabbed his face with both hands and held him firmly.

"What do you think you're doing, Brendan MacKinnon?"

"I'm kissing you." He lowered his mouth and set it on her soft lips. She weakened when his tongue fondled hers. Her warm mouth sent heat undulated through his body. He moaned at the pleasurable experience of her soft lips pressed on his. Timidly, she moved her tongue against his.

Brendan was so into kissing her he hadn't realized her hands pulled his hair. Was she trying to push him away again? Nay, she pulled him closer. He pressed his body against hers, wanting and needing to be as close as he could get. His hand meandered toward her breast and he felt the firmness of it beneath his fingers. He broke off the kiss before it progressed beyond his control.

With raspy breath, he searched her expression for a sign of truce. He didn't see one. Her eyes blazed, and he was uncertain if it was from anger or excitement. Brendan placed his head on her shoulder, his breath heated her neck and she shivered beneath him.

"Katie, if we don't stop, I'm not going to—"

She shoved him. "You better leave. I'm sorry, Brendan, for making you want to woo me."

"You're doing more than that, lass." Brendan kissed her again, but she pushed him away this time. "Are you still angry with me?"

"Aye." She declared it with such spirit that he couldn't help but grunt.

Briefly, he wondered if he should tell her he knew her betrothed and declare his own intention. Nay, he needed more time to figure out a way to convince her he meant to nullify the king's decree.

"I'll see you on the morrow, fairest Katie." Brendan left and felt better about the situation. Only now instead of fearing her wrath, he dreaded the fact he couldn't keep his hands off her. He stood outside her cottage and heard her mumble to herself.

"You're messing with fire and you will get burned. Madam Serena was right, the warrior is causing turmoil. Her prophecy came true. I met the vision of my dreams because of the child. A child I rescued, who caused me to take a somber mission."

Brendan tried to understand her words, but they didn't make much sense. He wondered what she talked about. Who was Madam Serena, and did she refer to him as the warrior? Had the lady made a prophecy about him? Her words unsettled him, and she continued to mumble to herself.

"Well, if I have to deal with turmoil, then I will at least cause him grief."

He looked through the window and contented she snuggled comfortably in her bed.

"I'll drive him crazed, and I'll begin at sunup." She smacked her pillow and settled to sleep.

He stood there for a long time and listened to the quiet of the night and rationalized her words. When he finally started off toward the keep, he smiled. So she wanted to drive him crazed, did she? He'd have to wait to see what she planned. If it was anything like what she'd done to that lady, he would have some laughs. One thing he was certain of, he had to stay alert and on his toes.

The next morning, Brendan found himself flat on his arse. He'd gone to the training field early that day so he could get to the hall early enough to keep an eye on Katie. His sparring session didn't go as planned, mainly because his attention wasn't focused on his opponent. Nay, his mind wasn't on his task at all. It was certainly a good thing he'd sparred with a seasoned soldier, instead of an inept beginner. He left soon after and trotted toward the hall.

He stalked her most of the day and didn't let her from his sight. Guilt plagued him throughout the night because she thought he wooed her for the guardian's name. What would she say if he told her the truth—that he wooed her because he wanted her? He also felt contrite because the deception hurt her. Before she slapped him, he'd gotten a glimpse of the hurt in her eyes. Once she accepted their fate, he would make it up to her. How he'd do so, he had no idea.

She sat across the hall, and he continued to follow her with his eyes.

"He's driving me mad, Janice. Can't you send him from the hall?"

"Kate, my name is Julianna."

"Oh, my apology, Julianna, but if he shan't leave, then I will. He watches me—"

Julianna grasped her sleeve. "Stay, I'll send him on an errand."

Brendan wanted to laugh when Julianna approached and asked him to go on the errand for her, but he nodded. All the same, he decided to give Kate a few minutes of peace. His hearing was beyond exceptional, and he'd heard their every word. He quickly left and went to the stables, where he'd been told Bonnie spent the morning. She was where she was supposed to be, helping the wolfhound master with the litter of pups. His promise kept, he intended to stop at Robin's on the way back. He hesitated to knock, but Tess opened the door before he changed his mind. She almost fell over at the sight of him at her door. He stood silent and willed her to leave by setting a stern look.

"I'm going to the keep to visit Julianna," she said.

Brendan thought she'd never leave. He wasn't one to visit and felt bad about causing her departure. She smiled before she closed the door.

"What are you doing here?"

Brendan knocked Robin back a step with a shove to his shoulder, their customary greeting. "I stopped by to say hello. Can I not do so?"

"Faigh muin, Brendan, you never stop by. What do you want?" Robin pulled a chair from the table, turned it, and sat astride.

"Can't a brother stop by to have ale with you?"

"All right, Brendan, here." Robin handed him a tankard of ale and poured one for himself.

Brendan regarded his brother warily. Robin knew him well enough to realize something bothered him. He hesitated. They drank and he was agitated, which wasn't foreign. He didn't know how to broach the subject he wanted Robin's view on.

"I'm glad Bonnie returned safely. She seems none the worse for it. We're fortunate Kate happened upon her."

Brendan nodded. "Aye, I, uh… I…"

"You're stammering, Brendan. Why don't you spit it out? You'll feel better." Robin laughed.

"I'm wooing Kate. Colin thinks it's because I'm trying to gain the knave's name, but—"

"The Kate, our Kate?"

"Aye, she's giving me a hard time though. I thought you might help me. You convinced Tess to have you, and she was hostile toward you." He couldn't look his brother in the eye. Instead, he studied his cup and swirled the ale.

Robin sobered. "Aye, Brendan, but it took me a long while. It wasn't easy, either. Women are peculiar."

"A while for what?"

"To realize that I loved her, and I didn't want to live without her."

"Katie's bonny and no other woman has made me want her this much," Brendan spoke in a gruff manner, and he hoped his face didn't display the discomfort he felt.

It must have because Robin smiled broadly. "I've never seen you this forlorn, Brendan. If I were you, I'd give up now, man, while you're still of sound mind." He laughed. "Are you wanting to marry her?"

"I thought about it," Brendan admitted.

"You have?" Robin's voice cracked.

"Aye, she hasn't responded well to my proposal."

"Why the hell not?"

"She wants to return to England to the king and have

her betrothed fetched. She said Henry arranged an acceptable betrothal, which he did. Yet, the match displeases me."

"I don't understand. Who is she betrothed to?" Robin cocked his head questioningly.

"The Barclay, Angus, damn it. She's said the betrothal is acceptable and wants to secure her father's holding. She must know who the betrothed is, but she hasn't said anything. How can I convince her to accept me when she finds me objectionable?"

Robin laughed derisively. "You objectionable? That is a problem, Brendan."

"I haven't spoken to her yet about my intention, but I will convince her. I thought you'd tell me how you went about it."

"I wish I could help you. When I tried to woo Tess, she was angry because I didn't talk to her. I just wanted her in my bed. After I realized that, I talked to her and made her accept me."

"Nay, that's not what I will do."

"Well, don't leave me in the dark."

Brendan placed his cup on the table and looked up. "I'll compromise her then she'll have no choice but to wed me."

"That's low, Brendan, even for you. She'll be angry and it will likely set you back."

"I'll deal with that." He stood abruptly and clapped Robin's hand and left.

Brendan walked to his favorite place, where he often pondered his problems. The view from atop the cliff was endless. He formulated a plan to win her acceptance. As he sat and stared at the landscape, his mind settled on an idea and it made him smile.

CHAPTER ELEVEN

The day of the celebration arrived. Brendan stood in the hall next to Colin and Julianna and waited for Katie's arrival. He resembled a skittish lad as he paced the hall, eager to get *it* over with. *It* was the plan he'd come up with—the scheme that would settle the matter of his and Katie's betrothal. The hall filled with the clan, but he ignored everyone around him and kept his eyes focused on the doorway.

Julianna was excited because her family gathered for the event. She all but shouted with joy when Sara, her best friend, and Sara's husband, Steven KirkConnell, from a neighboring clan, arrived with their children. Brendan watched her run through the hall to greet her longtime friend. His brother grinned at her joyous greeting and gave Steven a nod. Brendan pulled away from the wall to greet Steven.

Colin stilled him when he passed and stuck his arm out. "Is she still angry?"

Brendan stopped and frowned. "Aye, she called me Bryan again."

His brother slapped him on the back. "I'm sorry Bonnie told her about the wooing. She's just a wee mite and didn't understand. You should be thankful she didn't mention the betrothal, but that won't matter after tonight. Let's rejoice. I never thought I'd want to celebrate again." He poured a cup of ale for Brendan, then one for himself. "I couldn't believe what Kate told Julianna. Then I learned they beat my lass..."

"Katie went through hell. I cannot wait to repay that swine."

"It's about time someone took care of her and made her happy." Colin used his commanding tone, the one he'd used when they were in battle.

"Mayhap."

"Will you go through with it, Brendan?"

"Aye, Colin. I'm thinking about giving my sword arm a rest and concentrating on my other sword for a while."

Colin shook with laughter. "You remember me saying that?"

"Aye," Brendan recalled his jest on that long-ago night when they'd sat beside the fire on their way back from the border. His brother, Robin, tried to start a fracas between them, and Colin teased him about being surly. He'd never forgotten it. Brendan took a long drink of ale to abate his skittishness. That trait wasn't familiar to him and he didn't like it at all.

He pulled away when Kate came into the hall, but Colin stopped him.

"You know this will cause a war, don't you?"

Brendan shrugged his shoulders. A war it would be if Barclay insisted upon it. "Aye, I can handle Barclay and King Henry. A war it shall be, but Katie's worth it."

"I agree, Brendan, she is. You'll have our full support."

He kept his eyes on Kate as she moved through the room. "I tell you, she would flee if she had a suspicion of what I was up to. Hell, she wants Henry to have her betrothed fetched upon her arrival, which is why she won't be going to England. Nay, it's better this way. I'll marry her tonight. She won't have a chance to run, nor speak to Henry about her absurd idea. I will be her husband, not a damned Barclay. You know what else I'm thinking?"

Colin smiled at her when she waved. "What?"

"She should wear my tartan."

"Aye, Brendan, she should. Why don't you take care of it? I'll tell Father Tomas to come inside and join the celebration."

Brendan nodded and gave him a solemn look then walked to her. He wanted to laugh when she moved through the clan members to avoid him, but he cut her off near the buttery. She gasped when he took her hand and pulled her through the hall to the outside courtyard.

"What are you doing?"

"I need to talk to you, Katie." Brendan was in a hurry and walked as fast as he could. He led her down the path to her cottage, and when he reached it, he yanked her inside and slammed the door closed.

"What do you want, Barton?"

Brendan's jaw ground and he pierced her with his eyes. This night, he would demand she cease her game with the names. "You know my name. In fact, now that I ponder it, you say it outright when you're angry. Say it." He lifted her chin and forewarned her with his most stern look, not to test him.

"Uh...it's..."

He leaned closer and moved his face inches to hers, and used intimidation tactics to gain her obedience because he wasn't in the mood for her antics.

"B-Brendan."

"Aye, don't forget it again. You may fool others, Katie, but you're not daft. Your game won't work with me." He kissed her, but she shoved him away, which made him grin.

"Is that all you wanted to talk about? I want to rejoin the celebration."

Brendan pulled his tartan from his upper body and held it out to her. "I want you to wear this."

Kate's mouth dropped open when he stood before her bare-chested. It wasn't as if he was naked, but it was darned close. He wore a tartan on his lower body and boots on his feet, but he might as well have been naked by the way she surveyed him. He continued to hold the tartan out to her, while she gawked at him. His body responded to the caress of her eyes. Her eyes moved to his battle scars, his abdomen, his waist, and back to his face. Awed by his power, her breath ceased. As did his breath when she reached out and slid her hand over the muscles of his chest.

Brendan dropped the tartan. He picked her up, covered her mouth with his, and carried her to the adjoined room. They fell upon the bed, and his kisses became possessive. He couldn't get enough of her. She wrapped her arms around him and held him tightly. Unable to think clearly, he pressed his body against hers and reveled at her touches. The warmth of her kisses consumed him.

Briefly, he pulled his mouth away. "Katie, you're killing me." He quickly returned his mouth, never giving her a chance to respond. Her hands patted his chest and danced over his rippled muscles. He groaned at the agony of wanting her and of her soft hands touching him.

Heedlessly, his hands roamed the material of her gown until they reached her breasts. He cupped his hands, giving them a light squeeze, as he continued to kiss her hotly. Her back came up off the bed, and she bumped her head against his. He chuckled but pressed her back. Her eyes widened as he lowered the fabric of her gown. Once he revealed her beautiful breasts, he lowered his mouth to a light-pink nipple. His lips surrounded the hardened tip, and his tongue skirted the texture in sweet abandon.

He never wanted to stop. As he continued to mesmerize her with his mouth, he tugged at his tartan and threw it aside. His breath blew a hot trail from one breast to the other. He used his skill to keep her unbeknownst of his actions, but when his naked body caressed against hers; she heaved and tried to move him. Her attempt was paltry, which indicated she didn't really want him to move away.

Brendan pressed against her, his erection throbbed with need. Never had a woman affected him as she did. His mouth continued to nibble on her breasts, and he used his hands to excite her body by moving them over her curves. As his hand trailed along her leg, he pulled her skirts up, his palm shifted over the softness of her naked thighs. He looked into her eyes. Passion clouded them and made them even more beautiful. His mouth jerked over hers in a fierce kiss she responded to spiritedly.

Her enticed whimpers drove him onward, and he rubbed her innocence. Brendan was lost in a battle of sure will. His plan reverberated in his mind. He used his fingers, readied her, and blissfully stroked the heat of her. Kate's hands gripped his arms. Her passion took hold when she tilted her head back. Brendan had to do it. He had to continue to secure his rights as her husband, but something nagged him. His despicable scruples plagued him. He wouldn't continue without her acceptance.

"Katie, I want to make you mine." He stopped when his arousal reached her entrance. As he leaned over her, he caressed her with deliberate strokes.

She whimpered and her body reacted on its own accord. Kate pressed against him and willed him to proceed. She opened her eyes.

"Tell me you want me to make you mine." He searched her face for acceptance, but all he saw was ambiguity shadowed there.

A knock sounded on the door.

"Kate, Brendan, you're missing the celebration."

Brendan leaned his head against hers and fought the battle going on inside his body. She looked frightened now, which made him tense. He spoke in a terse voice. "Damn Gil to hell. Katie, do you want me to stop?"

"Aye, aye, stop."

He rasped at the thought *it* wouldn't happen. His plan to corner her into accepting him spiraled in a winless battle.

"I don't know what you thought you were doing…"

"Katie, have pity, will you? I can't breathe, let alone go." His grated breath forced his chest to contract.

She shoved him away. "Please…leave."

Brendan wanted to hold her, and to explain what she'd

felt was natural. Most of all, he wanted to explain that what they'd experienced was a sure sign they belonged together. But she was mortified and nothing he could say would change that.

He rose and his nakedness caused her to exclaim her abashment. She pulled the covers over her head and her voice muffled. "Get out, now!"

"All right, but don't return to the keep without that tartan on." After he slipped his other tartan around his waist and belted it, he left.

Gil leaned against a tree near Kate's cottage. He grinned with his arms folded across his chest and looked damned proud of his accomplishment. Just what Brendan needed—a way to defuse his anger. He strode purposely to him and struck him with his fist in his left eye.

"Cosh, Brendan. What'd you do that for?"

"You know damned well why. Why did you interrupt—?" Brendan couldn't continue, because Gil's laughter made him want to kill him.

"If you wanted to be alone, why didn't you just say so?"

"Go to hell, Gil." He marched away in an angry stride before his hands moved to Gil's neck. Aye, a good strangle would make the lad see reason.

Brendan almost made love to her and would be loving her right now if it wasn't for Gil's intrusion. When he reached the loch, he jumped in with his tartan on. The frigid water cooled his ardor within seconds. Aye, the fire dissipated and he could think reasonably again. He climbed onto the bank, lay back, and focused his eyes on the sky. Twilight canvassed the infinite stars twinkled in the abyss.

She wanted him, he conceded. How could he get her to agree? The answer evaded him. He should do what he planned then she couldn't say nay. It was low of him, but that didn't bother him. This night, she would become his, and he smiled at that. He recalled her beautiful body, ready for loving. A deep sigh attested his resolve. The lass had him running around like a lost sheep. Brendan scowled at that.

But damn it, if he didn't take her soon, he'd go mad.

CHAPTER TWELVE

The man bewildered her. Kate redressed and jeered at the tartan. She decided she wouldn't wear it, nor would she do his bidding. She picked it up, held it to her face and smelled his wonderful lingered scent. Just to show him he couldn't tell her what to do she folded it and placed it on the table. Dejectedly, she wondered what came over her. How could she allow him to touch her, kiss her, and do those marvelously wicked things? But at the time, all she could do was melt in his arms.

She didn't know why he affected her. She'd thought him to be crass and obstinate, which he was, but he was also sweet in his own way. What scared her was her attraction to him wouldn't be dismissed. He'd never make a good husband. She had to avoid him and return to England to her betrothed. Until she reached the king, she would have to deal with Brendan herself.

"Goddess, please help me keep my distance."

Upon that resolve, she fixed her hair and returned to the celebration. A mass of people gathered in the hall and the noise level rose. There had to be close to a hundred people within. All the tables were moved aside, and people danced in the center of the room. Gaiety abounded, and many toasted Bonnie. Kate skirted the dancers and saw her hostess amongst the guests.

"Kate, there you are. Where have you been? I've searched everywhere for you." Julianna smiled, her eyes shone with merriment as she watched the dancers.

"I, uh…was…" Her face brightened.

"I want you to meet my friend. Sara and I have been friends since childhood. This is Kate, the lady who saved Bonnie."

Sara hugged Kate affectionately. "I'm glad you rescued Bonnie. Julianna told me about your adventure. We're indebted to you."

"Oh, nay, I had to make sure she reached her home."

Gil sauntered toward them and grinned in his charming way. Julianna and Sara gasped at the sight of his swollen eye. He bowed slightly and stood close to Kate.

"Gil, what happened to your eye? It was fine an hour ago?" Julianna asked.

"Oh, Gil, you could use a little sympathy. Not that the ladies won't give it to you as soon as they see your bruised eye," Sara said.

He laughed garishly. "I ran into a…uh…a beast, aye, a great, big, hulking beast."

Everyone shared a laugh at that.

"Milady, Kate, would you take pity and dance with me?"

"I'd like to dance, Gelford." Kate curtseyed, and he took her hand. She noticed he shook his head and raised his eyes heavenward. She kept herself from laughing.

Sara turned and eyed Julianna. "Why did she call Gil, Gelford, Julianna?"

"Don't ask."

"Kate is beautiful. I'm surprised the men haven't barraged her."

Julianna laughed. "I'm not surprised at all, there's the very reason now."

Brendan entered the hall and scoffed at Gil holding

Kate's hand. He held it too fondly. They skipped to the tune and turned. Brendan's first thought was: *I will kill him.* His second was: *I need a drink.* He walked to the table, picked up a cup of ale, and chugged the contents.

"Thirsty, Brendan?" Colin chuckled as he leaned his shoulder against a wooden beam.

"Aye."

"I saw Gil's eye, nice shot."

"He deserved more than I gave him." Brendan glared across the room. Gil held Kate too close—it didn't sit well. Hell, he needed to calm down. "Is Father Tomas here yet?"

Colin raised a brow and grinned. "Aye, so when will you do it?"

"This night. I won't wait another night."

"She must agree, Brendan. She has to say the words."

"She will, somehow."

Colin caught Bonnie when she ran toward them and threw herself at him. He moved to the table. Brendan joined them and reached for another cup.

"Button, your uncle needs loving. Why don't you sit with him awhile?"

"Aye, Papa." Bonnie crawled onto Brendan's lap.

Brendan continued to leer as his woman danced with Gil. She seemed to enjoy herself, a little too much in his opinion. Everything about Kate made him cheerful, the way she moved, the way she laughed, and the way her eyes smiled. He was a besotted fool.

"Uncle, why are you angry?"

"I'm not angry with you, fairy." He touched her chin.

"Who are you angry with?"

"Gil."

"Why, did he do something bad?" She reached her hand behind his neck and gave him a gentle pat. He frowned at the gesture, which usually made him feel patronized.

"Because he's dancing with Kate."

"Why don't you dance with her?"

"I don't dance."

"Mama said you danced with her once. You want me to get 'em to dance with me instead?"

"Would you?" He felt guilty for using his sweet niece in such a way. "Nay, never mind." But before he stopped her, Bonnie jumped from his lap and scurried across the room. Gil released Kate's hand and lifted Bonnie. Brendan smiled at his clever niece. She waved to him from across the room, and he lifted his cup in salute. She giggled.

Colin stood near his table and conversed with Julianna and Sara, but Brendan paid little attention to them until he heard his name mentioned.

Sara gazed at the scene of the dancers. "Julianna, what's going on? Did I just see Brendan MacKinnon smile?" She cupped her hand over her mouth, but Brendan's hearing was superb.

"Aye, he even laughed yesterday," Julianna confided.

"It's a miracle."

"Nay, it's Kate."

"Poor Brendan." Sara laughed.

Colin shook his head at their comments and gave him an apologetic glance. Brendan didn't let their womanly gossip bother him. He couldn't stand to see Katie without his tartan on, it was driving him deranged. Before he marched toward her, he turned and reached a trunk behind him. He took out a tartan and made his way across the hall.

"I asked you to wear this." He held the tartan out to her. Kate smiled and touched his arm. His tension instantly unwound and he eased.

"You did? I don't recall."

"Aye, you know damned well that I did. I want you to put it on." His tone hardened, and he shoved the tartan at her.

She took it. "What if I don't do as you say?"

"Then I'll drag you out of here again and put it on you myself. Or better yet, I'll make sure the only thing you're wearing is me and my tartan." He waited.

She harrumphed and quickly placed the tartan around

her shoulders, the way Julianna wore hers, and looked at him with fire in her eyes.

"You are lovely." Brendan fixed the pleat on her shoulder, placed his arm behind her, and pulled her against him.

Colin was about to make an announcement. He jumped onto the table and held up his arm for silence. The hall became still. "Clan of MacKinnon, I stand before you the happiest man. I'm blessed with the women in my life. My wife Jules, you're the love of my heart. My daughter, Bonnie, I love you, Button. And the newest member of our clan, Kate, who will be considered a MacKinnon from this day forth. There are not enough riches in the world to repay you for bringing our daughter back. You are a lass of valor. For all that you endured for the sake of our child, it's only right we call you a MacKinnon."

Brendan smiled at his brother's words, mainly because Colin had gotten better at making speeches. But his smile widened when his clan chanted 'lass' valor.' Katie lowered her head and blushed at the attention. Brendan leaned forward and kissed her hard for several minutes before his entire clan. She thought to push him away but hastily walked away before he stopped her. Colin laughed boisterously when he sat back down at the table. Katie lifted Bonnie and their heads touched and they whispered. His demeanor softened, seeing them together.

A short while later, Katie sat at the end of the table. She hummed along to the tune the musicians played. Bonnie sat on her lap and was almost asleep.

Brendan nudged Colin's arm. "It's time."

"Are you certain, Brendan? Mayhap you should give it more thought and give her time to come to an understanding. Father Tomas can return. There's always tomorrow."

"Nay, I'm ready. I want to get it done this night." He advanced toward his adversary who sat unaware for the moment. Just how he intended to get her to say the words, he was unsure?

"Katie, I need to speak to you."

Kate handed Bonnie to Tess and followed him. He stopped a short distance away and waited for her to reach him. Father Tomas stood by them and he blocked her view of the clergyman. She tried to greet him, but Brendan stepped in front of her.

"Katie." He turned his back on the older gentleman because he needed a minute or two to collect himself and to explain. She glared at him, but he took her hand and placed the edge of his tartan over their joined hands. Her glare turned to a chaotic look.

"What do you want?" She tried to pull her hand free, but he held fast.

Colin and Julianna stood by Father Tomas and smiled. He thought they might give him away, but remarkably, they said nothing. She turned to him again, and he squeezed her hand tenderly. Kate appeared awkward, what with the onlookers around them. She curiously eyed him and his eyes bore into hers, but then he glimpsed Colin briefly. His brother gave a nod as if to say get on with it.

"Katie, you don't have to worry about meeting with Henry about your betrothed. I'm honored you brought Bonnie home. You're brave and have more courage than anyone I know. I honor you by pledging myself to you this day and I'll protect you with my life for the rest of my days."

"I don't believe I ever heard you speak as many words, Brendan."

"Tell me you love me." He squeezed her hand and kept his face serene.

"You want me to tell you that?" Kate cast him a panicked look. She stiffened and glanced at those who stood nearby.

"You love me, Katie, admit it. You need to say the words." He waited and stood firm in his resolve, willing her to say she loved him.

"Do I? Oh, I do, don't I? It's because of the vision. I love you, Brendan MacKinnon. How is it you know and…I didn't? I don't know why, because you're the most arrogant man I've ever encountered. What does my betrothal have to do with this? Oh, Goddess help me, the king will be wrath. Why aren't you saying anything? You're exactly like my vision—"

Brendan leaned forward and kissed her. He saved her from making a complete fool of herself. And it wasn't his usual suck-the-breath-out-of-you kiss, but a sweet sensual one she couldn't help but return. Father Tomas mumbled in the background, but she didn't seem to listen.

She shoved him away and returned to the table. Loud cheers rose in the hall, and she brightened with embarrassment by their stares. Mayhap she wondered why they looked at her strangely. She believed he'd announced their betrothal to his clan, but he'd done more than that.

When he asked Father Tomas to allow them to speak their vows, the Father hadn't questioned him. All was needed was his pledge and her declaration of love, which was why he'd provoked her. It had been easier than he'd thought. She said the words and pleased him. Brendan sat across the hall and pondered his actions. He hoped he hadn't made a mistake. When Katie found out what he'd done, she would be angry. It was too late now because he'd cast his fate.

The celebration went well into the night. Many of the clan's people congratulated her on her nuptials. Some of the older ladies touched her hair and said blessings of fertility. Thankfully, they spoke to her in Gaelic, and she hadn't understood them. If she had, she wouldn't sit happily across the room. He almost laughed aloud when she thanked them for their kindness.

Colin nudged him. "Brendan, I'm happy for you. I know Da's relationship with our mother affected us, and I never thought any of us would marry because of it. Now here we are, all married. I'm proud of you for doing the right thing."

Brendan scowled. "You're talking like a woman again. Being around your wife turned you soft. Och, you're right, I never thought I'd marry. Look at her, Colin. She's beautiful, intelligent, and is probably wealthy. What have I to offer the woman?"

"You are one of the bravest men I know. Kate doesn't need riches, but a man who will honor and protect her. Is that not what you pledged today?"

"Aye, but I'm thinking she will raise holy hell when she finds out. I don't want her displeasure."

"Too late now. You might've considered that before you tricked the lass into marrying you. I should take Bonnie off to bed, and you should take your lass to bed, too."

Bonnie fell asleep on Kate's lap, and Kate appeared as though she'd nod off as well. Colin approached and lifted his daughter. Brendan stood behind him.

"Come, Katie, you're tired. I'll walk you to your cottage," Brendan told her.

"Nay, the last time you did, you almost… Well, I'm certain I can find my own way."

"You'll get lost in the dark. Nay, I'll make sure you arrive safely." He didn't give her a choice but pulled her from her chair.

"Very well, Brendan." Kate couldn't walk fast enough and he had no trouble keeping up with her.

"Katie, we should discuss what happened at the celebration."

"What is there to discuss? I never agreed to anything, Brendan. Good night."

They arrived at her cottage and he released her hand. Kate opened the door and then slammed it in his face. He laughed at her display of wit. Unknowingly, she shut out her husband. A feeling of happiness forced his smile and he considered it would take him a long time to get back inside that door.

CHAPTER THIRTEEN

Brendan was utterly miserable. The two days following the celebration, Kate kept her distance. He gave her time to adjust to his family before he shocked her with the truth. Bonnie kept her busy, and he wasn't around much, which made his task easier. Julianna told him she'd left the hall with Bonnie, and they visited Tess. He relaxed and ate the rest of his food. Colin sat beside him at the table and discussed retaliation plans.

"She still hasn't told you? What's taking you so long, Brendan? You said you would get the name of that churlish-dog." Colin pounded his fist on the table.

"She'll tell me in time. I haven't seen her since the celebration," Brendan confessed.

Colin took a large gulp of ale and at Brendan's admission, he spit it out. "What?" He swiped his mouth with the back of his hand. "You've rendered me speechless, Brendan. Are you telling me you haven't bedded your wife?"

"Damn it, nay. I didn't have the heart to tell her we're married. She thinks we're betrothed. I'm giving her time to—"

Colin jeered. "There's no time for this cosh, Brendan.

You need to find out who the knave is. It's time you came clean and told her the truth. Damnation. Tell her you're not betrothed, but married. I cannot believe I agreed to this farce. She saved my daughter's life and I owe the woman, look what I allowed to happen. I'm not pleased about this. You must tell her the truth."

"All right, Colin, I'll tell her, and then I'll get the man's name. Christ Almighty, stop badgering me." Brendan hadn't meant to shout his frustration.

Julianna entered the hall and stopped upon seeing them. She hurried to the table and gave Colin a kiss before she turned to him. "Brendan, I need your help."

"What's amiss, Julianna?"

"Kate's cat is in the kitchen, and it's hissing at everyone. How did it get out again? I don't know where Kate is, and Dame Hester won't cook our supper until I get it out of there. Will you return the animal to her cottage?"

Brendan's jaw ground and he took his seat again. Why didn't she ask Colin? He was her husband, damn it all. Besides, he was a trained warrior, not a simpleminded fop to do mundane chores like retrieving a cat from the kitchens. And he gave the lass well-needed space. Now he'd have to take the damned cat to her. He supposed it was his responsibility—the cat belonged to his wife. He nodded at Julianna and stormed off toward the kitchen.

"There it is," Julianna screeched. The furry thing crouched under a wooden table.

"I see it," he said testily.

The cat hissed at them. Dame Hester stood aside and yelled for him to get it.

"You get it," he told Julianna.

"Nay, you. Are you afraid?"

"To hell with that." Brendan knelt down, grabbed the cat by its tail, and yanked it out. He held it under its front arms and heard Julianna and Dame Hester laughter as he left.

When he reached Kate's cottage, he stood beside the opened door and was about to enter when he heard his niece's cry. A small cauldron sat on the blazing fire in the hearth. Kate stood by it and added ingredients needed to make the paste to soothe the child.

"I'll add a pinch of a yarrow root to ward off infection and pinch of anise to soothe the sting. Oh, and a drop of wax to the mix to make it stick to you. How did you get stung, lovey?"

Bonnie whimpered beside her. "That lad, Sean, chased me again." She wailed and held her arm in the air as though it might fall off. "I ran to the tree and didn't see it. It hurts, Kate, make it stop."

"It'll take a few moments for the potion to simmer then we'll make you all better." Kate stirred the liquid, which formed into a thick paste. She slopped some into a small bowl and blew on it to cool it. After she applied the substance to Bonnie's arm, she set the bowl aside. "There, how does that feel?"

"Better, Kate. I knewed you could fix me. Sean best not come near me, 'cause next time I'll make him get warts."

Kate laughed and petted his niece's hair.

Brendan watched silently with a smug smile on his face. Was she a witch? The only person who used potions in their clan was Jinny, and he thought her a witch. Anyone who healed with such knowledge was considered such. Jinny brewed all sorts of potions and cared for their clan's illnesses. Many clansmen were leery of her, but they sought her when they needed medicinal attention. Brendan admired her skill, but Jinny was as superstitious as he was.

He followed his ancestor's practices to the limit. Luckily, he'd spoken to the elders and learned what he most wanted to know—details about how they went into battle. That's how he learned what symbols to paint on his body and to put soil in his boots. Dame Hester told him that her husband often did so because he never wanted his feet to leave his beloved Highlands. After hearing that tale, Brendan took up the practice and honored Harold's habit. He recalled Colin's strange expression when he'd seen him do it over the years.

His discovery of Katie being a witch comforted him. He set the cat down and continued to listen.

"If the boy bothers you again, you can fix it so he won't." Kate giggled.

"How can I do that?" Bonnie asked.

"You have to ask that after what we did to Lady D?"

Bonnie laughed with a touch of devilry in her voice. "Nay, I'll take care of 'em. He'll not bother me after I…"

"Now, don't do anything too bad. Your father won't be happy about it, and you don't want to have to sit in his chair."

"I won't, Kate."

Kate gave her an 'I-don't-believe-you' look, and laughed. "Oh, Trixie, there you are. I thought I left you at the keep." She petted the cat and collected her herbs from the table.

"Maybe I'll put thistles under Shawn's tartan."

Bonnie laughed at Kate's expression which made him grin. His niece ran through the doorway on her way to make plans for the poor lad Sean and almost knocked him over. She waved to him and kept moving. Bonnie's nursemaid, Emma shouted for Bonnie to wait for her. Bonnie's attendant couldn't keep up with her and chased after her. When would the lass ever learn?

Kate stood beside the doorway and watched Bonnie run amid the light rain. Brendan waited for her to acknowledge him. He filled the space in the doorway, and she backed up a step. He took his time admiring her bonny face, beautiful hair, and the clandestine look in her eyes. His body came alive, just standing near.

"Good afternoon, Katie."

She frowned and blocked his entrance. "Benton. What do you want?"

"Lass, when are you going to give up the farce?"

"What farce, My Lord?"

"Never mind. May I come in?"

"It wouldn't be proper."

"Aye, it would." He pushed the door open wider and shifted her with his arm.

"If you think just because we're betrothed—"

He kissed her quickly and cut her off. Brendan felt her eyes on him as he passed by. His tartan didn't cover much of him, and his soft-brown tunic's sleeves were rolled to his biceps. Her eyes shifted to a more modest part of his body, and her face brightened at her own boldness.

Brendan sat at the table, knowing she gawked at his back. His damned manhood knew, too. He wanted to talk to her and didn't need his desire taunting him. Not only did he wish to talk of their marriage, but he wanted to find out why she'd been placed in the care of her guardian. Henry should never have allowed Kate to go to the guardian, but if he hadn't, Kate wouldn't have saved his niece and she might, by now, be wedded to Barclay.

Hadn't Robin told him that Tess was more agreeable when he talked to her? Aye, he'd try, but his body had other ideas. He shook his head and vowed not to touch her.

"Would you care for a drink?"

"Aye, Katie." A distraction was just what he needed.

She poured water from a pitcher into a goblet and handed it to him. Brendan peered at the table and picked up the medallion he'd seen on her cat's neck. His hand covered the round width of the object, and he studied the emblem which appeared to be a spider. The craftsmanship was noteworthy; remarkably, the fine hairs of the spider's legs could be seen. He glanced up to find her regarding him.

"What's this?"

"I don't know what it is. My father sent it to me."

"Is it a memento?"

"Aye, it reminds me of him."

He picked up the parchment and read: *beware the friend with the black heart*. "What does this mean?" He nodded at the note.

"I haven't figured it out yet." She tried to take it from him, but he held it and turned in his seat.

"Yet?" He didn't like the way she emphasized the word.

"What are you doing here?"

Brendan let it go for now. He gave a puzzled look to the floor. What was she up to? He intended to ask what the rope and candles were for, probably for her conjuration. He smiled at that.

"I came to see if you wanted to go riding." When she didn't answer immediately, he asked again. "Would you?"

She took the medallion and note from him and placed them in her satchel. As she answered him, she collected the items from the floor. "I'm sure you have more important things to do than ride with me, Ben."

Had he seen the sparkle in her eyes? She dared to toy with him by calling him another name. "Nay, lass, there's nothing more important than you."

She brightened at his blatant remark. Brendan noticed her blush and his jaw clenched at her innocent reaction. She affected him, too. He leaned back in the chair and waited for her answer. Still, she hadn't given one.

"I'll sit here all day if you don't agree to go riding with me." Brendan rose and pulled her face close to his. His irritation at her calling him another name irked him. He gripped her neck but was careful not to hurt her. But damn it all, if she wouldn't call him by his name, he'd start yelling.

"Katie, I want to hear you say my name."

"B-Brendan."

"Aye, don't call me by anything else or you'll be getting a whack on your bonny bottom." He warned her in a playful tone.

She pulled from his grip. "You have no right to treat me so. I don't answer to you."

"Aye, you do. You're my wife."

"I most certainly am not your wife. King Henry betrothed me to another, and if you think you can nullify it by telling him you betrothed yourself to me, you are mistaken. You have no right to order me around."

As if he hadn't heard her, Brendan pulled her through the doorway. Henry would probably be irritated at Brendan's interference of his plans, but Henry owed him a favor, and besides, it was undisputable now since he'd married her. Hearing her say that angered him though. Damn it all, he should just tell her he married her.

"Come, I want to ride." Brendan led her to the stables by taking her hand. Kate continued to berate him on the way. He wasn't about to tell her anything, what with the mood she was in.

"If you think to take advantage of me because of your speech the other night, I won't fall for it, Brendan. I should tell you that—"

He stopped and jerked her body to his. "It's too fine a day to get upset, Katie. Let us enjoy the ride…" She opened her mouth and was about to say something when he kissed her. "…in silence." He continued to the stables and noticed the rain stopped and the ground all but dried.

"Seeing the horses reminds me of Ralph. I hope he fares well and isn't alone in the forest. Do you deem someone found him?"

Brendan nodded but didn't have the heart to tell her what he really thought. He prepared his horse and a smaller mare for her. Tugging the horses' reins, he led them outside. Once they mounted, he led the way to the glen where he often sat and contemplated his issues. The trees surrounding them provided shade from the sun high above. He noticed her gaze toward the cliff where the sunshine sparkled between the leaves of the distant trees.

Kate didn't speak during the ride, and he was left to his thoughts. When they reached the cliff, he dismounted, and let his horse's reins loose. She stood beside her horse and wouldn't go near the edge of the cliff, but she watched him walk to the very rim.

"Come here, Katie."

"Nay, I'll stay put, the view is lovely from here."

Brendan walked to her, took her hand, and pulled her to the edge of the cliff. She dug her heels into the ground.

"Don't make me go near the rim. Please, release me."

Her fear was evident in her tone, but he paid it no mind.

He scooped her into his arms and carried her to the threshold. Her eyes squeezed shut.

"Are you going to throw me over the edge?"

Brendan chuckled and shook his head. "Now why would I do that, Katie?"

She stiffened, as unbending as a plank of wood, and he sighed loudly. He sat and arranged her on his lap, and set his arms around her waist.

"Please, I'm quite alarmed, Brendan, let me move back. I promise I shan't call you by another name again, only let me return to the horse." She hid her face in the crook of his neck.

"Katie, I have you."

"We're going to fall. I don't like being so high. Please, let me up." Her arms tightened around his waist. She wasn't pleased with her undisciplined reaction either and scoffed.

"You're afraid of heights? I'll have to remember that. It could come in handy, later." He laughed when she tensed. He rubbed his hand in a circular motion over her back and calmed her. "I won't let you fall, I promise. Look at the sight." He pointed outward.

Kate gripped his shoulders and opened her eyes, and hesitantly glanced around her. Her eyes widened and her breath caught at the sight. Brendan loved the view of his beloved Highlands. Several mountain peaks towered to the sky. Clouds of mist settled in the valley between the crests, and the sun reflected a rainbow in a high arc, from one mountain to another. The land was spellbinding. Her breath hitched when she noticed the sheer drop and she gripped his arm.

"This is my favorite place. It's where I come to relax and think, and to be alone. There are many people in our clan and it can sometimes be hard to be alone. That view is why we call this fairy land."

"I can see why. I've never seen such land before. Are you sure it's real?"

He chuckled low in her ear. "Aye, it's real. How are you

finding your stay?"

"It's been fine, everyone is kind. Your land is beautiful, and I enjoy being with Bonnie. I will miss her when I leave. I haven't seen you lately."

"I've been busy, that's not exactly true, but I kept my distance to give you time to get over your anger. It's been difficult. Aye, Katie, each night I found myself outside your cottage. I'd wait around all night with your warm kisses on my mind."

"You shouldn't speak so." She tensed when he moved. "Don't move. I'm afraid we're going to fall over the edge." Her arms tightened around him, which made him grin.

"Don't worry, I have you." Why did that statement make him sober?

He liked the way she held him. Brendan gripped her waist, feeling her soft curves. Being close to her did things to him, things he didn't want to control. She was the complete opposite of him: she, light and fair, soft and sweet—he, hard and dark, stern and obstinate. Everything about her radiated femininity, her scent, the attire she wore, her mannerisms, and soft-spoken words. He wanted her to touch him, to kiss him, and to desire him as much as he desired her. Guilt chased away his selfish longings.

"I want to know everything about you, tell me about your childhood."

She lifted her face and stared into his eyes and tried to read his sincerity. "There's very little to tell, Brendan."

He squeezed her arm. "Don't leave anything out."

She relaxed against him. "My father raised me. We have a small fief in Cheshire. It's not as large as some of the other lords' properties, but my father was more of a soldier and trained men for the king's service. We were happy until my mother died. Her name was Jocelyn and I've her looks. My father loved her very much. After her death, he gave me much attention and devotion. I miss him."

"Where is he?"

"He went on an excursion to the east and died there."

"How did he die, in battle?"

"I don't really know, our overlord said his tent was burned to the ground and they couldn't find him. My father's squire said he'd been hurt in an earlier battle and was being tended to when their regiment was attacked. Before my father sent his squire away, he gave him the medallion to give to me."

"Why did he send it to you with that cryptic message?"

"I've yet to figure it out, it's a mystery. Lord Ri...ah, my guardian wants the medallion and I don't mean to let him know I have it."

"What do you mean he wants it? Did he try to take it from you?" Brendan listened carefully and hoped she would reveal the man's name. She'd almost let it slip.

"He asked if I received anything from my father, but I didn't let on that I had. When I met Bonnie and discovered her plight, I had to return her to her family. It was also a way for me to leave my guardian. He's not a good man."

"Nay, he's not. I'll make him pay, Katie. You have my word." Brendan's jaw clenched with that vow and he felt her stiffen.

"I must tell King Henry about the medallion and what Lord...um, my guardian did to Bonnie. Mayhap he'll enact justice for my father's death and for abducting a child. It's the only way I can secure my future."

He leaned close to her ear and whispered, "Your future is secure."

"Brendan, I cannot involve you in this. My guardian might come after me for the medallion and it will become dangerous. I'll not involve the MacKinnons—"

"We're already involved. He involved us when he abducted my niece. Do you deem we'll let that go so easily?"

She sighed and shook her head. "I wish he never abducted Bonnie, then I would never have come here. You should let the king direct his judgment."

"That's not the way of the Highlanders. When I find out who he is, he'll pay for hurting you and Bonnie. I've made that vow. Aye, it will be sweet revenge. Tell me his name, and I will enact justice for your father, too."

"I don't want to talk about this anymore. Look at the scene before us. How can there be such evil in the land when the land is as beautiful as this? It's romantic."

Brendan nudged her chin toward him. She didn't know what he was up to until his lips touched hers in a gentle kiss. She sighed when he ran his tongue over her bottom lip. Aye, he had her, right where he wanted her.

"I'm captivated by you," he whispered against her mouth, and deepened the kiss and took full possession of her lips. He gently moved her back onto the ground, and lay on his side, kissing the most beautiful woman he'd ever seen, his own wife, at his favorite place in the whole Highlands.

The sky seemed to surround them as if they were surrounded by the heavens. Romantic, aye, it was romantic. Brendan couldn't get past that thought. Their passion took hold and their bodies swarmed with desire. He wouldn't hold back any longer and wanted to make hard, hot, passionate love to her. But he didn't want to scare her off again, and he realized at that moment, she was as absorbed by their kissing.

With deliberate movements, he shifted her gown, and when it was below her breasts, he pulled back to see the loveliness of them. He cupped his hand under her soft mound and leaned to take the exquisite bud in his mouth. Kate grasped his hair and held him in place. Passion flowed between them. Brendan continued to kiss her breasts, and she moaned at the pleasure of it. He chuckled at the sound of her enjoyment. He moved to her other breast and repeated the gesture.

"Katie, you're perfect." He continued to fondle her breasts and teased her with his tongue. Never had he been as tortured, as wanting to be inside her. He grinned at Kate's abandonment when she threw her head back in passion. The intensity built inside her, just as it built within him. He reveled the rest of his prize and set the garment away from them.

"Ah, Katie, just look at you, you're ready for loving."

Kate didn't speak as emotions must've made it impossible. How could he utter a word? His eyes retreated to the vee between her sweet, soft legs. There nestled was his greatest want. He reached down to caress her velvety folds and groaned at the moistness there. She wanted him. He shook with desire. Brendan thought he died right then, his mind instantly blanked, and his body grew heavy under her gentle caresses. Kate sucked in a breath when he pressed the tip of his finger inside her. She mumbled something about him doing it again, and he smiled widely. He hastily removed his tunic and tartan. She watched him with wide eyes and gawked at his steeled body. Her fear had fled, at least she didn't seem to be afraid. When she reached out to touch him, he groaned at the sheer pleasure.

Brendan brought her body against his. She heaved as his hardness pressed against every part of her. Her naked breasts pressed against his chest. He wanted to act nonchalant, but her sweet cries and reaction made him as unstudied as if it was his first time.

They lay on their sides and faced each other on the soft grassy spot before the rocky edge of the cliff. Brendan's hand cuddled her bottom, and he pulled her against his hardness, his mouth invaded hers again. He was strangely aware of his body and its increased pulse. She moaned when his rugged hand moved over her skin. Her lusty cries propelled him onward, and he rolled her onto her back. The sun shone on her hair and turned it golden. He lost control. If he didn't take her this second, he would lose his will before he ever entered her. With that thought in mind, he knelt between her legs, leaned over her body, and whispered into her ear.

"I want you. Do you want me to continue?" The soft burr of his voice made his plea sound raspy. His breath intensified.

"Aye, Brendan. I need—"

"Me, you need me, Katie." He touched her face and peered emphatically into her eyes.

"Don't let go of me."

"Never, I'll never let go." To reassure her, he clasped her tighter in his arms. Brendan resumed kissing her and sent her to the brink of ecstasy. He pressed his erection against her, and her whimper fueled his need even more. He throbbed with such intensity his legs trembled. Kate's body reacted, and she shook too. She was as affected as he was and it pleased him. He would hurt her, and the thought brought forth his grimace. He plunged forward to get it over.

"Hold me, sweetheart."

"Aye," she whispered.

Forcefully, he pressed onward and broke the barrier as gently and quickly as he could. Kate screamed. Brendan froze. He kissed her rosy lips and prayed to God he hadn't hurt her too badly.

"Katie, don't move, let the pain pass." He groaned at her slight movement. "I'm only a man, Katie, and I cannot take…"

Kate's warm breath tickled his neck, and he kissed her shoulder. She wrapped her legs around his waist and ran her hand down his spine. Brendan was stunned by her bold movements, and he enveloped her in his arms. His muscles tightened, but he held back and tried to resist the urge to ram himself inside her. Her every touch excited him.

"Brendan," her whisper sounded breathless. "I want to…to move."

Her hips shifted and he pulled out slowly. She made a sexy sound from her throat, a sound that almost sent him to heaven. He combated the pressure to release a growl. He pushed himself against her and reveled at the sensation of his length sliding into the warmth of her being.

"Katie, this feels…" He lost his thought when she moved her hands over his chest. His dampened skin tensed with each movement. Excitement built when she stroked his chest and pinched the hardness. "You're going to make me explode." He continued availing his body of hers and reeled in lust.

Katie's moans increased and her eyes glazed with the shocking sensations that even now entwined between her legs. He was awed by the sensitivity of her emotions. Her climax consumed her, and she threw her head side to side and moaned in delight. He knelt back, supported her legs, and watched her reaction with affection. He never witnessed such sweet abandon before. Amazingly, he kept control and waited for her to finish. How he maintained such discipline, he had no idea. He needed release and had reached his limit.

"Say my name, Katie," he demanded and wanted to hear his name from her lips. His body stiffened, and he was about to experience the same wondrous sensations she had.

"Brendan." Her sexy voice distracted him for a moment until she wrapped her legs around his hips. He drove into her slowly and his rod encased by her tightness. He threw his head back and yelled to the heavens. His shout echoed through the summit, and his breath was so deep that his lungs pounded his ribs. He gawked down at the lady who ripped his heart from his chest. Brendan rolled onto his back and squinted at the bright sky.

She regarded him. "What are you angry about now?"

"Katie, I know you wanted to marry your betrothed, but I wanted to tell you..." He glanced at her bonny face and admired her beautiful eyes. He thought how best to say it.

She reached up and touched his face. "What is it?"

Kate waited for him to continue, but he couldn't because he was entranced by the color of her eyes. "I'm trying to tell you... You cannot wed your betrothed because...you're already married." There, he said it. He waited for her screech of outrage. He moved his hands to protect the front of him in case she became angry enough to do him in again. Yet she didn't respond or yell, or anything. Had she heard him?

"Are you listening, Katie? I said you're my wife."

"I can't marry you, Brendan, not now, not ever."

"Why the hell not?" He shouted, but realized his folly. It didn't matter because she was well and good wed to him. He relaxed.

"I have to return to England and I shan't come back."

"You're not returning to England. Not now or ever. I'm your husband and it's my duty to handle your guardian and seek justice for your father."

Kate's bottom lip quivered.

"Don't weep, Katie. I promise you won't regret being married to me."

"I never cry," she said between hiccups. "My father always said he was proud of me because I didn't cry like most girls in our village. Now, look at me. I'm a weeping babe, and it's all your fault." She shoved his shoulder before she swiped her eyes. As quickly as he'd removed her clothes, she'd put them back on.

"It won't be so bad, you know," he said lightly.

"What won't?"

"Being married to me. I'll take care of you. You'll be happy with me for a husband, although, I've no idea how to be a husband yet. I want you to have our bairns."

"I can't have your bairns," she cried.

"Why the hell not?" Brendan's voice rose. She studied the summit directly across from her and dismissed him. "Katie, you need to understand… We are married. You are my wife in every sense of the word. Wedded, bedded, and properly blessed by the church. The priest said the blessing at the celebration. Father Tomas declared it before my clan. You said you loved me and spoke the vow. Do you deny it?"

Brendan gave her too much time to think, and her deliberation sent her to bawl. He scowled and pondered what to do. He set his arm around her shoulder and tried to soothe her. This was exactly why he'd married her at the celebration. If he revealed his intention, she would've refused him. And why shouldn't she?

He didn't like the path of his thoughts and peered ahead at the peeks. She pulled away from him. With fisted hands, he clenched his jaw and thought about what to say to make her accept him. He closed his eyes and could come up with nothing plausible. The only characteristics inbred in him were those of a soldier. Would a wife admire the ability to subdue a man with his bare hands? Would the size of his sword matter to a wife? Would she respect him because of his talent for hearing his foe at a great distance? He didn't believe she'd consider those traits laudable. When he opened his eyes again, she was gone. Well, hell. She disappeared. He wouldn't chase after her.

The sun shone on his nakedness. Brendan sat up and glimpsed a large hawk in the sky above. The hawk's wingspan was impressive and had to be several feet across. Its shadow passed over him and cooled him for a moment. The shrill shriek echoed from the summit. Brendan calmed enough to go and reason with his indignant wife.

Aye, she almost killed him with pleasure. He smiled, the rare occurrence becoming a habit of late. He claimed her at the celebration before all his people, but today she claimed him. How would he make her understand? But first, he needed to make amends for his boorish behavior. He dressed quickly, ran to his horse, and rode hell-bent toward her cottage.

When he arrived ten minutes later, she wasn't there. There was no sign she'd been there. Where had she gone? Brendan ran up the hill to the keep and entered. He found Colin in his chair, talking to Bonnie. Was he spending a lot of time with her because he missed her or had the little hellion gotten into more mischief?

"Have you seen Kate?"

"Nay, she's not here."

Before Colin asked what he was about, Brendan ran outside. He raced back down the hill, hopped on his horse, and rode speedily to the cliff. He retraced his steps, but couldn't find her. Had she been angry enough to try to go back to England? Panic set in, and he stiffened at his speculation. He realized he needed help, and for the first time, he'd ask it of his brother.

When he entered the keep again, he told Colin what happened. Colin sent out several sentries to search for her.

LASS' VALOR

But Brendan wouldn't stay inside the keep, so he rode out, and promised himself he wouldn't return without her.

CHAPTER FOURTEEN

The eerie dark forest made Kate feel so alone. Brendan's reaction to their encounter deeply affected her, and she hadn't felt so alone before. Good Goddess, she was married to him. She'd ridden for hours and tried to gain control over her anger and despondency. Why hadn't she realized what he'd done at the celebration? It was a sneaky, low-down thing to do, and she hadn't expected it. Of course, she hadn't known he was aware of her feelings for him. Still, she shouldn't have professed her love for him in front of all those people.

Mayhap she didn't love Brendan MacKinnon, but the vision she'd had all those years. That vision comforted her, oddly protected her, and made her feel loved. All Brendan did was made her be wanton and feel things a gently bred lady shouldn't. Horrified by her behavior and what she'd done, Kate wouldn't return to face him.

Sounds of the woods did little to cheer her spirit. Trees hid daylight from her view and shadowed the forest floor. Kate reached a freshwater pool in the middle of the forest, and she released her horse's reins. She knelt, cupped her hands, and drank. After, she sat against a tree and her thoughts took her back to him.

Brendan seemed to accept their marriage. Perhaps she

should accept her lot and admit being married to him wouldn't be as bad as she thought it might be. But he was an obstinate warrior who wore paint, probably raided her homeland, and was practically a heathen. Yet, she was attracted to him. Why had she let herself go completely, not caring about the result? How did he tempt her to give in to his will? As the questions ran through her mind, no answers came.

A tear slipped from the corner of her eye, and she wiped it away. She tried to meditate and evoke the Goddess' spirit to ease her troubled soul. But it was useless, there would be no settling her. Tired and restless, she was mortified. Sooner or later, she had to return to the MacKinnon holding, but what would she say to him when she did?

The sound of crackling leaves drew her attention. Her horse must've heard it too, because it startled and took off, leaving her to walk back. She stiffened at the sound again. Had Brendan found her? When her back came off the tree trunk to see who it was, someone lifted her by her neck. Instinctively, she put her hands up to ward off the attacker.

"Well, well, Kaitlin, I've found you at last. Did you deem you could run from me and I wouldn't find you? I knew where you went because you took the stupid girl with you. Where else, but Scotland? I've ridden this land in search of you."

"Lord Richard, I have nothing you want. Let me go," she demanded and tried to pull free.

"You know what I want."

"Nay, I honestly don't." She released herself from his grip and shuffled a few steps backward. He glared at her and the hairs on her arms prickled. Richard appeared to be alone, but his men must lurk in the woods. She thought to call out for help but thought better of it.

"The medallion, that's all I want. Where is it?"

"I don't have it."

"I'll have no more lies. Manik told me he gave it to you upon his return. This is not the time to play games, Kaitlin, but I'm pressed for time." He stepped forward.

Kate backed another step and searched for the best route of escape. Richard reached out and shoved her to the ground. He knelt and used his knee to keep her still. She gasped when he gripped the length of her hair. She shoved him and tried to roll away.

Richard struggled to hold her motionless. "I'm tired of your willfulness and shall make you regret it." He struck her face twice before he regained control of himself. She lay on the ground and tried to protect herself, but it did no good. When he struck her jaw, she cried out.

"Stop, stop it."

"Where the hell is it? I need the medallion."

"I don't have it here. I'll have to get it."

"I'm not a fool. Where is it, with those savage Scots?" He gripped her hair and twisted her neck. "Damn you, Kaitlin, I believe you have an errand to run." He rose, paced before her, and struck his fist in his hand.

Kate shuttered inside but tried to calm herself. She had to think of a way to escape him, but nothing came to mind. He grabbed her wrist and jerked her upward. She coward away, but still he held fast.

"Return to their keep and fetch the medallion. Come to me in no less than a month's time. If you don't arrive by then, I'll send my full army to your father's fief, and all your tenants will die. Do you understand?"

Before Kate responded, he yanked her hair again and pulled her against him. "I killed that boy, Manik, for his perfidy."

Kate cried out at Manik's death. She freed her hand and slapped Richard across the face with as much might as she possessed. "How could you? He was just doing his lord's service. You're despicable."

"He was a means to information. If you fail, Kaitlin, I'll kill you, and the savages, too. If the regent awarded me the land, I wouldn't have taken the child, and you wouldn't be here. They'll pay, they'll all pay." He laughed derisively.

"You took a child because the regent wouldn't give you land? What do the MacKinnons have to do with the land?"

He didn't answer. Richard pulled a dagger from his tunic and shoved her to the ground again. He lay on top of her and forced her to still. He kissed her neck and squeezed her breasts. Kate shoved him and rolled away. She gained her feet, and he secured her against him before she might flee. Her eyes darted beyond him in search of a way to bypass him.

"You could've had it all, Kaitlin, and instead you ran from me with that child. Now, I should take what I want and be done with it." He leaned away for a moment and held his dagger close to her chest. She struggled, and he slipped. His dagger sliced the side of her chest. Blood flowed through the fabric of her light-blue gown and soaked the material. He nodded and grunted his approval. She placed her hand over the wound to stop it from bleeding and the warmth covered her fingers. The sting brought tears to her eyes.

"Look what you made me do. You're a hellion, Kaitlin. I didn't mean to cut you, but 'twas your fault for your injury. Bah, there's no sense in taking you now. You'll return to my manor, and your injury better not slow you. You haven't much time." He laughed and rose.

Kate couldn't move. She fell to the ground and watched him stalk to his horse.

"Don't dally or be tardy. The fate of those people rests on your shoulders. I'll be watching closely, Kaitlin." Richard mounted his horse, laughed mockingly, and rode away.

She sobbed at the pain in her chest and the wound throbbed. Her bliaunt was stained with her blood and she gasped at the horrid sight. Her eyes fluttered and blurred, yet she fought against fading into a stupor. Somehow she had to make it to the MacKinnon's holding before she lost her senses. On her knees now, she crawled a few feet. She needed Brendan. No sooner had she thought that she slumped against the ground.

CHAPTER FIFTEEN

The night grew late, too late to ride amidst the darkened woods. Brendan couldn't see between the trees. He looked above and noted the heavy cloud cover. He needed to give up the search for the night because the view obscured. There was no way to find her in the darkness. Hours passed since she'd gone missing, and his concern tore at him. He rode back to the keep and hoped the sentry found her. Maybe she'd gotten lost in the hills.

When he strode in the hall, he noticed his brother's grim expression.

"Colin, have you found her? Is she here?"

"We found her, but… I'm sorry—"

"Nay, what the hell do you mean, you're sorry? I, I can't lose her. She better be all right." Brendan's eyes filled with pain. His eyes scanned the hall, and he gripped Colin's tunic. "Where is she?"

Colin released his tunic from his hold. "Brendan, calm down. We found her, but she's hurt."

"Hurt? Badly? Will she die?" The words rasped from his lips.

"She was stabbed and beaten. Jinny will tend her. She's a mess and lost a lot of blood."

Brendan shouted his denial. "Who would stab her?"

"That's a good question, but Burk found her in the woods near McGurdy's pool. They've only just returned, and you may want to wait before you—"

Brendan shook his head. "I want to see her now. Where is she?"

"She was taken to her cottage."

Brendan walked toward the door.

"Wait," Colin yelled.

But Brendan didn't wait to hear what he wanted. He ran from the keep, down the hill to Kate's cottage. His heart clanked in his chest the whole way. He opened the door and found Jinny and Julianna tended her wounds. They glanced at him as he entered.

Brendan marched to the side of the bed and gazed at her. Her hair was dirty and tangled, her lovely face bruised. His blood boiled at the sight. Someone hurt his wife, and by all that was sacred, he would find the knave and kill him. His breath quickened, and his eyes watered. He somehow suppressed the rage which tightened his body and instilled the need to act.

Jinny and Julianna didn't speak. He gentled a caress on Katie's cheek and kissed her forehead. His gut coiled because she appeared small and helpless.

"Brendan," Julianna said softly. "She will recover."

"Look at her, she's too pale. Don't speak falsely, Julianna. Is she dead?" He assessed her color and didn't discern she breathed.

"Nay, the wound is not as bad as we first thought. It's merely a flesh wound. Let us tend to her, move back and give us room." Julianna forced him to move aside, and he fell back into the chair beside the bed.

Brendan closed his eyes and thanked God she would recover. He resumed breathing, and when he opened his eyes again, he saw Jinny motion to Julianna.

"We've taken care of her wounds, there's nothing left for us to do. We'll come back later and check on her. Send for us if she needs us." Julianna realized he hadn't listened, so she and Jinny left.

Brendan stared at her for a long while, and didn't move, neither did she. The night crept onward and the weight of possibly losing her crossed his mind repeatedly. He approached the bed and sat beside her. Gently, he pulled back the cover and grimaced at the bandaged wound on her chest. She was fortunate the blade hadn't hit her heart. A few inches to the left, and it would have been fatal. He frowned, replaced the cover, and caressed the side of her face. Whoever hurt her would pay, he swore. He petted her hair with the palm of his hand, but she didn't awaken.

"Lass, you must mend." *I love you.* He blanched at his thought—he had never thought such nonsense in his nine and twenty years. He didn't know how to continue. Normally he'd demand, now he pleaded, and thought the unthinkable. Her unmoving form chased away his reflection.

"Katie, wake up. I want to talk to you." Nothing. She didn't hear his plea. Her breath shallow and indicated she was well into her slumber. He resumed his position on the chair and watched her for long minutes. Jinny and Julianna returned a short time later. Jinny checked her wound and asked if she awakened. Brendan shook his head.

"Why don't you rest, Brendan? We'll call for you if there's any change," Julianna suggested. "We will bathe her."

"I can't leave her."

"She's likely to sleep for a time. We've given her a sleeping potion. You're not doing her any good sitting here. We'll call for you the minute she awakens," Jinny said.

Julianna forced him to leave the cottage and took his hand and led him to the door. She gave his back a forceful shove. He scowled at her bold behavior, but she didn't fear him.

Brendan ambled to the keep. The night grew darker, and no moon provided light. It neared the midnight hour. He strode to his chamber, changed his tartan and tunic. He washed his face and realized how tired he was. When he arrived in the hall, his brother shoved him into a chair.

"What's going on, Brendan? Who would stab the lass?"

"I only found out today what provokes him. I cannot believe he came here. How did our sentry not sense him? The man is a sneaky dog."

"Is it the guardian?"

Brendan nodded. "Aye, she has no other enemies besides that knave."

"Why would her guardian come all the way to the Highlands to kill her? He couldn't want her that badly, could he?"

"There's more to his wanting her. Katie's father sent her a treasure. She said the man asked her about it, and she denied knowledge of it. The knave knows she has it. He came after her for it."

"What kind of evil man are we dealing with here?"

Brendan grunted. "He tried to force Katie to submit to him and abducted Bonnie from Henry's castle. What I don't understand is why he'd take your daughter? Why would Bonnie be important enough to risk his neck? If Henry found out he took Bonnie, the man would be executed. Katie has something else he wants—the treasure. I doubt the two are connected."

"What kind of treasure?"

"A gold medallion, it's a strange object. I'll bring it to you so you can look at it."

Colin nodded. "Aye, I'd like to see it."

Brendan noticed her cat on the way out the door and wondered how the feline had made it back to the keep. He picked up the furry creature. He carried the cat to her cottage and set it beside her on the bed. The animal purred and settled next to Kate. She adored the animal and her pet might soothe her when she awakened. He rummaged through her satchel and found the object along with the note. After he checked on Katie's progress, he returned to the keep. Colin remained at the table and he handed the object to him.

"Here, it's a strange object. She said it was from the east. I saw it earlier and questioned her about it."

Colin assessed the medallion and turned it over. "Why do you deem he wants it? Is it valuable?"

"Mayhap, it's made of gold. He doubtless wants it, but he didn't tell her why. When I questioned her about it, she said she hasn't yet figured out why her father sent it to her. Her father was killed in the east, mayhap over this. I get the sense she might suspect the guardian. There was a message with it, beware the friend with the black heart. She doesn't understand what it meant."

Colin flipped the medallion over again and squinted. "There's a clasp." He removed his dagger and pressed the point into the hole. The medallion clicked, and Colin opened the ends. A piece of parchment fell out.

"What is it?" Brendan leaned forward.

"It looks to be some kind of map. I cannot understand the writing. Do you deem the man is after her for this?" Colin held the parchment up. "Mayhap he killed her father for it, but her father already sent the medallion to Kate. Seems likely to me."

"Why else would he chase her here? How does the knave even know about it? I don't like this one bit, Colin. Aye, he's after the map. I cannot leave her now; else I'd chase the man down and kill him."

"We should go after him, but he's fled and is long gone by now. You must get your wife to tell you."

"I will, and then we'll go. Vengeance will be mine."

Colin nodded in agreement.

CHAPTER SIXTEEN

Kate lay in a semi-sleep state, her mind blank and devoid of pain. How was that possible? Why did the cold of the night not penetrate her? She didn't feel the cold, nor did she want to wake, but she heard someone call her name. The lids of her eyes seemed too heavy and she couldn't open them.

"Katie, wake up, lass."

She tried to move but was weighted down as if something pressed her. Was she still in the forest? She forced her eyes open a slit. It wasn't too bright, so she opened them more.

Brendan's voice gentled. "That's right, Katie, wake up. Come on, sweetheart, open your eyes and look at me."

She focused on him. He sat beside her and she glanced around the room. He was alone. How had she gotten there? The last thing she remembered was Richard in the woods, his threats, and his attack. He'd stabbed her. Her eyes widened. Brendan caressed her cheek.

"Brendan," she whispered.

"Aye, you're safe in your own cottage." He lifted a cup of water to her mouth, and she tried to drink deeply, but he pulled the cup away.

"Thirsty," she groaned the word out.

"You've been ill for two days, lass. If you drink too

much, your stomach won't handle it. How do you feel?"

"Tired." She closed her eyes.

When Kate opened her eyes again, she sat up and adjusted to the darkness. She noticed Brendan asleep in the chair next to the bed with his legs propped on the bedside. How could she miss him when he overwhelmed the room? She pushed her legs aside and tried to stand. Her left side stitched when she moved. She noticed the chamber pot on the floor. With shaky legs, she made her way to it. She picked it up and stumbled to the other room. After she took care of that business, she tiptoed to bed and tried not to awaken Brendan.

"What are you doing?"

Kate jumped at his hard voice and lurched forward. "I'm...I had to..."

Brendan lifted her and settled her back upon the bed. "You were wounded. You cannot get out of bed and traipse about. Are you hungry?"

"Starved," she uttered.

He chuckled and walked to the door and shouted for Gil. Brendan gave instructions and returned to her side. "Gil will bring food."

"What happened?"

"Someone beat and stabbed you. You don't recall?" There was a touch of disdain in his tone.

"Aye, I do. I shouldn't have gone off into the woods, but I was angry with you. I needed to be alone and think."

"Katie, I didn't mean to be hurtful that day. You killed me with pleasure, but you left before I regained my wits and I searched for you to make amends."

"Well, I was on my way back when—"

Gil's knock interrupted her. Brendan strolled to the door, took the food from Gil. He returned to the sleeping area and placed the food on the nearby table. She picked at the food and he tore pieces of bread and handed them to her. Her appetite appeased, but she wanted to continue her explanation and get it over with.

"I suppose we should talk about what happened at the cliff."

Brendan stopped her with a finger to her lips. "Katie, I didn't mean to anger you that day. When I recovered, I went to find you, but I couldn't. I panicked and had Colin send the sentry to search for you. They found you stabbed and beaten. Was it your guardian?" His calm tone rose to an infuriated level.

She nodded. "After I left you, I rode around and found a small pool. I sat beside it and considered what…what we did. He grabbed me before I might flee and told me that he wants the medallion. He said I must bring it to him, otherwise…" Kate reached for the goblet of water to soothe her dry throat.

Brendan shifted and sat beside her. "Otherwise what?"

"He'll invade my father's fief and kill my people. Then he'll track me down and kill me. I refused him and I told him I didn't have the medallion. He struck me and said he knew I had it. That Manik told him I had it. He killed the young soldier…Manik died trying to protect me." The thought of her father's squire's death provoked tears to trickle from her eyes.

"Who was Manik?"

"My father's devoted squire. He brought the medallion to me after my father's death. I don't know why my guardian wants the medallion, but if he wants it, it must be important. I should give it to him."

"Damned right he wants it. Nay, you'll do nothing. The only thing I want you to do is tell me his name." Brendan cupped her cheek. "Please, lass, be reasonable."

"Nay."

"Nay?" He sounded shocked she disobeyed him.

"I won't involve the MacKinnons."

"I already told you, we are involved."

"I'm sorry, Brendan, if you're angry, but I'll not tell you."

"I'm married to the most stubborn lass alive. I won't give up, Katie, and I'll keep asking. Now, do you need anything?"

"You. Will you hold me?" Kate didn't want to think about the mess before her. She just wanted Brendan to hold her, and to pretend all of her problems had been nightmares shaken away with morning's light. He stretched on the bed and cuddled beside her. She smiled as he held her lovingly. He kissed her cheek and leaned his face against hers.

"Katie, what am I to do with you? You're making this too hard. It can be easy, you know. As your husband, it's my duty to protect you and see to your problems."

"I'll not speak of it further. I just want you to hold me, Brendan." Kate knew it was only a matter of time before he'd realize being married to her would cause him heartache. She had to return to her people, and she was certain he wouldn't leave his. When the time came, her problems wouldn't concern him. She was sure of it. She would see to her own difficulties, without the aid of her so-called husband.

"Are you a witch?"

Kate gasped at his question. "What did you ask me?"

"I asked if you were a witch. You are a wise-woman, like Jinny. I saw you mix the herbs and heard you speak of a goddess."

She turned toward him. "I fear to admit my ability to you or anyone, but I suppose you could say I am a witch. I prefer healer. My mother was, and my grandmother, too."

"Katie, there should be no secrets between us. A wife should tell her husband all. Don't fear to share yourself with me. I'm glad you're a witch. Aye, you've bewitched me. Do you cast hexes? Jinny doesn't but teases she's capable. Or at least, she says she won't do curses to hurt others."

"It's against my belief to cast hexes or curses. My ancestors decreed: Do your will and harm none. I only use my skills for good or for healing."

"Ah, so you won't cast a curse on your guardian then?" She shook her head. "What are the candles and rope for?" Brendan pulled her back against him, and she cuddled beside him.

"I use them to pray to the Goddess. She is supreme, the

giver of life, all that is good in the vastness of life. I find praying to her soothing, and she guides and protects me."

Brendan chuckled. "Well, your goddess hasn't done such a good job at protecting you lately. But you have me now, I'll protect you." He kissed her tenderly and sealed his vow and melted her heart. "Katie, mayhap if I told you something about me, you would trust me."

"I want to trust you, Brendan. What is it?"

"I'm as superstitious as you. Aye, we Highlanders are most serious about these things. I live by my ancestors' creed, especially when I go into battle which is why I painted those symbols." He laughed at her expression, which showed her surprise.

"So I'm supposed to trust you now that I know you're a superstitious man? Have you any other secrets you're willing to reveal?" She laughed.

"One secret at a time, lass."

Kate sighed and closed her eyes. Perhaps the arrogant warrior had a heart.

Being married to Brendan had to be the worst of all fates.

Each morning, Kate awoke to find Brendan gone, but he'd return each evening and badgered her for Richard's name. She refused to speak to him about it. Not that it mattered, because he would just stare with his icy stone-faced look. Once again, she found him gone when she awakened. After she applied a salve Jinny left on her wound, Kate dressed and prepared her morning fare.

She hastened about her morning ritual and lifted her hands in prayer to the Goddess for solace. Once she relaxed enough, she pulled her satchel toward her and opened it. Inside, she rummaged for the packet of old spells Madam Serena gave her. There were spells to heal, spells to bring good fortune, but not one spell to change a man to a more softhearted spirit. Although, the spell to cast evil spirits away might work to turn Brendan into a more docile husband. She laughed when she came to the love spell.

A knock at the door startled her, and she hastily put the parchments in her satchel. She didn't answer right away, and Julianna entered. Kate rose from the floor and hurriedly gathered her meditation tools. Another woman stood with her.

"Good day, Julianna."

"I'm sorry I didn't think you were here." Julianna took her hand and led her to the woman. "Kate, this is my sister, Laila. She's been at the KirkConnell's keep and only returned this morn. I wanted to introduce you. Garrick, that's Steven KirkConnell's brother, finally asked her to marry him. They will wed in two days."

"It is nice to finally meet you, Kate. Bonnie hasn't stopped singing your praises since I came home this morn. Thank you for all you've done for her."

"How could I not help her? It's nice to meet you as well. Are you excited about your marriage?" Kate smiled at the lovely young lady. The sisters didn't look alike, because Laila's dark hair gleamed, while Julianna's was much lighter.

Laila smiled. "Oh, aye, I fell in love with him when I was five and ten. It has taken me a long time to get him to propose. I had faith though and used every wile to snare him."

She laughed at Laila's lightheartedness. "What's your intended like?"

"He's splendid. When I was younger, I would sit and watch him all day. He's handsome. Finally, he took notice of me."

"I'm glad you succeeded if it's what you want," Kate said.

"He has the gentlest nature. I've never heard him yell once, but he's a warrior like the others."

"Well, Brendan yells all the time and always scowls."

"Oh my, I heard you wed Brendan, you poor lady."

Kate laughed at her concerned look. "Aye, but I don't

want to be. Ah, be wed to him that is, and he used trickery to gain my hand."

Laila giggled. "I've known him for a long time, and can certainly understand why. Who wants to be married to a man with a permanent frown?"

"Oh, will you two cease, he's not that bad." Julianna pushed her sister's shoulder and for that, she received a grin. "I admit, he is rather hard to get along with."

They moved to the table and sat. Kate poured them a drink and saw Trixie reenter the cottage. "Brendan doesn't deserve the problems I'll bring to him."

"Oh, dear, it sounds as if Kate is in dire need to talk. Come, tell us, Kate, what's wrong. We are your friends. We shall hold your confidence." Laila set her cup down and nodded.

For some reason, Kate saddened at that. They were her friends, and she felt connected to them. Julianna took her hand, and Laila moved closer. Suddenly, the wall she'd built up crumbled down.

"My guardian wants a medallion my father sent me from his excursion to Egypt. I've been given a month to return with it. If not, he'll send his soldiers to my father's fief and will kill our tenants. He also said he would find me."

"He sounds evil." Laila took her other hand, and they tried to comfort her.

Julianna squeezed her hand. "He is evil, Laila. He took my baby."

"I'm going to have to take the medallion to him. I cannot chance him besieging my home. I'm not sure how many soldiers he has, but it's likely many. His forces are second in number, under Lord de Guylet's. I believe he killed my father for the medallion."

"That's ghastly. Why does he want the medallion? What is it? It must be worth a fortune for him to be interested in it." Laila leaned back and looked to ponder it.

Kate reached for the wrapped medallion in the center of the table. Funny, she'd left it wrapped in the satchel, but now it was on the table. She handed it to Laila. "There's a map inside."

Laila studied it for several moments. "It looks ancient, and the locations are probably not even there any longer. It's in all likelihood useless."

"What do you mean useless?"

"I read all sorts of historical literature. Colin brings me tombs and pamphlets from Edinburgh. Men have found ruins of temples in the holy land during the crusades. If this is a map of such a place, it's likely covered by hundreds of years of sand or already pillaged or sacked."

Kate laughed so hard, tears came to her eyes. "Then I'd gladly hand over the map to Richard, but it makes me saddened my father might've died for this scrap of a map. My father's squire told me he was killed shortly after he showed the medallion to Richard."

Julianna rose and moved around the table to face her. "Kate, don't make the same mistake I made. When I first met Colin, I too had a situation I needed to resolve. I would've fared better had I told Colin about it from the start."

"I told Brendan about it, but there's nothing he can do to help. I must find out what happened to my father, and if indeed Richard truly killed him. Only then can I think of my future."

"Don't be so sure, Kate. Brendan is an intelligent man."

Kate didn't want to admit she couldn't trust him. No one could help her with this situation. Richard wanted the medallion, and she had the means to stop him from hurting others. She had to remember that and do what she could. If she couldn't find a way to gain an audience with King Henry, then she would confront the devil himself.

She changed the topic. "I haven't met George yet. Bonnie told me that you had a pet goat. Mayhap I should ask Bonnie to introduce me to him."

Julianna's face saddened. "Oh, don't do that, Kate."

"Why ever not?"

"George died when Bonnie was missing. He was old. I

haven't had the heart to tell her yet. She will be upset when she hears and I'm hoping she doesn't realize it for a long time."

"Oh, how horrid. Bonnie said he liked to eat your tablecloths and that you smacked him. I looked forward to meeting the animal."

"Aye, I miss him. He was endeared. When I first came, I couldn't stand him. He kept entering the keep, and I kept ousting him. We were good friends in the end." Julianna dabbed the corner of her eye.

"I'm sorry, Julianna."

As if they conjured up the little minx, Bonnie ran through the doorway. They stopped talking and she hugged Kate. Her eyes shined with mischief, and Kate wondered what she'd been up to.

"Kate, I saw Sean on the corral fence, his feet hung over the side, so I snucked up on him and tied his boots together." Bonnie grinned at her trick.

"You did? What did he do?"

"He didn't know 'cause I was real quiet-like. Then when they were knotted good, I shoved him off the fence." She giggled.

Kate and Laila laughed.

Bonnie smiled wickedly. "He tried to chase me, but he couldn't run, 'cause you know why?"

Kate grinned. "Nay, why?"

"'Cause his boots were tied together."

"You're a clever girl." Kate ruffled her hair and laughed again.

"I'd watch your back if I was you," Laila chimed in.

"Aye, he'll want to repay me back for that." Bonnie's smile disappeared when she noticed her mother's frown.

Julianna gave a motherly look: the kind that meant, 'wait-until-your-father-hears-about-this.' Bonnie was indeed in trouble. "You know what you need to do."

Bonnie nodded solemnly. "How long do I gots to sit there, Mama?"

"For the rest of the day and you'll apologize to Sean later."

"Aye, Mama." Bonnie left and they knew where she was going—to sit in her father's chair.

"How is it she speaks English so well, Julianna?" Kate asked.

"I often spoke to her in English, because it was a habit. When she learned to talk, she didn't stop. She babbled morn, noon, and night in Gaelic and English. I thought Colin would leave our keep to reside in the barracks. He asked me if all children spoke incessantly." She laughed.

"She's just like me when I was a child." Kate smiled then sighed. "I used to get into all kinds of mischief."

"God help us all," Julianna retorted.

Laila giggled at her sister's tone. "Why do you say that?"

"Because now we have two hellions in our clan, one was enough."

CHAPTER SEVENTEEN

Brendan MacKinnon teetered on the edge of madness. Kate besotted him and he was unsure what to do about it. He sat in the meeting and half-listened to what his brother said. When Bonnie entered the hall and ran directly to Colin, she sat on his brother's lap. The lass was up to no good if her troubled expression gave an indication.

"Good day, Button. What are you doing here?"

"Mama said I have to sit in the chair." Bonnie touched her father's face and gave a sorrowful gaze.

Brendan suspected her ploy to distract her father. She'd used the same tactics on him repeatedly.

"I suppose your mother will tell me what you did?" Colin grinned and hugged his daughter close.

"Aye, Mama will tell you."

Colin nodded and resumed his discussion. "Kate's a stubborn lass to be sure."

"I've tried to get the bloody man's name, but she'll not say. She won't speak to me now and hardly says a word to anyone. I've ruined it, mucked it beyond repair, and can't fix this when she won't accept me."

"I don't envy your plight, Brendan, and wish I had useful advice. I received a missive from Henry. He's coming for a visit. We'll find out the damned guardian's name soon enough. Let us enjoy Laila's wedding. Henry should arrive soon after. It won't be long now."

Bonnie shifted her father's face to look at her. "Honey's coming?"

"Aye, he misses you. Shhh, lass, I'm talking to Brendan."

Brendan almost laughed. He hoped his daughter when he had one, resembled his sweet niece. Although, Bonnie's hellion nature often tried his patience. The thought of having a child of his own made him smile. "I will try to reason with her. I'll see you later."

He strolled to their cottage, but Kate wasn't there. She must have had company because cups sat on the table. Brendan took a seat and lifted the medallion. The piece of gold caused many problems for him and Kate. He was reassured Henry would soon give the name and he would enact his revenge on the churlish-dog. His hand tightened around the object.

Brendan spent the afternoon on the training field. He'd take his mind off his wife. He spent the rest of the day trying his sword and worked on his maneuvers. When he finished going through the paces, he returned to the cottage rejuvenated and wanted to reassure himself she hadn't left. He entered quietly and moved like the wind—unseen and unfelt. When he spotted Kate asleep peacefully in their bed, the tension eased from his body. He hastily shed his garments and lay next to her.

During the long night, he contemplated their issues. The lass was riddled with flaws. Aye, she was stubborn, obstinate, and adorable. She cried all the time and couldn't remember a person's name if she'd etched it on her arm. Damn it all, he was in love with his wife. It struck him like a boulder hitting his hard head, and although he'd denied it, he couldn't fight it any longer. He promised himself she wouldn't weaken him. But then he contradicted himself. If anything happened to her, he'd hold himself culpable. He had to protect her at all costs.

His entire life was of warring. All he did each day since

he'd turned five was train for war. He wasn't one to dally over enjoyments such as women or ponder a family. Why did he feel so damn bleak then? He had nothing to offer the beautiful woman lying beside him in the bed. He wasn't a laird—just a soldier. Why would she love him? Somehow, he would convince her she belonged to him. He was nothing without her, nothing but a soldier, nothing but a man with no joy in his life.

There were plenty of soldiers to go around, though he was a superb warrior. Nay, he was nothing without her, without Kate. Brendan rose and kissed her lightly on her head. He left the cottage just as the sun streaked the gray sky with its morning light.

CHAPTER EIGHTEEN

The day of Laila and Garrick's wedding arrived with sunshine as the clans of the KirkConnell and the MacKinnon joined through marriage. The clans' people were in good cheer and Kate was glad she'd joined the celebration. They arrived at the KirkConnell keep early enough that they assisted Sarah in the wedding preparations. Sarah greeted her, and she watched Bonnie run through the hall in glee to play with Sara's son, Jamie. Kate sat at the opposite end of the table and smiled at the bride and groom. Their touching display of love envied her. Garrick didn't have reservations about showing his affection. Would that Brendan be so loving, but since he kept his distance, she didn't expect a show of tenderness.

Brendan sat on the opposite side of the room with several KirkConnell soldiers. He all but ignored her. She dispirited with homesickness and missed Lolly, Madam Serena, and being needed. The longer she sat by herself, the lonelier she felt, and the angrier she became with Brendan. He turned out to be a wretched husband just as she'd predicted he would be. How she wished King Henry sent her to her betrothed instead of her guardian. Her betrothed was likely someone similar to Gil, which would've been preferable. Gil danced with a lady. His manner was sweet-natured and his charm flocked the ladies to his side. None of the ladies dared to glance at Brendan, except for her. Why couldn't she have fallen in love with someone like Gil?

"Pardon, Milady, may I join you?"

She looked up to find Walt beside her. "Certainly, Walt. May I pour you ale?" He nodded, and she handed him a cup.

"I wanted to tell you I'm pleased you married Brendan, lass. He's done well for a wife. You are a blessing to him."

His sweet words brought a blush to her cheeks. "You're kind to say that, Walt. I haven't talked to you and I wondered…" A moment of awkward silence passed between them. She wondered how he was related to Brendan. They looked alike and Walt could've passed for his father.

Walt placed his cup on the table. "Aye, you can speak freely, lass."

"I noticed the resemblance between you and Brendan. How are you related?"

Walt laughed. "Aye, we're related by close lines."

"How is he not as chivalrous as you then?" She smiled when his eyes crinkled blithely.

"Give him time, lass. Brendan may be rough around the edges, but he has feelings for you. I can read him better than anyone, and you've set my lad on a jagged path. I haven't seen him beguiled before. He'll come around."

"Lady Kate, I need a dance partner. Would you do me the honor?" Gil placed his cup on the table and helped to pull her chair out when she stood.

"Will you excuse me, Walt?"

"Aye, lass, go." His laughter followed as she walked to the center of the room.

Gil smiled and led her around the dance floor. They moved in line with the dancers and ended up in front of Brendan who appeared unaffected by her dancing with Gil. She smiled and continued on with the dance.

The dance ended and Gil bowed. "You're a bonny lass to dance with me. You look beautiful tonight. I'm certain others have noticed."

Kate giggled. "Thank you, Gil, you're kind to say that."

Gil gasped. "Did I hear you aright? You called me by my given name." He placed his hand over his heart and pretended to be chagrined.

"I'm sorry about my travesty, but I had to put some effort into my plan to get out of telling you the man's name. Do you forgive me?"

"So it was all a ruse?" He burst with laughter. "I suspected."

Gil took her hand and kissed her knuckles. She pulled her hand back and saw Brendan approach. Daggers shot from his eyes. Gil turned his best grin and was about to say something when she spoke.

"Gil, I'm a married—"

"I cannot deny my attraction to you."

"Oh, I thank you for the compliment, Gil, but—"

"Lass, I'll make you howl your pleasure to the sky."

"Take your hand off my wife. No one will make Katie howl her pleasure to the sky but me." Brendan's voice rose well above those in the hall. Everyone stopped, the music ceased, the children stilled, all eyes fastened on them. Kate was mortified.

"Brendan, what goes?"

His answer was a sock to Gil's nose. Gil grunted at the blow and his nose bled from the impact. Brendan placed his arm in front of Kate and moved her back.

"Damn, Brendan, I think you broke my nose." Gil was handed a cloth for his bloody nose by Walt, who stood by and smiled as if the entire event amused him.

"It goes well with your black eye." Brendan shrugged, grabbed Kate by the hand, and pulled her through the hall.

Kate's mouth hung open in shock that he would strike his friend. She frowned and jerked his hand and stopped him from proceeding. "Why did you hit Gil? You hurt that boy."

He didn't answer. Gil's laughter rose as Brendan pulled her through the doorway. She ran to keep up with him. He practically sprinted, and she dug her heels into the grass to slow him. She tried to pull her hand free, but he wouldn't let her.

"Release me this instant." Kate pulled her hand from his and shoved him hard on his chest. Brendan grunted but stood anchored to the ground. His face showed no emotion, but his eyes glowered his anger. "What do you think you're doing?"

"What I'm doing?"

"You practically threw yourself at Gil, woman."

"I did not, all I did was dance with him. You had no right to hit him like that."

"No man will touch you, but me."

"Touch me? You haven't even spoken to me in days. I realize you're not interested in pursuing our marriage, Brendan, and believe me I agree. I don't answer to you, and if you—"

Before Kate finished her tirade, Brendan yanked her off her feet and carried her to the loch. She shrieked at his audacity. He set her feet on the grass. As soon as he released her, she shoved his shoulder but didn't move him at all. She fisted her hands at her sides and resisted the urge to strike him as he'd done to Gil. He motioned for her to sit, but she shook her head.

Brendan forced her to sit and pressed on her shoulders. He sat behind her with his arms around her waist. She sat between his straddled legs, the length of his legs touched hers practically to her feet.

"What the hell do you mean I'm not interested?" Brendan pulled her against him.

Kate kept her eyes on the water and hoped to distract her mind from his touches. "Why are you doing this? You're turning out to be a dreadful husband, Brendan."

"Lass, I want you." His whispered words made her shiver, and his warm breath next to her ear sent a tumultuous aura through her. She turned to look into his eyes.

"You don't mean that, Brendan."

His voice lowered and was roughly aroused. "Aye, I do.

You make me hard." To emphasize his statement, he placed her hand beneath his tartan. He wore nothing beneath it. He took advantage of their position and shifted his hands to hold her breasts.

Kate's stomach flipped and her breath caught. The muscles in her waist tightened in anticipation of his touch. She closed her eyes against the passion flowing through her body.

"You make me want to ram—"

"Brendan, don't say such things."

"I want to take you, and to hell with everything else." Brendan edged her bodice lower and uncovered her breasts. His hand gently caressed the scar above her breast. He groaned softly, kissed her shoulder, and trailed his lips to her neck. "I've missed you," he said hoarsely.

She moaned and leaned back against his hard body. His hands cupped her, and she reveled in the pleasure of it. He turned her in his arms and her body stretched over his. She tried to move off him, but he wouldn't let her. He shifted her back and took her nipple in his mouth. Kate moaned and threw her head back. With his hand supporting her back, he shifted her legs to his sides. She felt the hardness of him through the fabric of her gown. An exquisite yearning overtook her. She wanted him too.

He kept his mouth joined to hers while he loosened her garments. She abandoned all thought and reveled in the sensual touches of his hand over her skin. He lifted her, set her atop his erection, and lowered her onto him. Kate gasped when he slid inside her. A sense of power came because he gave up control, something she didn't believe he normally would do. He allowed her to move against his body and take pleasure. Brendan watched her with affection, and she couldn't control her emotions. She cried as their bodies joined.

"I love you." The words came easily to her. She held onto his firm shoulders and his strong hands supported her back. Kate groaned his name and found herself entwined in erotic pleasure.

Brendan took control from there. She gasped at the urgency of their movements. He lifted her with little effort and yet supported her body. Her cries of lustful torment provoked his intense thrusts. She wanted to triumph over him and make him as climatic as he'd made her. He grunted a manly response at his own release and didn't cease moving until his strength depleted. She fell against his chest and willed her breath to slow. With her face in the crook of his neck, she placed light kisses on his hot skin. He continued to hold her against him and his strength awed her.

"I want to stay like this for the rest of the night. Hell, for the rest of my life. I should have known I couldn't stay away from you, you're too tempting."

"Brendan?"

"Aye, love?"

"I don't know how you do it."

"Do what?"

"Make me want you so badly."

He kissed the side of her neck, and his mouth lingered for a moment. "We better dress before someone comes along."

Kate fixed her gown and helped him fold his tartan around his waist. His body looked magnificent in the moonlight, highlighting his smooth muscular chest. She couldn't resist and swiped her hand along the contour of his muscles, but he stopped her hand with his.

"If you don't cease, I'll..."

"You'll what?"

He grinned. "Do you want to do it again?"

Kate laughed a girlish giggle, which made him smile. He pulled her back against his chest and she faced the loch. With his hands wrapped around her waist, he leaned his head against hers.

"When this is over...after we dispatch the fiend, you'll be my wife in every way. Won't you, Katie?"

Kate didn't like the anguish in his voice. She didn't want

to love him, didn't want to deceive him, and most of all didn't want to get hurt. Once she returned to England, she wouldn't return. Her duty would force her to leave her husband. He squeezed her arm to get her answer.

"I must gain justice in my father's name and give the medallion to King Henry. I will return to my people." She'd spoken softly and tried not to anger him.

"I will gain justice for your father. You're my wife, and you should leave it up to your husband, me."

"I will not. This began with my father and it will end with me," she said emphatically.

Brendan ran his hand through his hair in agitation and started to say something. He closed his mouth, turned, and left her standing by the loch.

She stayed at the loch for an hour and watched the moon rise higher. Brendan knew the verity of it, that she would leave him, yet he made no offer to go with her. Kate spent a restless night and swarmed with a surfeit of emotions. Brokenhearted at the prospect of leaving Brendan, she should never have given herself to him again. Each time they were together made it harder for her to accept her fate—she would leave the man she loved.

She was relieved they would return to the MacKinnon holding in the morning. After the morning meal, they readied to leave and she said her goodbyes to Laila. Kate walked to her horse and mounted it. Bonnie was allowed to ride with her, and she was thankful for the distraction. Once again, Brendan took to his coldhearted demeanor and gave her a stone-faced look.

As they rode along, they came across a group of soldiers. Kate listened to Bonnie's chatter and shushed her when she noticed them. Two soldiers held flags bearing the king's insignia. The Highlanders immediately stopped and waited for them. Kate tilted her head to get a better look at the procession and was startled to see King Henry ride up to Colin.

"Colin, Julianna, I have arrived."

Colin laughed and bowed his head to the king. "So we see, Henry. Did you have to bring so many men? My soldiers won't take it well that Englishmen are here on our land."

Henry grinned. "You know I always travel with many. Keep your warriors in line, Colin, because my men have been trained to deal with your sort."

"My sort? What exactly are you saying, Henry, that I'm—"

"Cease bunching your tartan up your arse, Colin. I jest. Where is my favorite girl?" He glanced around and spotted Bonnie on Kate's mount. With a tug on the reins, he turned his horse and approached. "My sweet little minx, I see you're well. Come to Henry." He put out his hands and Bonnie threw herself at him. Henry caught and hugged her.

"Honey, I'm happy you're here. Now Papa won't make me sit in his chair."

"What did you do to cause your father to punish you so? Nay, don't tell me. You look well, sweeten." He kissed her forehead and rode back to Colin. "I'm relieved she was returned unharmed. I had to come and see for myself."

"Aye, thanks to Kate. Come, Henry, let us continue on."

Kate smiled at the king's charming manner. He was a young king and might be considered handsome by some. She kept her gaze on him and followed the procession, but she noticed Brendan now rode beside her. Before she suspected his intention, he dragged her off her horse's back and settled her on his lap. He continued to ride toward the front of the procession. She didn't say a word, but when they neared Henry, Brendan kissed her, and it wasn't the sort of kiss one would expect, given they now rode next to the king. Affronted by his action, Kate pulled away and silently pleaded with him to behave. He laughed. The scowling warrior laughed as though he was happy. She'd never understand him, not today, not on the morrow, not ever.

They reached the MacKinnon holding, and she left her horse at the stable for the men to tend to. She quickly walked down the hill and entered her cottage. After she changed her garments and washed, she grabbed the medallion from the table and walked to the castle. As she reached the entrance, she heard yells within. Bravely, she ambled inside the hall and scowled at the group of men in raised discussion.

Henry paced in front of the hearth and gave Colin and Brendan a ferocious look. It didn't seem to bother either of them.

"I cannot believe Richard de Morris took my own cousin's child from my castle. What manner of man would do something so heinous? I'm shocked he would go against me, his king. Why would he do that?" Henry stopped his pace when he noticed her. "Oh, you must be Lady Kaitlin, come, I wish to speak to you."

Kate didn't like the fact that the charming king was now onerous. She disbelieved she heard the king speak Richard's name. Colin must've told him her guardian took Bonnie, and the king knew who her guardian was. Now that the information was out, she would speak to the king on her behalf and leave. She did as he bid and stepped before him, and curtseyed respectfully. "Your Grace, I'm honored to see you again."

"The pleasure is mine, My Lady. I was saddened to learn of your father's death. Lord Hawk was a worthy knight and a great vassal. He shall be missed."

"Sire, my father spoke graciously of you, and looked forward to your coronation." Kate relaxed when the king smiled even though the Highlanders scowled.

Henry sat across from where she stood. "I want to hear the details of—"

"I will speak on my wife's behalf," Brendan dared to interrupt Henry. He took her hand and guided her to a chair. Against her better sense, she sat quietly. Brendan whispered to her, "Katie, let me do the talking."

"Nay, I'm not a child, Brendan. I need no one to speak to His Grace for me."

"You're my wife and will do as I say." He gave her a feral frown.

Kate almost laughed. If he were a bull, his nostrils would be steaming. She placed her hand on his arm and affectionately patted him in a condescending manner. "Brendan, if you don't let me speak to the king, I shall cast a spell on you that will turn you into the most impotent husband."

"You wouldn't." He raised an eyebrow and gave her his stone-faced stare.

"Wouldn't I?" She smiled and hoped her lie worked. Brendan grunted and turned away. He now scowled at Henry, instead of her.

Henry and Colin whispered to each other before the king turned his attention... "Brendan, did I hear you correctly? Are you saying you married Lady Stanhope?"

"Aye, Henry, I did."

"You went against my edict knowing I betrothed her to Angus Barclay?"

Brendan nodded. "Aye, I married her. Why should the Barclay receive such a gracious gift, Henry? I admit at first, I thought about returning her to you, but then she bewitched me." Brendan smiled at Henry and laughed when she pinched his arm.

"I cannot allow you to be married to her. I shall rectify this at once."

"Your Grace, I had hoped—"

Brendan became ornery then and interrupted her. "I won't allow you to annul our marriage, Henry. She's pleased with the arrangement and won't gainsay me. Besides, you owe me a favor, do you not? I'm asking for your approval."

Henry muttered an expletive under his breath. To look at him, you'd think he delighted at Brendan's declaration. Kate hoped she was wrong.

"Why did I ever promise you a favor? I should have kept my mouth shut that day, but I was grateful to you for your aid... Well, if the lady is pleased to have the match then, of course, I'll honor it. You'll enjoy living in England, Brendan."

Brendan spit out the ale he'd drank and turned the

nastiest scowl at Henry. Kate almost laughed. "What did you say?"

"I said you'll enjoy living in England. Lady Stanhope's, ah, I mean, Lady MacKinnon's land is beautiful and most prosperous. Her father took great care of his people as will you. His knights are the best-trained soldiers in all my kingdom. That should please you, I imagine. Well, you can continue to train men for my service, as her father had. This has worked out well and to my advantage. I should've considered you for her husband, though it never crossed my mind." Henry nodded satisfactorily as if the entire arrangement had been planned by him.

"Henry, I never said I would leave the Highlands."

Kate sat emotionless. Brendan's rejection sunk her heart. He was too attached to his beloved land and his people to ever leave them for her. She wanted to yell, but the king smiled and winked as if he had a secret.

"I don't know what to do about Angus though. What shall I tell him? I all but promised him a bride… How about Brendan MacKinnon stole your wife and lands…?" Henry's brow rose in question.

Colin spoke up. "I'm sure you can find another situation that might be more beneficial to the Barclay. If you need assistance, the MacKinnons would be happy to make sure he ceases the raids on the borderlands."

Henry stifled a laugh. "We shall speak of it later. Right now, I want to speak to Lady MacKinnon about Richard de Morris. My Lady, will you enlighten us on why Richard would do something so horrid as to take my cousin's child?"

She shuffled away from Brendan and gave him a frown before she focused on the king. "Your Grace, I received a missive from Lord de Guylet saying I was to be placed in Lord Richard's guardianship. My overlord informed me I would stay with Lord Richard until he returned and then I would be taken to my betrothed." Kate turned a heated glance at Brendan before continuing, "Lord Richard said something about not receiving lands from the regent and that he took the child for revenge."

"Revenge for land? Oh, I remember now... Colin, when you and Julianna came, we were intent to settle the matter of Julianna's father's holdings, which were now hers by right, but she didn't want the lands... The regent didn't approve of Lord Richard's request. Why would he do something as rash as to take a child, a child under my protection, because he was denied the land? There was nothing to be gained by it." Henry shouted the last and banged his hand on the table.

He turned to Kate, and she sensed someone behind her. Brendan solaced her briefly.

Henry leaned forward and grimaced. "I sent Richard a missive and asked him to oversee your father's land until Lord de Guylet returned. De Guylet was to take you to your betrothed, and you were to remain at your home, on your father's lands. I didn't want to upset you by forcing you to leave when you had only learned of your father's death. I'm not heartless."

"At first, Your Grace, I was uncertain why he made me leave my home, but I discovered the truth. Pardon me, I digress. Let me tell you what happened. I arrived at Lord de Morris' home and discovered Bonnie in the chamber next to mine. The de Morris' didn't have children..." Kate continued to describe the events until she reached the part where she found Brendan in the forest. "...Lord Richard didn't intend to contact my betrothed or return me on Lord de Guylet's return."

Henry folded his hands and listened. The only sign to show his disgruntlement was the movement of his nostrils and the stir of the hairs of his mustache. He rose to his full height and gripped his hair in frustration. He knocked his chair back with a loud bang.

"That damned blighter, subjecting himself on an innocent woman and child. De Morris wanted the holding next to his land and parleyed with the Regent. The Regent decided against it and told him on the day of the summer fair, the day Bonnie went missing. He sought revenge against me and used Bonnie to get it. You say he attacked you in the woods?"

"He hurt her badly, Henry. We will repay him for his injustices. Katie has more to say…" Brendan nodded to her, but she stared at the king.

He gripped the chair and vehemently moved it so he could sit back down. Once he sat, he took a deep breath and seemed to regain his composure. "I apologize, Lady Kaitlin. Please, go on."

Kate nodded slightly and handed the medallion to him. "I received this medallion from my father. Inside, there is a note from him which says beware the friend with the black heart. My father's squire said that he and Lord Richard argued over it. There are also letters from my father, which mentioned Lord Richard wanted the medallion. I'm sure the object is valuable, and I thought you should have it."

"My Lady, your father was my loyal vassal, and he was killed for it, so its value is nothing."

Tears gathered in her eyes, but she quickly gained control of herself. "I thank you, Your Grace."

"Lord de Morris will be punished for his foul deeds. I will send my armies to him at once." Henry pounded his fist on the table and rattled the cups.

"That is all I ask, Your Grace, justice for my father."

Colin stood and shook his head. "Henry, there is no need to send your armies. Let me and my men hunt him down. Now that we know his name, we will find him and seek our own kind of justice. He took my daughter, for God's sake, and almost killed Brendan's wife. It is our right."

A fierce expression overtook the king, and Kate was uncertain if he agreed with Colin. "My Lady, will you excuse us. I don't wish to speak of this brutal subject in front of you."

Kate rose, but Brendan grabbed her arm. He walked her to the door and kissed her before she left. She walked numbly toward her cottage. At least the audience with the king was behind her. Richard would be killed, but it didn't affect her.

He deserved to die for the evil deeds he'd done. Still, death wasn't something she took lightly.

Once she reached her cottage, she set her rope and candles on the floor. She couldn't help but cry now that it was over.

CHAPTER NINETEEN

It was just the beginning—the start of an all-out war against Richard de Morris.

Brendan waited for Katie to leave before he put in his opinion on the matter. Henry didn't give him a chance to speak, because he rose from his chair and called his scribe forward.

"I shall send word at once. My army will find Richard no matter where he is."

"Henry, I'm Katie's husband, with your approval. You should let me bring de Morris to justice. We don't need your army. We'll take care of de Morris and it's only right we seek retaliation."

"But it's my fault, Brendan. One of my vassals abducted Bonnie, killed Lady Kaitlin's father, and hurt her. If I don't do something…"

"She's my niece and Katie's my wife. Let Colin and me handle this. You've done enough by giving me Katie's hand. I haven't thanked you yet, have I?"

A smile tugged at Henry's mouth. He broke into laughter. "Brendan, I've never heard you speak so, married life changed you. Colin, did I hear Brendan MacKinnon thank me? I must be at my castle, tucked comfortably in my bed, dreaming this. 'Tis a day I never thought I'd see, the day

Brendan became gallant."

Colin lifted his cup and offered a toast. "You did right by accepting their marriage, Henry. I didn't think you would honor it, but how could you not? Brendan saved your arse that day by the loch."

Henry gave a disheartened look. "You told them? I asked you not to, damn but you're a pain in the arse, Brendan MacKinnon. Me thinks the lady is none too pleased to be your wife."

Brendan laughed. "Aye, but given time she'll accept me. She's beautiful and courageous."

"Courageous indeed. I cannot believe I agreed to this atrocity. I should never have betrothed her to the Barclay either. Nay, I should've met the woman first. Fortune shined on you Brendan and your clan when you found her. She is beautiful."

"Aye, but she's more than that. She's obstinate, beyond stubborn, and drives me to distraction, and I can't get enough of her. So tell me, where exactly does this de Morris live?"

Henry laughed and continued to tease him. "Colin, did he say she was stubborn? It sounds like a match made in heaven if you ask me. Mayhap I should be relieved you're married to her and not I?"

"Don't jest, Henry. We should discuss retaliation plans." Brendan paced in want to learn the man's whereabouts. He needed to be on his way.

Henry poured a cup of ale and started to speak when Burk, Walt, and Gil strode into the hall.

Walt reported, "Forgive us for interrupting, Colin, but we received word English forces sit on our border, the McFies have them cornered."

"Aye, it must be de Morris. He's been on our land, perhaps he's waiting for Katie." Brendan took out his dagger and studied its sharpness. "He told Katie if she didn't return with the medallion within a month, he'd send his army to her home. I believe he's waited to make sure she left."

Henry shot to his feet. "When the hell were you going to

tell me this? I'll send my men to protect her home. Colin, you and your men have my permission to seek de Morris."

Colin nodded to the men. "We'll meet in fifteen minutes by the stables. Walt, get our men ready. Give the order of arms."

"I must take care of something first." Brendan left the hall and walked down the hill. He shoved the door to Kate's cottage open and strode inside. She sat in a circle, and he smiled seeing her there. He knelt on one knee and gave a good show of skin when his tartan bunched above his thigh. He said nothing, but pulled her into his arms and kissed her. Brendan tightened his hold on her and lifted her against his body. She lolled against him, not being able to fight the feelings he aroused. His kiss turned to a smile. He pulled back and set her on the floor.

"I must go. I don't know how long I'll be, but I wanted to say goodbye. You'll be here when I return? I want your vow, wife."

She sucked in a breath at hearing him call her such. "I'm certain I'll be here when you return, but I shan't give you a vow."

"Katie, I don't have time to argue with you. I need to know you'll be here when I return and to know that you…" There he was, pleading again. He ground his jaw. Caring for the lass would cause him much consternation.

"I wish to discuss not living in England, Brendan. My people need me and I must return to them. I would expect—"

He kissed her quickly. "I must go, we'll discuss it later. Don't get into trouble." He turned and strode to the door. Perhaps time would attune her to the idea of being married to him—mayhap a great deal of time.

On his way to the stable, Brendan was fit to kill. He took on his usual mien for battle. The MacKinnon warriors rode out ready for war, fully armed, primed for a battle. Many men wore the blue paint they favored. At least one hundred soldiers rode down the hill. Colin called the Kerr clan and a few of his other allies because he wanted to confront the clootie who took his daughter. The men were in a vengeful mood, many wore hardened faces, and exhibited a serious tone in their speech.

"Brendan, do you deem it's them?" Gil asked.

"It likely is. We'll see when we get there, I suppose."

"Aye, then we'll set it to right."

"Aye, Gil, we will."

"No one kills him but me," Colin commanded.

Brendan wanted to dispute his brother's claim, but he concluded he'd take care of it when the time came. Aye, the man was his and his alone to inflict vengeance upon. When they arrived at the convergence, Brendan jumped from his warhorse, landed on his feet, and surveyed the foes in the distance. Ellic McFie awaited in the clearing with many of his soldiers.

"Ellic, it's a fine day for a scuffle, wouldn't you say?" Colin nodded a greeting. "How long have they been here? Have they made a move yet?"

"They've been here for about two days. Nay, the Sassenachs sit in the woods and haven't moved. There are about fifty men on the rise beyond us, and more beyond." He tilted his head in their direction. "I say we send them to hell. I don't know what they think they're doing squatting on our land, but we'll ask questions later."

Colin nodded in agreement.

The Highland warriors lined the base of the rise. They sat on their warhorses, ready for battle. The English soldiers speckled the horizon with their colorful banners. Their shiny armor reflected the sun, which sent a glare over the hill.

"It'll be easy to pick them off." Brendan noted their attire.

Many held red banners with a lion encircled by leaves. Colin indicated he tried to recall if he'd seen the emblem before, but he didn't recognize it. The English soldiers notched their arrows.

"I'm awaiting the Kerrs. Have they arrived yet, Ellic?"

Colin asked.

"Nay, they're not here yet. Douglas sent word he had troubles of his own at present, and couldn't come, but he would send men with Cedric."

"There are numerous arrows pointed at us, they'll likely darken the sky when they let 'em loose," Robin said.

"Good, then we'll have shade on us while we battle." Brendan paced before them, stopped and shielded his eyes, and searched the rise.

Colin, Ellic, and Robin grunted roughly at his remark. Brendan hadn't meant to make light of their impending battle, but the comment lightened the mood a bit. He held his sword in hand, slashed it side to side, as was his usual habit, and in his other hand, he held a foot-long dagger. Brendan always grew agitated before they warred, and he couldn't stand still. He continued to pace in front of the soldiers, a habit that drove Colin daft.

"Will you cease moving?" Colin placed his arms over his chest and scowled at his movement.

He stopped and turned toward him. "Let's go, I'm ready."

"We're not," Colin clipped.

"What the hell are we waiting for?"

"I'm waiting for our other allies to arrive."

"You've more coming?"

"Aye, of course."

"We can take them now, why wait? We well out-number them."

"Brendan, you're always impatient. I'm waiting for—"

"All right, Colin." Brendan continued to pace.

When the other soldiers arrived fifteen minutes later, Brendan insisted they forge to the fray.

"I'm pleased to see our allies arrived. Not because we need them to war with the English, but because you make me dizzy enough to spill my guts in the grass." Colin chuckled before he mounted his horse.

Colin sounded the battle cry and for the next two hours,

the men fought tirelessly. Swords clashed. Arrows flew. Weapons collided. Blood spilled. The Englishmen were no match for the Highlander warriors, and their forces were severely incapacitated. Several knights retreated into the forest and Brendan lost sight of Colin in the foray. When he finally saw him across the field, Brendan was slaying a man in his customary technique.

Colin approached. "Damn, Brendan, you're more bloodthirsty than I am. Aye, you're a ruthless fighter. Have you found anything out?"

"Nay, the knaves aren't talking."

"Why don't you leave some alive so we might question them?" Colin frowned.

"If I must," Brendan retorted dryly.

Colin laughed. He turned to see a man come at his back but didn't have time to react.

Brendan flung his dagger into the man's chest, and he fell backward to the ground. It happened in a split second, and Colin stood shocked for a moment in awe at the sheer force of his throw.

"My thanks. I didn't see him coming."

"Don't mention it." Brendan knelt next to the fallen man and plucked his dagger free. He wiped the blood on the man's tunic and returned to the fighting.

When most of the Englishmen were either lying on the ground or running for the hills, Brendan eased off the fight. The day was victorious in that the English would at least abscond. However, they had yet to find out who the knights were and why they camped on their land. Brendan hoped it was the Englishman he sought. He carried a man by the scruff of his neck—the soldier's feet barely touched the ground. He all but choked the man, turning his face red. When he reached Colin, he threw the man at his feet. Then Brendan positioned his sword at the man's heart.

"You're in a murderous mood this day. Your glare alone could kill the man." Colin folded his arms over his chest and took a relaxed stance. "Who is this, Brendan, a friend of yours? A neighbor perchance?"

Brendan glared. "That's not humorous, Colin. Don't speak to me about living in England. I swear to you, it will never happen. This man can talk, that's all I know." Brendan wasn't thrilled knowing Henry wanted him to live in England, and he hadn't given it consideration. Nay, he'd not leave his homeland for anything or anyone.

Colin pushed Brendan's sword away from the man. The man backed a foot away. "Mercy..."

"I want answers," Colin demanded.

"Aye, anything, just get him away from me."

"Are you Lord Richard de Morris' men?"

"We serve Lord de Morris. We came here with him and he told us to await him."

"Has he returned?"

"He told us we would stay here, that he awaited someone. He fought today," the young soldier supplied. Sweat rolled down the side of his face and he swiped it.

"Do you see him, look around," Colin commanded.

The man leaned from his position on the ground. He glanced at the field and shook his head. "Nay, he must've retreated with the others. We were told to keep you busy."

Brendan approached with his sword. He wanted to do the man in, but Colin stopped him.

"I've learned a good lesson from Steven. We'll send this man back with a message."

Brendan backed away from the man.

"Although, now that I think on it, the last time I sent a message it wasn't heeded by the Sassenach. Besides, why give him a warning?" Colin slapped him on the back and walked away. "Lord Richard de Morris," Colin said aloud. "Likely, he's run back to England with his tail between his legs, the coward. We'll return home and get his exact location."

"Are we going after him?" Robin asked.

"Damned right we are," Brendan answered for Colin, as he approached to stand next to them.

"We should stop by the loch before we head home. I

don't want my wife seeing us like this," Colin told them.

Night fell by the time they reached the loch. Several wounded men sat by the bank of the water. Colin had two soldiers tend the wounds of the few who had been struck. He directed them to bind and care for those who needed it. The more seriously injured were delivered to Jinny for aid. Warriors bathed in the loch, and a good number of tartans and tunics littered the trees and bushes, drying in the night breeze.

The soldiers' guard was let down, being near their home. Loud shouts and rambunctious play came from the water. The men were boisterous in recounting their actions of the day. Brendan bathed and sat beside a tree. He regarded Colin as he searched for him and Robin. It became a habit of his, to speak to them after battles. Colin had been responsible for them for a long time and always looked out for them. Not that they needed it. Robin caroused in the water with Gil, and they laughed over a tale another warrior told about a man he'd slain earlier.

"Brendan, are you all right?"

"Aye, why shouldn't I be?"

"You did well today. I haven't seen you fight in a long time. I always enjoy watching you combat."

Brendan nodded. "I want to find the knave and kill him. I won't rest until I do. He hurt Katie, damn it."

"You'll have to wait until I get his location from Henry. Richard de Morris is going nowhere."

"Nay, he's not." Brendan lifted his dagger and studied it. "I want to put this in his heart."

Colin sat next to him. "We need to talk about you're leaving. You will accept the land Henry gave you, Katie's lands."

"Nay." He absently used his dagger to scrape mud from his boots. He didn't want to discuss leaving, because as far as he was concerned it was a closed subject.

"She'll want to return to her home. She has property and must see to her people. Kate is too honorable to let her people down, Brendan. Will you let her go?" Colin stopped Brendan's hand, and he dropped his dagger.

"Can you explain something to me? You love Julianna?"

"Aye, with all my heart," Colin declared and placed his fist over his heart.

Brendan frowned. "What does that feel like? I don't understand what kind of love you're talking about...is. I might love Katie, but I'm uncertain."

"I'm taken aback, Brendan, you really want to know?"

"Aye, did I not ask?" He wasn't really sure why he'd asked his brother about love, but now that they spoke of it, his interest piqued. The awkward subject didn't affect him as it normally would.

"I cannot describe the sentiment, but I can tell you that I would die for her then I'd go to hell for her. Knowing she's part of me makes me who I am."

"That's absurd, Colin, I don't feel like that." Brendan still enraged from the fight, stood.

"So you will walk away?"

He scowled fiercely at his brother and turned back briefly. "Aye, I detest England."

Colin called after him. "But you might love Kate more than you detest England, Brendan."

He ignored his brother's remark and strode toward the keep. When he reached it, his stride increased. He intended to find his wife and to release his pent-up sexual tension. Quietly, he entered her cottage and noted she slept. She lay in a cocoon of covers. No fire lit the hearth, but the night was warm and none was needed. Brendan wanted her intensely. With that in mind, he stripped his garments hastily and joined her on the bed. He took her in his arms and kissed her roughly.

Kate awoke not knowing what happened. He covered her mouth with his. Once she realized who kissed her, she relaxed and wrapped her arms around his neck. Brendan was in a frantic state of heated passion, and every part of his body demanded release. He tore at her nightrail and covered her scream with his mouth. The kiss wasn't gentle either, but she didn't mind. She was as rough and fervent as he. His hands touched her everywhere. She cried out when he gripped her breasts with both his hands and used his thumbs to stroke her nipples. His harsh breath sounded in the room. He needed to be inside her. Exhilaration overrode any thought to be gentle, and he spread her legs and entered her. He drove into her repeatedly and reeled from the excitement. Carnal lust urged on his primitive response.

Brendan stopped abruptly. "Katie, am I hurting you?"

Her response was to pull his head down to return his kisses. He resumed his thrusts and his body spun out of control. Katie reached the pinnacle of her orgasm, and she screamed his name. Brendan grunted in satisfaction at her reaction. He yelled his climax to the rafters, and his body fell on top of hers in surrender. Aye, she'd weakened him. She held him close, his head cradled by her neck, and she fondled his hair. Her breath heated his skin and it allayed him and he smiled. He didn't move but continued to lie on top of her.

Brendan was overwhelmed by what happened. He used her vehemently, and he'd never taken a woman like that before. It didn't sit well with him either. Guilt pressed him, yet he couldn't look at her face to assess her expression. After minutes passed, he finally pulled out of her and rolled away. That's when he noticed she wept.

"Katie, did I hurt you? I didn't mean to be brutal. I...answer me." What in God's name was wrong with him? He prattled like a lad. Well, hell.

Kate cried harder. "You always make me cry. I don't usually do so, but you always make me."

Now he'd done it. He hurt her so badly, she wouldn't stop crying. He had to do something to soothe her and he enclosed her in his arms.

"Shhh, I didn't mean to hurt you. I would never..." he trailed off hearing her speak.

"It was beautiful, I never felt so...loved," she whispered her declaration and sighed.

Brendan didn't know what to make of her claim. His jaw tightened. How could she say that after he'd been rough with her? He squeezed her arm gently, but wouldn't acknowledge such feelings for her. He loved her, but wouldn't admit it aloud. A warrior wouldn't speak such nonsensical words. Brendan leaned forward and pulled the covers over them. He settled next to her and fell asleep within seconds with a frown on his face.

CHAPTER TWENTY

Kate lay for some time and watched him sleep. She longed to tell him the truth; that she loved him, had loved him for longer than she knew him. At least since his vision came to her. She wanted to say it outright—she loved him with her whole heart and he gave her a sense of contentment. He made her feel loved. The way her body responded to his astounded her. She regarded the man next to her as he held her tenderly. Admittedly, she didn't know much about him, he was as shut-down as a besieged castle. He didn't display much of himself to anyone, nor did he talk of his interest or his feelings. Brendan placed a stone wall around himself and none saw his tender side. What would it take to bring down those walls? Kate was certain she wouldn't do so.

He has a good heart but doesn't want anyone to know about it.

Julianna's words came to her. Brendan kept to himself and didn't share his views with anyone. That thought saddened her. If only she could draw him out. Had his demeanor always been serious? Brendan needed someone to care for him and she wanted it to be her. But that wouldn't be. He had no intention of going to England with her. If only she might renounce her father's fief, and remain with Brendan, but that would go against her father's bequeath.

Once she left the Highlands, it was unlikely she would

ever return. Her life with Brendan was over. She mustn't let her heart soften toward him further. Yet, she snuggled contentedly next to him, knowing she didn't have much more time with him. She would enjoy the few days that remained.

The next morning, Kate awoke and found Brendan gone again. Just once, she hoped to wake in his arms and have him kiss her before he stalked off to train. She snorted at that because it would take a cold day in hell for that to happen. A ride would lessen her woebegone nature. She ambled to the stable and luckily the stable master tended to the horses in the corral beyond the building. Kate needed to settle her nerves and a long relaxed ride would help. She took a saddled mare and galloped toward the open field where bales of hay made a maze.

She kicked her mount into a full run and the horse jolted at her demand. Its hooves moved fast and blurred the grass below. The mare's powerful body leaped in the air and she snorted and whinnied as if she was happy at the exercise. Blessedly, the mare obeyed her commands. Kate enjoyed the freedom. She'd always loved to ride fast and her laughter echoed through the field. When she heard someone clap, she peered at the nearby hill and noticed Bonnie. Her attention refocused on her task and the enjoyment of jumping the bales, and she hadn't realized people stood behind Bonnie.

It was a great way to begin the day. A rejuvenated aura overtook her, and she was giddy with excitement. No one would ruin her mood.

CHAPTER TWENTY-ONE

Brendan sulked throughout the morning training session. As he made his way from the training field to the hall, he spotted a crowd gathered at the top of the hill. He wondered what they looked at. Bonnie sat on the grass and peered below. He sat next to her and drew her attention. His minx of a niece was mesmerized by the view, as were the people who stood nearby.

"What are you looking at, fairy?"

"Kate."

"Kate? Where?"

"There." Bonnie pointed to the field.

Brendan gazed to where she'd pointed to, and his whole body turned rigid. His lady flew through the air on a damned horse. Not just any horse, but the one horse Colin told him was onerous, and not yet tamed. The horse landed beyond the bale. Kate's sunny laughter reached him, she laughed at her victory. He realized his breath was raucous, deep, and flared his nostrils with anger.

"How long has she been doing this?"

His niece hunched her shoulders. "She's a princess."

"Aye, lass, she is a princess."

Bonnie giggled. "Do you love her, Uncle Brendan?"

His niece smiled sweetly at her question and he grunted.

Bonnie snickered at his response. Kate finally noticed the crowd on the hill and her face reddened. She rode up the hill and dismounted near him. The people behind them walked away when their entertainment came to an end. He scowled and hoped she realized her jeopardy. But she must not have, because she had a fat smile on her face. She sat next to Bonnie and placed her arm around Bonnie's shoulder.

"Good morn, Bonnie. Brendan. It's a beautiful day."

"Katie." He gave her a hard look.

"Why are you not off trying to find de Morris or on the training field? I'm shocked to see you here wasting your morn. What are you doing here?"

"I believe I watched a bean-sith trying to kill herself. Why would you endanger yourself?"

"I wasn't in danger. I always—"

"You'll not ride like that again, not on that horse," he ordered.

"I don't answer to you, Brendan. I'll ride whenever I want, and on whatever horse I choose. I enjoy riding fast and jumping over bales."

"Bonnie, return to the keep. We'll see you later." He patted her leg to get her moving.

Kate lifted her arm and was about to stop her from leaving, but his niece moved with amazing speed and ran beyond her reach.

"You had no right to send her away, Brendan. I promised to—"

"Katie, I mean what I said. I don't want you riding like that again. Now, give me your word."

She looked him in the eye. "No."

Incredulous, he said, "Nay?"

"I always ride so and have since I was young. I don't answer to you."

"Why is that? You're an obstinate lass, you know that."

"What are you talking about?" Kate clenched her hands and shot daggers at him with her eyes.

"I want your promise, now." Brendan doubted she

would make such a promise, but he stood his ground and gave a ferocious frown.

"I promise."

Brendan grunted his approval at her compliance.

"What did I promise?"

His jaw flinched and his scowl deepened. "You're the most confusing woman. If you don't know when you're in danger, I'll have to..." Brendan gave up. He pulled her into his arms and kissed her. He set her back on the grass, touched her gently, his kiss tender. His tongue caressed hers as though he tried to melt into her. Kate groaned. He growled.

He continued to kiss her. Lying next to her felt too darned good. Brendan's entire length squeezed the whole of her body. His hands held her head still so he could ravish her mouth, though gently, especially after last night. If he continued, he suspected he'd take her there where anyone could come along.

He pulled back, his mouth a scant inch from hers. "You make me forget myself, and where we are."

"Brendan, please, I..."

"I was rough with you last night. Are you angry with me?"

"You weren't rough. I thought what we shared was beautiful."

The woman pleased him. He was a wee bit astounded she liked rough sex and would have to remember that next time they made love.

"Promise me you'll not ride a horse astride again."

"I enjoy riding a horse like that, Brendan. I was perfectly safe."

"It wasn't safe, Katie. That horse wasn't broken yet and is not used to riders. You ride well. I didn't know." Maybe the horse was affected by her spirit and perhaps she used a wee mystic power to lure the beast into accepting her on its back.

She stared into his eyes, which pierced hers. "Why are you displeased, Brendan?"

He ignored her question. "Did you mean what you said last night?" His hands rubbed her shoulders and gently persuaded her to relax.

"What did I say?"

"That you love me. You said it on our wedding day, and last night." His eyes bore into hers in wait for her answer. Would she deny it? He didn't know why, but he needed to hear her declaration.

"Did I? I suppose I meant it. Though I believe I meant you made me feel loved. Aye, that is what I meant."

"What about now?"

"Now? You're asking me if I love you right now?"

"Aye, do you?" He felt assailable and didn't like the feeling of it either. Why had he set himself up for a letdown? He squeezed her shoulder to get her answer.

"Aye, Brendan, I love you right now, right this minute even though you're making it difficult."

"Now and forever?" A sudden urge to grin came over him. He pulled her chin toward him when she turned her face to look at the field. "Say it," he demanded.

She tried to hide the distress in her voice. "Now…and…forever."

He kissed her softly to seal her vow. His hair caressed her cheek when his lips touched hers. She looked at him with affection, and he realized how deeply in love with her, he was.

"I love you too, lass." Brendan flinched when he spoke aloud. But he had said it low and was unsure she'd heard him.

"Did you say that you love me, Brendan? I thought I heard you say—"

"Katie, I'm a warrior."

"I know what you are. Well?"

"Warriors don't love, they fight." He glowered at the thought they discussed the inane subject.

"They don't love?"

"Nay, I don't have it in me to love. I care for you though and want to see you safe. I will protect you. There's no foe I cannot best."

Kate laughed at his arrogance. "Care? Safe? Protect? You make me sound akin to a little girl in need of a father's protection. I don't need you for that, Brendan."

"What do you need me for?" He wanted her acceptance, mayhap because he hadn't been accepted by anyone except by his brothers. She didn't seem to know how to answer. "You need my protection, Katie. I cannot love you as you want, but I admit you're important to me."

"I am?"

"Aye, you are." Brendan kissed her again.

Kate became unbridled when the kiss turned passionate. At that moment, nothing mattered but the woman held in his arms. He wouldn't speak of his affections aloud again.

"Brendan." His brother, Robin, called from a distance.

Brendan ignored him because he didn't want to stop kissing her. He felt content. Aye, and safe from having to admit to himself the feelings she aroused.

"We're having a meeting in the hall in fifteen minutes," Robin yelled.

Brendan pulled away from her again. "You're my wife. I want to hear you admit it. You'll start behaving as a wife who loves her husband should."

"I should be angry with you for tricking me. I'll admit to being your wife when you admit you love me. And when I hear you say you'll live with me in England."

Brendan raised his brow. "Then you'll never admit to being my wife. I won't leave the Highlands for you, Katie. You will stay here with me. I expect you to obey and do as I say."

"Obey you? I haven't obeyed anyone since my father left four years ago."

"Four years?" He shook his head. Had she been alone all that time? "Katie, I have your best interest at heart when I direct you."

"Do you? You only have your interests at heart, Brendan. I didn't deem you would leave your beloved Highlands for me, so nay, I shan't admit to being your wife.

If I mattered as much as you say I do, then you would go with me."

Brendan sighed. He supposed what she said was true. "I have to go. I'll see you at supper." He rose and quickly walked off. On his way to the holding, Brendan realized he'd have to keep Katie away from Henry. She would surely ask him to annul their marriage, and he wasn't about to have that. Aye, the woman needed to stay away from the king or he'd be doomed.

CHAPTER TWENTY-TWO

Kate awoke the next morning and found herself alone again. She pulled the pillow he'd used against her chest and hugged it tightly. His warmth and scent lingered. Her brows furrowed as she wondered why he always left in the morning before she awoke. He definitely wasn't a morning person. After thinking that, she realized he wasn't an afternoon person or an evening person either. He was just downright grumpy.

She hurriedly dressed and wrapped the MacKinnon tartan around her in the usual fashion. On her way to the hall, women waved. With a self-assured smile, she returned their joyful greetings. She'd promised to meet Bonnie in the morning, and when she approached the castle, she saw her waiting on the steps. Her little face lit with a smile.

"Good morn, Bonnie."

"I didn't think you would come."

"I promised, didn't I? What do you want to do today?"

"I want to show you and Honey the new pony Papa gaved me."

"Your papa gave you a new pony? Was this before or after you returned?"

Bonnie nodded. "After."

Kate laughed. Poor Colin gave the child a guilt gift.

Didn't he realize it wasn't his fault she'd been abducted? His daughter was taken by a loathsome snake and every time she thought about the little girl being held at the de Morris' manor, she trembled. But she thanked the Goddess for sending her there and rescuing the sprite.

"Come along then. Did you say Honey was coming?"

Kate took her hand, but before they moved off toward the stables, the king strolled through the doorway of the keep with two guardsmen following. He dressed rather plainly and wore a dark-blue tunic over dark leggings. His brown hair tousled as though he'd just awakened.

"The sun has barely risen. I don't believe I ever woke this early. My Lady, Kate," he said and bowed, "Bonnie tells me we're to go riding. I hope you don't mind if I join you."

"Certainly not, Your Grace. I look forward to it. I apologize for riding at such an early hour. I hope it's not too early for you."

"When the little mite told me we'd go riding, I had no idea she meant at sunrise." He grinned, to show his manner lighthearted.

It seemed to Kate that she wasn't Bonnie's favorite person any longer. Instead of holding her hand as she usually did, Bonnie held the king's. She smiled at their special friendship. At the stables, the master came forward when they entered. He grumbled under his breath. For a moment, Kate thought he'd make them ready their own horses. Perhaps the master's disgruntlement had something to do with the king's presence? Highlanders didn't much care for the English, and here was the most English man of the lot. She smiled at that.

"That's Marvin," Bonnie cupped her hand and whispered. "He doesn't like ladies in here. He always tells me that I'm too wee to be inside."

Kate laughed. "I see a beautiful horse over there. That's the one I'll ride. Where's your pony?"

Bonnie shook her head. "Oh, nay, Kate, the ladies never choose her 'cause she's not easy to control. Mama told Papa that she needed more training before she would ride her."

"That doesn't bother me, she'll do just fine. Besides, I rode her yesterday and she did well." Kate held her hand out and offered the beautiful mare a small carrot end.

"Marvin," Kate called, "put a harness on her for me?"

"Milady, I cannot, my laird would never forgive me for letting you ride 'er. Pick another. There be a gentler mare in the next stall."

"Nay, she's the one I want. Get her ready, and Bonnie's new pony. Your Grace, which horse is yours?"

The stable master grunted.

"My men will ready my horse." Henry motioned to his squire.

"We'll wait outside." Kate took Bonnie's hand and strode into the sunshine.

Marvin brought two mounts outside and handed the reins to Kate. "I don't know anything about this. Brendan will have my arse on the ground if he hears of it," he muttered and walked away. "He bade me not to let you ride her. Nay, I know nothing about it."

Kate laughed at his obvious dislike for letting her ride the mare. She assisted Bonnie onto her pony and pulled herself up on her own mare. The mare whinnied and bucked a few times before settling down. She soothed her with a gentle stroke. The king walked from the stable holding his horse's reins, and he too mounted his horse.

"It's a beautiful day for riding. Shall we proceed, ladies?"

Bonnie giggled at being called a lady. They rode around the keep's walls.

"What do you think of my pony, Kate?"

"She's beautiful, Bonnie, and perfect for you. I've never seen a pony with fawn coloring before. Why she even has white speckles on her coat. You should call her Deer."

Bonnie giggled. "Dame Hester calls me dearheart, sometimes."

"Nay, I meant like a deer, you know, animals that live in the forests." Kate laughed.

Henry grinned.

"Aye, I like the name, I will call her Deer."

Kate smiled. She loved riding and at home, she often rode in the fields, similar to the one before them. A feeling of homesickness engulfed her. "Your Grace, I want to ask if I might be escorted by you on your return to England."

Henry pulled his horse to a stop. "Bonnie, we're going to sit on this hill, and you can ride your pony in the field. Be careful sweeten, your papa will be angry with me if you hurt yourself."

Bonnie gleefully rode ahead, and Kate dismounted. They sat on the hillside and watched her.

"I wanted to speak to you about this. I would be glad to escort you home, Lady MacKinnon."

"Your Grace, please, call me Kate. I thank you for your favor."

"Kate, you have a lovely name. My favor hardly repays you for saving my cousin's daughter. Bonnie means much to me. Now that I think of it, I believe it was your fate to travel to Richard's keep. You were meant to find Bonnie and aid her. I suppose you're angry with me for betrothing you to a Scotsman, but then you did marry another. Tell me, what does your husband say about your leaving?"

"I know not. Every time I broach the topic with Brendan, he changes the subject or ignores me. He's fond of his homeland and I don't believe he intends to leave it. He said he wouldn't leave, yet I must return to my people. Mayhap marrying Brendan wasn't such a good idea, but I'm not angry and am happy to have known him."

"Do you love him?" Henry watched Bonnie ride around the bales of hay, and didn't take his eyes off her while she rode on the field. Her laughter sounded.

"I suppose I do, but it matters not. I have an obligation to my father's people."

"Kate, I apologize for causing you distress by agreeing to your marriage to Brendan. But you are right, you have an obligation to your people. He may change his mind. Mayhap staying in Scotland is not worth losing you."

She blushed. "Oh, Your Grace, it's kind of you to say, but I sincerely doubt losing me would matter to Brendan MacKinnon. Have you seen him this day?"

"He left the holding. Colin and his men are on their way to Richard's keep."

"I see." Kate picked at the grass and tried not to show dejection at him leaving without a farewell. Why would he say goodbye? He answered to no one but himself. She was only his wife and probably not as important to him as his sword. Her sorrowful attitude of late was unbecoming. Where was the sweet-natured woman who made everyone around her joyous? She longed to return to her jovial self.

"He'll return before you know it, and you shall return home. I wanted to speak to you about your father. Hawk was a good man and I grieve for his loss. If only de Guylet hadn't sent him to Egypt, those damned holy wars have taken many of our men. If I were in full power, you can be certain I wouldn't have allowed more of our men to die for Rome's sake."

"Will you be all right with Bonnie? I want to return to my cottage."

"She'll have me out here for hours, no doubt." Henry stood when she did.

Kate waved to Bonnie and rode to stable her horse. When she reached her cottage, she stood outside and held the wood frame of the door. She wondered if there was a way to get Brendan to change his mind and go with her when she left. How would she accomplish that? Unless she used a potent spell, nothing would make him leave. It wasn't as if he loved her, not the stubborn Highlander. Better yet, a love potion would make him see reason. Nay, she couldn't give him a potion. If Brendan MacKinnon loved her, he would do so on his own accord.

"Goddess, send me the answer," she said aloud as she entered the cottage. She sat at the table with a frown. Trixie jumped onto her lap, and she petted her. Kate was pressed for time but didn't know when they would leave. If they left as soon as Brendan returned, she wouldn't have time to convince him that he loved her.

She realized she hadn't seen the vision once since she met Brendan. Not once during her morning ritual or when she meditated had she seen the vision. It was gone, probably for good. Had the spirits tormented her all that time? Perhaps her happiness wasn't part of the plan. Thinking of the past brought forth images of Madam Serena. Her vision had been accurate. She'd gone on a solemn journey because of the child, and she'd met the fierce warrior of her visions. She never counted on the heartache that came along with him. Then she remembered what Madam said: the warrior would cause her grief, but it was well-meaning. Did that mean Brendan MacKinnon loved her? Kate hurried and erected her circle. Maybe if she prayed hard enough, her answers would come.

CHAPTER TWENTY-THREE

Satisfaction was close, Brendan tensed with it. He peered ahead into the dense woods and listened to the sound of footsteps clanking wood planks. The de Morris holding was ahead and he motioned to the others and waited for the riders to near. He couldn't believe his eyes as he approached the manor. In a quick dismount, he assessed the guards and counted the watchmen. Colin, Gil, and Walt stood next to him, each gauged the inadequacies of the guard posted.

"They almost make it too easy." Brendan walked beside them.

They scaled the walls in the dark of night. The guardsmen never heard their approach. They subdued the ten men who protected the walls, and then they made their ascent on the keep itself. A barred doorway obstructed their view of the inside bailey.

"There must be another way in," Colin said.

They moved to the back of the holding where several MacKinnon men strode along the walls in search of another entrance. Most holdings had an additional entrance and they suspected this one had as well.

Gil motioned to Brendan. "I spotted a wooden doorway behind this large shrub."

Gil pushed the door, but it wouldn't budge. Brendan

stepped back and went at the door with his body. The door gave way as his large body forced the old wooden hinges to bend. They found themselves inside a small darkened chamber. Only three fit inside at once. Gil lit a candle and bent to place it on the floor. They were inside a small garrison where weapons were stored on shelves.

Colin directed the men to guard the room so Richard's soldiers couldn't get to it. The room led to a long hallway, which in turn, led to the main hall. A lady sat at the table, apparently unconcerned about their approach. Brendan stepped beside his brother as the MacKinnons instantaneously surrounded her.

"Where is Lord Richard?" Colin asked.

"My Lords, welcome, I am Lady de Morris."

Brendan wondered what Colin was about when he pulled the lady from her seat.

Colin grasped the woman's hair tightly and held her close to his face. His brother's look was enough to send the woman to a swoon, but she dared to glare at him.

"You're the woman who cared for my child?" His brother shouted the question and the woman's eyes widened.

"Did you care for the lass your husband abducted?" Colin shook the woman. "Answer me."

The woman screamed and hastily shook her head. His brother disbelieved her. Colin forcibly shoved the woman aside and she cried out.

Colin rasped with anger. "How could you beat a defenseless child? I should kill you."

The woman's fear sent her to a faint.

"Brendan, get me out of here before I kill the woman."

Brendan backed away from the table and forced his brother to follow. "Do you think de Morris is here?" He eyed the woman as he left, all but dismissing her as they searched the keep for Richard. Disgusted by the care of the manor, Brendan searched room to room.

Colin met him outside the room he inspected. "I cannot believe my poor bairn was held prisoner in this filthy pigsty.

I'm even more incensed. God has my gratitude for sending Kate to my bairn." He voiced his affront and shared a heated look with Brendan.

Brendan continued to search the upstairs chambers and ran across a maid who volunteered information on the whereabouts of de Morris. He joined his brother in the hall after a thorough search, after he assured himself the man withdrew.

"Colin, a maid upstairs told me Lord Richard fled to another keep located a few miles to the south. He's not here."

Colin gave the signal and they departed the de Morris keep. Brendan rode along in silence. Forty MacKinnon warriors trudged along on the mission. The mist made the air dense, but the early morning sun tried to cut through it. Brendan didn't mind the dreariness, because he was used to being in cold and wet weather. The closer they got to the holding they searched for, the more agitated he became. All were quiet, except for Colin.

Colin spoke softly, "I was enraged at the condition of the keep my daughter was held in. It makes me incensed every time I think of it. We should be close. Do you deem he'll be there?"

"If he's not there, we'll keep looking."

They reached the location, a keep enclosed by a stone wall. Brendan jumped from his horse and climbed a tree to get a better look. He surveyed the holding from the branches of the tree he scaled and watched the sentry posted for signs of weaknesses.

"Let us ride to the wall. We have the proclamation from Henry. That should secure us an invite inside." Brendan smiled at that knowing it wasn't true. No man, even an Englishman, would invite them inside given they looked ready for battle. Mayhap they appeared as though they had just fought in a hundred-year war.

Brendan stopped his mount next to his brother's, and the rest of Colin's men filed in behind them. A man approached the threshold of the rampart. Their size intimated many men, yet the large red-haired guardsman courageously leaned over the wall.

"Who goes there? What do ye here?" He cupped his hands and bellowed.

"I'm looking for Richard de Morris. Is he within?" Colin shouted as he looked up at the stout man and shielded his eyes against the backdrop of the rising sun.

"Nay, he's not here."

"Who are you?" Colin asked.

"Who am I? Who the hell are you? You've come to my wall, so you'll be telling me first, who you are, and what you want of Richard."

"I'm Colin MacKinnon. I'm going to kill Richard de Morris." Colin took his sword from his scabbard and aimed it forward.

"Rather blunt, are you not, Scot? Richard is a friend. What did he do to make you want to kill him?" The man leaned on the crenellation in wait for his answer.

"Send the devil out so I can kill him. I don't have to explain myself to you."

The man grunted. "If you want access to my keep, you'll tell me why."

Colin practically growled at the man. "He abducted my child and held her in the filthy pigsty, he calls home. He took her from the king's castle grounds, from under his protection. He threatened my sister-in-law's life and that of her tenants. He deserves to die."

"Well, damnation. I don't know where he is. He left a few days ago."

Brendan touched his sword's handle and itched to draw it out. "He lies. The maid said he'd left a few hours ago."

"Where did he go?" Colin shouted.

"I know not. He stopped by for a short visit."

"Who the hell are you?" Colin demanded.

"Harry Fitzhugh. See here, the man's not here. I won't have you storm my keep. You'll be on your way now."

"You haven't heard the last of us, Fitzhugh," Colin said

and turned his horse.

Brendan nudged his horse next to his brother's. "What will we do now? Should we storm the holding and see for ourselves? Let's overtake the keep. I'm ready to fight."

"Aye, I know you are, Brendan. We certainly will storm the keep, but not until I have my men survey Fitzhugh's holding."

"Why wait? We should rush in there as we did at de Morris'."

Colin's face turned stern, a look Brendan understood.

"I'm not an arse, Brendan, and won't rush in there without knowing how many men we face or what the lay of the land is. I won't risk my men's necks without knowing the details. Who knows what this Fitzhugh's soldiers number. Let us make them believe we retreated. We'll move to the woods and discuss our battle plan. I'll not leave England until I find the clootie."

Brendan grimaced. "Neither will I." He didn't particularly agree with his brother's plan, but Colin was sensible when it came to warring. Brendan was more a fighter than a strategic thinker, which was one of the traits he admired in his brother. Still, he was sure if they invaded the keep, Fitzhugh wouldn't thwart them. He wasn't about to contradict his brother's reason and decided to keep his thoughts to himself.

They rode into the woods and made camp. Colin, Walt, and Gil crouched next to a drawn layout of the keep inscribed with a stick on the ground. Colin marked the posted guards. "How many men do you think Fitzhugh has inside?"

Brendan paced in his customary manner. "Will it matter?"

"Nay, but I need you at your best, Brendan. Do you deem you can put aside your strife for the man and the king's demand aside? You must focus on the coming battle."

"It's been put aside. Cease harping like an old woman. It matters not that I fight the English." To assure his brother, Brendan unsheathed his sword.

"I noticed flaws in the keep's design. We shouldn't scale the wall, but go behind and see what's there. Better to do the unexpected. We'll wait until nightfall."

"Aye, I agree. They'll expect us to come at the gate again or lay siege. Fitzhugh seems confidant his holding is secure, which makes me think he has a good number of soldiers inside."

"That could well be a diversionary tactic, Colin. I guess we'll see when we return."

The men rode hard back to Fitzhugh's holding when the sky darkened. Both men and beasts were aptly tuned for battle, and the anticipation of finding Richard de Morris lent a spark of energy to them. Brendan wiped the paint from his face because he wanted Richard de Morris to see his expression, to know his adversary, and to see the look of pure hatred when he killed him. When they reached the keep all was quiet, too quiet.

Colin whispered, "Something's amiss. Can you hear anything?"

"There's no one inside the lower bailey or atop the walls. I don't hear anyone about, yet it's early evening. There should be people milling about or a sentry posted. Do you deem it's a trap?" Gil said.

"Aye, it's definitely an ambush. Let's scale the walls and find out." Brendan's impatience wore him down and he paced while they discussed nonsense.

Colin shook his head. "I don't know how many soldiers Fitzhugh has. I'm hesitant to walk into an ambush. We know not if Fitzhugh has mercenaries or more knights inside."

"Let us storm the keep and find out." Brendan climbed the rampart of the stone crenellation, and no soldiers stood atop. He looked below to the courtyard, and no people walked along, not even a servant, soldier, or craftsman. "My senses tell me there is doom within, Colin. I can't deny my instinct." Brendan kept his eyes trained on the entrance of the manor but didn't see movement.

Colin motioned to his men and they made their advance

on the manor. They slunk down the walls, through the courtyard, and reached the door. They moved like shadows, hidden in the recesses of nooks along the way. It didn't matter, no alert sounded.

Once inside the keep, they found Fitzhugh. They stood and stared, Fitzhugh didn't move.

"Ah, Fitzhugh had a feast without us, lads." Colin's jest didn't gain a single laugh from Fitzhugh, or from his men. His voice wasn't at all jesting. Fitzhugh was dead, sitting at his table as if he enjoyed a fine banquet. Uneaten food remained on the table, and Fitzhugh was sliced at the throat. The attack killed him instantly.

"What the hell happened here?" Walt asked as he came from the hall that led from the back.

"It looks as though a friend might've turned on Fitzhugh whilst he enjoyed a fine supper. Let's find the servants, there must be some around," Colin said.

"My question is: where are his soldiers?" Brendan listened for sounds inside the manor.

As they scurried throughout the keep, they found several servants hiding in chambers above and below the main floor. They gathered them in a large chamber next to the hall. Fitzhugh's people appeared frightened and they crowded together in a corner. Brendan approached an older man, who looked as though he might offer information.

"Sir, I'm Brendan MacKinnon. His majesty, King Henry, sent us here to find Lord Richard de Morris. Has he been here?"

The man was aged. Brendan thought he might be hard of hearing, so he questioned him again in a louder voice. He hoped the man was forthcoming because the women looked as though they would swoon if approached.

"I can hear ye, no need to shout," he grumbled. "You say you're from the king?"

"Aye, we are. What happened here? Your lord is dead. Can you tell me anything?"

"What's your name, son?"

"Brendan MacKinnon, at your service." He rolled his eyes heavenward and frowned. Couldn't the man hear him? He said he had, yet didn't. Brendan decided to use intimidation tactics to gain his compliance. He stepped forward and towered over the man. Of course, the man's back hunched slightly and made him appear bent over.

The old man waved his hand at Brendan. "Back up, lad, I won't crane my neck to the likes of you, looking up at ye. Lord Richard was..." The man coughed and sputtered.

Brendan hoped to get answers before the man keeled in front of him. He stepped forward again and pounded the man's back, for which he received a grimace and the man's drawn-in breath.

A dauntless elder lady stepped forward. "Sir, let him be. Davy always coughs like that." She helped the man to a chair and turned to him.

Brendan thought perhaps the lady was the aged man's wife. She spoke rather loudly, likely from having to speak to her husband.

"Sir, Lord Richard was here earlier. He and Lord Harry fought. None saw Lord Richard kill him, but we know he did. After the servants set the food, they were directed to leave. We found our lord dead, and we were afeard Lord Richard remained, and that he would kill us, too." She stopped to pat Davy on the back and continued, "Lord Richard must've run off a short while ago. And many of the servants did as well."

"Where are Fitzhugh's soldiers?"

"My lord's men were severely decreased due to the crusade. He lost most of his wealth and hadn't paid the knights. Many left when their service ended." Davy supplied the information.

Brendan nodded. "Damn, he's gone again, Colin," he all but shouted.

The aged man didn't regard his aggravated state and mumbled absently, "The lot of them ran off and left us to see to the Lord. They be frightened of spirits and claimed the lordship's ghost would kill them. Our lord wasn't all that bad, was he, Mary?"

Mary didn't answer but gave a disgruntled look. So like a wife to disagree with her husband. Brendan envisioned Katie's expression, one of which rivaled Mary's.

"Is there anything we can do before we leave, old man?"

"Aye, ye might want to let the king know about our Lord. Have him send someone…" The old man commenced coughing again and Mary pounded his back.

Brendan nodded and followed his brother to the door.

Colin groused that he was in need of a good soak in the loch to remove the stink from being in such filthy keeps. Brendan couldn't agree more. After visiting Fitzhugh and de Morris', a good dip in the loch was well-needed. He wouldn't feel clean again until he returned home to his beloved Highlands.

As they left Fitzhugh's holding, several knights surprised them. Brendan pulled his sword free and took up the fight. At least, he was able to release his frustration at not finding Richard. He held his foot to a man's neck on the ground and used his dagger's butt to knock him unconscious. When he looked around for more foes, the fight ended. Colin motioned for them to move into the forest, where their steeds waited.

They rode to a clearing, an hour's ride from Fitzhugh's keep, and surveyed the damage to their men. Several men were wounded and needed tending. Brendan made a fire while Colin gauged their injuries.

Colin winced when he saw Walt lying on the ground. He ran to him and knelt beside him. "Walter, where are you hurt?"

"I'm struck in me chest. It doesn't bode well, lad."

"You'll be all right, Walt." He looked around for his brothers and assessed the wound.

"Nay, don't bother, 'tis a grave day for me, lad. I must speak to Brendan before I die. Get 'em for me." Walt's chest heaved.

Colin paced beside Walt and glowered. "Walt, you

cannot tell him. The news will destroy him."

"I cannot die without telling him. He deserved the truth long ago. I always promised I'd tell him one day, and that day is today. Get 'em now," Walt insisted in the strongest voice he could muster.

"Brendan," Colin shouted over the camp.

Brendan heard the shout and he strode toward Colin and Walt. He knelt beside Walt and noticed the blood soaking his tunic. "Are you all right? Got yourself injured?"

"Listen, lad, I have something to tell you…before I meet me maker."

"Walt, you won't die. Let us take care of you. Colin, send for Ben, he's good at tending wounds. We'll have you healed in no time."

"Nay, 'tis a fine day for death and I will meet it like a man." Walt grabbed Brendan's tunic and pulled him close.

Walt's strength amazed Brendan. Even with his injury, he forced him closer. Brendan helped him to a sitting position and held his shoulders.

"I should've told you years ago, not now when it matters not… Och, I never had the heart. Your mother and I… We had an affair long ago. I loved her more than any woman. You're not Donald MacKinnon's son."

"I'm not?" Brendan spoke low as the words sunk into his mind. Not Donald MacKinnon's son. He searched Walt's face for verity and looked into his own gray eyes. Now that he looked at Walt intently, he realized he looked at an older version of himself. Why hadn't he realized the resemblance between them before?

"Nay, you're my son. I want you to know how p-proud I am of you, l-lad." Walt's voice broke on the last word and he sobbed.

Brendan slouched at the news and released Walt's shoulders. "You're my father? Not Donald MacKinnon? I don't know what to say."

"Aye, Maggie gave you to me, but I couldn't tell you ere now. I shouldn't have kept it from you, but I was sworn to take it to my grave. I always w-wanted to claim you."

"Why... Why didn't you tell me?" Brendan sank back and scowled intently.

"Maggie made me promise not to tell you. I uh..." Walt weakened and his voice faltered.

Colin leaned over him and joined the conversation. "Walt, you've always been like a father to us, all of us. We care about you, too."

"You're good lads. Continue to care for...each other. You are good s-sons." Walt closed his eyes, the pain in his chest evident on his face.

"Walt," Brendan shouted and shoved Colin out of his way. He sprawled over him and called his name. It couldn't end like this, he needed to speak to him, wanted to tell him how much he respected him.

Walt whispered, "Lad, I lost my love...don't lose yours. Do you hear me, son?"

Brendan nodded. Walt's breathing ceased. His blood covered Brendan's tunic, but he wouldn't release him. Colin tried to get him to discharge Walter, but he wouldn't budge.

"Brendan, he's gone. There's nothing we can do for him now. Release him."

He shook his head. "How could I have not known?"

Colin didn't answer. "We have to get him on a horse and away from here. We'll take him home and bury him. He must be placed with honor."

Brendan didn't listen. Seethed with hostility, he wanted to pound something. "You are not surprised by his news. Why? Did you know? How long have you known?" His voice lowered and forewarned his brother of his rage. He wanted to flail Colin alive. His chest butted against Colin's aggressively, they'd come to blows. As anger increased his actions, Brendan couldn't help his enraged reaction.

Colin shoved him backward and returned his furious look. "Back off, Brendan. You don't want to do this. I won't lie to you, but you'll get indignant. Damn it to hell, if I told you long ago, you would've overreacted. I didn't want to upset you, and besides, Walt made me promise not to tell you. I would never deceive him."

"Mayhap I don't want to know this," Brendan groaned out and backed up a step.

"I should've told you when I found out Walt was your father. I learned of it before you told me about our ma's plight. Do you remember? It was when Julianna left me and I was a wreck."

"Aye, I remember. He made you vow never to tell me, and you disregarded my feelings on the matter? Were you ever going to tell me?" Brendan's throat constricted.

"I know not, Brendan, but Walt promised Ma he wouldn't tell you. He never did. I couldn't go back on his request, but I suppose I would've eventually told you. Walt was a man of honor, Brendan. You should be proud he was your father. Count yourself blessed you weren't born from Donald MacKinnon."

"I should have spent more time with him, Colin, and be his son as I would've liked. Dammit, I find out when it's too late and when it doesn't matter."

Colin placed his hand on Brendan's shoulder apologetically. "It's not too late to honor him. Come and help me get him on his horse so we can take him home."

They lifted Walt on his horse and tied him with rope to keep him from falling. Brendan retreated. He mounted his horse and kept his gaze ahead. All those years he lived a lie. He would've been honored to have Walt as his father. Instead, he lived with rejection from a father he'd craved attention from. Fortunately, he'd had his brothers while rearing, but Donald's rejection affected him. He'd never gotten over his supposed father's dislike. Donald's aversion was the sole reason for his demeanor, but he couldn't help that. It had been best to remain distant, unnoticed, and thereby unaffected by his father's harsh manner.

As he rode home, Brendan thought of the times he'd spent with Walt—the battles they'd gone through together, the nights they spent by the campfire when hunting, and the times they drank ale and jested with the soldiers. Walt entertained him with stories from his childhood and jested about his difficulties when he'd been learning to fight. Brendan would miss him sorely. He was the father he'd always wanted but never had.

CHAPTER TWENTY-FOUR

The entire MacKinnon clan attended Walter Ross' burial. Most ladies cried and some of the men had a tear, too. Walter, their beloved commander-in-arms, held in the highest esteem by the clan's people died a warrior's death. Father Tomas' heartfelt words rang true. Walt died in battle as a strong warrior should. It was the wish of all Highland warriors to do so, and according to their custom, they shouldn't be mourned—if they died doing their duty. Colin always kept that oath. Whenever his men died in battle, he didn't mourn them, because it was an insult. It was a sad day for the clan and a dismal day for Colin. Not only because of Walt's death but because Brendan became distant toward everyone, even him.

Colin stood by Julianna. She resisted her sorrow. Walt was like a father to her too, and she would miss his gaiety and counsel. He helped her adjust to Highland life when she married Colin. Colin squeezed her hand and tried not to appear grim. His wife watched Brendan, who stood obstinately erect and showed no outward emotion. Brendan kept himself in check, his eyes downcast as if he searched for a sign from the wooden box. It wasn't to come.

When Walter was placed in the ground, Brendan turned and marched away. His brother strode past Kate and didn't give her a glance or greeting. Upon their return, Brendan stayed in the barracks, and according to Julianna, he hadn't visited Kate. He suspected this would happen. His brother's standoffish attitude would cause more problems, but Brendan didn't seem to care. Colin wanted to go after him, but Julianna stopped him.

"Colin, let him be. He needs time to adjust to the fact that Walt was his father and has died. He must do so before he can properly mourn him. Let him alone for a while."

"I cannot. You know how he is; he's going off to sulk. I cannot let him. He might not ever return." Colin stared after his brother.

Julianna caressed his chest with a gentle stroke. "He needs time, Colin, he'll return when he's ready."

"Brendan doesn't have time. Kate wants to return to England. If Brendan doesn't go to her soon, she'll leave without him. I don't like that de Morris is still on the loose. He intends to kill her. Until we dispatch him, I'll worry about her."

"I know, Colin, but it's his decision. Mayhap she should go without him. Henry will protect her until Brendan comes to his senses."

Colin walked beside her and held her hand. She was right, but he felt somewhat responsible for what his brother was feeling. He should have told him the truth years ago.

"Colin, Julianna." Henry approached them in the lower bailey. "I need to discuss Kate and our departure with you."

"Aye, I know what you're going to say, Henry. Come to the hall."

Julianna stopped Colin. "I'm going to speak to Bonnie. She's upset about Walt's death, and she somehow found out about George."

"Ah, the poor Button. Come for me if you need me." He entered the hall with Henry in tow and turned to him when he reached the trestle table. "When will you leave?"

"On the morrow. I agree with Kate, she must return to her people. I'm not pleased with the way Brendan is handling this. Mayhap I should send a missive to Rome. I caused her much heartache by accepting her marriage to Brendan and now I regret it. Unless Kate relinquishes her rights to her father's lands, she'll have to tend to the tenants and servants. I don't deem she will refute her responsibility, she has honor."

"You're right, Henry. You'll ask Pope Innocent for an annulment? The price is likely going to be costly. Is Kate wealthy enough to pay such an indulgence?"

Henry placed his arms behind his back and paced, much like his brother Brendan did. "Nay, but I will aid her. It's the least I can do."

"Henry, I haven't asked for much in the years we've known each other, but I ask you now. Don't send the missive yet. Give Brendan time to deal with the death of his father. He loves Kate, and he will regret her leaving. He'll come to her."

"I will wait to send the missive to Rome, but he better not take too long."

Kate strode inside the hall and stopped when she reached them. She curtseyed to Henry and bowed her head to him. Colin took her hand and gave it a supportive squeeze.

"Your Grace, have you decided yet when we shall leave?"

Henry stepped forward. "On the morrow, we shall go. I will travel with you to your home and will continue to have my soldiers protect your land until Richard is captured. Your home is vulnerable since your father's knights are still in the holy land, but my men should be in place and watchful should Richard try something."

"Some of my father's soldiers returned, yet likely not enough to protect the people. I thank you, Your Grace. Colin, you have my gratitude for allowing me to stay here. I shall always remember your clan and your kindness."

"It is I who should thank you, Kate. We'll have a feast this night so you can say farewell to the clan. They will be sorry to see you go."

"Not all your clan, Colin. There is one in particular who doesn't feel that way."

Colin flinched at her forlorn tone. Damn his brother for hurting her. They owed the woman much for saving Bonnie. If Brendan had to live in hell in repayment, then he should do so—even if it meant living in England. "My brother needs time, Kate. You understand that, don't you?"

"I do. Please, tell him that I..." Kate's emotions sprung forth and she wept. "I'm sorry about Walt's death. I only spoke to him a few times, but he was an honorable man."

Colin's heart tightened at seeing her distressed. "Aye, he certainly was. Take rest for the feast. Try not to let my brother's conduct unsettle you. He'll come around."

Kate nodded and left. Colin stalked away. He needed to find his wife, and warn her about the night's festivities. The unfavorable duty of telling his daughter her friend would depart distressed him. He didn't want to cause Bonnie's unhappiness, especially since this day brought her much sorrow in learning of Walt and George's deaths. Better to get it over with before she found out on her own.

CHAPTER TWENTY-FIVE

Kate deliberately disobeyed Colin and hadn't gone to rest. She'd retrieved her candles and rope, and ambled to the stables. She wanted to get away and took the mare out for a ride. The mare trudged along slowly. Kate wasn't in a hurry to get where she was going. When she reached the cliff, she dismounted and took her belongings from the saddlebag. She walked hesitantly toward the edge, and when she reached it, her breath hitched in her throat. It was a long way down, but she had the courage to confront her fear and look below her. The wind blew around her, and she stepped back.

Once her rope was set and her candles positioned, she sat in the center. She hadn't tried to light the candles, because a strong wind whipped around her. The Goddess' elements were around her, except for fire, but that didn't matter. She raised her hands and chanted the prayers that came easily to her lips. After she gave her benedictions to the Goddess for keeping her safe, aiding her in helping Bonnie, and allowing her to meet her vision, she opened her eyes.

The last rays of the sun glared over the ridge with its beautiful splendor. Now, she had to say goodbye. She cleared her throat and spoke as loudly as she could, knowing he was there. She only hoped that he heard her words.

"I have come to say farewell. Do you hear me, Brendan?

LASS' VALOR

Madam told me about you, and my vision made me love you before I even knew you. You are as obstinate in life as you were in my visions. How I shall miss you. I will always remember you." Kate's words echoed through the crest of the cliff. She rose and collected her rope and candles. Before she strolled away, she glanced at the now darkened summit and promised she wouldn't dwell on her decision to leave.

Kate rode back to the keep. When she arrived, supper had been delayed. She hastily took her seat at the table. Her perseverance in trying to remain serene throughout supper was impossible. The clan members came to say goodbye, as well as the KirkConnells. Everyone surrounded her, all but Bonnie, who sat on the floor with her elbows on her knees and her hands perched her chin. Her sweet face downcast and she wouldn't look at her.

Kate left the crowd and sat next to Bonnie on the floor. "Lovey, I…"

Bonnie peered absently across the hall and paid her no attention. Kate touched her hand and smiled.

"Walt died."

"I know I'm sorry." Kate held her hand and leaned her head against Bonnie's. "He was a brave soldier and a good man. I'm sure he's with the Gods, probably fishing with your Uncle Walden." She hoped her words made the girl smile.

Bonnie sighed. "George died, too. He was the best goat."

"Oh, I'm sorry, lovey. I know how fond you were of him."

Bonnie sniffled. "And now you're leaving. I will never see you again." Her voice barely broadcasted the words.

Kate kept tears from falling. "You know I must go. I have a…clan that needs me, just as your clan needs you. You wouldn't want them to be sad, would you?"

"Nay, och I am sad. I won't ever see you again. I heard Papa and he said I am not allowed to leave our land again. I cannot go with Mama and Papa to see Honey. You live far away." Bonnie sniffled her cry away.

"Well, then I shall have to come and visit you then, won't I?"

"You promise?"

Kate sighed and couldn't help but be despondent. She lied to the little girl, and it broke her heart. Not that her heart wasn't already shattered. "I do, but it may be a long time before I return. How about I leave Trixie here? You know how much I adore her. If I leave her here, I'll have to come back. She won't replace George in your heart, or Walt, or me, but she might make you feel better."

Bonnie knocked her backward with a sprightly hug. Kate wrapped her arms around her and took a moment to revel in hugging her, smelling her soft hair, and feeling her little hands holding hers lovingly in return. She set her back on the floor and rose. Before she strolled through the doorway, Kate turned and gazed at her. She wanted to memorize her last view of her dear friend and her sweet little face.

CHAPTER TWENTY-SIX

Brendan stayed in the forest for a fortnight and contemplated the heartache he'd suffered. His head filled with strife as he thought about the years of lies and deceit. His body tensed and he didn't want to see or talk to anyone. Since he'd left Walt's burial, he'd sought the solace of the woods and camped alone.

He walked to the edge of the cliff, sat, and threw his legs over the rim. As he gazed at the far-stretched mountains and mist that lurked below, a sense of calm came. The sky brightened and the expanse cloudless. His mind cleared and he could think without intrusion from others. *Katie.* His heart commiserated and he recalled Walt's last words: *Lad, I lost my love, don't lose yours.* Brendan already lost her.

He missed her, but he'd made the decision to renounce his claim. He lay back on the ground with his legs hung over the cliff's edge and focused on the blue sky above. Winter was coming and a chill blew its wrath around him. Yet he felt nothing. He was numb. *Katie.* Why wouldn't his mind cease thoughts of her? She left him and returned to her people. When he faced life again, she wouldn't be there.

The devastating news of his parentage forced him to accept his place. Not that he didn't care about Walt, but that his brothers weren't blood-related affected him. He counted on them his entire life, through the hardship of losing their parents, the battles and wars with other clans, and now knowing the truth of his real father. A lifetime of lies swallowed him whole and he wasn't about to be released from the torment.

His brothers were from a different father. No wonder Donald MacKinnon hadn't cared for him. Yet Donald MacKinnon hadn't shown Robin much care either. His only concern was Colin taking over as laird. What the hell was he thinking? They would always be his brothers, no matter what occurred in their lives. Even if someone declared they had different mothers, he wouldn't let his relationship be influenced by any circumstances.

Colin shouted his name. His brothers approached and sat next to him. Robin took the other side, and they swung their legs over the cliff side. Brendan immediately sat up and waited for someone to speak. His brothers remained silent and probably wondered how to begin.

Minutes passed, and finally, Colin spoke, "Where have you been? We've been here every day looking for you." He gripped his shoulder in a brotherly gesture.

"I traipsed the woods like an arse," he confessed quietly.

"Are you all right? We were worried," Robin said low.

"I had thinking to do."

"We'll always be brothers. Nothing will change that," Colin said adamantly.

Robin agreed with a nod.

"We don't have to talk about any of it, Brendan," Colin said.

"We will if you want to," Robin put in.

"Nay, there's no need. It was hard to accept at first, but now I understand what I must do."

"Let's return to the keep then. Bonnie's asked for you every day and the clan misses you." Colin moved back to stand and waited for them to rise.

They rode to the keep, each silent. Neither Colin nor Robin broached the subject of Walt or Kate. His brothers likely feared he would retreat to the forest again, and they wouldn't find him by the cliffs. Brendan considered he should reassure them, but he didn't.

Julianna served supper when they entered. The hall quieted, except of course for Bonnie, because once she spied him, she yelled and ran to him. Brendan picked her up and kissed her cheek.

"I missed you, Uncle."

"I missed you, too, fairy."

She squealed in delight when he threw her in the air and caught her.

"Kate's gone, Uncle," she whispered against his face. Brendan didn't respond and she nudged his chin. "She belongs with you, with us."

"Button, she's where she belongs. England is her home." Colin took Bonnie from Brendan and sat her on his lap.

Brendan sat on the bench at the center of the table. He focused on his supper and tried to remain unaffected by his niece's unhappiness.

"Why does she belong there? She's a MacKinnon, Papa, you said so. Bring her home, Papa, please. She wanted to stay, I know she did."

"Did she tell you that?" Colin looked at her oddly.

"She was sad when she left."

Colin placed her in a chair beside his. "She is your friend, Button, and you miss her. But Kate returned to her people. Of course she was sad, she cares greatly for you." Bonnie stood up on her chair and wailed. Colin picked her up, but she wouldn't stop crying. "Bonnie, she's all right, I'm certain she is well. Don't worry about her, lass."

"Nay, Papa, she's not all right. I need her... Uncle needs her...we do..."

"I know you both do," Colin whispered. "But you'll have to wait until your uncle goes and brings her back."

"Make him sit in your chair, Papa, until he does."

Colin laughed at her demand. "I cannot do that, Button. My brother is mule-headed."

"Kate loves him, Papa. Does he love her?"

"Aye, Button, he does. He doesn't realize it yet. Give him time to understand it."

"Aye, Papa." She rubbed her face on his tartan.

Brendan observed his brother holding his daughter and heard their discussion. There was nothing to assuage his niece's distress—they were both miserable. She had to understand he and Kate were not meant to be together. In time, she would understand.

Whenever he looked at Bonnie, she reminded him of Kate. They were both innocence and sweetness. Nay, he wasn't worthy of Kate. Being a bastard, he had nothing to offer her. Likely, she was as rich as the damned English king. He would ask Henry to annul their marriage at the soonest. His fate was decided in the forest, and he'd abide by it, whether he was miserable or not.

He left the hall after the meal and slept on his old pallet in the barracks. Restlessly, his mind reeled with visions of Kate, and his integrity plagued him. He couldn't sleep. In the morning, he arose more cross than he'd been the day before. When he reached the hall, he found Colin dawdled by the table. Julianna attended Kevin, with Bonnie pestering her by her side. Robin and Tess sat with her, and Tess tended to their son. His family congregated, seemingly in wait for him.

"Colin, I want to take care of Walt's sword. Where is it?"

"In the scullery. That's where Jules has my weapons stored these days." Colin grinned.

Brendan grunted at that.

"Why did she put them in the scullery, of all places?" Brendan enjoyed hearing about the cat-and-mouse game between his brother and Julianna. She would move his weapons to an inconspicuous place, and Colin would have to find them. His brother grinned before he answered.

"You know how she feels about weapons hanging in the hall. Remember when she put them upstairs? I promised I wouldn't put them back in the hall again, and she suggested the scullery. I wouldn't deny her request. I think Jules does this to irk me, or maybe take my mind off things."

"She's a sweet lass, Colin."

"You have a sweet lass too, Brendan."

"Nay," Brendan shook his head. "I've decided against it. I don't want to talk about...her. Right now, I want to throw Walt's sword in the loch. Do you wish to come?"

"Aye, of course. Robin will want to come, too." Colin backed off the topic of Kate, at least for now.

Brendan waited while Colin explained to Robin what they would do. The three of them rode to the loch, and on the way, his brothers didn't harass him regarding Kate. Relieved, Brendan put his mind to the task at hand. He dismounted and walked to the water. Not a ripple floated atop the water's surface, even the wind stilled as they approached the edge of the bank. They stood beside each other. Brendan placed his foot on an aquifer and held Walt's sword above his head with both hands.

"I'll miss you, Walt, you were a good man," he said low.

"Here, here, one of the greatest warriors of our time," Robin agreed.

"Colin, here, you do the honors. You're our laird." Brendan handed Walt's sword to him, but Colin returned it.

"Nay, it's your right. He was your father."

"He was a father to us all. It is an honor." Brendan grasped the heavy sword with both hands and swung it in the air with its tip facing the heavens. "You lived a good decent life, Walt, and died a warrior's death. Your sword will remain here for you whenever you need it."

He flung the sword in the air, and it tumbled into the blue sky. The sound of its movement through the air swooshed and a great splash rose when it hit the water's surface. The ripple of the splash circled where the weapon sunk to the bottom.

"Walter Ross' sword will be encased by the spirits of our ancestors for all time. All its victims' blood will be washed away, and will secure his spirit entrance into heaven," Colin assured them. Their ritual completed.

They stood silent until the ripples faded. A light lap of the water reached the bank's edge. Brendan was comforted by the ritual. Pride filled him with Walt's spirit.

Brendan spent his days on the training field and worked off his frustration and tried his best to vanquish thoughts of Kate. He barely concentrated on using his skills. Not that his opponents knew that was the case, they were bested anyway. Nay, while he crossed his sword with the other men, his mind wasn't on the task at hand. He shoved Benjamin's face in the mud and his mind wandered.

Nighttime was the worst. Each night, he'd retreat to the cottage she used and sat in the chair and see her form on the bed, her bonny face whilst she slept. The woman haunted him and intruded on his existence. Damn it all, he thought as he continued to push Benjamin's face into the softened ground. He couldn't cease thoughts of her, even now he was agitated at the thought she was probably at Henry's castle being courted by a fop. Someone else would love her, kiss her, and touch her. She would cook for him and smile sweetly. She would bear a deserving man strong sons and sweet daughters.

"Brendan, your suffocating Benjamin. Ease up a wee bit." Colin laughed but didn't make a move to assist his expended soldier.

Brendan swallowed his indignation and released Benjamin. Faigh mein, his state of discontent rendered him a danger to those he trained with. He knocked another adversary to the ground and stalked away.

Colin regarded him from the wall. He smiled when Robin approached and knocked his shoulder.

"Is he there yet?" Robin asked.

"Almost."

"Let me know."

"Aye," Colin agreed.

Colin walked to the keep to enact his plan and found Gil

and Brendan in a fracas on the ground. Brendan drove his fist at Gil's mouth and split his bottom lip. Gil licked the blood and laughed, which incensed Brendan. Colin needed to stop their brawl before Brendan killed Gil.

"What the hell is going on here?"

"Nothing, Laird," Gil said honestly.

"Nothing? Gil, move away from Brendan. He's not in the mood to entertain you this day. What did you do to rile him?"

"I asked him a question and he pummeled me. It's not my fault he's hot-tempered lately," Gil said and spat a good amount of blood on the ground.

"What did you ask?"

"I asked him when he was leaving for England. I told him if he didn't want her, I did and I wouldn't mind living in England as long as the lady was mine."

"Well, hell. Brendan, what did you reply?"

"His lip bears my reply," Brendan said testily.

"Gil, cease taunting him. Brendan, I want to see you in the hall now." Colin strode inside.

"Brendan."

"Aye, Gil."

Gil shoved him. "I didn't mean it. She's your wife and I'm trying to get you to be reasonable. You love her. Och, why don't you go to her? You're miserable. I've never seen you akin to this."

"I'm an arse, that's why. I shouldn't have taken my ire out on you, Gil." Brendan irritably ran his hands through his hair.

"I can take it. I'm going hunting with the men and probably won't return for a few hours. Think about it, Brendan, the lass awaits. You didn't see her face when the king told her you left. I saw her riding with Bonnie that day, and it nearly broke my heart to see her deserted." Gil walked away and left Brendan staring after him.

Brendan entered the hall and sat next to Colin. The hall was empty save for the two of them until Robin strode in a few minutes later. Brendan poured himself ale and sat back and waited for his brother's attack.

"Is this an official meeting?" he asked sarcastically.

Colin grunted and gave a heated stare. "Damned right it is. We're going on a journey. Once we meet with King Henry, I'm going after Richard. The knave has to be somewhere and Henry will tell us where we can find him."

"You're saying you want to go to England to search for him?" Brendan waited for his brother's response, which came with a nod.

"Whilst we are there, you'll have to do a wee bit of arse kissing, Brendan, if you want her back. You married Kate. Have you forgotten that? Do you take the vow lightly and dishonor her? I'd never reason someone as superstitious as you would go against fate. Bonnie brought you two together, it is your destiny."

"Destiny or not, I'm not worthy of her." Brendan slumped in his seat and couldn't bring himself to look at them.

"What the hell does that mean, Brendan? Of course, you're worthy. She's probably devastated you haven't come for her and is likely feeling rejected. Women are funny that way."

"I am a bastard."

"Aye, you are. You crushed that poor lass' heart."

"Nay, I was born a bastard, Colin. She doesn't deserve my stigma and I have nothing to offer. I'm only a soldier with no future. You heard her...she has land and wealth. What can I offer her?"

"That's a load of cosh and you know it." Colin punched his jaw before Brendan knew what was coming. He didn't flinch.

"Will you go with us or do I have to drag your arse to England?"

Brendan frowned at his brother's bluntness. "Aye, I'll go, but I will return after we kill that son-of-a-bitch."

Robin scoffed and banged the table. "You cannot return,

Brendan."

"How can I leave? This is where I belong, my home. Who will protect the clan?"

"You belong with your wife. Is that why you won't leave? Because you have a duty to protect the clan? Brendan, we have many soldiers and allies. The clan's protection takes many, not one."

"Are you saying you don't need me?" Brendan's ire forced him to shout, but the words struck him as though he'd been hit over the head with a mace.

Colin released a waspish breath. "I will always need you. You're my brother, for God's sake. But you're also one hell of a soldier, and of course, we would want you to stay to protect us. Your wife has no one, save Henry, and he's busy tending to his kingdom. She's alone with no family to protect her, and yet, she must run her father's holding. Her husband should be there, protecting her, helping her, and God forbid, loving her."

"Brendan, remember what you told Colin when he wasn't sure if he wanted Julianna? You said to leave him alone and if he loves her he will go. That's what we're doing. Come, Colin, let him stew in his own stupidity." Robin pulled Colin's arm and they left him sitting alone.

Brendan leaned his head back against the chair and closed his eyes. A smile came and he almost laughed aloud at his brother's strategy. He'd pulled a similar ruse years ago when Julianna left Colin, and his brother wouldn't acknowledge his feelings for her. Well, whatever they'd planned worked. It occurred to him—he couldn't live without Katie. He envisioned her sitting on the floor inside her rope, the way she spoke when she was angry, and the devilry in her eyes when she was up to something sneaky. He didn't want to be without her, didn't want to be lonely anymore.

"Uncle, look what I made."

He opened his eyes and found Bonnie a foot from him. She held a bowl and whatever she'd placed in it, stank to high heavens. He glowered and peered inside the bowl. An insect's leg floated atop the crushed gruel. He bellowed a laugh. "What do you have there?" He reached for her and placed her on his lap, but set the bowl away from them, as far on the table as he could place it.

"I made a potion like Kate does. Do you know what it's for?"

"Nay, what?"

"It's going to bring Kate back." She grinned at her accomplishment.

"What did you put in it? It smells...ah, not too good, lass."

"I put a crushed up insect, some of Papa's water from his flask, the one he won't let Mama touch, and Dame Hester gaved me leeks too."

Brendan burst with laughter and imagined her crushing a cricket. If Colin found out his daughter touched his flask of brew, she'd be punished for a week. No wonder it smelled bad, with leeks too? He ceased his laughter when he noticed her hurtful expression.

"Well now, fairy, do you know what?" He put the question to her because it was always what she'd say to him.

"Nay, what, Uncle?"

"Katie would be proud of your success. Your potion must've worked because Katie will return." He caressed her hair and thought his niece would make one hell of a witch when she got older.

Bonnie shouted gleefully. "Are you going to get 'er, Uncle Brendan?"

"Aye, but I have to live in England now, not here. I promise to bring Kate for a visit in the spring. Will that make you happy?"

Her answer was to turn on his lap and hug him. He smiled at how happy he'd made her. If his niece went to such lengths to bring back Katie, he could at least be agreeable and assist her.

CHAPTER TWENTY-SEVEN

Brendan rode beside Julianna and Colin on his way to his new home. He wasn't thrilled at the prospect of living in England. Fortunately, neither his brothers nor Colin's soldiers teased him about it on their journey. If they had, he would've pounded them to the ground.

They neared Parkville Convent, and Julianna asked Colin to stop and pay their respects to Mother Superior, a nun whom Julianna had an ongoing relationship. She hadn't seen her in two years and wanted to thank her for helping Douglas' wife, Isabel, with her problem earlier that summer. Julianna also needed a break from riding and Colin wouldn't deny her. He let her have her way and insisted they would only stay a few hours, which would give them a bit of rest from travel.

Julianna rang the bell by the gate to summon the nuns. "Please, be chivalrous." She gave him and Colin a glance that meant they'd better do as she said. "Oh, here comes Sister Margarite. She's taking her old sweet time. How I remember her from when I lived here, she'd take forever answering the gate." The sister finally arrived and smiled. "I've come to see Mother Superior, Sister Margarite."

"Aye, child, come this way."

Brendan followed Julianna, and he breathed in the scent

of the old stone building. They were led to Mother's office, and Colin approached a small bench beside the wall.

Julianna laughed. "This is it, Colin, the punishment chair, the one I told you about."

"Ah, so that's the infamous chair. Bonnie is spoiled having to sit in my chair." He chuckled.

"Mother used to make me sit in it like you make Bonnie sit in your chair. That's why I always smile when you threaten her with that punishment."

"It's no wonder I like your Mother Superior," Colin said as he settled on the bench. "It's horrible, lass, no wonder you disliked it so much."

Mother Superior stalked in the room. She flopped in her chair and peered over her steeped fingers.

"Mother Superior, we were passing by and I thought I'd check on you. I wanted to thank—"

"Julianna, it's good to see you. I'm glad you're here. I need your help, dear child."

"Anything, Mother. What's wrong?"

"There's a young lady here, who can't seem to cease crying. She hasn't stopped since she arrived. I abhor a crying girl. You never cried when you were here."

"What's wrong with her?"

"She has a broken heart and won't heed me. I pray every day, and I'm certain God is listening and yet… Even Eloise hasn't been able to help her over her distress."

"I'll try to help, but I don't know what I can do," Julianna said.

"Try to reason with her, that's all I ask. Laird MacKinnon, you're looking…healthy. Are you treating my girl well?"

"I try to keep her happy, Mother."

"That's all she could hope for, Laird." Mother gave him a pat on his shoulder as she walked by. Julianna followed. "Julianna, come, I'll show you where the girl is. She's one of the girls who came with Isabel and stayed on. MacKinnon, make yourself comfortable. You may be here a while," she confided in a whisper.

Brendan sat in 'the chair' and grunted. "This chair makes you wonder if someone put thistles on it. I better not sit on it too long else it's libel to break in half."

Colin snorted. "Not likely, Mother Superior would only use the hardest wood she could find."

"I believe I'll have such a chair made when I reach Kate's holding." Brendan grinned.

"Why would you do that?"

"For my own wee lass, who surely will cause me problems. With my wife's influence, I'm probably going to be waylaid by the two of them."

Colin laughed. "It's good to hear you speak so, Brendan. I look forward to seeing your children. Have you decided what you will say when you arrive?"

"Aye, I will tell her the truth. That she can't deny our marriage, not when she will have my bairn." Brendan let his smile forth.

"She's carrying your bairn?"

He laughed at his brother's mouth which hung open in shock. "Not yet, och soon enough I'll see to it."

Colin closed his eyes, but he spoke. "My wife better not keep us waiting long. I want to be quick about our travel and find out where that clootie hides."

Brendan grunted. "Aye, we'll find him soon enough."

Colin opened his eyes. "You're sounding awful patient, Brendan. I would say you're happy at the delay. I suppose you're not eager to face Kate."

"Damned right I'm not. I still haven't figured out exactly what I will say."

"Be forthright and honest. She'll listen."

Julianna returned a few minutes later and they set out for the final leg of their journey. Brendan was apprehensive about being in England and kept his guard up. He didn't believe he'd ever be content living there. When they reached the holding Henry gave directions to in Cheshire late that afternoon, the sun had dissipated. Brendan assessed his future home from the distance. Even though the land was cast in the shadows of dusk, the property appeared welcoming.

"Looks to be a small fief, but there are plenty of fields."

"God Almighty, she's going to turn me into a farmer." He couldn't keep the touch of irony out of his tone, and Colin laughed.

"Mayhap a farmer who knows how to war with the best of them."

"That is not funny, Colin."

He took his time and surveyed the manor house, which appeared large and well-built. Several flags adorned the turrets and steeples. At one time, it must've been a wealthy fief, for it was made of stone and its security was built to withstand sieges.

The posted guard stopped them when they approached the gate.

Colin rode forward, but Brendan stopped him. "Let me." Brendan dismounted and bid the rest of the men to do so. Though they'd only brought twenty men, they appeared hostile. Brendan couldn't help that—it was their usual manner.

"I'm Brendan MacKinnon and I—"

"Sir, we were told to expect you." The guard stepped back and motioned for them to enter.

"Who told you to expect me?"

"King Henry. He's in residence and hasn't left yet to return to Londontown. He told us to tell you he's within. Welcome, my lords."

Brendan nodded and strolled toward the entrance. He pushed open the large wooden doors and marched inside. For a moment, he stood still and gazed about him. The room's cleanliness and coziness reminded him of Kate. Everything in the room bore her touch. A large table sat in the center of the hall, on which sat three bowls, one at each end, and a larger one in the center. All held fruit and vegetables. Beside the hearth, dried flowers hung on pegs and scented the room with their fragrance. Around the room, various chairs sat beside windows and under tapestries of rich-colored scenes. There was even a woven rug in front of the hearth with several homemade books sitting atop it. An aura of pride overcame him.

"Brendan, Colin, you're here." Henry entered the hall through a doorway and stood nearby.

Colin approached Henry and bowed. "Henry, we came to find out de Morris' whereabouts. I aim to search for him, here in England."

Henry clasped his hands behind his back. "I knew you would. Very well, I'll have my chancellor look into Richard's holdings and inform me where the man is. Once we have a location, you can go seek him."

"That's all I ask, Henry."

The king raised a brow and settled his folded arms over his chest. Brendan wasn't sure why, but Henry smirked.

"Is there another reason you came, Brendan MacKinnon, besides wanting to kill Richard?"

"Damned right, I came for my wife. What chamber is she in?"

Henry laughed. Brendan frowned at Colin, who gave him a hopeful gaze.

"Why would I tell you that? Kate has all but said she wants to annul your marriage. She's been downright insistent. I've never seen a woman so forlorn in all my days."

"She's my wife and I insist you allow me to see her. You haven't sent the request to Rome for the annulment, have you? I won't allow it." Brendan took a defiant stance.

"You dare to make demands of your king?"

Brendan swallowed his ire. If that didn't beat all, Henry used his position to rile him. Aye, he was now his king, and there was no disagreeing with him. "Nay, Henry, I just want to see Katie."

"Very well, she's in her chamber, third floor, the only door there. Leads to a tower room where she dwells. I don't know what she does up there all day, but she spends much time secreted away. She's probably sulking over you. Why I really couldn't say."

He half-listened to Henry's jests and took the stairs in a mad rush. Although the manor was aged, it appeared well-tended, and even the steps had been daubed to seal the cracks. He stood outside her chamber, hesitant to knock, uncertain of what he'd say. All the words he'd thought of along the way suddenly absconded. Mayhap words wouldn't be needed. He opened the door and stepped inside.

Kate sat on the floor inside her rope, candles inside and outside of the rope dimly lit the chamber. Brendan noticed the few tables laden with bowls and pouches. He stood mesmerized for a moment before he approached. Stepping around a chair, he looked down. Her beautiful eyes were closed, her lips parted slightly, humming. She didn't hear him and was deeply into her meditation. Her light hair cascaded over her shoulders, and she held her hands to the ceiling.

"Katie."

Her eyes opened and rose to meet his. "Brendan, you startled me. What are you doing here?"

He knelt beside her, took her hand, and held it firmly. She tried to rise, but he wouldn't let her. He remained silent, content to stare at her. He'd missed her, and took in her beauty. He pulled her to the ornate bed a few feet away—she had no choice but to follow.

She started to speak but closed her mouth. He set her on the bed and lay next to her. He wanted to hold her a moment before he broached the subject of their marriage. Much needed to be said, most importantly, how much he loved her.

He felt her sigh.

"Brendan, I cannot believe you came. Oh, good Goddess, I asked the king to send to Rome for an annulment. You really shouldn't be here in my chamber."

He stroked her face and smiled. "Is that all you've thought about since we parted, our annulment?"

"Of course, what else should I have been thinking of?"

"Mayhap, my mouth doing this." He trailed light kisses over her neck. "And perchance you missed my body doing this." He pressed his body against hers. "Have you thought about how hot I make you feel when I do this?" He caressed her breast and stroked his hand over her stomach to her femininity. Forget talking, his arousal rejected everything but making sweet, passionate love to her.

Kate sucked in a breath and waited to see what he would do next.

"Mayhap you missed me?" he murmured in her ear.

She opened her mouth to respond, but his mouth took possession of her lips. So like him, not to give her a chance to respond. He easily coerced her to accept him and swarmed her with kisses, while he used his body to overwhelm her senses. Every touch scorned her attempt to reproach him. She wrapped her arms around him and deepened the kiss. He never wanted her to let go.

Brendan steeled his legs over hers, to keep them still. He wasn't sure if she was angry he'd let her leave or not. He shook with an urgent need—the need to remove her clothes and have her soft, hot skin against his. Her tongue responded ardently, it swamped him with raged lust, so excruciating and yet thrilling. He had to stop but didn't want to. She fisted his hair and tugged on it gently to get him to move closer. He berated himself and remembered what he needed to do.

"Love, cease, or I won't be able to stop. I want to talk to you." Brendan recalled what his brother, Robin, told him about how he'd gotten Tess to accept him. He removed Katie's hand from his hair and placed it on his chest. She moved it in circles, and he stilled it and placed his hand over hers. "I mean it, Katie, we must talk. Let us discuss this annulment you've asked Henry for."

When he didn't say anything more, she sat up and turned toward him.

"Brendan MacKinnon, I can't believe you left. I went to say goodbye to you at the cliff."

"I was upset, Katie, about Walt and needed to come to an understanding. I saw you that day, and heard your farewell." His voice was a whisper against her neck. He pulled her into his arms. Brendan caressed her cheek with his thumb and changed the topic. "I don't want us to be apart again, and we won't speak of an annulment."

"I can't have you here, Brendan. You must understand that," she said low, but wouldn't look at him. She turned to face a tapestry on the wall beside the bed.

He turned her face to him. "Understand what, Katie? Why can't I stay? I am your husband."

"Because I c-can't live with a man who doesn't l-love me."

"I'm not asking you to. I'm asking you to stay with a man who loves you very much."

Incredulous, she asked, "You do?"

"Aye, Katie, I would die for you, go to hell and back for you, as a husband should."

"Now, you're telling me this now?"

Brendan touched his head to hers. "Aye." He gazed at her affectionately with his usually cold-gray eyes. "I realized I loved you when we were on the cliffs and I'd gone off to think. I couldn't stop thinking about you, even though my father just died in a battle with Richard's men. I only found out that Walt was my father. You wanted me to leave my home, a place where I have always been accepted, well, by my brothers. There was much to consider."

"You never knew about Walt being your father? I had guessed he was your father when I spoke to him, but you hadn't introduced him as your father when we met on our arrival. Walt was indeed a kind man. I'm sorry you had to deal with that pain alone. You should've let me console you. That's what wives are supposed to do."

"I couldn't be near anyone then. He didn't tell me he was my father until right before his death. Walt and my mother had a liaison, and he made Colin promise never to tell me. Walt made a vow to my mother that he would never claim me and I lived my life believing I was Donald MacKinnon's son. He was a heartless dog. I had much to consider. You left, and I was angry. I didn't deem you'd accept me."

"Brendan, I hardly knew you when I told you I loved you. I didn't love you because you were a son of a laird. It certainly wasn't due to your charm or gentle nature either."

"Why do you love me?" he dared to ask.

Kate knelt on her knees and her expression softened. "I had this vision, you see, I'm much like my grandmother and my mother. We pray to the spirits of the earth, the sun, wind, water, and fire. I honor my Celtic ancestors and—"

Brendan reached out to take her in his arms, but she held him off. "Nay, let me finish. When my mother died, I prayed to the spirits to show me the way and guide me. Lolly, my attendant, was a good friend of Madam Serena's, a Celtic woman who was a friend to my mother and grandmother too. She showed me the faith, and as I learned to harness my beliefs, a vision kept appearing. It was of a warrior with dark hair and gray eyes—it was you. Madam had powers I never dreamed of. She said I would go on a somber mission and I would meet the warrior when I met the child. Now you know why I reacted strangely when I first saw you after you bathed the paint away when we arrived."

"I thought you were brazen or mayhap brave, Katie."

Kate smiled. "I was scared to my toes, but I was sent to you for a reason. At first, I thought it was because of Bonnie, but now I know why I was sent to you."

"Why is that?" He grinned.

"Because you need me. I was sent to make you happy and bring you back."

"I admit I was distant, have always been. It was hard to deal with Walt's death, and that he was my father. He was a good man, and we cared about him. I'm still torn up about it."

"I only spoke to him once, at Laila and Garrick's wedding. He came to me and told me how honored he was that his son married me. I felt graced by his kind words. Walt was a noble man." Kate took his hand and her eyes bore into his.

"Aye, he was. I didn't think I was worthy of you, being

born a bastard and…only when you left, I realized how much you meant to me."

"Oh." Kate turned and peered at the window casement. "So you didn't find Richard?"

"Nay, he got away. I worried he would send his army here, and you and Henry were in danger. He hasn't come out of his hole yet. Henry is having the chancellor find his location."

"Now that you're here, it's over, and we can…" She trailed off when he shook his head.

"But it's not over. Richard is still out there and I won't rest until I find him."

Kate sighed. "You really intend to stay here in England?"

"Katie, I want you to tell Henry that we will remain husband and wife and he shouldn't send to the Pope for an annulment. Aye, my place is with you, wherever that might be, even if it means living in England."

"Don't sound disgruntled, Brendan, it won't be so bad, being married to me."

Brendan laughed at the words she threw back at him, and he recalled saying such to her. He pulled her into his arms and smiled at the courageous woman he held. She needed his protection, and he would make certain she was kept safe. They lay still for a while, neither spoke, just enjoyed the silence. His body suddenly reminded him how much he'd missed her. A stirring of desire snuck into his loving caresses. He chuckled at the thought. She snuggled by his side, and his hand moved over her bottom. He shifted her onto her back, watched her thick lashes fan her cheeks, and her full lips part.

"I want you," he said hotly.

Passion clouded her eyes when she opened them. "I need you."

Brendan clumsily fumbled at removing her gown and his tartan. He stripped in a rush to feel her nakedness. Every hair on his body prickled when her soft body touched his. He didn't have the fortitude to go slow. He wanted to be inside her and retreat to the mindless aura of finding the pleasure only she brought to him. He touched her essence and it sent him to a state beyond reason. His arousal throbbed with the need to feel her warmth.

Kate moaned at the sensation of his breadth pressed against her. She pulled his shoulders and encouraged him to continue, but he didn't move.

Without opening her eyes, she whispered, "Now, Brendan, make love to me."

His body shuddered in sheer lust at her sweet plea. He drove onward and stopped when he could move no further. Incapable of speech, he reeled at the spectacular feeling. He wanted to stay there until he met his end, and his end came sooner than he hoped. His body took control, moving in gentle but forceful strokes. Every thrust inched him closer to euphoria. He was about to lose complete control. He touched her and willed she found pleasure before his need expelled him. Too late, he didn't hold back, and his groans of pure culmination sounded throughout the chamber.

His deep groans tangled with her pleasured moans. He helped Kate relinquish her caution. The orgasm swept through her and shook her limbs in an overpowering force. Minutes passed as he listened to their rasped breath, smelled his masculine scent mixed with her feminine fragrance. Brendan was content.

Kate ran her cool palm over his chest. She yawned and closed her eyes. Brendan rolled to his back, and without a word, he pulled her on top of him. She placed her cheek where his heart beat madly.

He laughed and said in a husky voice, "Damnation lass, if that's how it will be..." He didn't continue but smiled at her disgruntled look.

"If you don't like doing it, why do you insist that we—"

He stroked her arm as he thought how best to answer. "Don't like doing it? Hell, if I react like this every time..." He didn't finish, his lovely wife fell asleep. He joined her a minute later after he pulled the covers over them.

CHAPTER TWENTY-EIGHT

Kate awoke to loud humming. She opened her eyes and smiled. Was her scowling warrior humming? She giggled into her pillow, but he heard her. He stood across the chamber and leaned on the window casement. Something drew his attention. What held her enthralled was his naked body with every inch of his hardened muscles uncovered and on display. He continued to hum and walked to the tub which filled with steaming water.

Happiness bubbled inside her. She couldn't believe he'd come to England for her. The remarkable feat had to be an act of love. Madam was right, it all worked out. She'd found her vision, married him, and now she was uncertain what would happen. Would he find a place in her life? She would make sure of it, she promised herself.

"You're finally awake?"

"Why are you cheerful this morn?" Kate moved off the bed, approached him, and knelt beside the tub. She leaned her elbows on the rim.

"I'm beginning my life with my wife, a bonny lady, this day." He took her hand and kissed it, his warm lips tarried over her knuckles.

Kate laughed. "Brendan, you've never spoken so... What's wrong with you? Do you have a fever?" She felt his head to discern if indeed he'd gotten ill.

"Nay, love, if I'm hot, it's because you make me so. Join me." He patted the water and reached for her, but she backed away and shook her head.

"The tub is rather small and you take up all the space."

"I'm finished." He rose and dripped water on her.

Kate's eyes filled with love when she grazed his magnificent form. She jumped on the bed and squealed when he threw himself beside her. She touched his shoulder in a gentle caress.

"What will happen?"

"I'm going to make love to you until supper."

She laughed. "Nay, I mean, will you really live here with me?"

"As much as I detest England, lass, I'd live anywhere as long as I can be with you. Aye, I will live here and become the lord. I cannot believe I'm saying this."

"Does it distress you?"

"Nay, but I'll visit home, Katie, from time to time. I promised Bonnie we would visit in the spring. You should've seen the potion she concocted to make you return. She crushed an insect." He laughed.

Kate's eyes shone at the thought. "Oh, so that's where my spell went for bringing those you love back to you. I thought I lost it. I should have known Bonnie took it. Oh, I would so love to visit her in the spring. I shall miss her."

Brendan ran his hand along her leg until he reached her inner thigh. "Before we go down to the hall, I want to make you squeal again." He did more than that and she giggled when he tickled her knee. He discovered a few ticklish spots she'd hidden from him.

A knock sounded at the door and Colin shouted. "Brendan, Henry wants you and Kate in the hall in fifteen minutes. Did you hear me, Brendan?"

"Aye, we'll be down shortly." Brendan muttered, "I had no intention of leaving the chamber for at least another hour or two. Still, Henry is king, hell, he's now my king. I suppose

I shouldn't press his ire by keeping him waiting. We will continue this later." He leaned and kissed Kate's stomach before he rose.

"I wonder what Henry wants? Do you deem he found out Richard's location?"

"I hope so. I want to finish this. But who knows, Henry probably wants to annoy me and rub it in my face he's now my king. I assume he wants me to kneel before him and swear fealty. Damn him."

"Will you?"

"I suppose I must." Brendan wrapped his tartan around him, pulled his tunic over his head, and waited for Kate to finish dressing. He took her hand and guided her to the hall.

Henry sat at the head of the table and appeared lordly. He dressed regally and wore his official reigning expression. Kate greeted him with a curtsey and a smile.

"Your Grace, good morn. You're looking well. You wished to see Brendan and me?"

"Lady MacKinnon, I suppose I really cannot call you such, because your husband is not a knight, nor is he landed. I will have to rectify that."

Kate tilted her head and gave Brendan a questioned glance. "Sire, but you gave your acceptance of our marriage, and he will take over as lord here. I don't understand. Do you intend to separate us?" Sorrow instantly trounced her heart. She looked back at Brendan, but he stood and kept his stone-faced gaze on the king.

"What I wish is for you both to come to Londontown. I'm leaving today and expect you at my court within a week. By then, we should receive word of Richard's whereabouts." Henry rose, waited for their courtesies, and bounded to the door.

She looked at Colin, who smiled. "Do you know what this is about? What does he intend?"

Colin shook his head and walked through the door.

Less than four days later, they arrived at Henry's summer castle, Whitehall. It resembled a fortress rather than a king's residence. Kate heard there was a dungeon where the more heinous criminals were kept. Yet most offenders against the crown were sent to the Tower, in the heart of Londontown. Colin told her not to worry, that the king had many sentries. He also told her that this was the very castle where Bonnie was abducted. Kate's heart sank because the place held unhappy memories for Colin and Julianna. Still, Colin supported his brother and traveled to Londontown.

Kate and Brendan were shown to a chamber lavishly furnished. She paced along the bedside and every so often glanced at Brendan who paced the other side.

"When do you deem he'll call for us?" She'd whispered her question because she suspected someone listened. She got an unusual sense, and it was eerie being at the king's castle where there was no privacy. The walls closed in, and she was certain they were as thin as the rushes at the de Morris keep.

"When he's ready. Do you wish to go outside? We could walk the gardens."

"Do you want to visit the gardens, Brendan?"

"Nay, it was only a suggestion to take your mind off this."

Kate scoffed. She couldn't see her husband, the scowling warrior, walking amid the sculptures and hedges of the king's castle. He was out of place at the regal residence.

Colin knocked, and they both called to enter at the same time. He came in and flopped into a brocaded chair at the foot of the bed.

"What are you two doing?"

"Pacing," Kate said.

"Oh, God, I shouldn't have come here. He'll call you down near suppertime. There will be a feast tonight." Colin looked as though he'd laugh, but he refrained.

Kate sat on the bedside and surmised his expression.

Brendan fisted his hand and raised it to the ornate ceiling. "Why does he make us wait?"

They sat silent until Colin spoke, "We should await him in the hall. Many have come for the feast. He even invited the Shelmores, Brendan. Julianna is with her aunt in the hall."

Brendan nodded and clasped her hand. "The Shelmores are friends who live by the border. Julianna is related to them. Let us to the hall. It's better than waiting here."

The hall was crowded, and many flustered at Henry's imminent arrival. Colin stood next to her and spoke to Chancellor Hubert about politics. Colin grasped Brendan's arm to stop his stride, and Kate stepped in. She held his arm and took him for a turnabout of the room. Her intention to take her husband's mind from Henry's looming announcement eased him and she absently commented on the tapestries and furnishings. Even though Brendan nodded occasionally, he hadn't listened. He couldn't give a farthing about such things. Though she knew it, she continued to utter nonsense.

A creek of the door alerted them Henry appeased them with his presence. He walked in with his shoulders covered with a fur cape. He appeared foreboding.

"Your Grace," Colin said mockingly as he approached with Julianna and bowed. "Finally, you arrive. Brendan awaits your word."

"Ah, so the wagtail is anxious, is he?" Henry laughed and looked to Brendan at the end of the room. "Where is Lady Kate? Ah, your brother is blocking her from my view."

Kate grasped Brendan's hand and walked toward the king. She and Brendan paid their respects and Henry turned without a word to them. He seemed angry.

"Lords and Ladies," Henry bellowed from the steps of his dais. "Before we dine, I want to bestow a great honor this day, but before I do, I want to tell you a story."

All looked at the young king and moved closer to listen to his tale. Kate pulled Brendan toward the crowd, but he only let her get as far as the outer lying people.

"I have family who lives in Scotland, and one of those members is endeared to me." The crowd gasped as if he bespoke a longtime secret. "Her name is Bonnie, and she's my cousin's daughter, a wee lass. Whenever I see her, I can't help but fall for her delightful antics and sweet smile. She's a amusing minx. Unfortunately, she has an uncle who is just about as obstinate as they come. Many fear him, as did I. I shouldn't confess such and you don't wish to hear your king speak of fearing anyone. But honestly, a fiercer warrior I never met."

A hush of whispers hastened through the crowd.

Henry continued, "When I visited years ago, the soldiers played a jest on me and took my garments. They left me naked in the frigid water. At the time, I was beyond angry, and I swore to have their laird flail them all before me. But then, Brendan MacKinnon, the fierce warrior, happened by and I hadn't expected his aid. Of all the warriors, he had more hatred for me than any. Yet, when I asked him for help, he gave me his tartan...me, the man he most hated. I haven't forgotten it."

The lords and ladies stood before Henry baffled and silenced by his story. They didn't know what he intended. Kate didn't either. She gripped Brendan's hand and turned to whisper to him, but he shook his head and nodded to Henry.

"When my sweet Bonnie was taken from this very castle, I was devastated, and I blamed myself. A courageous woman faced danger to return the little mite to her family. Her honorable courage has made me realize that there is indeed someone for everyone. For she loves the fierce warrior and I intend to reward them both. Brendan MacKinnon, step forward."

Kate released his hand, and Brendan moved through the crowd. He stood before Henry, and as she approached to find out what was happening, the king asked him to kneel.

Henry took his sword and placed it on each of Brendan's shoulders, saying, "I knight you, Brendan MacKinnon, for your kindness to a king whom you didn't have to honor, but you received my friendship for it. Knighting you rewards your wife, for you are a peer of my realm. Rise, Sir Brendan."

Kate ambled forward and kissed his cheek. She grinned at the king. "I thank you, Your Grace. You haven't sent the missive to Rome, have you?"

Henry roared with laughter. "Are you certain you wish to be married to this blighter?"

"Aye, Your Grace, he's obstinate, but I care greatly for him. He will be a worthy husband and an asset to Cheshire."

Henry laughed. "You're a courageous woman, wanting to be married to him. Why, since I've known him, I've never seen him smile."

"Sire, he smiles all the time, at least, at me, he does."

Brendan pulled her aside. "Cosh, I'm even more English now, being knighted by Henry. I'm not sure I like it, Katie. I am unworthy of Henry's gratitude, especially since Richard is still out there. But I'm proud of you. You make me feel worthy."

"Brendan, you are worthy, always believe that. Regardless of Richard's capture, the king is indebted to you. I cannot believe he knighted you."

Her husband grunted, and she laughed at the surly look on his face.

They entered the dining hall and took their seats, on Henry's bench, in their place of honor. The servants set platters of food for the feast, and the revelry began. A small group of musicians played in the corner of the room and sent soothing music through the room.

A group of men returned from sentry duty and approached the chancellor. Hubert held them off with a wave of his hand, but the soldiers marched in a procession then parted when an older gentleman's armor clinked with his every step. He stopped behind them and removed his helmet.

"What goes here? Where is my daughter?"

"Sir, what right do you have to interrupt his majesty's supper?" Hubert bellowed.

The man cleared his throat and said sternly, "I was told my daughter is here."

Hubert moved aside and motioned for him to continue

forward. Hawk marched toward the group and stepped before the king. Kate hadn't paid attention to the commotion, and when she turned, she paled.

"Father?"

"Fairy?"

Brendan caught her before she hit the floor, she fainted dead away.

"You're Katie's father?" Brendan asked.

"Lord Hawthorn Stanhope, at your service." He faced the king and bowed. "Sire, what is going on here? Why is my Kate here and not home where I left her?"

"I am having a feast to celebrate Sir MacKinnon's knighting, and your daughter's marriage to him."

The man frowned like a clootie. Aye, a devil who wasn't pleased by Henry's news. Brendan held Kate's limp body in his arms.

"The hell you are. I gave no permission for her to marry him or anyone."

"You are dead, or at least, you were dead. I gave my permission." Henry stood, his face reddened. He didn't appear to like being told he needed Lord Stanhope's permission for anything.

"You must undo it," Hawk said and frowned at Brendan.

"He cannot. Our union was blessed by the church. We are married," Brendan said through clenched teeth. "She's my wife in every matter."

"Sire, he must lie, I won't believe it."

"I'm afraid he's not lying, Hawk. They married some time ago. I am but handling a formality by knighting him, an honor he deserves."

"Will you move out of the way so I can lay her down somewhere," Brendan shouted. He'd lost his patience with the two of them and wanted to take Katie away.

Hawk and Henry hesitantly moved aside. Brendan walked from the hall, holding his senseless wife. As he leaned against the wall, he considered the ramifications of her father's appearance.

Kate came to the moment he exited the room. She tried to get him to set her down, but he wouldn't release her. "Madam is never wrong," she mumbled.

"Katie, you need to rest a moment. I'll not have you fainting again," he commanded.

"B-but my father is alive. Did you see him...? I can't believe... He's alive or was I dreaming?"

"Nay, he's alive and well. You're not dreaming."

"Brendan, what will I tell him?" she whispered.

"About what?"

"Us."

"How about, I love him and we're married for starters?"

"Nay, I mean, I...of course, I love you, Brendan, but what if he doesn't consent. I'll have to get our marriage annulled."

"Here we go again," Brendan uttered.

He entered their chamber, and set her on the bed, then walked to the window where he looked out at the rainy sky. "Why did this happen now? It was all but settled, and I planned to take you home on the morrow."

A knock sounded at the door. Brendan opened it and found Lord Stanhope beyond the threshold. He moved aside to let him enter.

"I want to see my daughter."

"Father, please come in."

Her father took her in his arms and she wept, seeing him for the first time in many years.

Brendan stood beyond and watched their reunion. She wiped her eyes and returned her gaze to her father. He appeared aged, more so than she remembered. His hair grayed and his beard thicker. His eyes paled and weren't as blue as she recalled. Kate trembled from weeping.

Brendan kissed her cheek. "I'll be with Colin and Julianna—amusing Henry. Send for me, if you need me."

Kate nodded. "All will be well, Brendan."

He ambled away with hesitant steps and gazed at her before he closed the door.

Her father surveyed his leaving too, and when the door closed, he pulled her in his arms.
"Kate, you're unharmed? I worried about your safety and I thought—"
"That Richard would kill me? Is that why you put that absurd message inside the medallion? A lot of good it did." Kate found the courage to berate him. "Why did you do that? You caused a lot of woes, and not just for me."
"I feared Richard would come after you. Did he?"
"Aye, because you sent me the medallion. Did you not realize the jeopardy you put me in?"
"Mayhap, but I thought the king would protect you."
"How was he to do that when de Guylet hadn't returned and de Morris claimed to be my guardian?" Kate's anger rose. She wanted to yell at her father for his ill favor.
"I didn't know he would come after you for it, Kate."
"I became his ward and discovered he kidnapped a child from the king's palace, Colin MacKinnon's daughter. That's how I met Brendan, but King Henry had already betrothed me to another Scotsman, though that never came to be. Anyway, Richard came after me, and he threatened me for the medallion. He killed Manik. There is more but I'm afeared to tell you what he did to me."
"The vile man," Hawk shouted. "Has Henry had him tried?"
"He gave Colin MacKinnon permission to kill him for stealing his child."
"Get your belongings, fairy, we will leave this place at once. I long to go home. I'll find Richard myself, the beastly boar."
"I cannot leave. I'm married to Brendan and I won't leave him, Father. He needs me."
"Needs you? What about me? I need you, too."

"You need me? You left me alone for four years to care for myself. You don't need me."

"I didn't mean to leave you for so long, Kate. I cannot lose you now when I have only returned." Her father paced the room. She held back a smile when he mimicked Brendan's movements.

"Father, I belong with Brendan now. You knew I would wed, eventually. I love him, and he loves me." She pulled away and clasped her hands and willed her father's acceptance.

Hawk lowered his gaze to the floor. "You'll leave your father for this man?"

"Aye, when I told him I loved him, I promised to honor him, and I won't go back on my word even if that means disappointing you."

"Fairy, you don't know what you're saying. Mayhap I've jarred you by coming back from the dead. I will find another worthy husband for you."

"I won't leave my husband. He is worthy. If you want to leave, then go. I cannot stop you, but I wish you understood these people. They're good-natured and were kind to me when I had no one to turn to."

"I will repay their kindness by giving them—"

"Father, you're not listening. They want nothing because they feel they owe me for saving their daughter."

"So I'm to lose my daughter after you saved theirs? Is that the way of it?" Hawk asked angrily.

"You will not lose me, Father. I am married, but I shall visit. You can visit anytime. Brendan will bring me for a visit—"

"You married a barbarian Scot. What of my aspiration to have you married to a good Norman knight?" Hawk moved to the hearth and leaned against the stone.

"You spoke nothing of your aspirations of a Norman knight, nor did you say you disliked the Scots. Well, I'm married to a barbarian Scot, and that's that." Kate yelled loudly, her voice all but gave out.

He appeared stunned she raised her voice to him. "Where is my doting daughter? You're not the sweet daughter I left behind. You've changed; even your appearance has changed to that of a woman. I cannot fathom you being married to that giant."

"Father, I am grown. You must understand. You were gone a long time and left me to fend for myself. I should be wrath with you for leaving me alone, but you were only doing your duty. Please, understand it's what I want."

He nodded. "Come, let us return to the dining hall. You should finish eating."

Kate agreed and returned to the now silent hall. Many vacated it after the earlier commotion. As soon as they arrived, the king lowered his goblet and placed it on the table.

"Come, Hawk, Lady Kate, we will discuss this dilemma."

"What know you of this Brendan MacKinnon, Henry? Is he a worthy man as my Kate affirms?" Hawk accepted the goblet of wine given to him by a servant.

"You won't find a fiercer fighter or a more noble man. I'm related to his sister-in-law, Julianna. The MacKinnons are a peaceful clan, but they are a clan to be reckoned with if it so warrants."

"Has he fortune? Security of an army? What has he to offer my daughter?"

"He has no fortune, but none are needed where he dwells. These people live a simpler life, not as we do with our courts, entertainments, and wealth."

"So they're poor?"

"That depends on what you consider poor. Colin, Brendan's brother, is the laird. His clan prospers with crops, and he's been an adviser to Alexander."

"Alexander, their king?"

"Aye, so it might seem to you and me they are without means, but our kind of wealth means little to them. They take care of themselves and have an abundance of food and whatever they have a need of."

Colin entered the chamber and joined them.

Kate greeted him and asked him to sit next to her. She needed his presence but wished Brendan would return. As he ate, her father watched her and continued to berate Henry with questions. Kate couldn't eat a bite. She was relieved when Brendan appeared. He sat beside her and held her hand under the table, soothing her by rubbing his thumb over the top of her hand. His touch calmed her.

"Don't let him upset you. We'll get through this, Katie. Smile. Let us celebrate our union." Brendan spoke low so only she heard.

"How can I celebrate when he's being unreasonable? I must go, Brendan. I'll retire to our chamber." Kate pulled her hand from his and stood.

Brendan watched her leave then looked at her father. He observed him for a good length of time, but Hawk didn't take notice. He continued to eat and grunted at the king's words.

Colin tapped Brendan's shoulder to gain his attention. "He's as surly as you. Kate's wed a man akin to her father. No wonder she likes you." He guffawed at his jest.

"Cosh, Colin, keep your insults to yourself, otherwise, I might shove my fist in your mouth."

"Hell, Brendan, you're irritable. Let your wife sooth your testiness. I'll see to your father-in-law," Colin jested.

"Aye, I'm for that." Brendan couldn't leave fast enough. He walked quickly to their chamber, and found Kate crying, lying on a heap of coverings. He sat on the bed and took her in his arms.

"Love, it's not that bad. Your father will come around."

"I don't want to talk about him. I need you."

Brendan smiled at the sultriness of her plea. It was easy for him to dispel the strife as her words sent his body to fervor. She wanted release too, and let the carnal sensations overtake her body. He wanted to forget her father and everyone outside their door. He was as gentle as he could be, but she wouldn't let him. She urged him into a climatic state and was as forceful in her demands. Their lovemaking heightened and each reached the climactic sensations at the same time.

After, as he lay beside her, his heart beat frantically. He'd never let her go. Her father needed to understand. She clung to him, and wouldn't release his arms, so Brendan let her have her way. The room darkened into blackness as the night wore on. Still, she wouldn't let him go. He thought she slept because she didn't move or speak.

"I love you, Katie," he admitted aloud.

Kate bolted into an upright position and turned to him. "What did you say?"

Brendan frowned, but she couldn't see it. As her eyes adjusted to the darkness, she leaned closer. "Say it again."

"I love you."

"You've done it now, Brendan," she mumbled.

"What?" he asked as he pulled her back into his arms.

"Are you saying that because…"

Brendan cradled her face and nudged her chin so he could see her face. "Katie, how could I not love you? You have loved me since you had your vision. I'll not deny it, but you won't weaken me, love, do you hear?"

She giggled and lowered her mouth to his. "I won't weaken you, Brendan, I promise."

"And I won't be a farmer, Katie, do you hear me?"

She nodded against his chest. "Somehow, I can't see you tending the fields, Brendan. I'm not of a mind to change you. I like you just as you are…my scowling warrior."

He smiled at that.

CHAPTER TWENTY-NINE

The last thing Brendan wanted was to leave Katie. But Henry grew frustrated with the mood in his court. He suggested a hunting party for the men as a means of entertainment. Brendan kept his distance from Lord Stanhope who sat with his arms folded over his chest. The man glared at all who chanced to look at him. Brendan paced the great hall like a caged lion, watchful at the door for Katie. She wanted to be alone, she'd said, and Brendan appeased her.

Colin drew away from the table. "That's a fair idea, Henry, a hunt. I'll assemble the men."

Brendan reluctantly walked outside into the cool morning. The sky grayed and light rain speckled the ground.

Henry held his hands out and gazed above. "Perhaps we shall go on a hunt on the morrow."

"Nay, it'll stop soon. The day will turn brighter. The clouds are not that thick," Colin said.

Brendan led his stallion into the center courtyard and mounted it. He waited for the rest to join him and glowered at the thought of spending the day in boredom.

Lord Stanhope muttered, "They're not coming, are they?" The 'they' were he and his brothers. He would've taken offense at the remark, but drew a breath and withheld his affront.

"Damn me, I thought to escape them," Henry whispered to Colin.

Brendan presumed Henry meant him and Lord Stanhope. Colin laughed boisterously and gained hard stares from Henry's soldiers and grins from Colin's warriors. They forged ahead and rode in silence through the thick overgrown woods which bordered the castle walls. The king's hunting grounds didn't offer much of a selection of animals to hunt, and Brendan grew as bored as he'd been in the hall. He led the procession and gazed at each side of the trees. He pulled his mount to a stop and blocked those behind him.

"Men camp ahead about three-hundred feet beyond."

"You hear them?" Henry asked incredulously.

Hawk wedged his horse betwixt his and Henry's. "What's happening?"

Colin ignored him and asked, "Do you think they're Richard's men?"

"Could we be that fortunate?" Brendan countered.

"Advance in our usual formation, men," Colin ordered. "Let us prepare."

Henry nodded. "I find this exciting. I've never been involved in a fight before and wish to see you Highlanders battle." Fortunately, Henry's soldiers moved in and flanked him.

Brendan scowled at the king. "Your Grace, keep your voice low." He eased at Henry's sentry's gesture of protection. He didn't want to worry about the king if the fracas became intense.

"Henry, stay here, where it's safe," Colin directed.

"Nay, I shall go forth with you. My men will see to my safety."

Colin nodded and wouldn't gainsay the king. The MacKinnon warriors jumped from their mounts and readied for the fight. They used mud to cover themselves with dark painted symbols. The warriors held daggers and broad swords. Henry's eyes widened and he insisted he be included in their ritualistic ceremony. Brendan and Colin shook their heads at the king's request. Once he readied, Brendan paced in front of the soldiers in anticipation of war.

The afternoon grew dismal as the clouds thickened and the forest floor overlaid with a dense mist. The mist didn't stir when the warriors advanced on the enemy. Colin demanded again that Henry remain with his soldiers, away from the conflict, but he didn't concede and walked beside Colin's men. Lord Stanhope wouldn't stay behind either and marched behind them.

When the last warrior settled on the large branches over their enemy's camp, a bird took flight and fluttered its wings. The creature gave alert to those on the ground. Brendan raised a hand and listened to the men below.

A man rose at the scuttle of the bird, but he seemed to dismiss it. "Be on the alert, men." He walked to the fire and turned back and peered at where the bird landed. Mist shifted on the ground and rolled toward him. "The day grows eerie."

Two soldiers squabbled over a chunk of bread. The man cuffed them on the sides of their heads and took the bread. "You'll get nothing now. Settle down to rest, men, we'll get an early start. I want to regain my possession by the morrow and be gone before the king becomes the wiser."

As the camp quieted, the man sat by a fire amid his guards. They positioned around him and would give an alert if anyone advanced. He spoke to another, "How have I ended here, in the mist of Londontown? If I'd obtained the damned medallion sooner, I would be in the holy land by now. I should have the treasure. Instead, I sit here," he held out his hand, "in the damp woods awaiting that hellion. Kaitlin won't get away. I won't give up."

A man nearby said, "You should've known the woman wouldn't come."

Brendan tensed in realization the man was Richard.

Richard nodded at his comrade's conjecture. "I'm disheartened Fitzhugh wouldn't give aid."

"Aye, m'lord, you had to kill him."

LASS' VALOR

"Indeed." Richard shot a glance at the trees in the distance. "I thought I heard something. Shhh."

At once, men jumped from the trees and surrounded Richard and his men. Before he called his men to arms, Brendan and his brethren stood face to face with their enemy. Two of Colin's soldiers approached and took Richard's arms. Richard's men tossed their weapons near the fire and their lord struggled against to free himself.

"Release me. I'm Lord Richard de Morris. My men will cut you down at my command."

Colin frowned in disbelief. "I don't think so, de Morris. Your men have surrendered."

"Release me, I said."

Colin threw him to the ground but he scrambled to his feet. Brendan positioned his sword an inch from his chest and Richard stilled.

"I will tell you why you'll die by my hand, Lord Richard," Colin declared heatedly.

"You dare insult me?" Richard yelled.

"You took my child from the king's castle and kept her in that pigsty you call home. For that, you will face death this day." Colin gripped his sword and held it above his shoulder.

"Let me do the honor, Colin. He hurt Katie and tried to kill her father. I should be the one to end his life," Brendan said.

Richard stepped back and yanked his sword from its scabbard. He held it pointed at them.

Colin eyed Richard before he turned to him. "Aye, Brendan, the honor should be yours."

Brendan wanted a fair fight and signaled to the warriors to keep back. "Did you act alone, Richard?"

"Alone in what? Capturing the child? 'Twas easy," he boasted. "The king wouldn't care about a heathen child, or about Stanhope's daughter. Why would he? It doesn't matter now, I've lost the medallion, the child, and here I am facing you."

"It matters greatly. The child is the king's cousin and

Lady Stanhope is my wife. Were you trying to prove yourself when you forced her to submit to you? Then you stabbed her and left her for dead in the woods. You feed on the innocent and weaker, don't you? You're the devil's kin." Brendan regarded Richard's hand which tensed on the hilt of his weapon. The attack was imminent.

Richard's gazed turned scornful at his kinsmen who stood aside and watched the foray. When Richard noticed the king's liveried soldiers beyond them and Henry's look of disdain, the man's face whitened.

Brendan detected his immovable stance. Richard grew lax for a moment then repositioned himself and readied to strike. Brendan swung his blade in an arch and intended to slice him in the middle, but Richard sidestepped too quickly and he missed. Richard retaliated and jabbed his thinner sword at him. Brendan easily dodged his thrusts. Richard growled in frustration and ran at him. Before he reached him, Richard stopped short.

"Hawk?" He raised his sword and a fearless mien overrode his caution. A harrowing expression replaced the fierceness.

Brendan didn't lower his weapon, but kept his position and waited to see what Richard would do. Within a few steps, he would end Richard's life, but Lord Stanhope marched and stood between them.

"Richard," Hawk muttered with disgust. "You're a deviant daemon." He shocked them all when he spit on Richard. "That's for trying to hurt my daughter."

"You live," Richard said in awe.

Hawk frowned. "An Arab saved me. All this trouble, Richard, for a piece of scrap parchment and a mysterious treasure?"

"The treasure will be mine," Richard yelled. "I shall have it. No one will stop me."

Brendan stood near, and as everyone stared at the deranged man, the forest stilled and silenced.

"It was for naught, Richard, there's no treasure. The

medallion and map are invalid, but an artifice made by the Templar Knights. The map leads to a demolished monastery here in England. Perhaps the medallion is worth something if you melt it down," Hawk said mockingly.

"Naught but a demolished monastery? You lie." Richard's gaze gave no regard for his peril. "I shall be rich, richer than you, richer than the king."

"Richer than me, Richard?" Henry asked.

Richard's eyes scrunched when Henry stepped forward. He must've forgotten the king attended their scuffle.

"There was never a treasure. You gain only your death with your greed," Hawk said.

"Nay, nay, it's impossible, Hawk. I won't let you have the treasure. You lie." Richard ran at Hawk.

Brendan held his ground and shoved Hawk behind him. He allowed Richard to come at him, but at the last second, he shifted his blade in Richard's direction. He pierced Richard's waist and let his weapon drop to the ground. Richard stumbled and bumped into him. He tried to jab him with his sword, but the length didn't allow for an easy target. Brendan grabbed his sword's handle and yanked it from his hold. He threw it into the air, away from them.

Richard's breath heavy now, sent forth its steam in the cold air, and his exertion evident in his slumped form. Brendan stood ready for his advance. Richard threw his body at him and they ended on the mist-covered ground. The men shouted as the mist floated and swirled around them. None moved and waited for the victor to rise.

Brendan had enough of the tarry. He pulled a dagger from his boot, punched Richard in the face, and knocked him from his chest where he tried to hold him down. As Richard rolled back, Brendan gripped his dagger, took aim, and shoved the blade into Richard's heart. The man's eyes boggled and he stared at him for a moment. He breathed no more.

Brendan took a moment to catch his breath before he gained his feet. When his clansmen saw him rise from the cloaked mist, they cheered.

Colin clapped him on the back. "Well done, Brendan. The knave is dead?"

He nodded and bent to retrieve his dagger. His steps stirred the mist, and he yanked his dagger from Richard's chest. He made certain Richard was dead before he walked away to fetch his sword.

"Collect your leader," Colin said angrily to Richard's soldiers.

The Englishmen hurried to recover his body before they changed their minds about releasing them.

"Finally, justice is served," Colin said.

Brendan reached his side. "At last, the devil is dead."

Hawk approached and stood between them, and clapped them on the shoulders. "You fight well, lad. I owe you a debt as you saved me from Richard's sword."

"Nay, you owe me no debt," Brendan retorted and walked away.

CHAPTER THIRTY

Kate paced the length of the chamber she stayed in. She tried to reason how to convince her father Brendan was worthy of her hand. Nothing came to mind, and she dejected at the thought of disappointing her father. Nothing would sway him. She startled at a knock on her door. When she opened it, she hadn't expected to see her father. She opened the door wider and stepped back.

"Fairy, I need to speak to you."

"Father, please, there's nothing more to say." Kate moved into the room but turned when she reached the window.

"Aye, there is. I was wrong. I'll grant you married a strong man, but will he provide for you?"

Kate noted his smile. "Brendan is resourceful."

"You have my approval, Kate. You must love him to go against my wishes. I won't stand in the way of your happiness."

A tear slipped down Kate's cheek. "Oh, Father, I'm pleased to hear you say that."

"I imagine your man needs you about now. Why don't you go to him?"

"What are you talking about?"

"He killed Richard and left abruptly. His brother said he

always goes off after a fight. I don't know where he went."

"He wasn't harmed, was he?"

Her father scoffed. "I doubt anyone could inflict harm on that hardheaded Scot. I suppose I did well by you. It's safe to say I can return home and resume my life."

"Be well, Father." Kate leaned up and kissed her father on the cheek and ran from the chamber.

She ran most of the way to the palace gates but stopped a few times to catch her breath. With her skirts in hand, she ran through the trees that edged the castle walls. When she reached a clearing, she found Colin with Brendan on the highest part of the rampart. Colin climbed down a ladder and as he passed her, he winked.

Her breath caught at the height of the wall, but she had to brave it. Kate waited for Colin to walk away and grabbed hold of the ladder. When she reached the top of the wall, she sat next to Brendan and took his hand. "My father told me what happened. Are you all right?"

"Aye, I am now that you're here." He squeezed her hand.

"You killed Lord Richard?"

A tranquil silence fell between them. The end of the vendetta released Brendan from his vow and his shoulders relaxed. He kept his gaze on the distance and drew an easy breath.

"Aye, I did. You're a brave lass to come up here. You were terrified to sit close to the edge of the cliffs at home. I had to coax you to look at the view. We're up mighty high."

She peered at the steep drop in front of them, though it wasn't as tremendous as his cliff.

"You're not afraid anymore, are you?"

Kate smiled. "Nay," then she admitted, "Perhaps a little."

"Are you trying to be fearless? Why are you unafraid?"

She clutched his hand. "Because you won't let me fall."

Brendan grinned. "I'm pleased by your faith in me. You're the most valiant lady."

"I'm glad you think highly of me, husband."

Brendan brushed his shoulder against hers and kissed her. "I do."

"My father gave his approval of our marriage."

"I knew he would. When is he leaving?"

Kate laughed at the grumpy tone of his voice. "I don't know, probably soon. Why?"

"I want to return home and beget my sons. You won't see anyone for weeks."

Kate laughed harder. "I don't want to see anyone—only you."

Brendan lowered her back onto the wall. "Why don't we start right now?"

"Here atop the wall, in the rain?"

"Aye, it will feel good. It's dark enough, none are about."

Kate responded and pulled him close to kiss him. The rain hit her face and rolled between their lips. His hard mouth covers hers and turned over hers. He held her neck, with his thumb positioned in the center, and swept gently over her throat. Brendan lifted his head and peered above. The noise of a hawk's shrill shriek sounded overhead but obscured in the dark rainy sky. She spotted her father below in the courtyard, a good distance from them. He peered at the sky and walked away a moment later.

She placed her hand on Brendan's chest. "I dreamt about you for the longest time, you came to me in a vision when I was four and ten."

"What was I doing in this vision?"

"You scowled at me. I gave up ever finding you."

"Why?"

"Because my father left for the excursion and I didn't believe I would ever meet you and..."

"Did I kiss you in your vision?" He grinned and cupped her face in a loving caress.

"Nay, you didn't," Kate admitted.

"Then it couldn't have been me."

"Oh, it was you. I memorized every inch of you. Your

eyes haunted me, and your hair was slightly shorter, but it was you."

"You dreamed of me all those years?"

Kate nodded. She trailed her hand along his chest, up to his arm to his bulged biceps. "Aye, and I wasn't sure why you came to me. I've loved you for the longest time, I'll always love you." She closed her eyes and sighed.

"I love you too, Katie." He caressed her bottom and lowered his mouth again. After kissing her for a spell, he raised his head and grinned. "I can't wait to go home. Shall we leave on the morrow?"

"I'm pleased we'll return to your clan, Brendan, it's where we belong."

"Aye, you belong with me."

Brendan took her inside the king's palace and once there, he showed her how much he loved her. Kate slept soundlessly and hadn't heard him rise. When she awoke in the morn, he was gone. She frowned at the room.

The door burst open and Brendan strolled in. His eyes no longer looked cold and foreboding, but light and somewhat adoring. He took her hand, pulled her from the bed, and kissed her. "I'm glad you're awake. It's time to leave. You might want to say farewell to Henry and your father. They await you."

Kate scrambled away and hastily dressed. When she entered the king's hall, all was silent. Her footsteps sounded loud, but she ambled forward until she reached Henry and her father, who stood next to the dais.

"Your Grace, thank you for everything. I shall always remember your kindness."

"Be well, Lady MacKinnon. Take care of my friend." Henry whispered the last of his farewell. She smiled and nodded.

Her father took her in his arms and hugged her tightly. "I will leave this day as well. My men long to return home, as do I. It's been years since they've seen their families. I promise to visit, fairy."

"We shall expect you soon, Father."

Brendan took her hand and guided her from the palace. She smiled at Colin and Julianna who awaited on their horses, their men waited ahead outside the gate and eager to depart. Brendan helped her onto her mount and she was finally on her way home. Throughout the day's ride, a sudden ailment struck her. The scenery blurred and her stomach flipped from the motion of the horse, but she refrained to mention her illness to Brendan. The last thing she needed was his concern.

Travel to the Highlands was much easier on the journey than it was when she'd traveled with Bonnie. There was no fear of Richard's wrath or getting lost in the dense woods.

"You are tired. Ride with me and close your eyes." Brendan pulled her onto his horse and she cuddled in his embrace.

Brendan stopped on the rise before his beloved home and brushed his lips over Kate's. He stroked her face and awakened her. She slept the last two hours of the ride and stretched in his arms. He helped her from his mount.

"We're home."

She wore a smile on her bonny face. Life would be vastly different for him. Brendan was a soldier no longer, but a husband. One day he would be a father and have a family. The thought of it lightened him because he'd never dreamed to have such riches. Their cottage would be a joyful place where the wee ones would be loved. Brendan recalled her promise to her father before they left. Lord Hawk would visit and her happiness was assured.

They reached the holding. Kate clasped his hand and beamed with joy at their homecoming. He took the steps and released her hand.

"I need to change my garments." Brendan took the steps and hastened inside. In the chamber he used when he stayed at the keep, he knelt beside the trunk which held his laundered tartans. A voice drew his attention, and he spotted his niece at the window casement. He withheld the urge to bellow with laughter.

She leaned and peered out the window with a large tankard position on the edge. What in God's name was she up to? Brendan approached cautiously and hoped to get a glimpse. Bonnie leaned her head against the iron grill and tipped the tankard's contents.

"Lass, what are you doing?"

Bonnie startled and jumped back from the window. "Uncle Brendan, I ah, dumped my cup out the window."

"I see that, but who did you dump it on?" He laughed when he lifted her in his arms, but glared when he noticed the lad, Shawn, below the window casement.

"You must apologize, lass." He set her down and gave her a push toward the window.

Bonnie peeked down. "Sorry, Shawn."

Brendan replaced his tunic and a fresh tartan over his upper body. "That's all?"

She nodded.

He laughed heartily. "You're going to have to tell your papa about this."

She nodded again. "All right, Uncle, I'll tell him later."

He shook his head. "Nay, you'll tell him now." Brendan lifted her and carried her back to the hall where her father stood at the table with the ladies. Bonnie's expression turned grim and before anyone told her otherwise, she sat in her father's chair.

When his niece gawked about the room, she noticed Katie and immediately ran from the chair to her. She hugged his wife and bawled something about Kate's cat. "I missed you and knowed you would come back."

"I missed you too, lovey. Have you been a good girl?" Kate knelt and petted Trixie who rubbed against her leg.

"Aye, I been a good girl and took care of Trixie."

Kate laughed and hugged his niece. "Thank you."

Brendan gave Bonnie a 'get-on-with-it' look, and she walked to her father's chair and sat again. Colin approached

LASS' VALOR

and knelt next to his daughter.

"Papa," she said softly.

"Aye, Button, you'd best confess your wrongdoing. Your uncle appears displeased and I suspect you've done something disagreeable."

"I...dumped water on Shawn's head."

Colin laughed but stifled it. "Why did you do that?"

"I don't like 'em. Do I gots to sit in your chair?"

His brother sobered. "Aye, for the rest of the day."

Dusk dimmed the sky and the evening meal would soon be served, she'd only have to suffer a few hours of punishment. Brendan smiled when Kate approached her ally.

"Colin, may I sit with her?"

His brother nodded. "Don't make it too pleasurable for her, Kate."

"I won't, I promise."

At that moment, Burk entered the hall and walked directly to Colin. Brendan noticed the grim expression on his face.

"Laird, your attendance is needed. There's a grave matter."

Colin tilted his head at the soldier but followed when Burk turned and fled.

Brendan wondered what happened. He gave Kate a quick kiss and followed his brother outside. As he exited the hall, he noted several MacKinnon soldiers by the gate. They appeared ready for battle. "What's amiss?"

Colin turned. "It's not good, Brendan. Barclay came to claim his wife, and he says he'll go to war if need be to obtain the king's gift."

"Cosh, I knew it would eventually come to this. Well, let's not keep him waiting." Brendan walked to the stable where his steed hadn't even been settled. He mounted and rode through the walls. His brothers rode beside him and Brendan couldn't bring himself to speak about what was to come. The situation should prove humorous. He wasn't concerned Barclay would war with them. The cosh he was about to pull should settle the matter.

They reached the hill where Barclay waited with his men. Brendan noticed their hostility and almost laughed, but he kept himself circumspect.

"It looks as though they ready to war, Brendan."

Robin rode to his other side, and Brendan glanced from one brother to the other.

"We stand with you and won't let Barclay get his hands on Kate," Colin said.

Brendan grunted. "Aye, let us greet them then." He nudged his horse forward and his brothers followed. When he reached Angus Barclay, he stopped and circled him and the few men brave enough to set themselves apart with their laird.

"Angus," Colin said. "What do you here on our land?"

Angus grumbled and took his sword from his scabbard. Brendan almost smiled.

"I don't think you want to do that. Best put away your sword before my clan deems it a threat. You don't want to cause their ire." Colin nodded, but the man's eyes bulged.

Brendan sat on his steed and waited for Angus to address him. It didn't take long to get to the heart of the matter.

"Brendan MacKinnon, you stole a gift King Henry intended for me, my own wife. Because of you, I lost her and the lands he granted me. What say you to these charges?"

He rounded Angus again and kept a stern expression on his face. "Oh, aye, I stole the woman, but you wouldn't have wanted her. I saved your arse a good deal of trouble, Barclay. You should thank me."

Colin frowned at him, as did many of the MacKinnon men.

Angus' face reddened. "Thank you? And why should I thank you? You admit to stealing my intended bride?"

He nodded adamantly. "Aye, I surely do."

His foe's eyes bulged with anger. "You'll pay for the deed this day. You insult the woman. Why wouldn't I want her?"

Brendan kept his expression serious to better affect the Barclay. "Well now, because she's been nothing but trouble since I found her. She's a downright obstinate woman, and carps day and night. Aye, she's demanding too. I suspect she's even a witch. She's a mite cowardly and is afraid of her own shadow. Now that I think on it, Colin, mayhap we should turn her over to Barclay. Hell, we don't need that kind of woman within our clan."

Colin caught on to his ploy. "Aye, you're right, Brendan. We should fetch her. I'll not have the woman influence my wife or the rest of the women in our clan. Besides, her voice annoys me." His brother scowled and affirmed his statement with a nod.

Angus' horse lifted its legs and sidestepped. "The hell you say. She's a witch? We don't want such a woman in our clan. I have changed my mind."

Brendan hunched his shoulder. "You can't change your mind. You came here today for her, and I say we send her back with you. Colin, make him take her."

Angus's face reddened and he frowned. Brendan held in the urge to grin.

"You'll not tell me what I should do, lad. MacKinnon, you should learn how to control your brother. I won't take the woman, not if she's as you say. Do you speak the truth?"

Colin, at last, spoke up. "What my brother says is true."

Brendan rounded Angus again and bumped his horse into the laird's. "I suppose we have no choice but to keep her then. Are you sure you won't change your mind? She is beautiful."

Angus sheathed his sword and shook his head in defeat. "Nay, beauty or not, I don't need a carping woman, Brendan. I relinquish my claim to her. She's all yours."

"We won't have any trouble with your clan, Barclay. Don't traipse on our land with a change of heart. If you walk away, you forfeit the gift." Colin turned on his mount and hid his smile.

"Gift? Nay, the woman is unworthy of the bestowment. We won't trouble you further. Don't be thinking to drop her off on our land either. I'll have your word, MacKinnon."

"Aye, you'll never see her." Brendan leaned forward and jerked his body as if he'd strike Barclay and the man moved back. He almost laughed, but instead, rode to catch up with his brothers.

Colin chuckled at what transpired. "That was risky, Brendan."

Brendan grunted. "Barclay's a dimwit, but he wouldn't want Katie if I...I lied."

"Aye, you lie rather well, brother. Still, you're fortunate he fell for it."

Brendan grinned. "Remind me to tell you about the fight I got into with his men once. They told me all his sisters are shrews who harass him, and how superstitious he is."

"Sounds like someone I know." Colin nudged his horse forward.

Brendan kicked his steed's haunches to catch up to his brother. He was happy to return to his sweet wife, who contradicted all he'd told Barclay. As he rode through the portcullis, he dismounted and left his horse for the stable lad to care for. He and his brothers went inside the hall and stood stock-still at the view. Somehow, his wife, Julianna, and Tess ended up on the floor by the hearth. An empty jug of brew lay on its side in the center of their triangle.

Kate played with a decorative ruffle on her gown and giggled. Julianna's legs crossed at the knees, and her foot waved in the air, her slipper dangled from her foot. Tess threw her son's ball that Julianna made for him in the air and caught it. Their laughter made him raise a brow.

"Julianna, you must do something about the cobwebs on your ceiling," Katie said and snickered.

"You're so right, Kate," Julianna said, "If I can get my husband out of bed at a decent hour, mayhap I will put him to the task."

"I want to give Robin a task, but it won't be anything of

that sort," Tess chimed in.

Kate laughed. "If they ever come home…they should be here pleasuring their wives and seeing to our needs, but instead, they go off to war or some equally appalling pursuit."

Brendan kept himself from laughing outright at their conversation.

"We shouldn't forgive them easily when they return," Tess said stringently.

Brendan and his brothers stood transfixed, shocked more like, at the sight of their wives. The ladies didn't know they were being observed because they were too busy laughing.

Colin smiled then whispered, "They're sotted."

"Seems they are," Brendan agreed. "I believe I didn't lie about everything I said to Barclay. My woman is a wee bit of trouble. Should we give them assistance?"

"I say we let them suffer," Robin put in.

"Nay, I believe I'll enjoy myself this night," Brendan said, happily.

"Hah, they'll be in a besotted slumber before we get 'em to their beds," Robin said.

Colin shook his head, his arms folded over his chest. "Seems they found the brew I hid in the buttery. I was saving it for a celebration and it was the last jug."

"Aye, you'll have to visit Scottie to get more," Brendan suggested.

Colin frowned. "He won't give me anymore. I just got four jugs from him. We used three for Bonnie's celebration. Just look at them, they drank an entire jug amongst the three of them. Hell, they should be tipsy for the next week. That brew is potent."

Brendan laughed. "They don't even know we're here. Let's get them off the floor, shall we?" He approached his wife, and his brothers went to their wives. When the women finally saw them, they broke out in fits of laughter.

"They're out of control," Colin said with disgust.

Brendan nodded as he leaned to lift Katie in his arms.

Her head lobbed a few times before she settled it on his shoulder.

"Sweetheart, you're in for a pounder."

"Brendan, put me down. I can walk."

"Nay, you can't. You'll kill yourself walking to our cottage."

She giggled and smacked his cheek with her lips. "Don't you have faith in me?"

"Not at the moment, love."

Katie grinned a sideways smile and clasped her arms around his neck. She held him tightly and he pulled her hands loose and patted them to keep her from putting them back. Her womanly scent didn't override the smell of the brew, and his grin widened. Brendan reached the cottage at last and gently set her on the bed. Trixie jumped up, but he shooed her away.

As he went about lighting the hearth and candles, he heard her giggles. When he finally reached the bed, he was unclothed and was ready to join her. He lay on his stomach and watched her. Her hair came undone from its ties and tresses strewed about her face. She blew a tendril away and giggled again.

"Ah, love, you're no good to me now, not in your condition. You better sleep it off." Brendan rolled over and kicked the covers aside.

Kate rose and removed her garments. She paraded around the room naked, and he raised a brow at the sight of her bare bottom. A groan escaped him. She blew out several candles, most taking more than one attempt and marched back to bed. Kate crawled over him and straddled his hips.

"Husband," she said proudly when she leaned her head against his chest. "I dreamt about you for the longest time. I didn't understand why you always looked at me sternly, but now I do." Katie trailed her hands along his chest and distracted him. "I'll always love you."

"Katie, you don't know what you're saying. You had too much brew."

She scoffed. "Nay, I really do love you, Brendan. You're my own gentle warrior." She closed her eyes and he felt her breath tickle his skin when she sighed.

"I love you too, Katie." He caressed her bare bottom. "Did you hear me, Katie?" He smiled in the dark and realized his drunken wife fell asleep. Brendan shifted her legs and sighed himself. Instead of pleasuring his wife as he'd intended, he listened to her light snore. His last thought before he surrendered to his slumber, Angus Barclay would definitely have warred with the MacKinnons if he'd truly known what he lost.

EPILOGUE

MacKinnon Land, Highlands
August 1224

The rope was positioned in a six-foot circle, the four candles pointed in the cardinal directions. Her hands folded over her large abdomen. The vision cleared when Kate closed her eyes and focused on it. She saw his face unequivocally, the boy had dark hair, and his gray eyes twinkled with mischief. She smiled broadly and tried to memorize his face, his manner, and his traits. Suddenly, she felt a light brush against her lips.

"You're not visualizing another warrior, are you?" Brendan knelt in front of her.

Kate opened her eyes and grinned wickedly. "Oh, aye, I have seen a vision of another warrior."

"Who?" he demanded irritably.

Kate laughed. "He will be as strong as you, a fierce warrior with—"

"Who is he? I'll kill him."

"He's not even born yet." She patted her stomach.

"Oh, you mean my son," he qualified.

"Aye, of course. Who did you think I spoke of?" She

laughed because her husband was a bit miffed about the length of her pregnancy.

"Never mind. So you've seen a vision of our son?"

"My vision was clear. He'll be a strong, fine son to be proud of."

Brendan touched her stomach and kissed her cheek. "When are you going to birth him, Katie? I'm tired of waiting."

Kate giggled. "Soon, I suppose it won't be much longer, but he'll come when he's ready. Let's get rest." She wouldn't tell him she'd had contractions on and off for two days. Brendan would probably force her to bed. Kate would rather go about her routine and keep busy. Likely, Brendan would worry and she didn't want him to be concerned.

He helped her to her feet, placed the rope and candles on the table, and joined her on the bed. Brendan watched her settle to sleep and was apprehensive about the birthing. He didn't seem to be able to sleep and looked about the room. She sighed and wished he would relax, but that wasn't his nature. She stared at the herbs near the hearth, drying, and the bowls of concoctions she'd made to assist Jinny, because of all the recent illnesses.

During the night, Kate sat up and declared in a calm voice she was about to have their bairn. She nudged his shoulder and told him to fetch Jinny.

Brendan ran from their cottage naked until he realized he hadn't dressed. He returned a minute later and hastily put his tartan around him, kissed her, and said he'd return quickly.

Brendan was worn-out from lack of sleep and worry, and paced outside their cottage for hours in wait. The warm summer day did little to allay his unease. Likewise, the chirping birds, light breeze, and sunny skies went unnoticed. He, however, grinned sheepishly at Colin's green coloring.

"Brendan, I realize you're nervous, but will you cease

pacing? You're making my head spin." His brother closed his eyes and forced himself not to look at him.

"I'm not nervous, just bored. Katie will be fine, won't she?" He refused to give in to fears she'd succumb. "She's been at for over four hours. I know how long Julianna took birthing Bonnie and Kevin. I don't think I can stand the wait."

Colin pulled himself from the ledge and stood beside him. As he spoke, the cottage door thrust opened. Brendan dismissed him without a glance. Jinny motioned him forward and wiped her eyes as she and Julianna left. She appeared to be crying. Women were sentimental.

Brendan waited until they left before he approached his wife. "Are you well, Katie?"

"Aye, Brendan, I'm well."

"And my son?"

"He's a fit lad, Brendan, strong and healthy."

Brendan moved to the bedside and glanced at the bairn fussing in her arms. He took his son and held him, the babe's head lobbed. He started screeching.

"Cradle him in your arms," Kate instructed. "We need to love him and show him affection."

Brendan shifted him and looked into his son's eyes. He couldn't tell what color they were, but they were light. His head held a few tufts of dark curls.

"He's a fine lad, Katie, you did well."

"Me? He resembles you and…" Kate laughed when the baby let out a loud cry, and Brendan quickly handed him back. "…he has your disposition." She smiled and positioned the babe against her breast.

The only noise to be heard was the sound of the suckling babe. Brendan watched his wife and son quietly for a moment. "Thank you."

Kate frowned. "You mustn't thank me. I only did my duty."

"Now I must do my duty."

"What's that?"

"Protect you both with my life, and have a chair made for our son, who will likely be bent on trouble like his mother, and of course, work on begetting a daughter." He laughed when she pinched his leg.

Kate smiled. "Enjoy your son for a while then we'll see about a daughter."

"Do you think he'll like the cliffs?"

"Nay, nay, you mustn't take him there, promise me."

Brendan smiled and suspected he and his son would have many secrets. Katie would scold him to no end. Instead of promising her, he kissed her longingly, while he caressed his son's head.

"I promise you, my son won't have a father like Donald. I'll teach him everything and show him how much he's loved. He'll be a fine MacKinnon warrior with courage and strength. We should call him Walt. Aye, to honor my real father. Walt would like that."

"He would, Brendan. Very well, we'll name him Walter. I love you."

He kissed her again and sealed their pact. "I love you, Katie." The words came easier. "Now and forever. You've given me a son who will have as much valor as you."

AUTHOR'S NOTE

Dear Readers,

I hope you enjoyed the Pith Trilogy. It was my first foray into writing. I loved Colin, Douglas, and Brendan's stories and their fearless heroines. The early 13th century is perhaps my favorite time period to write in, and to me, the most romantic.

Happy historical reading,

Fondly,
Kara Griffin

OTHER HISTORICAL TITLES BY KARA GRIFFIN

~LEGEND OF THE KING'S GUARD SERIES~
CONQUERED HEART – Book One
UNBREAKABLE HEART – Book Two
FEARLESS HEART – Book Three
UNDENIABLE HEART – Book Four

Critically Acclaimed Scottish Romance Series
~GUNN GUARDSMAN SERIES~
ONE & ONLY – Book One
ON A HIGHLAND HILL – Book Two
A HIGHLANDER IN PERIL – Book Three
IN LOVE WITH A WARRIOR – Book Four

~THE PITH TRILOGY~
WARRIOR'S PLEDGE – Book One
CLAIMED BY A CHARMER – Book Two
LASS' VALOR – Book Three

Coming Soon
Mystic Maidens of Britain - Series
PENDRAGON'S PRINCESS – Book One
THE GOOD WITCH & THE WARRIOR – Book Two
A KNIGHT'S LOVE – Book Three

Lairds of the North - Series
THE SEDUCTION OF LAIRD SINCLAIR – Book One
SEVEN LASSES & A LAIRD – Book Two
MAKING HER A MACKAY – Book Three
KIERAN'S STORY – Book Four

The Marvelous MacLeers (series)
Keepers of the Kingdom (series)
Daughters of Dunfeld (Halloween anthology 2020)

What readers are saying...

MYSTIC MAIDENS OF BRITAIN SERIES
PENDRAGON'S PRINCESS – Book One
5 stars - I loved reading this medieval fantasy! A magical story of castles and kings, of a princess born with a mystic gift and a prince with a real live dragon kept hidden from the rest of the world. Well written and romantic, this book is very entertaining. - PPeters Reader Review

LEGEND OF THE KING'S GUARD SERIES
CONQUERED HEART – Book One
5 Stars - WOW! What a great start to a series, this book is fast paced action, but then what did I expect, Kara Griffin writes strong minded and compassionate characters and embroiled them into adventure and romance. -Ann L.

UNBREAKABLE HEART – Book Two
5 Stars - A sensational story of love and forgiveness. A roller coaster of emotions, a swoon worthy hero, and a heroine who gives our hero a run for his money. The author did an awesome job in transferring the anger and devastation Makenna was feeling as well as the love that eventually conquered their hearts! - Maria (Books & Benches

FEARLESS HEART – Book Three
5 Stars - I recommend to everyone. Heath and Lillia are perfect together. Friar Hemm is amazing. The Guardsman intoned together. It's a sad, tearful, astounding, amazing book. - Reader Review

UNDENIABLE HEART – Book Four
5 stars - Really good book; enjoyable read. I hadn't read one of Kara's books before, but I'm glad that I picked this one. I enjoyed it and it kept me engaged. I would highly recommend this book to anyone who hasn't read Kara's books before. - Reader Review

GUNN GUARDSMAN SERIES
ONE & ONLY – Book One
5 Stars - I love everything about this story Grey and his guards oh my god!!! They are to die for! If you love highlander HEA with a lot of twists

and a beautiful love story filled with strong fierce loving men and independent women then this is definitely for you! - Reader Review

ON A HIGHLAND HILL – Book Two
5 Stars - This book had a great storyline, with humor, action, intrigue and of cause a tender romance. I will be reading more work by Kara Griffin for sure. - Julie D.

A HIGHLANDER IN PERIL – Book Three
5 Stars - This book has intrigue, mystery, murder and incredibly romantic scenes that you will have a problem putting it down until the very end and then you will wish it had another chapter so you could keep reading the story. I did not put it down until the last word was read. I recommend this book to any who enjoy historical romance with intense intrigue and suspense. - Jusnana

IN LOVE WITH A WARRIOR – Book Four
5 stars - Talk about realism, romance, passion, a heat of battle, and remarkably accurate history. This fast paced and adventurous plot moved quickly and kept me interested all the way through. These two alphas make you laugh, cry, cheer and rant! - Romantic Renay

THE PITH TRILOGY
WARRIOR'S PLEDGE – Book One
5 stars - Much swooning and mischief under the Plaid issues---along with danger, intrigue, and romance that will steam your glasses - Past Romance

CLAIMED BY A CHARMER – Book Two
5 stars - Enjoyed!....every bit, moves along no wasting time in the story. Kept me wanting to know what or who is the other enemy besides one of her relatives. - Reader Review

LASS' VALOR – Book Three
4 Stars -Lass' Valor was a thoroughly enjoyable read. Kara Griffin did a wonderful job with the character development and storyline, spinning a tale full of adventure, love and a little mystic. - KVD Reader Review

ABOUT THE AUTHOR

Kara Griffin has been writing for over 20 years, publishing many novels, and has received praise from readers and reviewers alike. She's been married for 30 years and has raised 3 wonderful daughters, who are on their own paths to love. Her second grandchild, a wee lass, joined the family in February.

Kara's love of history led her to research her Grandfather's heritage and found her Scottish roots. Ever since, she's loved learning about Scotland's history, good and bad. She enjoys writing about the heroes of the past, honor, courage, and love.

When she's not writing, she enjoys reading historical romances and watching any sort of historical drama and spending time with her family. Her writing partner, a fat tabby named Pearl (a kleptomaniac) can usually be found trying to steal items from her desk.

If you enjoyed this story, please take a moment to post a review on your favorite book site. Reader reviews are important and much appreciated. Thank you.

Made in the USA
Coppell, TX
14 February 2020